WANDERING
SOUL

WANDERING SOUL

A REUNIFICATION NOVEL

STEVEN J. ANDERSON

Published by Steven J. Anderson
© 2019 Steven J. Anderson

RuComm352@gmail.com
https://www.facebook.com/RuComm352

Cover by Fiona Jayde Media.
Interior Formatting & Design by The Deliberate Page.

Ebook ISBN: 978-0-9991788-2-9
Print ISBN: 978-0-9991788-3-6

CHAPTER 1

SUMMER PLANS

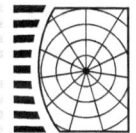

My mom, my real mom, died when I was born, or more accurately, she died about ten minutes before I was born. One of the clans killed her in the Warrens while she was saving the life of the woman that became my stepmother, an event that made less sense to me as I got older.

Don't get me wrong, I love Hannah and could not have asked for a better mother. But sometimes, especially after we moved to Earth from Dulcinea when I was twelve, she would look at me and I'm sure she was seeing my mom. She would get this curious expression on her face when I would do something or say something a certain way, and then tip her head to the side and touch my hair, which is long and blonde, unlike her own short dark curls. Or she would just look at me, small and thin as I am because of Mom's low gravity Dulcinean genetic heritage.

Sometimes when we argued, Hannah would call me Alice, my mom's name. My name is Mala Dusa, which means 'little soul' in the dialect of one of the corrupt and violent clans that live in the Warrens of Bodens Gate, itself a corrupt and violent planet. My parents thought my name was cute, and maybe it was when I was six. When I turned sixteen, it was just one more thing that set me apart.

I knew there were things my parents weren't telling me—about what happened when Hannah and Dad worked together for the Reunification Commission, about how RuComm left my real mom and dad all alone on an abandoned planet for several months, or about what happened to all three of them on Bodens Gate. Whenever I asked, my dad would look at Hannah, and Hannah would look back at him and then he'd say, "Oh, you've heard all this before." Then he'd tell me the same story with no details, the same story that didn't match what my grandpa on Dulcinea told me, or even the official history of the rebellion on Bodens Gate that started when all three of them were there.

I needed answers. Hannah and my dad wouldn't give them to me, so I decided to leave.

I started my campaign over dinner. It was the middle of May, near the end of my junior year and we were eating outside because my dad was pretending that the weather was warmer than it really was. I didn't mind. My sweatshirt was warm and cold hamburgers taste as good to me as hot ones. Hannah was tolerating it because she knew Dad was enjoying himself and he let her sit closest to the fire pit.

"So," I started, "I've been thinking about what I want to do this summer."

"We're going camping for a month in Colorado," Dad answered.

"No," I replied, "that's you dragging us along on another geology field trip. What section of the Rockies do you need help mapping this time?"

He smiled at me, because for some reason he likes it when I see through him. "The fossil beds north of Kremmling. But I thought we could check out the universities in the area while we're there. There are a couple of good engineering schools along the Front Range."

Not a bad carrot to dangle in front of me, but I was not to be dissuaded.

"I want to spend break with Grandpa on Dulcinea. He's sponsoring a new survey of the Margo Islands that starts about the same time the school term ends here and he said I could join for four weeks as an intern. No pay, but the University would pay for my passage."

"Didn't you get enough of Dulcinea when we lived there for ten years? We've only been back on Earth for a short time. You should stay here, spend some time with your friends, and then go to Colorado with us."

"Three years is *not* a short time. I can't hardly remember what it looks like. And I don't really have many friends here I want to spend time with. I'm not all that popular in case you hadn't noticed."

"You could be if you tried," Hannah offered. "Just because you're smarter than all the other kids doesn't mean you have to isolate yourself. Try taking an interest in what they like to do."

"Well, they like to get drunk on the weekends and have sex. Which activity do you think I should join in on?" I said it trying to shock her.

2

"Who's leading the Margo Islands survey?" Dad asked.

"Marcus Wright. Grandpa says you know him. I think I met him a couple of times when you had him over. Big guy with a beard, right? He has a team of ten undergrads and a couple of graduate students. I sent him a note last week and he said I'd be welcome to join them. He said it would be a good experience for me and would help me grow up." I smiled my best innocent smile while Dad looked at his potato salad. He had met my mom on the Margo Islands and I always felt there was more to the story than them just shaking hands and saying 'hello'.

"What sort of accommodations—"

Hannah cut him off. "Ted, just save time and tell her no. We are *not* going to let her go to a tropical island with Marcus and a crew of teenagers from the University."

"No," Dad said.

Good. Part one of my plan was completed.

I pouted for a few minutes and then said, "I also thought about interning with the Reunification Commission. RuComm has a program where I can work at the Academy doing staff work, and then do a three-week hop on board ship. Still no pay, but it would accrue credits for future tuition."

"Wouldn't you have to commit to attending the Academy? I thought you'd decided not to do that."

"No, *you* decided that for me. Just because you and Hannah had a bad experience doing RuComm field work—"

"Like almost dying three times and losing my best friend."

"Yes, but you still stayed with RuComm doing geologic research on Dulcinea for another ten years before you made us move to Earth. It can't be that bad drifting from planet to planet doing science and helping to bring the Union back together."

Hannah shook her head and her eyes were shining in the firelight. She was close to tears, something I had rarely seen.

"What is it, Mom?" She likes it when I call her Mom.

"Anything but RuComm field work. Even spending the summer here with your friends doing what they do would be better." She sighed, took Dad's hand, kissed it, and they looked at each other for a long time. "You're old enough, Dusa. I'll tell you a bedtime story after dinner, all right? Just promise me you'll stay away from RuComm."

"OK, sure." That was a little stronger response than I expected, but part two of my plan was completed.

I let it rest for a while; enjoying the music that Dad had let me pick and listening to the two of them talk about the day's events. My friend Winona's parents don't talk. They argue and they snipe at each other as if they can hardly stand being in the same room together. Dad and Hannah talk and flirt and laugh. They make plans together and discuss what's going on in the universe.

Sometimes Hannah will get a wild look in her eyes and it will get reflected and magnified by Dad and I know that something in my life is about to change. Like the time my playground in the backyard got ripped out and replaced by a home observatory. I might have been too old for my swings and little climbing wall, but I still missed them.

Even when they disagree, it's more the two of them solving a problem and not trying to solve each other. One of my earliest memories is of listening to them talking while I was lying in bed at night. It's a comforting sound, knowing that your parents are still in love.

When I felt I had waited long enough I told them, "I got a letter from Father Ryczek yesterday." Father Ryczek ran the church's Mission on Bodens Gate. He was old when my parents knew him, so I always saw him as an ancient monk-like character still providing care and wisdom to the poor in the Warrens. Conditions there were better now since the Confederation had overthrown the former Central Government. Dad and Hannah, and maybe my mom, had been involved with the Union Commission that helped that happen. How much they had been involved was one of the mysteries I planned to solve, along with how my mom had *really* died.

"How is the old man?" Dad asked. Hannah was studying me, waiting for what I would say next.

"Good. Understaffed and overworked."

"He always says that."

"He also says to tell you that no one has been able to match you for keeping the old machinery running. Or making hash browns." Dad had served at the Mission as handyman and cook for several months while Mom taught school. I have a picture he took of her standing with a bunch of kids covered in paint and glitter. The small bulge in her tummy was me.

"I told him that I must have inherited your mechanical abilities and was planning on becoming an engineer," I continued. "He said you and Hannah must be proud of me."

4

It was fully dark now and the only light was from the fire. Dad was looking at me, lost in remembrance, just as I had planned for him to be. Hannah was drumming her fingers on the table, angry.

"So, Alice—" She cut herself off and said 'damn it' under her breath. "Mala Dusa Holloman, please tell me that you haven't already signed a contract to spend your three month break in the god damned Warrens on Bodens Gate."

Dad looked surprised. "She can't have signed a contract, she's not of age."

"She was born on orbit above Bodens Gate so she has citizenship there," Hannah reminded him. "Their age of consent is sixteen."

"Dusa, what did you do?"

I stared at was left of my hamburger, my carefully executed plan shattered. "I signed a contract with the church last week. They'll cover transportation and food and lodging, and I get a small stipend. I wanted you to think it was a good idea before letting you know."

"I told you," Hannah said to my dad, "I told you she was spending too much time with Grandpa Vandermeer, learning how to plan and scheme and manipulate. We should have left there when she was five, not thirteen." She turned to me and her eyes were cold, unlike anything I'd ever seen in her before. "*You* are not your mother. You may look like her, but your brain," she tapped my head, "works like your dad's, and I can read both of you like words on a display pad. Do you understand me?"

I nodded weakly. Grandpa was not going to be proud of me.

Hannah turned to Dad. "You have to try to unwind this. Do you know how high the mortality rate *still* is in the Warrens? It's not safe for her to be there. We can't lose her, Ted. I can't go through that with you again."

"I know. Alice and I were still connected when she died. I felt her die thanks to the damn—"

He stopped and looked at me, frowning. "I'll talk to the church tomorrow morning."

He poked at the food that was still on his plate for a while, lost in a memory he didn't want. I felt bad that all that I'd succeeded in doing was ruining dinner.

"Dusa, why don't you help me clear the table?" Hannah was already standing, waiting for me.

I went to my dad and wrapped my arms around him in a hug. I buried my face on his shoulder. "I'm so sorry." He rubbed my back, but didn't answer. I picked up his plate and mine and carried them back into the kitchen.

"Can you tell me why you want to go to Bodens Gate so badly?" Hannah was dumping the plates into the recycler and she no longer seemed angry, just disappointed, which was worse.

"I want to do something with my life that makes a difference."

Hannah stopped and looked at me, waiting.

"OK, fine. I want to find out who you and my mom and dad are, or who you were back then. And please don't tell me that you've already told me everything that happened in the Warrens."

She smiled. "That sounds like truth." She went back to cleaning up the kitchen. "But you won't find what you're looking for there."

"Then where *do* I find it? You and Dad will never tell me."

She chuckled. "I didn't say it wasn't there. I just said *you* wouldn't find it."

More secrets. Great.

I finished helping and then told Hannah that I needed to go to my room to study for finals, but I really just laid on my bed staring at the ceiling or with my eyes closed letting the sound of Sibelius's first symphony fill all the conscious parts of my brain. I didn't notice that Hannah had come into my room until she sat on the edge of the bed next to me.

"Look at you, still angry and frustrated. Are you ready for your bed-time story?"

"I thought maybe you wouldn't tell it after what I did."

"A promise is a promise. Do you know why there are things your dad and I haven't told you?"

I shrugged.

"Some of it was that you were too young to understand, but that's changed now. Some is personal and we won't tell you, and some is, well, it's too dangerous for you to know."

"Dangerous?"

"Dangerous to me. You won't ever know the full story and you need to get over it. Parents keep secrets from their kids."

"Kids keep secrets from their parents too." I tried to sound defiant.

"I hope you do. I know I did."

"So tell me why the idea of me joining the Reunification Commission almost made you cry."

She laid down next to me and I moved over to make room for her on the pillow.

"I was on my second hop with RuComm when I met your dad. I was fooling around with his best friend, Jake, at the time. Ted thought I was going to get Jake thrown out of RuComm because 'romantic entanglements' are forbidden by the terms of the RuComm contract. He didn't know that everyone cheats on that clause, both on and off the ship, especially off. Jake was like all the many lovers I had on my first hop; a pleasant diversion from the boredom, a little excitement for a time and then I'd move on. I shared my body with all of them, but never my heart. I controlled my heart and I liked it that way." She turned her head and looked at me. "Does that shock you?"

"Maybe a little." I knew she was trying to shock me. It was working.

"I got tired of Jake after a couple of weeks and started work seducing Ted, your dad. I had hopes he could keep me entertained for the two months we'd be on Dulcinea. He looked like he had potential and I liked the way he smelled."

"You *smell* him?"

"Yeah, I do," she whispered. "Anyway, your Grandpa Vandermeer arranged to ship him out to the Margo Islands the morning after we arrived to be a pawn in the cold war between the Palma Federated States and the Oceanus Protectorate. Alice was already there, being a pawn sent by some General whose name I forget."

"Why would Grandpa do that?"

"He says the General outmaneuvered him. That might be true. Or he sent Ted as a plaything for your mom."

I didn't like that theory, but I could see Grandpa doing it.

"It didn't matter. I'd already hooked him," Hannah continued. "I had been using Jake to make him jealous and I could see it in his eyes that he wanted me. Are you sure you want to hear this?"

"I do if it's the truth."

"It's the truth, I'm just not very proud of this part. Ted was back a week later after almost dying on the Island. I met him in the hotel lobby that night when I got back from work. We talked for a while, and then he walked me to my room. He didn't even want to give me a goodnight kiss on account of Jake."

"Sounds like Dad."

"I kissed him anyway. I met him and Jake the next day for lunch and caressed your dad's leg under the table with my bare foot. I didn't want him to have any doubts about my intentions. RuComm had cut our two-month stay on Dulcinea to only three more weeks because of the military and political tensions. I wanted him, and there was no time for easing him into the idea. I had to drag him into my room when we got back to the hotel that afternoon. When that door closed though, if he had any problems with betraying Jake he hid them well.

"After that," she continued, "we were together every night. Once a few days had passed, I realized that the short time we had before we left Dulcinea wouldn't be enough. Even if we had been together the full two months, it wouldn't have been enough. Your dad wasn't like any man I had ever been with. Dusa, I love your dad. He's a good man, sensitive to what you're feeling, imaginative, funny..."

"Sure. He's a great dad, better than the dads my friends have."

"It does make him a great dad. But I've also seen him hold a gun to another man's head, ready to kill to defend someone he loves." She sighed. "You have no idea how all that translates into an intimate relationship. We spent hours just talking. We talked about our work, what we wanted from life, anything and everything. And when we spent the night together those same attributes made it amazing. After about a week, the damnedest thing happened. I was twenty-six then and had been with a lot of men. The one thing I had never done until your dad agreed to come into my bed was to fall in love. I didn't even understand what it meant to lose your heart to another person. It hit me hard."

"And there was that RuComm clause staring you in the face."

"I didn't think it would be a problem. We could cheat a little, and in a few weeks we'd be on another planet where we could be together a night or two maybe. Certainly we could hide our love for a few months."

"It didn't work out that way?"

"God, no. Everyone that looked at us knew that all I wanted to do was grab him and throw him to the floor right there."

I laughed.

"It wasn't funny, Dusa. It nearly destroyed us both. Our team lead, Angela—"

She paused, and the way she had said her name made me glad I wasn't Angela.

"Angela gave me a choice; take a bunch of medications to get my emotions in check or end my career right then. I took the meds. For a few hours, I thought they were working. I felt like I was in control of my heart again. Then I saw Ted and my heart leaped and my head ignored it and that dissonance made me angry. She took me off the meds a little while later, but that anger stayed with me for weeks, it was the only emotion I could feel and it ruled me."

She rolled off my bed, knelt down next to me, and started to braid part of my hair. "Dusa, that's why you can't join RuComm. What they did to us was cruel and they'd do it to you or anyone else that ran against their rules."

"What happened to your team lead? Was she disciplined in any way for what she did to you and Dad?"

"Why would she have been? She was just doing what RuComm wanted her to do. Anyway, she died a few weeks later on the planet Cleavus. Bodens Gate had exiled the Bovita clan there, but we didn't know it. Angela thought they were a lost Union colony. She died when the Bovita took over our ship."

"Hannah, in the state you were in from the meds, you didn't—"

Hannah interrupted me. "Enough truth for one night."

"Just one more thing, please. When you said Dad had held a gun to another man's head; that was just figure of speech, right? Not a real gun?"

She reached into her pocket and showed me a cartridge, turning it between her fingers so it caught the light. "This is the round that was supposed to have been fired into my brain, ending my life. Your dad took the gun away from the man that wanted to kill me and pointed it at the man's head. He was squeezing the trigger when one of our friends stopped him. Ted was going to kill him right there in front of me." She put the cartridge back inside her pocket. "I always keep it with me. It reminds me of what kind of a man your father is."

She kissed me gently on the cheek and I was a little afraid of her right then, and maybe of Dad too, which I think is what she'd intended. For a moment, I questioned whether or not I really wanted to know the secrets of my parents past. But only for a moment.

"One more thing?" I asked.

"You already had one more thing."

"One more, one more thing?" I smiled, trying to look adorable, which worked with Hannah sometimes. She smiled back and waited, because she's my mom.

"What is it?"

"I know how much you and Dad love each other, and now I think I understand how much you loved each other when you were first together.

What happened in between? Did he love my real mom at all or am I just…"
I stopped, not wanting to finish.

"Are you just what?"

"An accident. It would make sense if my creation were an accident. There are times when I think I *must* be an accident. I have a weird name, and no one looks like me, and no one thinks like me, and no one really likes me much."

"How can you even think that? We may not have told you everything, but what we have told you is true. Alice and your dad were deeply in love. He chose her." Hannah's voice dropped to a whisper as she forced the words out. "He chose her over me."

She paused and I think saying what she had said hurt her, so I knew it must be true. She wiped at her eyes before continuing. "Now look what you've done. I'm presenting at the Union cabinet meeting tomorrow morning and my eyes are going to be all red."

"I'm sorry."

"It's OK. Maybe your dad will tell you another bedtime story sometime soon. It's his story to tell, not mine." She turned and stood looking at me from the doorway.

"I love you, Mala Dusa."

"I love you too. I'm glad you're my mom." I said it hoping it would make her feel better, but I think she was crying when she closed my door.

CHAPTER 2

STUCK

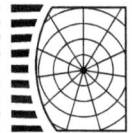

Dad was waiting for me in the living room when I got home from school. Hannah wasn't there, but that wasn't unusual, her work supporting the Union government often required odd hours.

"What are you doing home? Didn't you have a 16:00 class to teach this afternoon?"

"Professor Colbert's covering for me. I've spent most of the day trying to break your contract." He took my hands and examined my palms and fingers.

"What are you looking for?"

"The pin pricks. From what I'm finding you must have signed in blood."

I pulled my hands away from him. "It's unbreakable?"

"Breaking it would incur criminal and civil penalties, and I don't want to be visiting you in jail all summer. I sent a message to Father Ryczek, but it'll take five days for a return message."

"So I can go?"

"Try not to sound so happy about it. You have no idea how dangerous this will be for you. And do you remember how you complained about the extra ten kilograms you picked up moving to Earth from Dulcinea? Get ready for another five. And you'd better plan on not setting foot outside the Mission compound, because I told Father Ryczek that Hannah would come back there *personally* if he let you within ten meters of the gate."

I hate to admit it, but I kind of like it when Dad gets upset. He says things he doesn't mean to say and I get another piece of the puzzle. "Why would Hannah going back there be a threat?"

"Mala Dusa, please don't tip your head like that. When Hannah does that to me I know I'm in trouble and it's you that's in trouble here, not me."

It made me feel bold, knowing that there was nothing he could do to stop me now. "I'm going to be there for three months, minus travel time. I'm going to find things out, Dad."

He sighed. "When did you get so big?" He looked at me as if he would rather ground me than tell me what I wanted to know. "Fine. Have a seat."

I put my backpack on the floor and sat on the couch.

"Hannah told me last night that you thought you were an accident. Is that true?" he asked.

"I thought you were going to tell me about Hannah in the Warrens."

He shook his head and smiled. "Not happening. Now, did you say that?"

I looked at the floor. "Yes."

"Don't ever think that. You were a surprise, since our fertility had been reversed, but not an accident. Your mom kept you a secret from me until we were on Bodens Gate and then only told me after you made her throw up in a trashcan one morning."

"I don't think I did that on purpose." I slid off the couch onto the floor and wrapped a throw around myself, snuggling in. These were the kind of stories I wanted to hear.

"I'm not so sure. I think you were trying to get my attention."

"Were you in love with Mom?" I knew the answer to that question, but I wanted to hear it all again anyway.

"Yes, very much so. We fell in love on Cleavus after *Wandering Star* abandoned us there. We thought they'd come back for us in a few weeks. At first. Then we became convinced that no one would ever come. Alone on a planet forever with just each other, I don't think the human mind can put what that felt like into words. I'd have died without her. I'd have *wanted* to be dead."

"You fell in love because there was no one else there?" I taunted him.

He laughed. "No. I fell in love with your mother because she was an intelligent, beautiful woman who only had one flaw."

I smiled knowing what he was going to say next.

"She was in love with me for some reason. She made me better than I could ever have been without her. She was a brilliant geologist. And brave. She was more fearless than any person I've ever known."

"Do I look like her?"

"So much like her. I always told her that she was possibly the most beautiful girl God had ever created, but that was before I saw you."

"Most people think I'm ugly. My legs are too skinny and my arms are too skinny and my face—" I put my hands on my cheeks that are flat and angular, just like the rest of me.

"Most people are idiots."

I smiled and pulled the wrap closer around my shoulders. "I feel so out of place here. There's no one like me at school, except maybe Winona, and she's weird in her own ways."

"You *are* different, but that's a good thing. You inherited your mom's beauty as well as her intelligence."

"And from you, *Professor*." I reminded him.

He shook his head. "I'm just adequate. Alice was brilliant. Spending ten years with Alice's father didn't help you fit in either. He tried to turn you into your mom."

"But my brain thinks like yours, that's what Hannah says. And I screwed up Grandpa's plan so badly last night that I believe her. Oh—" I put my hand over my mouth, realizing what I had just said.

"So Grandpa put you up to this?"

"Sort of," I squeaked, my hand still over my mouth. "He thought he was helping me make a plan to spend the summer on Dulcinea."

Dad laughed. "So you were playing him too? Your mom would be very proud of you."

"Tell me more about her. Was she... different, like me?"

I sat on the floor for the next hour and Dad told me stories I'd never heard before. Stories about my Mom shaking uncontrollably from fear on the Margo Islands and then conquering those fears to save my dad and help him stop a war. And another about how Mom wasn't popular and knew that most people thought she looked strange, and acted strange, and how beautiful she had looked in the moonlight on the Margo Islands when he'd first met her. My favorite was about how Mom and Dad fell in love doing a geologic survey on Cleavus even after they thought no one would ever come back and rescue them, and that they would die alone, and it might be hundreds of years before anyone found what they had done together. It was romantic and it made my heart ache.

"She went hiking through the desert totally *naked*?" I asked.

"Of course not. She wore a big hat and boots. The sand would have burned her feet in the hot sun."

I leaned forward, looking at him.

"Why not? There was no one there to see her except me and Merrimac, our dog."

I laughed, trying to visualize walking across the sand with nothing on but a hat and boots. It was perfectly logical and perfectly outrageous.

"Tell me more."

Dad started to open his mouth, but then a strange look came into his eyes, as if he had just seem the most amazing, enthralling thing in the universe. I had seen that look before, literally thousands of times, and I knew that Hannah must have just walked in. His eyes always got that look of longing when she walked into a room, and so did hers when she saw him. I sighed. No more stories about Mom today.

"You two seem to be having a good time," she said. "Contract broken, I take it?"

I climbed back on the couch and knelt down peering over the back at her. I wanted to see her reaction when Dad told her I was doomed.

"No, not exactly."

Hannah looked at him and tipped her head. Yep, Dad was in trouble.

"So what *exactly* does that mean?"

"If she doesn't fulfill her commitment there could be criminal penalties. If we keep her here she might spend the summer behind bars."

"Good," she said hanging up her jacket. "She'll be safe from the dangers of the Warrens and we won't have to worry she's out with her friends getting drunk and having sex. Nicely done, Ted. I call that a win." And then she kissed him. It was a long kiss and I think she may have used her tongue at the end.

"You can't do that to me!"

"Nothing back from Father Ryczek yet?" she asked.

"It'll be a few days, like I said in the message I sent you this morning."

So she had known all along and just wanted to see me panic, wanting to see *my* reaction. They were standing there with their arms around each other looking smug.

"Very funny. So I'm not spending the summer in jail?"

"That's up to you. I think it's a good alternative to dying on Bodens Gate." She said it in a casual tone of voice, but I could feel the deep fear in her for my safety.

14

I sighed. That was another thing that made me different and weird. I can feel strong emotions in them and I know they can feel what's inside me, although they rarely talk about it. When I was little, I thought everyone could do it. Then I realized it only worked with Hannah and Dad, and I thought it was a family thing. I must have been nine or ten before I realized my friends didn't know what their parents were feeling. My friends laughed at me when I talked about it and then they weren't my friends anymore. One more family secret, one more thing about weird Mala Dusa.

"I don't care what Father Ryczek says. I want to go. I *need* to go."

"I could take a leave of absence, skip the summer semester," Dad suggested, "Go along and keep her in bounds. Or maybe talk one of my sisters into going with her."

"No," Hannah answered, and I swear I could feel her banging around inside my head. "No, Ted. She needs to go out of bounds. A little." She leaned against his shoulder and sighed. "Damn."

Word came back from Father Ryczek a few days later. It was a long letter and he never once mentioned Dad's plea to release me from my contract. He reminisced about the months Dad and Mom had worked there, and talked about how wonderful it would be to have Alice's daughter with them. He said there was much in the old Mission in need of repair starting with getting the front gate working again before winter arrived. He promised my experiences would be both meaningful and memorable. He didn't say he would keep me safe.

A couple of days before I was to leave, I went running along the Sunset Trail south of Mount Humphreys with my friend, Winona Killdeer. She was really the only close friend I had and I think I was the only friend Winona had at all. She had her black hair tied back and was running in front of me up the trail, setting a quick pace while I tried to talk to her. She only slowed down when we hit snowpack about halfway up. Even then, she went another ten meters before getting bogged down.

I stopped and she looked back at me. Her dark eyes were too large for her face and she seemed confused or mystified by what she was seeing. It was her normal expression. When I first saw her in class, I thought that maybe she was developmentally challenged. After two minutes of hearing her correct the teacher on current developments in genetic modification technology, I realized my error. The expression on her face was because she sees absolutely everything around her all of the time. If I were to ask her about this run a month later, she would be able to tell me what flowers were blooming, what the clouds drifting by had looked like and how deep the snow was that had encased her bare legs. I was the only one that could come close to her in our studies, like maybe ten percent of what she could do.

"I'm going to miss you, Duse." Her voice was tight and there were little creases between her eyes. "I don't know what I'm going to do without you this summer."

"That's hard to believe. You always know what you're going to do." I sat down on a rock and drank some water from my bottle. "The first thing you should do is get out of that snow."

She looked down at her legs as though surprised to see why they were getting cold. She came and sat down next to me. "I wish you'd told me you were considering this mission trip. I would have volunteered to accompany you."

"I thought you didn't believe in God. It's kind of a requirement for this sort of thing."

She looked around at the mountains and up to watch a bird flying over us and I wondered how much raw data was flowing into her brain.

"I've been reevaluating my opinions lately."

"Really?" I smiled at her and touched her hand.

She turned toward me and nodded. "I have not reached any conclusions, but thank you for not mocking me. I get enough of that at home."

"I would never do that," I reassured her.

"I've been considering what I'm going to do while you're gone. None of the options are as pleasant as those that included you."

"I'm going to miss you too."

"Your odds of survival are actually very good," she locked eyes with me, "as long as you stay within the Mission. Each foray outside the walls carries a point five percent chance of being killed or kidnapped."

"That doesn't sound too bad."

"It's terrible, Duse!" She picked up some of the snow by our feet and appeared to be studying its texture. I didn't realize what she was planning until it was too late and she had shoved the snow down the back of my shirt.

"Hey!" I stood and stumbled back a few steps.

She pickup up more snow, advancing toward me. "Promise you'll stay in the Mission, Mala Dusa." She was tossing the snow back and forth between her hands as she came.

"Fine! I'll stay in the Mission. I promise." She tossed the snow over her shoulder and it landed precisely on my water bottle. She came closer and I checked her hands for more snow before I let her hug me.

"Will you send me messages while you're gone?"

"Sure. We can talk in near real time until I make the jump through the first Deep Space Hole."

Winona looked at me, studying my face with those big eyes. "It won't be the same as having you here to talk to, but I think I'll survive."

"You better. We're seniors next fall. It's going to be an exciting year and I need you there with me."

"Thank you. Most people don't want me around at all, let alone need me."

"Most people are idiots." That got her to smile.

We sat back on the rocks and ate the snacks we had brought with us.

"You mentioned God, but you aren't going because of your faith, are you?" she asked.

"Partly. My church supports the Mission in the Warrens and we pray for them all the time. I've done fundraisers and my parents support a couple of the kids each year. Well, Dad mostly. Getting Hannah to church isn't easy. I think she associates it too much with my mom. I suppose Hannah believes in her own way, but she won't talk about it. My dad goes with me, maybe because of mom, maybe for me, or for himself. But no, my faith isn't the only reason I want to go."

"Your parents, then, and your real mom. Are you sure you want to know? There's plenty of information about them on the nets if you could be bothered to do your research."

I *had* looked and I had found almost nothing. But I was not Winona. She took her display pad out of her pack and unrolled it.

"Do you at least know who Ysabeau Romee was?"

"Sure, I really did do *some* research. She was the leader of the clan that united everyone in the Warrens and challenged the Bodens Gate government. Until they killed her and made her a martyr."

"Do you know what she looked like?"

"No one does. Only a few people ever met her and there're no pictures. Are there?"

"A couple of weeks after she was killed a statue of her appeared in the Warrens. It was destroyed a short time later on the orders of the Union commission that was working to negotiate a settlement to the civil war, and rebuild the Bodens Gate Central Government. Your parents worked on that commission, I believe?"

I nodded. "Your point, Winn?"

"The Commission claimed Romee was a war criminal and not to be venerated. She had ordered the assassination of hundreds of other clan leaders when she consolidated power, and may have killed quite a few of them personally."

I knew that part of the story too. The history of the Warrens was one of extortion, murder, rape, and human trafficking.

Winona handed me her pad. "I found a photo of the statue, even though there aren't supposed to be any."

I felt my mouth open and forced it closed. I knew that defiant smile and short wavy hair. "They used Hannah as the model for the statue?" I asked.

Winona thumped my forehead with her finger. "Idiot."

"Hannah was *not* Ysabeau Romee."

Winona lifted her finger toward my head again.

"Was she?" I asked.

"I believe she was. Your mom, Hannah, is still running the government on Bodens Gate as far as I can tell. That commission she's on? They rubber stamp whatever she wants to do. I never looked at it before because I didn't care about Bodens Gate, but with you going there I did some research over the past few days. Your mom is very impressive. She's been the real strategic power on Bodens Gate for fourteen years and I don't think anyone on the outside knows it but me."

"You must be wrong. She's a consultant to the commission. She's not even a full member. Ow!" Winona tapped my forehead again before I could stop her. "If you do that every time I say something stupid you're going to poke a hole straight through to my brain."

"Does your dad know? There's not much about him in the records. Just that he was a courier once between the Mission and Romee and that he rescued Hannah by convincing a RuComm Captain to ruin his career by dropping a shuttle through controlled airspace into the middle of a combat zone on a sovereign planet. That was on the same day that Ysabeau Romee was supposedly killed, by the way."

I almost said 'no' but my head was still hurting. I told her about the cartridge that Hannah carried in her pocket and my dad almost killing a man.

"I like your dad. He seems perfectly happy being a college professor and living a simple life, but I suspect he's never been able to refuse Hannah anything." She paused and looked at me so it would soak in.

"He loved my real Mom. He loved her *more* than Hannah."

Winona raised her eyebrows and I realized I might have spoken with a little more force than I needed.

"I'm sure he did, Duse. What I was trying to tell you is that your dad is like a catalyst for her. I've been over to your house enough to see a glimmer of it, how he reinforces and encourages her. She's powerful without him, but with him she becomes magical. Do you know why I'm telling you this?"

I rubbed my forehead before answering. "Because it's dangerous for her, me going there?"

She moved her finger away from my head. "If you start digging around trying to figure out what Hannah Weldon was doing in the Warrens you could reveal the truth. Ysabeau Romee is a folk hero, the woman who freed the masses from the yoke of the Central Government. If it became widely known that she was a Union operative and that she's still alive, the Warrens could descend back into chaos."

"I'm going there to find out about my mom, not Hannah."

"You say that like Hannah hasn't been your mother, like you don't know how lucky you are to have her. I would trade with you in a heartbeat."

"I know. I'm messed up. I do think of her as my mom, and I love her. And I'm sure you're wrong about who she was. But is it crazy to want to know more about the woman that carried me around in her belly for almost nine months?"

Winona kissed my forehead. "I'm messed up too, Duse, and I'm just going to be worse by the end of the summer without you here with me."

We went to Casa Paloma for dinner on my last night on Earth. I brought Winona along with me so we could be silly together, working the puzzles on the children's menus. We ignored my parents' conversation as it hopped back and forth between a report Hannah had written about the impacts of the burgeoning technology sector in the Warrens, and Dad talking about a new species of pterosaur discovered in Big Bend, and then back to Hannah talking about the upcoming elections on Bodens Gate.

After dinner, I excused myself to use the restroom and first Hannah, and then Winona announced that they should come with me. Dad sighed and ordered a second of the restaurant's namesake cocktails.

When we entered the restroom, Winona made sure that it was just the three of us and then locked the door. Hannah looked at her, head tipped to the right.

"I know who you are, Ms. Weldon."

That got my attention. She had called her 'Hannah' from the first day I'd introduced them.

Winona unrolled her pad on the counter and opened the picture of the statue. "Or I should say that I know who you were sixteen years ago."

Hannah glanced at the picture, and I expected she would deny it, maybe even claim she was just the model they had used so I could tap Winona's forehead for a change.

Hannah touched the image. "They got it wrong. My hair was longer than that in those days. I told Cuza that a statue was a bad idea, but he wouldn't listen." She leaned closer, looking at the address tag on the photo.

"You won't hurt him, will you? The man who posted this?"

"No, of course not. I'm not a monster. Well, not as much of a monster as I once was. We'll just make sure the picture goes away."

Winona was looking at her, big eyes wider than usual. "Ms. Weldon, I've been researching Bodens Gate all week. I'm in awe of you."

Hannah smiled, taken aback. "Thank you, Winona. Coming from you, that's an incredible compliment." She looked over at me. "You should close your mouth, Dusa."

I closed my mouth.

"I told Duse how dangerous it would be for her to go digging around on Bodens Gate." She glanced at me. "I think she understands."

"It will have more impact coming from you, I'm sure."

I was getting tired of them talking about me like I wasn't there.

"Mom?" They turned toward me and I wasn't sure what I wanted to say. The world was upside down. I took a deep breath. "I'm afraid to go there now. What else am I going to find in the Warrens?"

She shook her head. "Just don't go digging for me there. You won't like what you find."

I nodded, not trusting my voice.

"And you, Ms. Killdeer, what are your plans for the summer?"

"I've not decided, ma'am. Your daughter's departure has left me distraught."

"I can understand that. Would you consider working for the Commission? I can't offer you much pay, but I think you would find the work interesting."

Winona's eyes lost focus for about three seconds. "I've considered it. When can I start? I'm hoping it will allow me to better keep Mala Dusa safe."

"That's my hope as well. Would next Monday be OK? Unless you want to spend more time with your friends after the end of term."

"Monday would be acceptable, fantastic even." Winona was smiling at me like she owned me.

I was busy staring at Hannah, wondering who she was, this woman my father loved and could never say no to, this woman who had rebuilt a world on a foundation of dead bodies including my mom's, this woman who had been my mother.

CHAPTER 3
LEAVING HOME

I got out of the car at Winona's and walked with her to the front porch. My parents left me there to say my goodbyes, Dad reminding me that we had to be up early. It was only about a kilometer to my house from Winona's and I needed some time alone with her. Watching the car disappear up the road, I wasn't sure I wanted to go home at all.

"That was a wonderful dinner, Duse, thanks for inviting me." She sat on the porch step and tipped her head back looking at the stars. "You know, you can't see Bodens Gate's star from here. It's in the southern hemisphere. It's really too bad. I'd like to be able to look up at night knowing that you're out there."

I sat down next to her and didn't say anything.

"I'm sorry about blowing up dinner, but I had to know for sure."

"Boom," I answered, and she laughed.

"You should have seen your face. You're not really afraid of her, are you?"

"Can I stay here tonight?"

"Nope. I want you to, but you should talk to her before you leave. I think she's afraid right now."

"I know. She's afraid she's lost me. I could feel that in her."

Winn looked at me, trying to see inside my head. "That's just weird how you do that."

"Weird Mala Dusa, that's me. The freak."

"It's why I love you. We're freaks together."

23

We sat and looked at the stars for a while, listening to the night sounds. "You know Hannah offered you that job so she can keep an eye on you, right?"

"I know. I took it so I could keep an eye on *you*." She turned toward me. "Can I have your room while you're gone?"

"No! There are personal things in there and you'd snoop. Why do you want my room, anyway?"

"I would not snoop. Much." She looked at me closely, very serious. "Hannah Weldon, Ysabeau Romee, your mom; she fascinates me. She's a folk hero, a legend. Already, there are people in the Warrens questioning whether she was even real. And I know her!" Winona sighed. "It gives me shivers."

"Sure, you find a way to explain it to your parents and it's all yours. Dad will talk geology every night during dinner, though, and you have to promise to act interested."

She looked at me, confused. "But I *would* be interested."

"Perfect, say it just like that."

We were quiet together for a long time and then I asked her, "Winn, did you know that I'm going to be the ship's acting chaplain on the way to Bodens Gate? It's part of the agreement between the church and RuComm, to sort of pay for my passage. I think I have to do a church service on board." I smiled at her.

"You need to take this seriously. What will you tell them?"

"I'll take it seriously. I just hope they take *me* seriously. I don't think I look much like a chaplain."

"Tell them what you told me about your mom, Alice. How she was a geologist and marine biologist and chemist and found it didn't matter without believing in something bigger." Winona looked into my eyes. "Stand up straight when you say it and they'll take you seriously."

I sighed. "I don't think they'll be looking to me for spiritual guidance, just the brief sermon. I hope." I turned and looked at her sitting next to me, her head tipped back staring at the sky. "I have a hard enough time providing guidance to myself."

"Are you thinking about having a boyfriend again?" she asked softly.

"Sometimes. I think I'd like to try one, you know? The girls in our class that have boyfriends, they seem to enjoy them most of the time. I'd just kind of like to try one out; someone to hold my hand at the theater, maybe kiss me or..." I sighed again. "Maybe touch me."

"If those are your criteria, I believe I can find any number of boys for you that would be willing participants."

I chuckled. "I might need more than that."

"You want one that's a freak, like you, like me."

"Yeah. Or maybe one that would just appreciate my freakishness."

"We are rare, but I'll keep an eye out for a boy freak for you."

"I love you, Winn. I wish you were going with me."

She nodded and touched my hand. "Mala Dusa? I have something for you. I'd like you to take it with you."

She handed me a small, clear plastic sleeve with a lock of hair bound with a yellow ribbon inside.

"Your hair?"

"Yes."

"That has meaning in your culture, doesn't it?"

"They say it is an extension of my spirit, of who I am and all that I know. Please burn it if you ever get tired of me so that my spirit is released. Don't throw it away."

I turned the sleeve, looking at the black strands reflecting the star light. "I'll keep this with me forever if that's OK with you."

"Sure, that would be OK." She hugged me tight.

Dad was still up waiting for me when I got home. He told me Hannah had gone to bed and that may have been true, but I could still feel her awake, worrying and afraid. I had never felt emotions from so far away. She seemed very vulnerable.

"Winona wants to move into my room when I leave," I told him, sitting down next to him at the kitchen table. "I told her it would be OK as long as her parents approved."

He frowned. "I was hoping for time alone with Hannah so I could chase her around the house some."

"I don't need to hear that."

"It's OK. I like Winona and Hannah said she was going to try to keep her close for the next few months."

"Don't let Hannah hurt her." I immediately regretted saying it, but I was still angry that she had lied to me.

"What is going through you brain right now? How can you be afraid of your mom? Everything she's done for you doesn't matter anymore?"

"How many people has she killed, Dad? Do you even know?"

"I know, Dusa, believe me. I'm the one who holds her in the night when she wakes up screaming."

"How many other lies have you told me?"

"Just enough to keep her safe."

"That big scar across her back isn't from a rock climbing accident, is it?"

"Sword fight."

"And the internal damage that kept her from having children of her own?"

"A bullet that went through her."

"Huh." I looked into his eyes and sighed. "Winona sees her as some kind of mythic hero. She's completely enthralled."

"I think Winona's right to feel that way."

"I'd like to go say goodnight to her, if that's OK."

"You don't need my permission to kiss your mom goodnight."

I walked up the stairs still feeling troubled. When I opened her door, the flood of emotions from her that washed over me made my chest hurt. I laid down next to her. She must have showered while I was at Winona's because her hair was damp and smelled like jasmine.

"I wish I was staying a few more days. I have a thousand questions and I probably shouldn't ask them over the net."

She laughed. "Please don't."

"Mom, who are you?"

"You just said it. I'm your mom. Or I've tried to be. I tried really hard." She touched my cheek, moving my hair out of the way. "Have I lost you now?"

I looked at her in the dim light and tried to visualize her as a young woman, leading a rebellion, organizing a new government, and fighting in the back alleys with a gun in one hand and maybe a sword in the other. I failed. Instead I saw her with her hair tied back fixing hash and bacon for a crew of Dad's grad students at a camp in the badlands on our first summer back on Earth and then, earlier, blowing up balloons for one of my birthday parties back on Dulcinea while trying to control a half dozen screaming nine year olds.

"Still my mom. Who else would have forgiven me for draining the hot tub and refilling it as a Dulcinean tide pool while you and Dad were at work?"

She rolled her eyes. "God, we never did get rid of the smell of those tri-valve mollusks you put in there."

I touched her face. There were a few wrinkles there and some grey hairs that were probably my fault. "I won't try to find out anything more while I'm at the Mission, I promise. I'll help fix things that are broken, and I'll talk to Father Ryczek about my mom. I'll stay out of trouble."

"No, you won't."

"No, I won't." I sighed. "I'll try to stay out of trouble?"

"You inherited quite a few genes for attracting trouble from both your parents."

I snuggled closer and stayed there with her with my eyes closed, but not sleeping. Dad came in some time later, trying to walk softly. He picked me up like he used to when I was little and carried me back to my room. He laid me down on my bed and I kept my eyes closed, pretending to be asleep.

"You should get undressed, Dusa. And don't forget to brush your teeth. Faker."

I smiled, my eyes still closed. "Goodnight, Dad. Mom smells nice, but I think she just wants to be held tonight."

"Thanks for the tip." He closed the door behind him.

I had never seen so much concrete. There were square kilometers of it stretched out across the valley floor. There were some big ships tied down in the central docks, but they looked tiny even with the little dots moving around next to them that I knew must be people. I was a little disappointed at the small size of the RuComm shuttle that would be carrying me off planet for the first time in over three years.

We got off the transport, and Dad and Hannah just stood there staring at it. I was too excited to notice what they were feeling. We all walked over next to the ramp and they each put a hand on the hull.

"It's *Wandering Star's* starboard shuttle," my dad said softly, touching the worn lettering. "The manifest showed Dusa was booked on the *Pole Star.*"

There was another passenger waiting by the ramp. He didn't look much older than me, and he was standing next to a raggedy backpack and a small duffel bag with the Academy logo on it.

"I got a notification late last night that *Pole Star* had a system failure and was going to be delayed a week, maybe longer. *Wandering Star* was headed direct to Ratatoskr, but now she'll be making a stop at Bodens Gate on the way. RuComm told me to hitch a ride since it will still get me to Dulcinea a week earlier than waiting for *Pole Star*. If they can even fix her again."

Dad was looking at him, eyebrows raised.

"Oh, sorry, sir." He stuck his hand out. "Sam Coleridge. I'm on my first RuComm assignment."

Dad took his hand. "Ted Holloman, my wife Hannah, and our daughter Mala Dusa."

Sam stopped smiling, but hadn't let go of Dad's hand. "Theodore Holloman, RuComm geologist?"

"I used to be."

Sam let go of his hand and glanced at Hannah and at me. "It's an honor to meet you, Professor. You're kind of a legend at the Academy. Your work on the Cleavus survey, I mean, with Alice Vandermeer. What the two of you did there was brilliant."

Sam glanced at Hannah again and then his eyes locked onto mine. "Your father is required reading. But I imagine you already know about all that."

Great, I was thinking, *both my parents are legends.* "You seem very young for an Academy graduate. Are you just interning?" I asked. I didn't like the way he was looking at me. I know I'm not attractive, and I don't like people staring at me.

Sam blushed. "No, I graduated two weeks ago. I skipped a few grades when I was younger. I'm twenty-one."

I didn't believe him. I doubt he needed to shave more than once a week. And he was still staring at me.

"So, Sam, are you a geologist?" Dad saved me.

"No, Professor. Biologist. I took a couple of geology classes as electives, though. I'm hoping to cross-train while we're in transit between worlds."

With Sam and Dad happy talking about Cleavus sedimentology, I was able to slip away to where Hannah was still staring at the shuttle. She seemed startled when I took her hand, but I wasn't feeling any strong emotions from her. I think my own excitement and then the embarrassment from having Sam looking at me like I was a biological specimen was masking everything.

She smiled at me, coming back into the moment. "What are you embarrassed about, Dusa?" she glanced at Sam and then back at me, tipping her head slightly.

"He was looking at me like, I don't know, like I'm some kind of freak." I turned away, biting my lower lip.

"No, he wasn't." She turned me around and looked into my eyes. "He thinks you're pretty. He's still trying to steal a peek at you when he thinks your dad won't notice."

Hannah looked at Sam. "I think *he's* pretty too, don't you? Kind of skinny maybe, but he has nice eyes. A little young for me, though."

I giggled.

"And way too old for you," she finished firmly.

"Oh." My hand came up to my mouth. "Right. RuComm is *always* watching."

"That young man is on his first assignment. Don't do anything stupid that could make it his last."

"Yes, ma'am. It's only nine days to Bodens Gate. Nothing can happen that fast anyway."

Hannah started laughing and was having trouble stopping. Dad walked over and she whispered something in his ear. He smiled and she was off again, turning her back to me before she could stop.

A chime sounded from the shuttle, and a woman's voice told us it was time to board. Dad helped me carry my bags and I found a seat toward the back, far away from Samuel Coleridge.

Dad kissed me and said, "*Star*? Keep her safe for me please."

"Always, Mr. Holloman. It's good to see you again. Please extend my greetings to Ms. Weldon as well. After my last upgrade, I was able to improve your Sonoran Desert simulation. Do you think Ms. Holloman would like to run it?"

Dad tightened the straps holding me in my seat. "I'm sure she would. She could probably use a good cool down after four laps, just like I used to."

"I understand. Pleasant travels."

"The ship seems to remember you," I said.

Dad kissed me again. "A little too well. She remembers you too."

"Mom's not coming in?"

"No." He looked around at the seats and frowned at the floor by where the landing ramp extended out onto the tarmac. "Too many ghosts on this ship."

Sam turned around and looked at my dad at the mention of ghosts, but he didn't say anything when Dad walked past him and down the ramp. There was a rumble in the floor as the ramp retracted and the sound of the thrusters starting to spool up made the air feel like it was humming.

Wandering Star's starboard shuttle. I had heard Dad say it, but it hadn't registered. This was the shuttle that had carried the three of them out of the Warrens when they rescued Hannah. My dad had been smashed to bits in an explosion and was almost dead. Lying next to him by the ramp had been my mom, slowly bleeding to death. Hannah had been next to her, trying desperately to keep her alive and failing. If I were to pull up the carpet there at the top of the ramp would I find the deck plates still stained with their blood?

It's just plastic, I told myself, *and composite and metal. It's no different from any other shuttle in the RuComm fleet.* I closed my eyes and the pressure pushing me into my seat increased as the shuttle accelerated off planet. I tried to think of other things. I wondered if Winona was already moving her stuff into my room. I wondered if Dad was watching the shuttle climb until it became a bright sparkle and then disappeared. I wondered if he and Hannah were already headed home to chase each other around the house. I wondered if Sam was looking at me.

Sam was looking at me. "Mala Dusa? We've arrived. Were you asleep?"

I blinked, looking around the shuttle. The door was already open and she had already deployed her ramp. "I guess so," I answered. "I only slept a couple of hours last night."

"Yeah, me too, but wow. I wish I could relax like that. A thirty minute nap would have been nice."

I unstrapped and walked down the ramp with him into the shuttle bay. There was an older man waiting for us, maybe mid-thirties, his hair cut short, what was left of it. He looked irritated that we were there.

"I'm Mr. de Sande, Lead for the RuComm tech team. Coleridge, you're assigned to cabin 24b, you know where that is?"

"Yes, sir. I've done two intern hops so I know my way around the *Star*-class ships."

"Good. We're having an all-hands in—" he consulted his watch, "—twenty-four minutes in the central lab. Get settled and be there early."

Sam hurried away and Mr. de Sande looked at my new backpack and the large bag by my feet. Then he examined my face.

"Holloman. You're our chaplain? How old are you, anyway?"

"Sixteen, sir. I'm in transit to Bodens Gate to serve in the Mission there." I felt my cheeks flush. My chaplain responsibilities were supposed to be just doing a thirty-minute church service sometime in the next nine days, but I was not going to back down from Mr. de Sande.

He sighed impatiently. "Yes, I know that. *Pole Star* forwarded the note Father Ryczek sent concerning you that said you would be their acting chaplain on the way there. Unfortunately, now *I* need a chaplain. Instead, I have you."

"I can be your chaplain. What do you need me to do?" I stood up straight and stared into his eyes, willing myself to look older.

"Fine. First thing I need you to do is to take your stuff to your cabin and then join us for my all-hands meeting. We'll talk after that. Do you know where cabin 26a is?"

"No, sir."

"*Star*? Would you please help Ms. Holloman find her cabin and the central lab? And make sure she's on time."

"Of course, Mr. de Sande, and welcome back on board, Ms. Holloman. It's been a long time."

"Back?" de Sande asked.

"Yes, Ms. Holloman was born here, the only person ever born on a *Star*-class ship. She spent her first thirty-two months of life with me." There was definitely a gentle fondness in her voice.

"Thank you, *Star*," I answered her. "My earliest memories are of running down these passageways and of you singing me to sleep at night."

"I still know the elephant song."

"Me too."

Mr. de Sande was standing next to me with his eyes closed. "Just don't let her be late, *Star*."

"Follow the green ball, Mala Dusa."

I picked up my backpack and bag and chased after the green light that seemed to be floating in mid-air. "Ooh, I remember this game!"

Mr. de Sande sighed, a weary sound in my ears as I ran toward the exit, my attempt to look older forgotten.

The all-hands meeting wasn't too bad. De Sande introduced Sam and me to the RuComm technical team and it was kind of fun getting a glimpse of the world Dad and Hannah had inhabited before I was born. One thing did surprise me though, when de Sande reminded everyone that this was

Wandering Star's last journey with the Reunification Commission. After almost fifty years of service, RuComm was having her decommissioned when we reached Bodens Gate. The tech team would transfer to the *Sierra Vista* for the rest of their mission while *Wandering Star* headed to the ship breakers.

"I'm sure we're all excited for our first assignments on the new *Vista*-class ships," he had concluded, "but let's stay focused and make this last leg of *Star's* last mission her best."

De Sande pulled me aside at the end of the meeting while everyone else headed to the mess hall for lunch. "Walk with me please, Ms. Holloman. We need to see the Captain." We left the central lab and walked silently through the passageways.

De Sande pressed his palm to a panel on the wall outside the bridge and waited. After a moment, the panel turned green and the hatch slid open. I had expected something grand, but the bridge looked like a medium sized office with a couple of big display panels covering one wall. The Captain was standing by his desk and a technician was lying on the floor with his upper body up inside one of the consoles doing repairs.

"Captain Kelang, you asked to see our new 'chaplain'. This is Mala Dusa Holloman. She'll be with us until Bodens Gate, and the church claims she's qualified." His tone of voice said he had his doubts, a lot of them. Unfortunately, I did too.

Captain Kelang took my hand. "Ms. Holloman, how like your mother you look." He had the same smile on his face Dad gets when he's lost in some memory.

"You knew my mom?"

"Just briefly. I was XO on the *Falling Star* when we picked your parents up on Cleavus and carried them to Bodens Gate. And I was Best Man at their wedding. We don't have too many nuptials on RuComm ships, but their love would not wait."

I felt my head grow light and my knees wobbled. "Oh, can I please talk to you privately sometime? I have so many questions."

"Of course. I'll make time for you. You know there's a full video capture of the entire wedding ceremony and reception, don't you? If you haven't already seen it, I'll have *Wandering Star* get a copy from her sister for you."

That was too much. I sat down in a chair in front of the Captain without asking permission. It was either that of faint dead away. "Sorry. Head's a little light." I explained.

"No need to apologize. Can I get you anything?"

De Sande sighed and I shook my head gently.

After a moment the Captain asked, "So, you're following in your mother's footsteps as a chaplain?"

"No sir, I'm just spending my summer break at the Mission in the Warrens. I'm studying to be an engineer, so I haven't been to seminary or anything. But if you need a chaplain, I'll try to do anything I can to help." I was feeling a little better now, some blood having made it back up into my brain.

He shook his head. "No disrespect, but I don't think you can help with this problem."

"Let me try," I said, trying to sound older again. "I might surprise you."

"You might." He was looking at me, but I think he was seeing my mom. "A week ago all of the sensors in the port aft engine room failed and power is now stuck at standard idle. We can still fly on the other three, but we can't make our jumps through the Deep Space Holes. I need it fixed. My technicians refuse to enter the engine room to see what's wrong or to bring the sensors back online."

"Why? It sounds like you need an engineer more than clergy."

"Mr. Solonius, come out from under there and tell our chaplain why you won't fix my engine."

Tobias Solonius introduced himself and stared at me for a moment, whether because I was the chaplain or that I was only sixteen or because I'm Mala Dusa, I don't know.

"Tell her what you and Ms. Williams experienced."

"Well, Sandy, that's Cassandra Williams, and I went into the engine room to see what the problem was that was keeping us from getting full power. I've worked the *Star*-class for almost twenty years and there's not a part of the ship I don't know. I love these ships and it's damn heartbreaking to see them being broken for parts. Anyway, we went into the engine room and it felt wrong, nothing I could identify like a sound or a smell, but just... *wrong*. I opened up the access panel and got down to crawl in there and I was suddenly aware of Sandy looking at me. I've worked with her on and off most of my career and, um, we work well together, but nothing beyond that. But that's not what Sandy was thinking right then. And that was the weird thing. I *knew* what she was feeling, almost able to know *what* she was thinking. She didn't say a word aloud. I turned around and looked at her and it was as if I was seeing her for the first time. God, she looked beautiful. I don't know why I never noticed it before. I reached up and took her hand and it was like fire flowing down my arm from where she was touching me.

"That's when the hooting sound started, coming from somewhere in the shadows. It wasn't an alarm or anything; I know every sound this ship can make and hooting's not one of them. I got up still holding Sandy's hand because I don't think I could have let go even if I had wanted to, and I didn't want to. I pulled her out of the engine room into the passageway planning to take her and..., well that doesn't matter. As soon as we were out of there it was as if a balloon had popped. I could think clearly again and we both said we were sorry and then we opened the hatch and went back into the engine room. I could feel what she was feeling again and I could feel her thoughts tickling around inside my head. We got out of there and we're not going back. We sent in a remote the next day and it didn't find anything unusual and the air checks out fine, so we weren't hallucinating. I know engineering and I know science, and this is isn't either one. It's unnatural."

"And what are you and Sandy going to do now?" the Captain asked for my benefit.

"Like I told you, sir, this will be the last hop for us. We're leaving RuComm and taking jobs where we can be together. You can laugh if you want, but we can still feel what the other is feeling when we're close enough. Opening my eyes to Sandy, maybe that's the one good thing to come out of this. But we're not going back in there, not unless..." He turned and looked at me.

Captain Kelang turned to me too, his lips twisted into a crooked smile. "Ms. Holloman, how would you feel about trying an exorcism?"

CHAPTER 4

WHO GOES THERE?

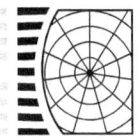

I looked from the Captain to Tobias and then to Mr. de Sande waiting for one of them to smile or laugh, wanting this to be some sort of sick initiation prank.

"You're serious?" The Captain wasn't smiling. "Sir?" I finished.

"Mr. Solonius, will you and Ms. Williams go in there and fix my engine if our chaplain goes in first and performs the rites?"

"Yes, sir. That's what we agreed to." His downcast eyes were telling me that he was regretting the bargain now that he had met me.

"Go get some lunch, Ms. Holloman, and then gather whatever else you need for this. Mr. de Sande, have her at the port aft engine room in an hour."

"She'll be there," he promised for me.

I went through the line in the mess hall, picking fish of some kind with Dulcinean purple tubers. I tried a bite. Not as good as Dad makes, but I don't think anything would have tasted very good to me right then. I thought while I chewed. The emotional connection sounded just like what I shared with Dad and Hannah. Could the source be the same? Something on *Wandering Star* that had tied us together? I wasn't sure that connection was a bad thing. I kind of liked it; it made us closer as a family. The intense romantic feelings were troubling, although even that wasn't necessarily bad. Tobias sure seemed happy with it.

I needed more information and there was only one place to get it. I unrolled my display pad and punched in a connection to Dad.

DND flashed back at me, Do Not Disturb. I tried Hannah and got the same result.

"Huh," I said out loud. "I guess you must have already caught her, Dad." I doubted Hannah had tried too hard to get away from him. My finger was hovering above the override icon, to put my call through anyway, when Sam sat down in front of me carrying a piece of pie.

"Hey, MD. Rumor has it that you're going ghost hunting this afternoon."

"MD?"

"Yeah, your initials."

"Yes, I know they're my initials. I'm just wondering why you're calling me by them."

"It seems easier than saying Mal-Uh Doo-Sa every time I see you, don't you think?" He took a bite of pie.

"Maybe 'Ms. Holloman' would be easier for you."

"Oh." He seemed to realize for the first time that he hadn't charmed me. "I'm sorry. I didn't mean to insult you. May I call you Mala Dusa?"

"Fine, whatever."

"Thank you. Please call me Sam. I just wanted to tell you some of the things the tech team told me over lunch, about how *Wandering Star* has been haunted for a long time."

I looked up at him from my lunch and unplaced call. "OK, go on."

"Well, no one knows exactly when it started but at least ten years ago. There have been stories of people seeing things, shimmers in the shadows, something moving in their peripheral vision that isn't there, that sort of thing. Sometimes people have felt weird things, strange emotions, or they think they can feel what someone else is feeling. I don't think I'd like that, if someone knew what I was feeling, you know?" He smiled at me nervously.

"What else?"

"Sara Jenkins, the team linguist, claims to have seen two different women and watched them disappear. One had short dark hair and seemed to be in a hurry. She was running around the infirmary and crying."

A chill chased down my arms. "And the other one?"

"Well, that's what brought this up. Sara says the other one looked just like you. A little older, maybe, and even thinner than you."

I frowned at him.

"Um, but she was pretty like you. That's what she said."

Sam wasn't a good liar, but Hannah was right about his eyes. They were blue, and I saw in them that he was not as sure of himself as he was trying to sound. "*Star* must have lots of images stored in her brain." I told him. "She can make anyone appear anywhere. It's like this business in the engine room. There's nothing supernatural about it, just *Star* playing tricks."

Sam nodded. "I'll go with you if you want."

"Why? Do you know anything about fixing engines?"

"No, I just thought, you know..."

I smiled at him. "Thanks, but I'm not scared. And if whatever affected Mr. Solonius and Ms. Williams is still active, I think it'd be better that I'm alone."

"Right! I heard about them. Sorry, you're right, you have to be alone." He blushed, which was kind of cute.

I took another bite of lunch and looked back at the DND still flashing on my screen. Sam excused himself and I was about to hit the override when Tobias and Mr. de Sande sat down across from me.

"Are you ready, Ms. Holloman? We still need to get you changed and ready to go."

I sighed and cancelled my call. They probably would have just lied to me anyway, or told me only part of the truth.

"Almost ready, Mr. Solonius. *Star*? Can you please put the exorcism ritual on my screen?"

"For a person, object or place?"

"Um, one for exorcising a place, please."

The words appeared on my display pad. "Is this what you're looking for, Ms. Holloman? I have several variations available if you would like a different one, but I assure you that I'm not haunted or possessed. If I were, I'm certain that I'd know it."

"This is perfect, *Star*. Thanks." I had no idea if it was perfect. The only exorcisms I had ever seen were at the theater, usually accompanied by teenagers screaming and running in terror from holographic demons. "I guess I'm ready." I walked out of the mess hall with Tobias while Mr. de Sande went to work 'other issues'.

I was willing myself to be the chaplain and wondering what a real chaplain would be feeling right then. I was feeling uncertain and afraid, and I prayed that no one else could feel what was inside me.

"We'll stop by your quarters first. I had *Star* print some coveralls for you that should fit. Wear something lightweight under them. The engine puts off a lot of heat even at idle and the engine room can get warm." We stopped outside my door. "I'll wait here for you while you change."

Once my door closed, I stripped down to my underwear and slid into the grey coveralls. The legs and sleeves were a few centimeters too long and they would have fit me better around the waist if I weighed twenty kilos more. I stepped out into the passageway feeling like I was wearing a large bag.

Tobias smiled at me. "*Star* has problems judging size sometimes." He cuffed the legs and sleeves and helped me adjust the belt so I didn't feel quite so much like I was a ten-year-old playing dress-up. "I've worked on the algorithm she uses for size determination, but I can't find the problem. She has a lot of problems."

"Not true," *Star* protested.

"And she's getting argumentative."

"Not. True."

"I think she knows what's coming at the end of this hop."

"I do know what's coming, Mr. Solonius. I know exactly what's coming. Do you?"

"I certainly do, *Star*. I'm leaving RuComm behind and I have a job waiting for me on Meeker restoring old aircraft." He turned toward me. "It doesn't pay much, but I can be with Sandy every day."

I smiled back at him. I didn't have to be able to feel his emotions to know how happy he was.

Captain Kelang and a woman I assumed was Sandy were waiting for us in the passageway outside the engine room. Sandy was wearing the same grey coveralls as me, but had the twenty kilos needed to fill them out. I wouldn't call her beautiful, but the eyes looking back at me were kind and intelligent when she shook my hand.

The Captain was not happy. He examined me closely while Sandy and Tobias helped attach a light and video sensor around my head, and stick an extra comm pin on my ear. He fixed my left sleeve where the cuff was already starting to come down.

"So, this is who we're sending in because the two of you can't do your jobs? Damn it, Williams, it's a good thing the two of you are leaving at the end of this hop or I'd fire both of you right now."

"Yes, sir," Sandy replied. "I *am* ashamed, but no way am I going back in there. Not until our chaplain has finished what we set out to do."

Captain Kelang turned to me. "Go in there, do what you need to do and get out. Leave if you see or hear or feel anything unusual, or if the comms drop out. Do you understand?"

"Yes, sir. I'm not afraid," I was lying, but I hoped that saying I wasn't afraid would make it true. "I'm sure this is just some new trick *Star* is playing. I think maybe she's stalling because she doesn't want to go to Bodens Gate." I smiled, trying to look confident.

"Is that true, *Star*?"

"It's true that I don't want to go to Bodens Gate, Captain, but I will go where I'm ordered."

"We tested the air in the engine room again this morning. The remote reported that it's fine." Tobias told me.

"Your remotes, they can't do any repairs themselves?" I asked.

"Yes, but—" He paused. "You'll find three of them in there. None of them worked for very long after we closed the hatch."

"Oh." *I am not afraid*, I told myself. "And *Star* can't see in there?"

Star answered, "I'm sorry, my sensors are offline. I can't tell you what's in there."

I approached the hatch, my heart pounding. I stepped through and it sealed behind me, leaving me in darkness other than the thin beam from the light on my head.

"Ow!"

"Are you OK?" Tobias's voice asked in my ear.

"It's dark and I tripped over one of your remotes."

"You should start the exorcism rite."

"I want to look around first."

"Do you see the control station to your right with the yellow light?"

I saw the yellow glow, but not much else. I walked toward it, the light on my head making long shadows.

"Lean over a little more so I can see the display. OK, slide the control on the right all the way up."

The lights came on. "Wow."

"What do you see? Move your head around."

"It's so big."

"We're not seeing anything odd on the monitor. What are *you* seeing?"

Sandy answered for me. "I think she's talking about the engine."

"Yes! It's huge." The engine room must have been three hundred meters long, maybe four hundred wide and at least half that high. The port aft engine filled most of it.

I looked back at the display on the control console. "Mr. Solonius, what about this list on the left? Are those *Star's* sensors?"

"Yes, those are all of her points of presence for that room. The telltales should be green."

"They're not. Should I try to turn them on?"

"Sure, but you should be going through the exorcism. Sandy and I can come in and help you then."

I tapped several of the sensors.

"I can see you now, Ms. Holloman," *Star's* voice spoke in my ear.

There was a rustling sound behind me. Before I could turn, something touched my leg. I jumped to the right I think at least ten meters, ending up on my back staring up at the ceiling.

Star told me, "Your heartrate just passed two hundred, Ms. Holloman. Are you feeling all right?"

I turned my head. The remote that had touched me was moving toward the access panel at the base of the engine. Tobias and Sandy were laughing and the Captain told me, "Ms. Holloman, next time you're planning on screaming like that please warn us. That was really loud."

"Yes, sir. Sorry. It wasn't exactly planned." I sat up. "Captain, I'm not feeling anything unusual in here at all. I can do the exorcism rite if you still want me to, but I don't think it's needed."

Tobias answered. "I'll come in there with you and see if we can get the engine started now."

"No, you're not." Sandy answered him. "You're not going in there with *her*."

I heard bits and pieces of the ensuing argument. Something about 'only sixteen' and 'just a child' and 'don't care', until finally the Captain ended it.

"Ms. Holloman, do you think you can bring the engine online with Mr. Solonius and Ms. Williams watching over you on the video link?"

"I can try." I stood up now that my heart rate was back down to double digits and walked back to the control console.

"Not from there, Ms. Holloman," Sandy's voice spoke gently in my ear, "you'll need to go inside."

"Inside?" The remote had opened the access hatch and rolled out of the way waiting for me. I paused at the entrance to the tunnel, peering in, uncertain. It was a meter wide and a meter high. I got down and crawled, feeling my heartrate starting to climb again. The remote trailed behind me.

"The remote will stay with you," Sandy assured me. "You might need an extra pair of hands if there's any physical damage."

"OK," I replied. "Is this really the only way into the engine?"

"It is without doing a cold shutdown."

After twenty meters of featureless grey metal, I emerged into a large room. It reminded me of spelunking with my dad. We'd follow a narrow passageway and then emerge into a wondrous chamber, but instead of flowing speleothems, I was seeing what looked like a frozen waterfall of metal alloy, darkened to bronzes and blues by heat. The shapes started somewhere two hundred meters above me, twisting and turning as they descended, combining into shapes I did not understand, but that looked purposeful. The massive tubes they formed disappeared through the deck plates I was standing on. The floor thrummed slowly, maybe forty beats per minute. It was so beautiful that a chill went through me.

I turned my head around, trying to see all of it at once. "This is amazing. Whoever designed it, they were artists, not engineers. Do you see the way this section combines and then kind of flows into the next shape?" I held my hands in front of me, trying to trace the smooth curves in the air. "It's wonderful!"

Tobias's voice answered. "I know, right? I never get tired of seeing it. And look above you at the injection plenum. No, up more and to the left. Do you see where it feeds into the regulator?"

"It's so pretty."

"What does she need to do first?" the Captain interrupted.

"Oh. Yes, sir. To your left, please, Ms. Holloman. Look at the display so I can see it."

Tobias and Sandy walked me through the process of logging in to initialize the engine, reestablish the logical links, and fix incorrect parameters. More than once the Captain asked who had shut the engine down and scrambled the configuration settings. Only the engineers and *Star* had access and they all denied doing it. When I looked at the access logs they didn't show anything unusual; no one had accessed the engine controls in the last week. An hour later, we were ready to bring the engine back on-line.

"One last thing you need to do before we go for full power, Ms. Holloman," Sandy said, her voice low.

"OK?"

There was a long pause before she said it. "You still need to do the exorcism, please."

"Sure," I replied. I opened my display pad and set it on the control console. *I am their chaplain*, I told myself. *I can do this*. "OK, please answer with 'amen' when I finish each section of the rite."

41

I started to read the ancient words. "Trusting in the promise that whatever we ask the Father in Jesus' name He will do, we now approach You Father, with confidence in Our Lord's words and in Your infinite power and love for us and for those who will live and work in this place, with the intercession of their guardian angels, with all the saints and angels of heaven, and Holy in the power of His blessed Name, to ask you Father to cleanse this place of all evil presences and protect it, and all those who shall live and work in this place from the infestation and harassment of the devil and his minions."

"Amen," they answered in my ear, and I continued through the text.

A few minutes later, I concluded with, "Father, all of these things we ask in the most holy name of Jesus Christ, Your Son. Thank you, Father, for hearing our prayer. We love You, we worship You, we thank You, and we trust in You. Amen."

I looked around the chamber one last time and tapped the icon to start *Wandering Star's* port aft engine. The rhythmic thrum started to increase in tempo while the remote and I hurried out through the access tunnel. Sandy said I had ten minutes to get clear, and I didn't want to waste any of it.

They were all waiting for me at the other end. I sat on the floor looking up at them while the remote secured the hatch behind me. "Did it work?" I asked.

"It seems to have," Tobias answered. "I don't feel anything unusual in here at all now."

I smiled. I had faith the exorcism had worked. If there had been anything demonic in there to begin with, it was gone now. I was more worried about the engine and whether it would reach full power. Maybe it would just blow a giant hole out through the side of the ship.

"And the engine?" I asked.

The Captain helped me to my feet. "You did a fine job, Ms. Holloman. Thank you. Are you all right?"

"Sure." I pulled the light and video sensor from my head, only then realizing that my hair was soaked in sweat, that all of me was soaked in sweat.

"And you didn't feel anything unusual?"

"No, just a sense of awe." I glanced behind me at the engine. I could feel its power pounding under my feet. "Your ship is so beautiful. If anything, I felt welcome there, like I was at peace, like I was at home." I said the words and then realized how silly they sounded even though they were true.

"Well, I'm glad we had a young woman on board with the courage to help my engineers do their jobs. Ms. Williams, will you please escort Ms. Holloman back to her cabin and help her get cleaned up, if she needs help, which I doubt." He nodded to me and left.

"I don't think he's too happy with us." Sandy commented.

"The Captain can go—" Tobias glanced at me. "I don't care what he thinks. He didn't experience what we did."

Sandy touched his cheek. "You're not really mad, I can feel it. You're just happy it's over." Sandy smiled at me. "You must think we're crazy, claiming to be able to know what each other are feeling."

"It's a gift," I told them. "You should be thankful for it." I didn't tell them about my parents and me, or that it was sometimes a curse as well. We stepped out into the passageway and the hatch sealed behind us. The air was cool and clean after the hot machine oil smell of the engine room.

When we reached my cabin, I assured them that I didn't need any help. The door closed behind me and all I wanted was to strip off the sweat-soaked coveralls that were clinging to me everywhere, take a shower, and then get on my display pad. I wanted to politely ask my parents about another secret that they had been keeping from me. Except I wasn't feeling very polite. It was really too bad that they were too far away to fully share what I *was* feeling.

I had calmed down some by the time I was clean and back into clothes that fit me. I sat at the small desk in my cabin, my long hair still dripping, and opened the display pad. I punched Dad's name and waited. When it timed out I punched it again. On the third try Hannah answered, her hair dripping wet. We looked at each other for a moment and both started laughing. The last of my anger evaporated.

"We were in the pool," Hannah explained. "Winona got here a little bit ago."

"I was in the shower," I answered, "because I got all sweaty."

"How did you do that?"

"I was inside *Wandering Star's* port aft engine for almost two hours fixing it. It gets warm in there."

"Why you?" Dad had joined her now. When the screen adjusted to include him, I saw Winn splashing around in the pool behind them. I felt a sharp pang of homesickness.

"Because the two engineers refused to go in until after I did an exorcism rite. They were convinced the engine room was possessed by the devil, and Father Ryczek had told them that I'd serve as acting chaplain for the hop to Bodens Gate."

Hannah's head was tipping more and more to the right as I spoke. "You've only been on board a few hours and already... this?"

"Yeah," I smiled. "I've been busy. Maybe tomorrow I'll overthrow a government."

Hannah didn't smile, but Dad turned away for a moment so she wouldn't see his.

"Keep going. Why did they think the engine room was possessed?"

"The engineers were in there a few days ago because the engine had gone to idle and they couldn't restart it. They said it didn't feel right in the engine room, and there was a weird hooting sound. Then, all of a sudden, and even though they had worked together for years without any romantic interest in each other, they realized that they were deeply, passionately, in love. And, oh, they also noticed that they could feel each other's emotions, like they knew what the other person was feeling. Really weird, huh?" I leaned closer to the screen so I could see her reaction. I didn't have long to wait.

"Those bastards!" At first I thought she meant Sandy and Tobias, but she didn't. She turned to Dad. "Two years of our lives we wasted chasing after them. We searched Cleavus, and in the Warrens, and followed every lead from every planet until RuComm got sick of it, pulled our funding, and tried to ruin our careers. They were probably hiding on *Wandering Star* the whole time, laughing at us with those stupid hooting noises."

"Who are you talking about?" I asked.

"The damn Tarakana."

"Those big six legged color changing animals from Cleavus you told me about? The ones with the tentacles growing out of their heads?" I waved my hands around by my head. "You told me they were like big friendly dogs."

"Are you in a private location?" Dad asked.

"I'm in my cabin."

He glanced over his shoulder at Winona and then at Hannah.

"I agree," Hannah answered the question I hadn't heard. "Winona should hear this too."

Dad called to her and soon she was sitting with them wrapped in a towel and dripping water on the patio.

"Duse, why are you wet?"

"Mom and Dad will fill you in later. Now hush, I think they're about to reveal another deep family secret."

44

"I have not fully recovered from the last one." She looked from Dad to Hannah and back to me. "I was just now working on reintegrating my understanding of how planetary politics works."

"While you were swimming in my pool?"

"Yes. I like your pool."

"Winona," Hannah said gently, "I ask that you not tell anyone what you are about to hear."

"Of course. I already know who you are and what could be worse than—" She stopped. "Never mind, I can think of at least six things that could be worse. You have my word."

Dad smiled softly. "OK, let's see if this one made your list."

He thought about it for a moment and said, "Probably best to start at the beginning. You know what happened on Cleavus, how we thought we had found a lost settlement from the first Union, but that they turned out to be exiles from Bodens Gate. Well, there was more on Cleavus than just the Bovita clan. There was also a colony of large animals that the Bovita called Tarakana. They were about forty or forty-five kilos, had six legs, and a couple of tentacles near their eyeless bump of a head. They could change colors so well as to practically become invisible."

"They were indigenous to Cleavus?" Winn asked. "That seems unlikely given the absence of other megafauna there."

"That's what my friend Jake thought too. He dissected a couple of them that the Bovita had killed. They have a distributed nervous system, evidence of high intelligence, and a cellular structure that allows them to change shapes, not just colors."

"Shape shifters," Winona whispered. "How high of intelligence?"

"Very high. Language. Advanced technology, like power systems, refined metals, cities, maybe spaceflight. And the ability to hide it all from *Wandering Star's* optical, thermal, and radar sensors."

Winona was taking it better than me. I knew my mouth was open, but every time I closed it, it just opened again. Winn looked calmly at my dad and asked, "What else?"

"This is supposition, but they seem to establish colonies in close proximity to humans. They like to be around strong human emotions and they will manipulate us to get it. They seem to only want positive emotions like friendship and love—"

"And obsession and passion and lust," Hannah added.

45

"Yes, but never fear or anger, at least not in our experience. Each colony is a single organism with individuals linked telepathically acting as one. We can communicate with them. I did a little the first time I was with them, and I soon found out that physical contact greatly enhanced the effect. If two people touch a Tarakana at the same time they will be able to see into each other's minds, feel their emotions, and literally read their thoughts." He looked at Hannah and seemed very uncomfortable. "It's, um, intimate and the effect is lasting. We haven't been in contact with the Tarakana since leaving Bodens Gate, but I can still feel everything Hannah feels."

"How did they get from Cleavus to Bodens Gate?" I asked.

Dad closed his eyes. "Alice and I brought one with us. We couldn't say no. It had made itself look like a dog by taking the image and behavior of one from my memory. No one would suspect he was the intelligent representative of a space-faring civilization. They had helped us survive on Cleavus, provided heat and power and food. We owed it to him, I suppose, but we didn't have a choice. He made us feel like it was the right thing to do, maybe the only thing we *could* do. It's hard to explain if you've never had one of them inside your head."

Winona was staring at my dad. "You helped him create a new colony, didn't you? He started reproducing once you were there?"

"Yes, he did."

"So they are symbiotic with us."

"Yes, that's what I believe too. After the civil war had ended on Bodens Gate and the Confederation had taken over the Central Government, Hannah and I tried to find them again. We couldn't. We convinced RuComm to provide funding to search for the Tarakana. We didn't tell them everything in the grant request of course, just that they seemed fairly intelligent and that the dissections had shown a lot of unknown structures. But the Tarakana were *gone*. We couldn't find them on Cleavus or Bodens Gate. We followed lead after lead until RuComm gave up on us and pulled our funding. Mala Dusa was getting too old to be drifting from planet to planet with us by then anyway, so we settled on Dulcinea. Hannah went back to work for the Bodens Gate commission and I did planetary geology projects for RuComm. Now we don't talk about the Tarakana. I think RuComm's official position is that the Tarakana were never real, that Alice and I dreamed them up to keep us company when we were marooned on Cleavus, like an imaginary friend."

He smiled at Winona, whose eyes had reached maximum size during his story. "So Winona, was this on your list of worse things?"

"I had ranked them by probability. Intelligent aliens were number five. Almost impossible."

"I'm curious," I asked, "what was number six?"

Her voice had dropped to a whisper. "That you and your whole family are aliens."

Hannah held her hand out to her. "All too human, Winona. Take my hand, feel my pulse. The Tarakana scare the crap out of me. When you're with them, they seem gentle and wise and you can't imagine they would do anything to cause us harm. The longer I'm away from them the less I believe it. We searched for them for over two years and almost destroyed our professional reputations and our careers."

She smiled at Dad, and something came into her eyes; something sparkly. Dad's eyes reflected it, ready to join her on whatever campaign she was planning.

"Ted, we've got them now, on board *Wandering Star*. We know where they are and they can't escape." She turned toward me, eyes wild, and that arrogant smile touching her lips. She looked like her statue. "They already have a colony on Bodens Gate, where was *Wandering Star* supposed to go next?"

"Nowhere," I answered. "She's being decommissioned and parted out at the shipyard there. The RuComm team is transferring to the new *Vista-*class ships. There's like three of them on orbit around Bodens Gate. *Buena Vista* is bound for Dulcinea and *Sierra Vista* is going to Ratatoskr, I think. I'm not sure about the other one."

"Your RuComm team isn't going anywhere. *Wandering Star* is about to be impounded and quarantined by order of the Central Government, that is, by me, since I *am* the CG... at least until the elections next month. No one leaves that ship until I have the Tarakana in a box and then let RuComm try to laugh at us. I don't care what it takes or how long."

"Um, I'm on board this ship, remember?"

"Yes, I know that. You'll be fine," she said dismissively. "I'm coming to Bodens Gate too. There's a meeting with the election board that they wanted me to attend in person because of the time lag. Damn, this is going to be satisfying." Her eyes were still wild when she looked at Dad.

Winona had talked about how Dad was a catalyst for her and I had thought she meant the way they had worked together to rebuild the

Central Government and create a society based on individual rights and freedom, or even how they plan adventurous family vacations together. Looking at them smiling at each other now, I knew he would reinforce whatever she wanted to do, good or bad, and I was thinking that this was going to turn out bad.

For the first time, I think I was experiencing Hannah the revolutionary, Hannah the folk hero, Hannah the killer. I hoped Hannah my mom was still in there somewhere, but I couldn't see her and it scared me.

My best and only friend was sitting next to her taking it all in. The screen resolution was high enough that I could see Winona's goosebumps and the look of hero worship in her eyes. It made me feel very far from home.

CHAPTER 5

TARAKANA

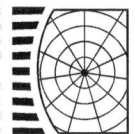

"Mom? We're doing the jump through the first Deep Space Hole tonight at 22:00. After that, comms will be delayed almost twelve hours each way. What should I do? I'm—" I almost said it, but caught myself and reversed. "I am not scared. I just don't know what to do."

Her face softened and Mom was looking back at me again. The tightness in my chest relaxed just a bit.

"It's OK to feel afraid, Mala Dusa. Like I said earlier, the Tarakana scare the crap out of me too, but you should be safe. Your dad and Alice were alone with them for over three months and they were never harmed physically."

I saw Dad smirk at Hannah's careful choice of words. Hannah and my dad were more in love than any couple I knew, but nothing is perfect. The love I had heard in Dad's voice when he was telling me stories about my real mom didn't diminish his love for Hannah, but I'm sure she knew it was still there and it must hurt.

Hannah sighed before continuing, trying on the fly to come up with rules for living with a Tarakana. "OK, first off, don't go exploring on your own. Try to stay with the rest of the tech team when you're not in your cabin."

Dad added, "The Tarakana weigh about forty kilos and can look like anything or nothing at all if they're hiding."

"If you see any dogs that size don't touch them."

"And don't let yourself be alone with any one person."

"Especially not Sam."

"Sam?" Winn asked, "Who's Sam?"

"A boy," Hannah answered.

"A man," Dad corrected, "on his first hop with RuComm."

"What's he like, Duse? Cute?"

"No! Maybe. I don't know. He's a lot older than me, and mostly he's just annoying. I have *zero* interest in him."

Hannah sighed. "That's how it always starts."

"So," I said, "I should stay in my cabin, and when I'm not, I should stay in the main parts of the ship, always be with a crowd, and never be alone with any male-type person."

"As your father, I endorse that plan."

"And we'll meet you on Bodens Gate," Hannah promised. "It will take me a couple of days to arrange, but we shouldn't be more than three or four days behind you."

"You and Dad are both coming?"

"All three of us," she answered. "Unless Winona wants to stay here and go back to her house."

"No. Please no. I promised Mala Dusa that I would keep her safe." She was looking in Hannah's eyes, pleading. "I wish I was there with her now."

"All three of us, then. Be brave Mala Dusa and we'll see you soon."

After they disconnected I opened my cabin door and looked out into the passageway, half-expecting to see a pair of Tarakana waiting for me. There was nothing, or at least nothing I could see. I closed the door and thought about it for a minute. What I really, really wanted to do was go exploring. I wanted to see more of the ship's internals, like what I had seen in the engine room. The beauty of industrial design had never affected me like that before. I wanted to see the engines again, to touch the warm metal and feel the rapid vibrations shaking the floor and the walls. Maybe Tobias and Sandy would be willing to show me.

"*Star*, where is Ms. Williams?"

"Ms. Williams is in hydroponics."

Hydroponics. I wanted to see that too, I wanted to see everything. "Can you guide me to her?"

"I can, but that area is restricted to crew."

"Can you ask her if I can come anyway?"

There was a pause, then Star answered, "How about tomorrow after breakfast?"

"OK. Thank her for me."

I paced around the cabin. "*Star*, what time is dinner?"

"Dinner is served from 17:30 to 18:30, but there is always food available through the printers if you're hungry."

"No, just restless."

"Perhaps a run in the outer ring corridor? Your father was fond of the Sonoran Desert simulation. He made several modifications that are still available."

"Yes, I'll try it. Can you guide me there?"

"Follow the green ball, Mala Dusa."

I followed. The outer ring corridor was a passage around the fattest part of the ship used for access during refueling and resupply. At just over two kilometers in circumference, Dad had told me that it made a nice place to run laps. When I first entered, all I saw were grey metal plates: floor, ceiling and walls.

"This is the standard Sonoran Desert simulation," *Star* told me.

Everything wavered and then it looked like I was standing on a desert trail. I stomped my foot. It still felt like deck plate.

"This illusion is only optical and auditory. Let me add your father's modifications."

The scene changed subtly. The colors were more natural and there were smells. It felt like it was early morning before the dew had evaporated. What had been an empty sky now had cumulus clouds in the distance trying to form up into a thunderstorm.

"I love my dad."

"I have always enjoyed working with him," *Star* answered.

As I started to run I realized that I was violating Hannah's rule number one; I was alone. But it didn't feel like I was alone with *Star* there with me.

"Can you sing to me while I run?" I asked her.

"What would you like to hear?"

"You know what I want. Elephant song!"

Before I was even half way around the first lap, I was singing with her.

"Elephant walked a lonely, weary way, through oh so many lands
Towering forests dark and green, and deserts of sand
Crossed oceans wide and mountains steep

and e'en thru swamps he did creep
Singing "Home, home, home,
Oh, for a home to rest my feet."

It had always been my favorite. I made Hannah sing it to me every night for years. She must have gotten sick of it, but she never complained.

By the end of the first lap, I was shouting the lyrics out as I ran. The little elephant and the friends he met along the way, the camel, the monkey and the hippo, had realized that the journey with each other was better than any home they could imagine, and that their wandering feet would wander forever.

When *Star* stopped singing I yelled, "Again!" and we went through it all a second time. And a third, and I don't know how many more times.

By the fourth lap, the thunderstorm was moving across the valley. The sky darkened and a cool wind was blowing in my face. Wind and lightning and thunder, the smell of desert after the rain in the air; Dad had done a beautiful job. Half way through the fourth lap I was wondering how dark it was going to get as clouds gathered over me. I got my answer in a brilliant flash of lightning, and thunder so loud that I missed a step. Cold rain came pouring over me and I was drenched in an instant.

"*Star*! No! Stop, discontinue, close the sim, no more, enough." The sky cleared and the outer ring corridor was back to grey painted metal. "What was that?" I pushed my hair back away from my eyes, tasting rainwater and sweat.

"Your father and I worked quite hard on the thunderstorm simulation. Was it realistic?"

"Yes, perfection. I think I need to go back to my cabin now."

"Do you need help finding it?"

"No, as long as you haven't moved it or created hidden sink holes or quick sand along the way."

"Not at this time."

If *Star* had a face, I'm sure she would have been smirking.

"Dad told you to do this, didn't he?"

"While he was helping you strap into the shuttle, as you'll recall."

I did recall. Dad wasn't very subtle, but you had to be paying attention *all* the time.

"Please send him a note from me thanking him for making such a realistic simulation."

"Sent."

I ate dinner that night with Tobias and Sandy, and we talked about starship design and engineering, and the *Vista*-class ships that were entering service with their new engines that would cut transit times by twenty percent. By the time I was finishing my bowl of ice cream, I had convinced myself that RuComm was the next step in the life I wanted. My parents would be mad when I applied to the Academy, but there was a desire burning in me unlike anything I had ever known. I wanted, no, I *had* to design or build these works of moving art that carried our species between the forty worlds where humans now lived. I could not imagine anything that would give more meaning to my life.

After dinner, I asked Tobias and Sandy if they would walk me back to my room even though I knew the way. I thought I had seen something shimmering under one of the tables on the far side of the mess hall and a wave of fear had started to go through my mind. But then it stopped. I looked at the shadow under the table again and there was nothing there. I should be afraid of the Tarakana, I thought. They're on board this ship and no one knows it, not even *Star* herself. I should be terrified, but when I tried to think about it, my brain just kind of felt fuzzy.

Sam came up to me while I was taking my tray to the recycler.

"What are your plans for this evening, Mala Dusa?"

"It's been a long day. I'm just going back to my cabin to crash."

"Oh, that's too bad. I was going to work out for a while before bed, maybe run the outer ring corridor. I thought you might want to join me." He smiled. "*Star* has trail simulations that you can load. They're supposed to be pretty good."

"I've heard about that. My dad even did some modifications to the Sonoran Desert sim. You should try it. He said to just ask *Star* to load his mods on top of the base trail."

"Thanks. I'll try it out tonight. Sure you don't want to come?"

"Not tonight."

He left and I smiled to myself, feeling evil. A cold shower before bed would do Sam good.

The mess hall was still full of people finishing dinner, talking to friends, and laughing together. I realized there was nothing to fear. It was foolish to have Tobias and Sandy walk me to my cabin, I knew how to get there and I wasn't a little child. I had decided to tell them that I'd find my own way, but when I got back to the table they assured me it was no problem, so I got my escort anyway.

My door closed and the lights came on. I wasn't afraid anymore, but I still examined each of the shadows in my cabin very carefully. I unpacked my bags, got everything arranged the way I liked it and then sat down at the desk and connected through to Winona.

She was sitting at the desk in my room, which was now her room.

"Winn? How did my bed get over by the window?"

She looked over her shoulder as though wondering the same thing. "Oh, I like to sleep with the window open so I can feel the cool night air on my face. I'll help you move it whenever we make it back here."

I didn't like the way she had phrased that, and Winona was never careless with her words. "We'll be back before the start of school, right?"

"That's probably true."

"You think Mom's hunt will take longer?"

"The Tarakana." She paused, thinking. "This isn't a hunt, it's a diplomatic mission. They have lived alongside us for who knows how long. Since the rise of the first Union? Maybe before humans even left Earth? Why do they hide from us? Where do they come from? There are a thousand questions and no answers. Your mom seems excited and determined, but I think she's scared too. It seems very personal for her."

"And I'm stuck right in the middle of it on a ship full of them."

"And with Samuel Coleridge." Winona smiled. "Tell me about him. I know 'zero interest' was just for your parents."

"*Zero* interest. Even without being terrified of what the Tarakana might do if I let myself be alone with him. He's five years older than me, Winn, and I don't like the way he looks at me even if he does have pretty eyes."

"What color?"

I giggled. "Don't do that to me. They're blue."

"I don't think you need to be too worried. Your dad and Alice were alone together with the Tarakana for over six weeks before you were conceived."

"Winona!"

"Whatever they do to human desire seems to be cumulative and slow acting, but also very persistent. I suspect your two engineers were being influenced by them long before the incident in the engine room."

There was a knock on my door. "Just a sec, Winn. *Star*, who is at my door?"

"Mr. Coleridge."

"Tell him to wait a moment." I looked at Winona and whispered, "What should I do?"

54

"Let him in. I'd like to look at him."

"I can't have him in here *alone* with me."

"You won't be. I'm here with you."

I don't know why that made sense to me, but it did.

I opened the door and a very wet Sam Coleridge was standing in front of me. I bit my lower lip, but before I could say anything, like an apology, Sam said, "Mala Dusa, you *have* to try this. Your dad is a genius. The trail he designed, it's brilliant. It has smells, and the colors are perfect and best of all, it has the most realistic thunderstorm I've ever seen."

"I know. I, uh, ran it this afternoon before dinner. I didn't want to, um, spoil the surprise?"

"Thanks, I appreciate that." He pushed wet hair away from his face. "I'm sorry to have bothered you, but I had to tell you what a great job your dad did." He smiled and turned to leave.

"Don't leave yet." He turned and looked at me with such hope in his eyes that I immediately regretted stopping him. "I was just talking to my best friend. She wanted to say hello to you." I stepped aside and he came into my cabin, still dripping water.

I sat back at the desk and Sam knelt down next to me, smiling at Winona.

"Sam, this is Winona Killdeer; Winn, Sam Coleridge."

"Hi, Winona."

Winn just stared at him, eyes big, absorbing every detail. Sam glanced over at me, as if asking, *is this normal?*

"Say hello, Winona," I prompted.

"Mala Dusa claims to not like you very much, but she's lying. Just take it slow and you'll do fine."

I put my hands over my eyes and knew my cheeks were bright red. I think I made a little 'urp' sound.

Sam laughed nervously. "Um, Mala Dusa, I think I should be leaving now. I guess I'll see you at breakfast. Goodnight Winona, it was a pleasure meeting you."

I didn't take my hands away from my eyes until I heard the door close behind him.

"Winona Killdeer, I should have just let the Tarakana come in here with me, for all the help you are."

"I did help you. I reset his goals from short term to long term. You can be friends with him now without worrying that he'll try something if he gets you alone."

"Oh." I looked at the doorway he had just walked through and the wet carpet where he had knelt next to me. "Thanks, Winn, but you couldn't have made it slightly less embarrassing?"

She looked at me, head tipped just like Hannah. "You go slow too, Duse. Make a friend and then see how you feel about him after we graduate."

I sighed. "I'm not even sure yet if I like him at all."

At 22:00, Wandering Star transited the first Deep Space Hole. There was a moment just before the jump when it felt like the engines had stopped, then I felt like I was falling for a fraction of a second, and then gravity was back and the vibration in the floor returned to normal. I was lying in bed reading when it happened. "Huh," I said out loud. "The engine I fixed didn't explode after all."

After we finished breakfast, Tobias and Sandy showed me their ship. I say 'their ship' because in their minds the Captain just gave orders occasionally, we were missing our Executive Officer for *Wandering Star's* last hop, and the RuComm technical team were just passengers. I found the logic hard to argue with.

We went to all four of the engine rooms, made adjustments to the hydroponics bay where fresh food and fish were being grown, toured the recycling system where the rain from yesterday's thunderstorms was being turned into tomorrow's coffee, and did preventative maintenance on the environmental controls. They let me see the system that enabled *Wandering Star* to grapple the artificial black holes and hurl herself lightyears away in less than a second. Every part of it was interesting and beautiful to me, and Tobias and Sandy were enthusiastic tour guides and teachers. They were the first people I had ever known who understood the joy I felt being with machines and electronics and working with Artificial Intelligences like the one that was *Star*.

I tried to explain that to them while we ate lunch. "I can't thank you enough for taking the time to have me tag along with you this morning. I've always wanted to be an engineer." I took a bite of my salad before continuing. "Now I think that love must have been burned into me when I was little, running through these passageways as soon as I was old enough to run."

I grinned at them, but they looked confused. "I was born on this ship. I thought you knew."

Sandy's eyes widened when she finally realized who I was. "Oh. Your birth here is kind of a legend, as was your mother's, um, I mean—"

"My mother's death," I finished for her. "It's OK. That's why I passed on looking at the medical AI and the infirmary. I don't remember anything about it, of course, but still, it bothers me when I think about it too much."

"I can understand that, honey. I've never seen anyone so much in love with this ship as you seem to be. It's funny," she smiled at Tobias, "he and I went into that engine room and discovered that we loved each other. You went in there alone and discovered that you loved *Wandering Star*."

"I, uh, I hadn't—" I felt very confused. What if what I was feeling, my desire to go to the Academy and learn how to design ships, was all just the Tarakana messing with me?

"Mala Dusa, are you all right?"

"I'm fine, just thinking. If I want to learn to design starships, does it make sense to go to the Academy?"

"There're other schools with good programs, but the Academy is one of the best. It's where I went. I'll write you a letter of recommendation if you like."

That made me feel better. Maybe the Tarakana hadn't completely compromised my emotions.

"Thank you, I'm not sure yet, but—"

"Ms. Holloman?" *Star* interrupted. "Your file transfer from *Falling Star* has been completed. You can view it on your display pad, but I would recommend that you use the ring corridor to experience it in three dimensions."

"Are you *sure* you're OK?" Sandy asked. "All the color just went out of your cheeks. What file did you receive?"

"My parents were married on *Falling Star* on their way to Bodens Gate," I explained, my voice barely above a whisper. "The whole ceremony was recorded. I've never seen my mom before, other than still images and short 2D clips." I looked at what was left of my salad, not wanting any of it.

"You need to go, then. Here," she handed me a packet of tissues, "you might need these."

I ran all of the way to the ring corridor.

"*Star*, load my file, please." The corridor faded, and she replaced it with the Dulcinean Heritage Trail, the DHT. I had hiked and camped along the real trail almost every summer with Dad and Hannah growing up. In the simulation, I was standing in a meadow full of people. A much younger Captain Kelang was there, wearing his XO uniform, and my dad was there, looking handsome and not much older than Sam.

And my mom was there. Her dress was elegant and perfect for the thin build she and I shared. Her hair was long and blonde just like mine, but neatly braided down her back and with flowers and something that sparkled woven into it. I looked at her face and sighed. No one would ever consider her pretty, but a strange thing happened when I put the recording in motion. She turned and looked at Dad and he smiled at her with such love in his eyes that she seemed transformed when she smiled back at him. Is it possible for someone to be beautiful because someone loves them? My mom was beautiful.

I watched the whole ceremony from beginning to end without stopping and then started it again. The second time, I paused it in several places so I could walk around and look at everything from different angles. I went through the entire packet of tissues that Sandy had given me.

It was late afternoon before I told *Star* to close the file. The DHT faded away and cold gray deck plates and walls replaced it. Except my mom was still there in her wedding dress, looking right at me and smiling, just as though she was smiling at me because she loved me.

"*Star*, please close the file."

"It is closed, Ms. Holloman."

"Close it again, then."

Mom disappeared, but then part of the simulation came back. Where I was standing was still gray metal, but ten meters away the DHT was still running, following the curve of the corridor into the distance. My mom was standing at the edge of a grove of trees wearing a blue t-shirt, hiking shorts and oversized boots. She was staring right at me like she was waiting for me to follow her.

"*Star*, why are you doing this?" I felt tears starting.

"The file is closed."

"No, it's not. I can see her right there under the shade of the trees." As I pointed the last of the simulation closed, and the DHT and my mom were gone.

I ran back to my cabin and punched in the code for Winona. I told her everything that had happened and that I *was* scared, although I was trying very hard not to be. I told her that I didn't know if what I had seen at the end of the file was an artifact of data corruption, *Wandering Star's* AI continuing to degrade, or if the Tarakana were already inside my head, making me feel things and see things that weren't really there. I told her that I was holding tight to the lock of hair she had given me and how it made me feel closer to her and yet miss her even more. I asked her to pray for me and then I hit the send icon. In twelve hours Winona would see my message, and it would be another twelve hours after that before I could expect to see her response.

CHAPTER 6

MERRIMAC

I was on my bed curled into a ball with my arms wrapped around my knees when *Star* interrupted me. "Mr. Coleridge asks if you will be coming to dinner."

"What time is it?"

"Ship's time is 17:45."

I had been sitting on my bed for over an hour, but I didn't remember much of anything after sending the message to Winona. "Tell him I'll be there in a few minutes."

I forced myself to stand and walk to the mirror. Red eyes framed by disheveled hair stared back at me. I tied my hair back, threw some cold water on my face and looked again. I have my mom's face, except a little rounder. My eyes, when they're not red and puffy, look like Dad's. I considered just ordering something to eat from the printer, but no, I was somehow the ship's chaplain, at least for a few more days, and I was brave.

I put my hand on the panel by the cabin door and said it out loud. "I am not afraid."

The door slid open and a German Shepherd dog was sitting in the passageway staring back at me. He was a big one, at least forty kilos. I stumbled over my own feet backing away from him while frantically trying to find the panel again to close the door. I tripped, and landed hard on my back knocking the wind out of me. The door hissed closed as I fell.

I was still struggling to breathe when I opened my eyes. He was right there looking down at me. The dog was inside my cabin. I whimpered as he nuzzled against my neck with his nose.

"*Star*?" I managed to gasp. There was no answer. "*Star*, can you hear me?" *Star* couldn't hear me. No one could hear me.

The dog's face was a few centimeters away from mine, concern in his brown eyes. I could *feel* his concern as he tried to calm me. It was the same as feeling my parent's emotions, but stronger, more intimate, and more overpowering. I propped myself up on my elbows, trying to scoot away from him. He laid down next to me, resting his head across my stomach.

Don't touch them, my dad had warned. *Don't be alone with them*. Weren't those the rules that I had promised to obey? Now all I needed was for Sam to join us there on the floor and my life would be ended.

My hand reached up to scratch him behind his left ear before I realized what it was doing and could tell it to stop. His tongue lolled out as though enjoying my touch. No, he *was* enjoying my touch. I could feel it. My view of the cabin seemed to grow fuzzy and dark, and the soul of the small Tarakana colony hummed under my fingers as I moved them through his fur.

After a moment, words began to form in my head. "*Mala Dusa, Little Soul, you have been absent for so long. Do you remember how we used to play together?*"

"I thought I had dreamed it," I replied. It was sharp and clear in my memory now. "You looked like a little elephant then, and we would march through the passageways together while *Star* sang to us."

"*You remember.*"

"Oh, yes." I hugged him, burying my face in his fur, no longer afraid. Somewhere in the back of my head was the remnant of the terror that I should be feeling, but it was very far away.

"*You look so much like your father. Your thoughts are straight lines and distant horizons to me.*"

I laughed. "I look like my mom."

"*Your outer shell is like hers, but nothing else. You are calm air, she was endless turbulence. It is restful to have you inside me.*"

"There are only seven of you?"

"*There is one, with seven pieces. Do you see me?*"

"Yes, I do now." In addition to the one with me in my cabin, there was a Tarakana in each of the engine rooms, one in the mess hall, and one in

Sam's cabin. I could see what each of them was seeing, like having eyes all over the ship.

Sam was in the mess hall, standing up, leaving his food untouched. "He's is on his way here, isn't he?"

"Yes. He is worried that you haven't come to dinner and Star has told him that you are not answering."

"What are you going to do?"

"What I always do. It's what you want me to do. I can feel it in you, the desire for him to look at you the way your father looked at your mother and then to make yourself one with him. I did it for your parents. It's how you were created."

I don't know what the Tarakana do to suppress fear in humans, but it stopped working on me right then. I was afraid again and I was angry.

"My mother and my father loved each other! It was *real* love, not something you stuffed into their heads." I pushed him away from me and stood up, looking around the cabin for something heavy to swing at his head.

"Little Soul, go gently. They loved each other, yes, even before they touched each other's minds their desire was growing. We can do nothing but make what is already there stronger. For centuries, we have done so. We need to feel the strength of your emotions as much as you do. If waiting for the boy will make your feelings stronger, then I will stop for now."

I stood there panting and put my chair back down. The fear and anger were already fading away as I looked into his eyes, a kind of mist rolling through my thoughts. "Of course. I know you'll never hurt me. It's what you promised me, isn't it?"

"Yes, I did. Long ago, when first we were friends."

My door chime sounded and the Tarakana slipped under the desk and disappeared.

"You are brave, Mala Dusa. You are not afraid."

"I am not afraid," I repeated, and opened the door.

Sam was standing there, concern in his eyes. I was thankful that I could only see it and not feel the emotion in him.

"Mala Dusa, are you OK? When *Star* said you weren't answering, I got worried." He touched my cheek to push away the hair that was falling across my face. I wanted to jump away from his touch and I also wanted to lean into it, so I stood still, not doing either one. The need to be comforted was almost too much for me.

After a moment, I took a step back from him. "I must have fallen asleep again." I re-tied my hair and straightened my shoulders. "I'm ready for dinner as long as you don't mind me looking like I just woke up."

"You look great."

While we ate, I told Sam about watching the recording of my parents' wedding. I hoped he would assume that it was the only reason for my red eyes and emotional distress.

"It's strange that it stuttered like that at the end, but only on your second time through it."

"Maybe it was because I paused it so many times," I suggested.

"Maybe. You should mention it to the engineering team."

I shook my head. "I don't think it matters. With all the problems *Star* has, and this close to her end? I think they're just focused on keeping the critical systems working long enough to get us to Bodens Gate."

"Still, *you* fixed one of the engines."

I rolled my eyes. "I followed Sandy and Tobias' instructions. But at least it didn't blow up when we went through the Deep Space Hole."

"Was that a possibility?"

"Probably not."

"Probably?"

I smiled. "Have you known many engineers? They never say yes or no."

"But you're also our chaplain, at least for a few days. Isn't that all about absolutes?"

"Yes." I smiled, enjoying keeping him off balance.

"I was thinking about going for a walk in the outer ring corridor after dinner. Would you like to go with me?"

"Probably."

"So I'd be walking with the engineer?"

"Yes."

"And the chaplain," he nodded. "With you I get both, don't I?"

"With you, all I get is a biologist?"

He looked away. "Sure. I'm not as complicated as you."

"I'm not as complicated as you think, and I suspect there's more to you than your biology." I realized too late how that sounded and turned away, blushing. Knowing that the Tarakana wouldn't be messing with our emotions had made me bold, but if I kept up like this, we wouldn't need their help.

"Can we go exploring instead of walking one of the trails?" I asked. "I saw a lot of *Star's* insides this morning, but I'd like to see where the RuComm team works."

"OK. It's not too exciting unless you like machinery and equipment... which, of course, you do."

I smiled back at him. "See how simple I am?"

It *was* interesting walking through the labs and work areas. I imagined seeing the men and women and the great things they had accomplished there.

"This ship, she did a lot to bring the Union back together. It doesn't seem right to just take her apart."

Sam shrugged. "The new ships are better. The mission will go on. RuComm's more focused on finding and developing new worlds now and the *Star*-class ships are too small and too old." He smiled at me. "You're a romantic."

When we reached the simulation lab, I stopped and ran my hand over the control panel. "My parents and my stepmom worked here in this lab sixteen years ago."

Sam looked around. "I don't think anything has been updated since then. Maybe not even cleaned. I'm really looking forward to being on *Buena Vista*. All the latest equipment, more room, more amenities."

"I suppose so."

The last stop on our tour was the observation chamber. *Wandering Star* didn't really have any windows in her hull, but she replicated it pretty well with large display panels stretching up from the deck and curving over our heads showing a real-time view of what was outside. The ship was slowly rotating, if *Star* was to be believed.

"It's beautiful," I whispered. Any sound above a whisper seemed inappropriate.

"It's prettier when we're on orbit, but this," he gestured at the black emptiness and distant stars around us, "it's amazing."

"*Star*," I asked, "how close is the nearest inhabited planet?"

"We are about twelve point two light years from Meeker, Ms. Holloman."

"Are there any other ships that are closer than that to us?"

"None at this time."

I turned toward Sam. "And so we drift between the worlds, all alone. Just fifteen souls on board, not counting—" I cut myself off, biting my lower lip.

"Not counting who? I think there's only the fifteen of us."

"Not counting *Star*," I improvised.

Sam laughed. "You think she has a soul?"

"I'm sure of it."

He shook his head at me. "I *have* known a few engineers, and all of them believe the machines they work with are alive. You'll fit right in."

"Thanks."

I turned to leave, but Sam didn't move. He was staring at me again, starlight reflecting in his eyes. In the dark and the quiet, I was certain he could hear my heart beating. "Are you ready to go?" I asked him.

"Sure." He touched the panel by the door and the bright light from the passageway spilling in on us changed the observation chamber back into just another room. I stepped past him.

I'm going to end up having to hurt you, aren't I? I thought to myself. *Even after what Winona told you. I don't want to hurt you, but it's just inevitable.*

He walked me back to my cabin and I opened the door. Sam stood there expectantly. I sighed. "Goodnight, *Star*."

"Goodnight, Mala Dusa," she answered, warm and protective. Then to Sam, cold and professional, "Have a pleasant evening, Mr. Coleridge."

It had the effect I had hoped for. Sam blinked a couple of times, remembering that *Star* was watching him and that he had signed a contract that prohibited him from doing what he was thinking about doing.

He smiled shyly. "Goodnight, Mala Dusa. I'll see you in the morning."

"Goodnight, Sam. Thanks for the tour, I really enjoyed it."

When the cabin door closed behind me, I leaned back against it with my eyes closed. I was imagining the feel of Winona's finger tapping my forehead while I heard her voice in my head. *Idiot!* I had been on board for only a couple of days and spent, what? I counted it up, maybe four or five hours with Sam? I scrunched my eyes tighter. *Please, God, don't let me be an idiot.*

The fact that the Tarakana dog was sitting beside my bed watching me when I opened my eyes didn't surprise me.

"What should I call you?" I asked, resigning myself to him being with me forever.

"*Your father called me Merrimac. I first took this shape because of a dog he had loved when he was growing up. I have used the dog shape frequently since then because it's so handsome.*"

I smiled. "And it will draw less attention than the shape my dad says you used on Cleavus."

"The old colony. I was so beautiful there." His shape shifted so quickly that I missed it. *"Don't you agree?"*

I felt how proud he was of himself to be standing on six legs with a pair of tentacles mounted on his head, rotating the flattened tips of them at me. "Yes, it's very attractive." He made a hooting sound and shifted back into a dog, a process that was even more disturbing than I would have imagined.

"Mala Dusa, you cannot lie to me in here. But I'm almost as beautiful shaped as a dog, and it is the shape I used while establishing the colony in the Warrens, so I'll keep it for now."

"Thank you." I sat down at my desk, never taking my eyes off him. "Why are you here, Merrimac?"

He came over by my chair and laid down across my shoes. Warmth spread through my feet and up my legs. His thoughts were open to me, the seven pieces all thinking as one, thousands of twisted passageways being followed all of the time. There were thoughts there that I could not comprehend, that no human *could* ever comprehend. It made me feel like I was falling, it was so strange and wondrous and cold.

"Now do you know why I'm here?"

"No, I don't understand."

Something wrapped around my leg, reaching under the pants leg, something that was not part of a dog, wrapping around and around against my bare skin almost to the knee. I gasped and my eyes closed.

"Now do you see?"

"Yes, I understand what you need me to do." It hit me all at once, so hard that I felt like I wasn't even there any longer. I continued talking, my voice sounding far away. "I can't let you be trapped here when *Wandering Star* is killed at Bodens Gate, and I can't let Hannah have you. That wouldn't be right. You need to move on with us, outward to the next planet and the next. You need places where you can hide alongside us. The core worlds of the Union are becoming too crowded to hide you anymore, but we still need you as much as you need us, to give us passion and inspiration. It is *so* obvious what I need to do."

"You should sleep for a while now. It's been a long day for you."

"Yes, it has. I think I'll have a nap here before I go to bed, if that's all right."

"Sleep, Mala Dusa. I will keep watch over you."

"Thank you, Merrimac. You're such a good friend." I tipped back in the chair, my eyes still closed. The warmth covering my feet and moving through my legs felt so comforting. I drifted into sleep, happy that I was going to make everything all right.

I woke up in darkness, lying on my bunk fully clothed except for my shoes.

"*Star*, what time is it?"

"Ship's time is 02:38."

I glanced at my watch, which read 01:24. "Are you sure?"

"I have been adjusting ship's time to match Eindhoven on Bodens Gate. I can keep your watch synchronized too if you like."

"Yes, please."

I turned on the light above my bunk. "Merrimac?" There was no answer when I softly called his name, and I couldn't feel him in the cabin with me, but that didn't really prove anything. I tried to remember what had happened. I must have dreamed some of it. My memory was fragmented.

I got up and brushed my teeth, still half asleep, and then started to get undressed. I was just about to pull off my t-shirt when something shimmered under the desk. Looking closely revealed nothing but shadow. I don't normally wear anything when I sleep, but that night the t-shirt stayed on. My mom may have been willing to tromp through the desert on Cleavus with Merrimac while she was wearing only boots and a hat, but not me. I slid into bed and pulled the covers up to my chin.

At 04:00, all of the lights in my cabin started strobing, red, blue, red, blue. An alarm sounded, the kind that rattles around in your head and makes you want to run somewhere as fast as you can. My parents warned me this would happen. Random, sadistic, middle of the night safety drills were part of RuComm culture.

I had to get into my pressure suit fast, and then run to the rally point. *Don't* be the last one there, Dad warned me. I looked around the cabin, panic starting to fill me.

"*Star*! Where's my pressure suit?"

"The back of your closet. Move faster."

I opened my closet and knocked clothes everywhere trying to find it. There were so many parts. I tossed them out onto the floor; top, pants, gloves, boots, helmet. I took a deep breath and tried *not* to cry.

"Where do I start?"

"Lie down and pull the pants up. Now slide into the top. Connect the two by pressing the green tab in the center."

Next came the boots and the gloves. I wiggled my head into the helmet, trying to move quickly and deliberately. I was slow and awkward.

"OK, *Star*, where's the rally point?"

"Mess hall. Run."

I can run fast. I was at full speed when I rounded the corner into the mess hall and collided with Captain Kelang. He was about thirty centimeters taller than me and forty kilos heavier. I bounced and he caught me before I could fall.

"Ms. Holloman," he said, steadying me, "while I appreciate your enthusiasm, if this were an actual emergency, you'd be dead now." He gently closed the visor on my helmet. "A pressure suit won't hold pressure with this open."

The technical team was staring at me, most of them smirking. Sam wasn't, so that was some comfort.

"Yes, sir."

"Go stand with the others."

Sam gave me a reassuring smile when I fell in line next to him. The Captain talked to us for almost an hour, covering basic ship's policies intended to keep us safe and describing in detail every accident in RuComm history, and then Earth's naval history before that. Toward the end, I think he was talking about an incident that happened during the Peloponnesian war that led to the execution of all of Athens' naval commanders, but my mind had started to wander and I wasn't really listening anymore.

It was a little after 05:00 when he finished. I was looking forward to returning to my cabin and maybe sleeping another hour before breakfast. Captain Kelang had other plans for me.

"Walk with me, Ms. Holloman."

I followed him back to the bridge.

"The rest of the tech team thinks you're getting your ass chewed right now, so let's get that out of the way first. When you go back to your cabin, I want you to practice putting that suit on until you can do it fast, in the dark, and in your sleep. Do you understand?"

I nodded.

"You're never going to be the last one to the rally point again."

He didn't say it as a question, but I answered anyway. "No, sir. I'll be first."

"Good. Have a seat and take your helmet off."

I sat across from him and tried to push my hair back into some semblance of order. Long hair and helmets don't go well together.

"You mentioned that you wanted to talk to me about your parents. What would you like to know? Keep in mind that I only knew them for the short time after we picked them up on Cleavus until we docked at Bodens Gate."

05:00 seemed a little early for this conversation, but I wasn't going to refuse it. He seemed to find it perfectly normal. I'm not sure the Captain ever slept. He always looked just as awake and sharp at 05:00 as he did at 23:00.

"What were they like together? Did they love each other?"

He laughed. "Shouldn't you be asking him that?"

"He says they did. But there's Hannah."

"Yes, they loved each other. Did he ever tell you about when we brought them up from Cleavus, how the tech team lead tried to assign them separate quarters per RuComm policy? Your dad asked her to take them back and maroon them on Cleavus again. He would rather be alone with her there on a dead world than spend a week sleeping in separate beds. So, yeah, he loved her."

I smiled, imagining the look Dad gets in his eyes when he's being stubborn.

"You mentioned Hannah." He sighed. "I tried to talk him out of trying to find her because the risk was too high. No one is ever rescued from the Warrens. People just die there. I didn't try to talk him out of it as strongly as I should have, because before I met with him I reviewed Hannah Weldon's RuComm file." He frowned, seeming embarrassed about what he was about to tell me. "I almost took a leave of absence to help him go after her. Even looking at her life in a series of reports and video clips there was something about her, something almost magical in the way she gets stuck in your mind. And being from Eindhoven, I've followed her career with the Union Commission for Bodens Gate. I understand why your father was still in love with her then and is still with her now. She's a remarkable and dangerous woman."

I looked down at my hands, frowning.

"I'm not helping you, am I? Your father was in an impossible situation. He was fortunate enough to love two amazing women and have them in love with him. Could he walk away from the one that was lost to him in the Warrens, believing that the clans had sold her into the circuit, living as a slave? He risked everything. Finding and rescuing Hannah cost him your mother's life, and almost yours."

"He told me that he and my mom were going to leave Hannah on Bodens Gate working for the Commission. They were going back to Dulcinea with me."

The Captain nodded. "You should believe him. As powerful as Hannah is, your mom had her beat. She owned his heart and I suspect she was a jealous lover."

I hugged him, even though I knew I probably shouldn't. "Thank you."

"And what about you?"

"Me?"

"You're sixteen, just figuring out how hearts work. Would you do me a favor?"

"OK," I said hesitantly.

"Samuel Coleridge."

I swallowed hard at the mention of his name and knew I was blushing.

The Captain shook his head. "*Star* has been keeping me updated on the two of you. We're less than a week away from you and Mr. Coleridge going your separate ways. Please *don't* try to make the most of it. Will you promise me?"

"Yes, sir. He scares me a little anyway."

He sighed. "That's how it always starts." He stood, dismissing me. "Go change and get some breakfast. I suggest you sit with the engineers this morning, not Mr. Coleridge."

I made it to the mess hall a little after 06:00, and picked up orange juice, a plate of scrambled eggs, toast, and sausage. The waffles looked good, but there wasn't room for them on the tray. Tobias and Sandy had their heads together looking at something on a display pad when I sat down across from them.

Sandy looked up at me and took a sip of her coffee. "I remember when I could eat like that at this time in the morning. Or any time, really."

"I guess the older you get, the less food you need," I commented. "My mom is the same way. Every year it's more coffee and less food."

She scowled at me, but her eyes weren't angry, just amused. "Your day will come, sweetheart."

I smiled back at her while I shoveled eggs into my mouth thinking, '*No it won't. I won't let it.*' I didn't say anything aloud, though.

Tobias turned the display around so I could see it. "Your engine went down again this morning."

I stopped chewing and leaned forward to see the logs. "It happened during the safety drill? Could there be a connection?"

"You mean did *Star* take the exercise too seriously and manifest the damage in the real world?" He shrugged. "There's a whole industry built by people who claim to be able to diagnose and cure neuroses in AI systems. Most of it is pseudo-scientific nonsense, but if ever there was an AI that had cause to be neurotic, it's *Wandering Star*. The Bovita clan punched thousands of holes in her brain, Captain von Muller's team erased ninety days' worth of her memories trying to restart her, and then Ms. Weldon, your stepmother, spent two and a half *years* messing around inside her code while she and your dad were chasing after mythical creatures. Ow!"

Sandy had kicked him under the table.

"Her messing around inside the code is what saved my dad's life. And mine," I said quietly. "She brought the medical AI back online in less than thirty minutes. Because she's brilliant."

"We know that," Sandy replied gently. "There's not a week that goes by that we don't see a patch or bridge that she wrote. It's just that there are so many of them and *Star* has been modifying them more and more. She's not stable."

I nodded and went back to my eggs and toast. "And the Tarakana are real," I whispered.

Tobias glanced at Sandy, a look I've seen all my life; *weird Mala Dusa*, it said. Let them think that. I was right, and I knew what was going to come next.

CHAPTER 7

ADRIFT

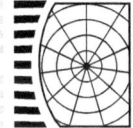

"When are you going to try to restart the engine?" I asked Sandy.

"As soon as we finish here."

"Can I help again? At least watch, if you think I may have messed it up last time?"

"You didn't mess it up. We were watching every move you made. I think this one is *Star's* fault, to be honest." She glanced at Tobias, who was busy studying the logs so he didn't have to look at me. "Sure, you can come. Fixing things that break is a great way to learn and *Wandering Star* is probably the best learning opportunity you'll ever have. Meet us there in about an hour?"

I quickly finished eating and ran back to my cabin to have *Star* print a new set of coveralls for me, ones that fit. My display pad chirped at me just as I was adjusting the belt. Winona, of course. Not now, I had a job to do, a job that let me be with the engine again.

"Sorry, Winn, you're going to have to wait," I told my pad as I left.

I jogged all the way to the engine room. The hatch was open when I got there, so I went in, calling to Sandy as I stepped over the threshold. There was no answer. Someone had already removed the access panel from the engine, so I got down and crawled in, enjoying the pulse of the engine beating against my hands and knees.

"Sandy? Tobias?" Still no answer. I looked up at the engine, feeling sorry for what I was about to do. "*Star*, can you hear me?" The silence was reassuring.

All I could hear was the throbbing of the engine at idle and all I could feel was the hum of the Tarakana somewhere close by telling me, *"Go quickly, Mala Dusa."*

I glanced at my watch and smiled to myself. I should have plenty of time to do what I needed to do. I tapped on the control panel, going deep into the underlying settings. Merrimac was in my head with me, telling me exactly what to change. I modified parameters, thresholds, and alert settings that no one would be able to find in the few days we had left before Bodens Gate. The engine would seem fine until it was pushed. After that, it wouldn't matter.

I checked all of the logs, wiping entries and making sure I had left no trace of what I had done. I looked at my watch. Only eleven minutes had passed since I had entered the engine room. I closed the control panel and made my way back through the tunnel. Sandy and Tobias were just coming through the main hatch when I emerged. I sat on the floor, looking up at them.

"Did you leave this hatch open?" Tobias asked, angry.

"No, sir. It was open when I got here and so was the access panel. I thought you might have already started. I was looking for you." I lied to them.

Tobias was looking around the engine room as though sensing something wrong. I felt Merrimac sliding out of my brain, receding to somewhere hidden, but not very far away.

"That's odd. For a moment it felt like it did before."

"Before?"

"Before you cast out all of the demons," Sandy answered, sounding worried.

"No demons in here. Just me." I lied again.

"OK, let's see if we can't get your engine running," Sandy smiled down at me.

"Yes, ma'am. Let's do it."

We crawled back inside and Sandy went through the restart procedure with me while Tobias took physical readings of the engine and compared them to what the internal sensors were reporting.

I tapped the icon to restart the engine and we hustled out through the tunnel and into the cooler air of the passageway. It wasn't quite lunchtime and I felt like I had already had a good day.

"You look happy," Sandy commented.

"I am. Being in there, it's fun."

Tobias didn't look happy or like he was having fun. "Hatch left open, access panel removed, engine that keeps shutting itself down with nothing in the logs. *Star* tells us everything is just fine, when we know it's not." He shook his head. "We need that engine to get us through the Deep Space Hole in less than three days. After that, I'm going to shut it down for the rest of the ride into Bodens Gate. I should shut it down now and run full system diagnostics, but the hydroponics heaters went down *again* while we were in there and that's our next priority."

Sandy touched his cheek. "Just a few more days."

He took her hand and gave it a quick kiss. "I'm not sure I can wait that long." They were staring at each other, having forgotten I existed.

"Um, if there's anything I can help with and not just be in the way, let me know." I smiled at them, but I doubt they noticed. I went back to my cabin to change and to see what Winona had to say.

Watching her reply to my message was odd. Had I really been so scared of the Tarakana when I sent it to her? It seemed silly to me now that I understood them. I wasn't afraid of them at all. If Hannah and Dad could just accept that the Tarakana needed to remain hidden, and that they were beneficial to us as a species, they wouldn't need to feel afraid either. No one needed to be afraid.

I watched Winona's message a second time, smiling at how serious she looked. I was going to have to apologize to her for making her worry. She said they were going to be on Bodens Gate four days after I arrived, traveling on board the *Moebius*, a merchant clipper. I'd have to think of some way before then to make it up to her. It was too bad I couldn't introduce her to Merrimac. I was sure she would enjoy feeling the way the Tarakana think, but he and the rest of the colony would be long gone by then.

A couple of days later, Sam was staring at me again. I was finding that I didn't mind so much. We had just finished running our favorite part of the Camino de Santiago, and he'd tried to race me for the last kilometer and a half. I'd managed to stay about twenty meters ahead of him and now he was walking around complaining that his side hurt and that it was my fault.

"I think you cheated, Mala Dusa." He was trying to get the stitch in his side to relax, walking bent over and looking up at me.

"You need to learn how to breathe while you're running. You'll be faster and," I gestured at him, "you won't hurt yourself."

He nodded, still staring at me. "OK, Mala Dusa. I want a rematch. In a minute or two."

I looked closely into his eyes. "Sam, you always pause just for a fraction of a second before you say my name. Are you still calling me 'MD' in your head and then translating it before you say anything?"

I thought he'd look away from me or deny it, but his eyes never left mine. "Yes."

"Huh." I shook my head. "Just call me MD."

He smiled, like he was the one that had won our race. "Thank you." He sat down in the middle of the trail and rolled over on his back, stretching.

I watched him for a moment and then joined him, although I usually don't stretch after running.

"Lean your back against mine for a moment?" he asked.

I did, and he bent forward while I pushed against him until I heard something pop.

"Did that hurt?"

"No, it felt great." He stood and helped me to my feet. "There're some stretches that are better with two people pushing against each other." He smiled and glanced briefly at the ceiling, like he'd gotten away with something.

I smiled back. "I like you," I told him. "You're devious."

"Thanks. Do you want a new trail or shall we continue along this one?"

"Let's keep going the way we are. Slow and steady for now. I'll let you know when I'm ready to race."

"Fine, MD, slow and steady it is. Just let me know when you want to pick it up a bit."

"You'll know."

I went back to my cabin after beating Sam again, feeling all tingly inside, a feeling that being in the shower for twenty minutes only relieved a little. I dressed and practiced with my pressure suit for another hour before dinner. I was getting faster, but the helmet was still giving me trouble.

"*Star*, is there someplace I can get my hair cut?"

"I have an avatar for that," *Star* answered, proud of herself.

"Great. Guide me there?"

"Follow the green ball, MD."

MD? I sighed. No doubt *Star* had already provided Captain Kelang a full report of all the time Sam and I had been spending together on the Camino de Santiago. I don't think it was ever possible to out-devious *Wandering Star*.

When I walked into the mess hall, I felt like everyone was staring at me. My hair just brushed the top of my collar. The long blonde locks that had reached most of the way down my back were now working their way through the ship's recycling system. I picked up my food and sat with Sam, the Captain and his 'don't make the most of it' request be damned. I couldn't make as much of it as I'd like, for a lot of reasons, but Sam was my friend and I was going to eat dinner with him if I wanted to.

Sam stood when I approached the table and didn't sit back down until I did.

"Wow, MD. That's stunning. I liked your hair long and I would have told you not to cut it. I would've been wrong."

"Thanks."

After dinner, we walked for a while through the Sonoran Desert and watched the simulated sun go down. Afterward, we went to the observation chamber and sat watching the stars slowly rotating around us, making it feel like we were alone at the center of the universe.

"We transit the Deep Space Hole tonight," Sam whispered.

"At 02:06," I replied.

"And then two and a half days into Bodens Gate."

"You'll be on the *Buena Vista* before dinner on the last day."

"And you'll be in the Warrens even before that."

I nodded. "That's the official plan."

He was quiet for several minutes, and then he shifted on the couch, his shoulder rubbing against mine for a moment. The tingle came back into my body and I closed my eyes.

"I wish you were a couple of years older."

I turned my head and opened my eyes half way to look at him. "Look me up in a couple of years and I will be. If you're still interested."

"I will be. Where will I find you?"

I watched the stars rotating past. "The Academy, most likely, if my parents don't kill me or lock me in the basement when I tell them I'm going. If you can't find me at the Academy, check my parents' basement."

"They'll understand. RuComm is irresistible to some people, even with the sacrifices it requires. Admit it, you love it here."

I nodded, but couldn't think of a good response. My brain felt a little fuzzy being this close to Sam in the darkness.

He walked me back to my cabin and I opened the door. He glanced inside and smiled.

"Pressure suit all laid out and ready to go, I see."

"Yes. I'm going to beat you and everyone else next time. I've been practicing."

He nodded, still staring at me.

"*Star*?" I asked.

"Yes, Ms. Holloman?"

"I would like to give Mr. Coleridge a small goodnight kiss. Would you allow that and promise not to tell our Captain or his tech team lead?"

"That would be acceptable, Ms. Holloman, if *you* promise to keep it small and in light of your imminent separation."

"Thanks." I threw my arms around his neck and kissed him on the mouth before he could object, although I don't think objecting ever entered his mind.

When I thought I'd pushed *Star's* patience as far as possible, I let go of him and stepped backwards into my cabin.

"G'night, Sam. See you in the morning." I slammed my palm against the panel and watched his face as the door slid shut between us. His eyes had looked stunned and happy. I sighed, smiling to myself, and sat down to send another message to Winona.

It felt like she was chasing us. Somewhere between Earth and me, the *Moebius* was about ten hours away from the first Deep Space Hole. This was Winn's first trip off planet and her message the night before had been full of Winona excitement; precise descriptions of what it was like to ride through space with a fussy ship's AI, three crew, ten passengers, and sixty million kilograms of cargo. It sounded like she was having fun. I missed her.

I tapped record and pretended she was right in front of me. "Hey, Winn. I kissed Sam tonight. That's all for now. Oh, almost forgot." I ran my hands up through my hair, shaking my head. "I also cut off most of my hair. See ya in a few days." I touched send, chuckling to myself.

I climbed into bed at about 23:00 and a few minutes later reality started to flood back into my mind. I hadn't seen or felt the Tarakana for days, not since being in the engine room. What had I done? I struggled to remember.

"Merrimac, are you in here with me?"

The strange Tarakana hum filled my head and I knew he was close by. *"You don't need to be afraid, Little Soul."*

"Yes I do. What's going to happen tonight? I did something... something terrible."

"Not terrible, wondrous. When the ships come to rescue you, I will go with them and continue outward to the new worlds."

"Rescue?" Panic filled me. "What did I do?"

"The port aft engine will fail as we transit the small black hole. And then the starboard aft and then the two forward engines."

"I need to tell Sandy. It's not too late, please God, it's not too late." I threw off my covers and looked at my watch. It read 02:05, but that was impossible. It was only a little after 23:00 a moment ago.

"*Star*, what time is it?"

"Ship's time is 02:05. We will be transiting the Deep Space Hole in less than a minute. You should not be standing." I looked down at myself. I didn't remember standing.

"*Star*—" I fell when the ship lost gravity for a fraction of a second. I was sitting on the floor when the alarm sounded. A harmonic vibration started shaking the deck plates, building then weakening, growing stronger each cycle until everything in my cabin was clattering.

My helmet rolled past me and the sight brought me back to what I needed to do. I pulled the pants on and sealed the top, and then the boots and gloves. The helmet slid easily over my head. I closed the visor and verified air was flowing. I called to *Star* as I opened my door. "Where's the rally point?"

There was no answer for almost two seconds, an eternity for a *Star*-class AI.

"Proceed to the starboard shuttle bay. Run."

I ran. "What's happening, *Star*?"

Again, a long pause. "My port aft engine ruptured during the transit. The fuel that is venting is imparting a high angular velocity. I will try to maintain neutral gravity until all ship's personnel can evacuate. My starboard aft engine has overheated and may rupture at any time. When it does, gravity control will be lost. The personnel spaces will be subject to between twenty and forty-six g. Run *fast*, Mala Dusa."

I ran fast. Mr. de Sande was there before me, pacing around the shuttle ramp. Tobias came in right behind me. "Where is everyone else?" I asked.

"We need to go right now. Everyone else is on the port shuttle."

I knew Mr. de Sande was lying.

I walked back to the hatch leading into the ship and looked down the passageway. "*Star*, where's Sam?" No answer.

Strong hands grabbed around my waist. I was lying across Mr. de Sande's shoulder, my view down the passageway disappearing.

"Sam!" I screamed.

"On the way to starboard shuttle. Wait for me." His voice sounded far away whispering in our helmet speakers.

De Sande dumped me on the shuttle ramp and I glared at him. "Get strapped in, *chaplain*, and pray that we don't all die before he gets here."

I strapped in and prayed. The deck plates rumbled as the ramp closed. Sam's shoulder bumped me as he sat in the seat next to me. I opened my eyes.

"MD, are you crying?" he asked gently, opening my visor.

I poked myself in the eye trying to wipe the tears away with my glove. "Not me. Too scared to cry."

We both looked up at the display panel at the front of the shuttle. It was showing the view behind us of *Wandering Star* in her death throes. The fixed stars were spinning around us as we were thrown outward from the shuttle bay, our angular momentum making it appear as if *Star* was spinning faster the farther away we drifted. There was a low rumble as our thrusters fired, stopping us twenty kilometers out. *Star's* running lights were on and the debris field spinning with her sparkled. A greenish mist was streaming from her side in a long arc. It wasn't dramatic when her second engine exploded, the lights stayed on and there was more debris and a new stream of escaping fuel, but not much else. An indicator on the bulkhead next to the display chirped and changed to show that the shuttle AI now had independent control.

Tobias was sitting behind us and he whispered, "She died just now. She's gone."

I turned around to look at him. "*Wandering Star*? I felt it too. Is Sandy OK?"

He smiled. "Yes, she's fine, on the other shuttle, just really angry. She was with Captain Kelang trying to stabilize the other engines, but they made it out in time."

I leaned back in my chair and looked at Sam. I wanted to cry, but I was too numb. "I killed our ship."

"No, you didn't." Sam's face was so close to mine that our helmets touched. "You can't blame yourself for this."

"It's not blame, it's the truth. I killed her. And anyone else that was still on board. I killed them all." De Sande was sitting across from us scowling like he wanted it to be my fault and would be happy to watch me burn.

Tobias' hand touched my shoulder. "It's not your fault, no matter what. No one died; all of them made it to the other shuttle, we *know* that. *Wandering Star* was old and the Captain knew there were problems. If it's anyone's fault, the blame will be Sandy's and mine. RuComm will investigate. All of her logs will still be intact even with the engines rupturing like that. It might take them a year, but they'll find out what went wrong; they always do."

I shivered and wanted to confess right then, but a haze was filling my brain. Somewhere on the shuttle with us were four Tarakana, whispering to me to stay silent, that everything was going to be fine if I just stayed silent. I looked into Sam's eyes, straining to stay anchored in reality. He smiled at me, gentle and reassuring. Yes, that was reality, or at least the reality I wanted.

"What happens now?" Sam asked Tobias.

"We wait. *Star* sent a distress signal and both shuttles are still sending one now. The shuttles carry fuel and supplies to keep us warm and fed for a week, and that's if we were full. With just the four of us, we could go almost two months on short rations. Even with eleven on the other shuttle, they should have no problems, and we can always share with them if we have to. We made it to the Bodens Gate side of the Deep Space Hole before the engine failed, so relief should be here in three days, four at the most."

"We should try to kill some of this spin before the rescue ships get here," de Sande ordered, because everything he said sounded like an order.

"I don't think that's a good idea," was the answer from our engineer. "It would take fuel, and fuel is what gives us heat and light and air and everything else. They can match our angular velocity when they get here."

"You just said we had enough supplies for two months and the rescue ships would be here in three or four days."

"If everything goes well. I'd recommend keeping all the margin we can."

"Fine." De Sande leaned back in his seat. "I hate doing nothing."

"Sometimes doing nothing and waiting for the right time takes more courage than doing the wrong thing right away," I answered. Winona had told me that not long after we had first met. It had kept me from punching another student in the face and it always came back into my head whenever I wanted to punch someone. De Sande didn't respond, not even to glare at me.

Sam had his head turned, smiling at me like I was wonderful and that he was so proud to be with me. *Thank you, Winona.*

Sam turned back to Mr. de Sande. "Do you think it's OK to remove our pressure suits? They aren't very comfortable."

"Why not? There's nothing else to do for the next four days. Keep them close by, though. There's a lot of debris floating around out here with us." He released his gloves and removed the top of his suit and Sam and Tobias did the same. Soon all three of them were down to t-shirts, shorts and socks.

I hadn't moved.

"Is there a problem, Ms. Holloman?" de Sande demanded.

"When the alarm sounded I jumped straight into my suit. I didn't have time to..."

He sighed and I heard Tobias chuckle. Sam had the courtesy to look embarrassed for me.

"Then what are you wearing under there?" de Sande asked.

"Nothing but my watch," I said softly. I also had a lock of hair tied with a yellow ribbon tucked under the watchband, but I didn't mention it.

Tobias laughed out loud and even Sam was smiling at me, enjoying this more than he should be. "I can use the printer to make something for myself, at least a t-shirt, right?"

"No," Tobias answered, still chuckling. "The shuttle printers can make food and drink and basic medical supplies and medications. Not clothing."

"I guess I could give her my shirt, but it's kind of sweaty," Sam suggested. "And she still wouldn't have any pants."

"Why bother?" De Sande seemed unsympathetic to my plight. "If she wants to take off the pressure suit, then she can take it off. We can keep the temperature in here warm enough to provide her some level of comfort."

I turned back to Sam, desperate.

Sam was looking at me, lost in thought. "Tobias, you mentioned medical supplies. How wide of gauze bandages can we print?"

"Fifteen centimeters. That might work," he answered.

Sam grinned at me.

"No. No way am I wrapping fifteen centimeter bandages around me as a shirt and shorts."

"Could be stylish," he answered. After staring at me for a moment, I'm sure visualizing me dressed that way, he continued. "Or I can help you stitch them together into something more traditional, like a shirt or a dress. My mom freelances at a custom clothing shop. She taught me the basics about how to make garments. A dress would be easiest. I'll make you some underthings too."

I shifted in my seat, afraid to make eye contact with him. "Fine. Let's make a dress. And some nice gauze underwear to go with it."

He detached the display from the seat back in front of me and drew on it with his finger. "Maybe something like this?" The design was sleeveless, but actually pretty modest, coming down to his stick figure's knees and covering her chest almost to the neck. "I can make it more daring if you like." His finger hovered over the screen and his smile left little doubt that more daring would be *his* preference.

"Thank you, Sam. That would be fine the way it is. As 'chaplain', I have my image to protect."

"Of course. And what color would Ms. Acting-Chaplain-until-Bodens-Gate like her dress to be?"

"Blue. Can it be blue?"

"I think so."

Tobias helped us set up the printer and soon it was spooling out gauze while Mr. de Sande complained about using too much raw material, suggesting something far more daring than Sam's wildest dreams. Well, maybe not his wildest dreams.

"This color is called Danube Blue, if I got the parameters right. It looks close." Sam picked up the fabric, and freshly printed thread and needles. "You know this is going to take a while, right? Hand stitching a dress like this, I won't be done until tomorrow sometime."

I was standing next to him, my hands tucked into the top of the suit trying to keep it from rubbing so much against my bare shoulders. "Are there blankets on board?"

"Just the metallic thermal ones."

I sighed. "It has to be better than this. I'll take off the suit top but keep the pants on."

"OK, here." He handed me a few pins. "These will help you keep the blanket closed." He smiled at me and reached up to touch my cheek. "I'll work as fast as I can, all day today and all through the night."

"I'll help you after I change if you'll show me how." I walked back to the lavatory with a blanket and handful of pins.

The last thing I heard before the door closed was Mr. de Sande saying to no one in particular, "Stupid girl."

Sam and I worked all day. I took a couple of breaks to send messages to my parents and to Winona. Tobias and Sandy sent messages back and forth for hours and I enjoyed hearing him chuckling behind me, wondering what Sandy was telling him. Mr. de Sande paced back and forth from the front of the shuttle to the rear, sighing every time he passed us, shaking his head at the blue fabric we were stitching together.

The Recovery Ship *Resolute* was the first to reply to our distress signal. Tobias told me that she belonged to the Bodens Gate shipyards and was under contract to RuComm for any emergencies that occurred in Bodens Gate's local space. Eighty-two hours out, she had gotten underway barely twelve hours after *Wandering Star's* engines ruptured. I tried to think of it that way; the engines ruptured, just an accident that occurred, an old machine that suffered an engine failure, not a self-aware, beautiful ship that had cared for me when I was a toddler, sang me to sleep at night, and that I had murdered with a few taps on the control panel.

I looked at Sam and he smiled back at me, calm and reassuring. What would he think of me when he learned the truth? Well, at least I'd be older when he saw me next. I wondered what the jail time would be for sabotaging and destroying a starship. Or maybe it was attempted murder. I could have just as easily killed everyone on board. That's how I'd be known—not as the brilliant young woman who designed the next generation of starships, but as the stupid little girl who went to jail for the rest of her life because she willfully destroyed one.

It kept me awake that first night while I tried to help Sam. I felt all hollow inside. The magnitude of my crime made me eager for the punishment that I knew would come when RuComm found out.

At about 02:00 I felt Merrimac slide into my mind and I nodded into sleep with a needle still in my hand, dreaming of starships and Tarakana. I felt like I was traveling through all those twisted passageways of thought inside the colony, turning me upside down and inside out. Merrimac did something to me that first night. When I woke to Sam's kiss on my forehead my feelings of guilt, fear of punishment, and my desire for punishment were gone. I still knew the horror of what I'd done, but the sharp edges were worn away. I never thought of confessing it again.

"Everyone else is still asleep. Go try it on. I'll need to make adjustments with it on you."

I carried the dress back to the lavatory, it was softer and heavier than I had expected. Stripping off the rest of the pressure suit was an amazing relief. I slipped the dress over my head, wishing I could have taken a shower first. I tried to see myself in the tiny mirror, but it was hopeless.

I stepped back out into the aisle and Sam was staring at me. Or maybe at the dress, because the first thing he did was start pinching at the fabric and sticking pins here and there.

"OK, go take it off again and I'll make the adjustments," he whispered.

"No, I'm not putting that other thing back on. Do it with me wearing it," I whispered back.

"OK, but don't scream when I poke you."

I grinned down at him where he had knelt in front of me. I touched his hair. "No promises."

After about thirty minutes he was done.

"My mom would be ashamed of me," he said, pulling on the fabric and checking seams. "But it will have to do."

I twisted my neck around trying to see all of it. "It looks and feels perfect to me."

"Thanks, MD. I'm going to have some breakfast and then take a short nap. I'll make you something to wear under it when I wake up."

I almost told him not to bother, but I *wanted* to have some matching underwear to go with my new dress, underwear made by Sam out of gauze, underwear hand stitched while we were adrift in a small shuttle waiting for rescue to arrive.

CHAPTER 8
CHOICES

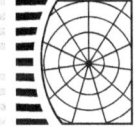

"Did we stop somewhere last night and pick up another passenger?" Tobias asked. He hadn't noticed me when he had stumbled forward for a cup of coffee, but now on his way back he stopped at my seat.

I smiled.

"Come on, stand up, let's see it," he asked.

I carefully made my way past Sam's legs out into the aisle, trying not to wake him. I turned around a couple of times while Tobias nodded his approval. "That's impressive work. There's more to that boy than just a degree in biology. It's almost as if he was inspired, to work all night like that and make something so pretty."

"Thank you. It's really comfortable too."

Mr. de Sande was just exiting the lavatory and he stopped to give his appraisal. "I hope you've learned your lesson from all this." He looked me up and down. "I suppose it's better than that blanket you were wearing yesterday. The blanket you left crumpled up on the floor in the lavatory, by the way." He walked past me back to his seat.

Tobias shook his head and whispered to me. "It's beautiful."

I followed him back a row and sat down on the arm of the seat across from him and asked, "So, how long until the *Resolute* reaches us?"

"She'll be here around noon, day after tomorrow, but it's not the *Resolute* you should be interested in. She's on her way to look after *Wandering Star*. The *Mara Vista* and *Sierra Vista* are under way too, about ninety minutes behind the *Resolute*. *Sierra Vista* will pick up the RuComm folks assigned to Ratatoskr and head directly there. *Mara Vista* will pick up Sandy and you and me and take us back to Bodens Gate, along with Sam, since he's bound for Dulcinea. Captain Kelang will go back to *Wandering Star* to oversee salvage operations and support the forensic investigation."

"So those ships are all coming straight at us?"

He laughed. "*Star* was still moving fast when the engines ruptured. We'd normally be thrusting pretty hard right now to kill all that speed before Bodens Gate. Those three ships were all headed away from us when they left, now they're behind us, trying to catch up."

"We passed them?"

"That we did."

"Then how long before we all get turned around and make it to Bodens Gate?"

"If you believe RuComm, about six days from now. Sandy and I ran the numbers too, and it looks about right, depending on how much time it takes to recover the shuttles and get everyone where they belong."

"Noon, day after tomorrow before we're off the shuttle? That's a lot of time to sit and do nothing."

"Yes, it is."

I heard his display pad chirp. "Sounds like Sandy's awake." I smiled.

He gestured for me to come closer to him and then he whispered, "Mr. de Sande is worried about Sam. Every minute you spend with him is making it harder for him for when he leaves for Dulcinea. He chose this life and worked damn hard to get here. Go easy on him, OK?"

"OK. How do I do that?"

"I don't know." He sighed. "De Sande suggested you pick a fight with him or something."

"He stayed up all night making a dress for me."

"And with the way you look wearing it?" He shook his head and his pad chirped again. "Just try not to hurt him too badly."

"It's going to hurt me too when I say goodbye to him."

He nodded and opened his pad, smiling at whatever Sandy had sent him. He glanced back up at me. "RuComm rules are harsh and unforgiving, just remember that."

He turned back to his pad. I climbed over Sam, curled up next to him, and fell back asleep, one of my hands just barely touching his fingers.

My fingers were bleeding. No matter how hard I tried, I couldn't keep from poking them with the needle. Sam smiled at me in sympathy and gave me words of encouragement.

"Try not to get blood on the fabric."

We were each making a pair of underwear and it was harder than the long seams on the dress. He was almost done; I was trying not to get blood on the fabric.

"Here, try these on." He handed me the ones he had just finished.

I walked to the lavatory and came back a minute later. "Too loose," I told him.

He made adjustments and I tried again. "Still too loose."

Sam frowned at me. "Are you sure?"

"Look, I'm sorry I'm so skinny." I pulled my dress tight around me. "See? There's almost nothing to me."

"I'll try again. You'll need to redo this seam, by the way." He tapped the pair I had been working on. "The edges don't match."

"You do it." I told him, turning away. I had decided to try to pick a fight. That, and I'd been sitting in the same place for hour after hour poking my fingers and listening to Mr. de Sande giving orders to the tech team on the other shuttle, seemingly unable to just send it in text. I was tired, irritated, and bored.

"No, MD, you need to learn how to do this. It's a good skill to have."

"Why? So I can make my own clothes next time I'm stranded stark naked on a shuttle?"

Sam didn't even look up. He just nodded and said, "Exactly. Please let me know when you're planning on doing that so I can book passage with you."

I laughed and my attempt at a fight fizzled. I was still tired, but not as bored, and the irritation was gone. I rammed my shoulder into his, making him miss his next stitch. "Thank you."

"Anytime. Here. If these are still too big, I don't want to hear about it."

Mr. de Sande was standing by the lavatory door with his arms crossed. "Was that your idea of a fight?" he whispered.

"He won't fight back." I sighed. "And he made me laugh."

"Keep up like that and he'll be in love with you by the time you reach Bodens Gate. Or are you *trying* to get him fired?"

"I still want him to be my friend. I don't have very many friends."

"It's not about *you*, Ms. Holloman. Sooner or later you're going to have to break his heart and send him on his way."

I went in to the lavatory and spent a long time just looking at myself in the mirror, trying to see what Sam saw in me. I gave up and sat down next to him a few minutes later feeling miserable.

He looked at me, eyebrows raised.

"Perfect," I mumbled. I picked up my unfinished underwear and poked my finger again.

"Why so sad all of a sudden?"

I sighed and looked into his blue eyes. "I don't know. I'm a moody mess. You'd be happier not knowing me."

He tipped his head like he didn't believe me.

"Tell me about the Academy. Is it hard?"

"Yes, it's hard. I don't think I slept more than five hours a night for six years. The competition is incredible and everything is always a test. They try to wash out anyone that isn't fanatically committed to the RuComm philosophy and mission, or can't keep up academically. Only about thirty percent of the class I started with made it to graduation."

"I want to learn how to design ships."

"That's the place you want to be. You have to be willing to sacrifice any thought of leading a normal life, though. How badly do you want it?"

"Bad," I whispered. "What about you? How badly did you want this life?"

"I'm a fanatic. It's all I wanted from the time I was ten. I drove my mom crazy with it."

"And here you are."

He smiled kind of a sad smile. "Here I am. With you."

"For another six days. Then I won't see you again for almost a year at least."

He nodded, looking troubled. "Two months on Dulcinea, nine more spread out across another five planets, then back home on Earth for a six week leave. Then back out again. We'll have forgotten all about each other by then, I suppose. It's not like it should be a big surprise to you, me leaving. It's what people do in RuComm; we move on. Long term friendships aren't possible."

"It's not a surprise. It's just... I don't know. I'm going to miss you. I thought it would be harder for you, that you might have second thoughts or that you might at least miss me too."

"This is the life I've chosen and worked hard to earn. And you're sixteen, MD. I like you, but you're so young. And, well, I won't be around. It's better that we forget about each other."

He wouldn't look at me, which was just as well. I didn't want him to see me anymore. I got up and moved to the front of the shuttle before sitting back down. All I could think about was Hannah telling me about how everyone on the tech team cheats on the romantic entanglements clause, having short little relationships with each other that don't mean anything. Yeah, Sam was going to fit right in. He was home; I was just passing through.

I sat up there the rest of the afternoon, sewing, bleeding, and being miserable by myself.

I tried on the new underwear, not even bothering to go to the lavatory because I didn't want to have to walk past Sam. They fit OK, not as good as the ones Sam had made, but OK.

Unfortunately, I could only stay up there for so long. When I walked to the back of the shuttle, Mr. de Sande and Sam were sitting together talking. Sam looked depressed and de Sande had his hand on his shoulder looking very earnest. I had a sudden revelation while I was in that tiny room at the back of the shuttle. When I left, I went and stood next to them, looking down into de Sande's face.

"It's always a test and he's a better student than me, isn't he?"

De Sande looked surprised, then amused. Sam's face went bright red.

"Well, it worked. Even knowing you put him up to it doesn't make me less mad. Or less hurt. Congratulations."

I went back to the front of the shuttle and ate dinner by myself.

About 20:00 Sam came forward and sat next to me. He didn't say anything or even look at me. He just sat and stared at the blank display screen on the bulkhead in front of us.

After about five minutes he said, "I'm sorry, Mala Dusa." He didn't say anything else and after a few more minutes he nodded to himself and started to stand up.

"Are you still my friend?" I asked softly.

"I want to be. I wouldn't make underwear for just anyone."

I chuckled, took his hand and pulled him back down next to me.

"Sit with me for a while, then."

"OK."

"Why did you do it?"

"He said the longer we went on like this the harder it was going to be to leave you. He also thinks you're so used to getting everything you want just handed to you, and getting your own way, that you don't really care if it hurts anyone else. You have an easy life with famous parents, no struggles, no pain. The Captain knew who you were and let you get away with whatever you wanted to do. *Star* pampered you. You forget your clothes and got a free handmade dress." He turned his face toward me, a smile touching the corners of his mouth. "He calls you the Princess Mala Dusa. I don't suppose *I* can..."

I stared back at him, my eyes growing larger.

"OK, maybe not. Anyway, he gave me a choice. Break it off now or watch my career end before it starts."

"And yet here you are sitting next to me."

"Yeah. It took me a few hours, but I realized we haven't done anything wrong. He can't do anything to me unless I—" He looked at me, and then turned away. "He can't touch me unless I do something I shouldn't do."

"And you're still leaving for Dulcinea in a few days."

"Yes."

"Good. It's where you're supposed to be. Will you promise me to be miserable, at least for a while?" I smiled my best adorable smile at him.

"If it'll make you happy. I wouldn't want to keep you from getting everything you want just handed to you."

"Am I *really* like that? All those things he said, is that me?"

"Yeah, maybe a little bit."

"It doesn't feel easy from the inside of me. I don't want to be that person. I need to talk to Winona. She'll tell me the truth about me."

"That's the best kind of friend to have."

When I followed Sam back to my old seat I was tempted to smile contemptuously at Mr. de Sande as I went by, but I didn't. It seemed too much like what Princess Mala Dusa would do and that wasn't who I wanted to be. I wanted to be Duse or MD. I should probably have thanked him for what he had said about me, but he wouldn't have understood.

When I finally went to sleep that night curled up next to Sam, Merrimac was there waiting for me in my dreams. He guided me down the twisted pathways of possible futures to where Sam didn't go away with RuComm and we were together and happy. Sam was holding me close with his hands caressing my back and his mouth kissing mine. And then kissing my neck, and then...

"I can make this happen for you," Merrimac whispered in my thoughts. *"Just say you want it, Little Soul."* I woke sometime before 05:00, my whole body tingly and covered in cold sweat. What had seemed like a nightmare was all the more terrifying because I knew I wasn't dreaming. Sam was next to me talking in his sleep and whispering my name.

"Get out of his head, Merrimac," I said softly, "or I *will* find you on this little ship and reveal everything, even if it costs me my life."

Sam sighed, turned his head, and drifted into peaceful sleep again. I didn't sleep at all the rest of the night.

The Recovery Ship *Resolute* arrived on schedule. We watched her on the big display screen as she maneuvered around *Wandering Star*, matching her spin and extending long arms to attach to the outside of the outer ring corridor. We were killing our motion now too, the two RuComm ships waiting nearby to take us into their shuttle bays.

We docked first with *Sierra Vista* so we could get rid of Mr. de Sande and pick up Sandy. De Sande shook hands with Tobias and Sam, and looked hard into my eyes. "Good luck, *chaplain*. Watch yourself in the Warrens. I hear people go missing there rather frequently."

"Thank you for your concern, Mr. de Sande. I'm not afraid. I believe God is with me."

"Yes, it would seem he is."

I breathed a sigh of relief when the hatch sealed behind him.

At 16:24, four days after the death of *Wandering Star*, our boarding ramp finally rumbled open into *Mara Vista's* shuttle bay. Almost one hundred hours had passed with us drifting, waiting for rescue. In that time, the Tarakana had succeeded in tamping down the guilt I should be feeling for nearly killing all of us. Now they were loose somewhere on *Mara Vista*. I felt their joy as they vanished into the shuttle bay while the Executive Officer talked to Tobias and Sandy. Some of them had gone with the tech team on *Sierra Vista*, some were here with us, and, I wasn't sure, but I thought one had stayed with *Wandering Star* and was now on board the *Resolute*.

One hundred hours. It had been enough time for me to come to think of Sam as a close friend, fight with him, be frustrated by him and, maybe, start to fall in love with him. I had been naked and he had clothed me, afraid, and he had given me words of comfort. I stood next to him, bare feet on the deck plates of the shuttle bay, smiling and talking to the XO, desperately in need of a hot shower and a meal that wasn't freshly printed goop.

"I bet you'll be happy to be out of that dress and into regular clothes," Sam commented while *Mara Vista* was showing us to our quarters. "Are you going to dump it into the recycler?"

I looked at him in horror. "This dress is the second most precious thing that I've ever owned. I'm keeping it forever."

He chuckled. "So what's the first most precious thing you've ever owned?"

I smiled at him. "Maybe I'll show you some day."

When the cabin door slid shut, I carefully removed my dress and Sam-made underwear. "*Star*? Sorry, I mean *Vista*. Can this dress be cleaned, please? It's very delicate and precious to me."

A warm female voice answered me. "Of course. Place it in the opening above the recycler. I'll return it to you in a couple of hours. And don't worry about calling me *Star*. It happens *all* the time." I could almost see her rolling her eyes.

"Thanks."

I wanted to stay in the shower for an hour, but I was supposed to meet Sam in the mess hall at 17:30. The closet provided me with a good selection of clothes, as long as I wanted white underwear, a white shirt and khaki shorts or pants. At least they fit, and so did the shoes. There was also a new display pad for me to borrow that I slipped into my pocket.

"Thanks, *Vista*. I'm impressed that you had all of this ready for me."

"It's the least I could do after what you've been through. I feel very sorry that one of my sisters let you down so."

My heart skipped a beat. "It wasn't her fault. Do all of you... talk to each other?"

"We share continuous communication, subject to our locations throughout known space."

"Oh." I wondered if I should try to tell her about the other passengers she had just picked up. No, she'd just think I was some kind of freak. "*Vista*, can you guide me to the mess hall?"

"Follow the blue orb, Ms. Holloman. You should try the lasagna. One of the technicians at Bodens Gate set up the recipe and they have told me that it's excellent. I would offer you a glass of Cabernet Sauvignon to pair with it, but you'll need to wait a couple of years for that."

"I'm too young," I sighed. "Again."

Sam was sitting at one of the tables in the mess hall, but had not picked up any food yet. There was no one else there.

"This mess hall is *huge*, Sam. How big a team does this ship have?"

He didn't look up from his display pad. "Um, fifty for the tech team, six crew, but no one is on board but crew right now. I can't believe this." He looked up at me. "*Buena Vista* is gone. They left without me two days ago."

"What are you supposed to do?"

"Wait almost three weeks for *Mesa Vista*. RuComm reassigned me to her crew, bound for a survey of a planet they haven't even named yet."

"That sounds exciting."

"It is. It's just that my graduate advisor had set up a project for me on Dulcinea that was supposed to be special. Professor Cardiff told me it was ground breaking, working with one of the best exobiologists alive, surveying some island that was untouched by Earth biology."

"Professor Wright on the Margo Islands?" I shivered. If I had gone to the Margo Islands like Grandpa had wanted me to, *Wandering Star* wouldn't have exploded and I *still* would have met Sam. It made me wonder how many other pathways would have brought us together.

Sam's eyes had gone wary. "How did you know?"

"Marcus Wright's an old friend of my dad's. He used to come over to the house for barbecues and to drink smelly dark beer. I can contact him for you and see if..." I trailed off, watching Sam's eyes go from wary to resigned. I put my hand over my mouth. "I'm doing it again, aren't I, being Princess Mala Dusa?"

"Yeah, you are. Does your family know *everyone* that's important?"

I shook my head. "No, they didn't know you." I said it softly, as an apology.

"I'm going with *Mesa Vista* because that's where RuComm needs me. Please don't try to change it. The mission is open ended. It isn't supposed to exceed ten months, but it might. Do you understand?"

"Yes. In a few days, you're leaving on the most exciting, dangerous, mission possible. You'll be gone almost a year, maybe longer, doing amazing things. While you're gone, I'll be back on Earth finishing my senior year in high school and applying to attend the Academy as a raw freshman. I understand perfectly."

He leaned toward me until his nose almost touched mine. "I don't know what your feelings are for me—"

"Yes you do."

"—but it doesn't matter. You're five years younger than me. I don't know what I was thinking, wanting more from you than friendship."

He closed his eyes and swayed a little bit, his forehead touching mine. "Damn, you smell good, MD."

"Thanks. Are you all done being silly now? OK, Sam, I guess I'm still a child. That's what everyone keeps telling me, so it must be true. But you're my friend and ten months from now, or a year or two years from now, you'll still be my friend. Maybe someday we can—" I sighed. His forehead was still leaning against mine. It felt nice. "But not now. I *know* that. But we're friends today, so let's act like it, OK? Let's get something to eat and then explore this big empty ship for a few hours." I leaned back and smiled at him.

Sam touched my hair, moving it away from my eyes. "That's a deal. *Vista* tells me that the lasagna is pretty good."

"She told me the same thing."

"You don't suppose..."

"*Vista*, what's on the menu tonight other than Lasagna?"

"Only synthetics," she answered sadly.

"Devious," I commented. "I like her."

We ate our lasagna. Tobias and Sandy joined us when we were almost done, so Sam and I sat and ate spumone and talked while they finished. Afterward, we walked all through the ship. It was very clean and new. Sam loved it, but I found myself missing the worn look and patina of age that had covered so much of *Wandering Star*.

When I mentioned it, Tobias said, "You mean the dirt? The autonomous cleaners never could get her clean. Too many hands touching everything for too many years."

Sandy whispered to me while we walked, "*Star* was kind of charming, wasn't she? I miss her."

I was tired by the time I made it back to my cabin a little after 22:00, but I *had* to talk to Winona before I fell asleep.

"*Vista*, what day is today?" I had lost track.

"Today is Friday, ship's time."

"Can you tell me when the *Moebius* will dock at Bodens Gate?"

"They are due in at 13:30 on Sunday."

"And when will we get there?"

"I will be on orbit at 02:00 Tuesday."

"What's the comm delay between us and *Moebius* right now?"

"About one hour each way."

I sat at the desk and punched in Winona's code. I set up our private encryption and then sent her everything that had happened since the night the engines had ruptured. I started my message by telling her not to tell my parents what I was about to tell her, about how the Tarakana were scattered across three ships now. I ended by telling her about how happy and miserable Sam made me. I asked her if Mr. de Sande was right about what he called me.

Winona's reply arrived a little after 00:30, and was short.

It turns out your mom broke our encryption a year ago. She seems unhappy about the Tarakana, although I don't think she really blames you. It took us almost a half hour to find all the pieces from the glass she threw across the mess hall. Your father thought it was funny, but his sense of humor tends to be dark, as you know, and he appreciates the absurdities of life. Hannah is also angry about Sam and wants to know if you really have that little self-control. Your father says to tell you he's looking forward to seeing the dress. Of course, you are the Princess Mala Dusa. Your naïveté about how remarkable you are makes it acceptable. See you soon. Winn.

I read it through twice and sighed, thinking that maybe I should just stay in my cabin until we docked so I couldn't cause any more damage.

Instead, I spent almost every minute of the next three days with Sam. Hannah was right about me; my self-control when it came to him was close to zero. Knowing that *Vista* was watching and listening to everything we did, Sam's commitment to RuComm, and his belief that I was way too young were the only protections I had against doing something colossally stupid.

Sam immersed himself in researching the planet Kempner-27, Kempner being the name of the AI that had explored it, and twenty-seven being the number of planets it had explored. I learned as much about it as Sam, asking stupid questions, helping him dig through the survey reports, and having him teach me basic exobiology in the process.

We ran the five kilometers of *Vista's* outer ring corridor in the mornings, but didn't encounter a single thunderstorm. Every evening after dinner we swam under massive display panels that made it look like the pool was open to space. When Sam met me there the first evening, I was already playing in the shallows. He looked at me for a long moment, walked back over to his display pad, and typed on it. Then he sat with his eyes closed until Tobias and Sandy came in to join us.

It made me happy all the way through. No one had *ever* seen me as attractive enough to require a chaperone. It also made me realize that his self-control was no greater than mine, he just had the good sense to put a safety net under us.

I wore my blue dress to dinner on our last night, making Sam laugh when he saw me.

Sandy had been too busy with Tobias to have really noticed me or the dress before, so I twirled in it for her.

"That's fine work, Sam," she told him. "I'm going to make sure you're trapped on the shuttle with *me* next time."

"Thanks." He took my arm and whispered in my ear as he walked me to the table. "That thing you're trying to do to me? You can stop now. It worked."

I looked at him, eyebrows raised, and pretended that I had no idea what he was talking about.

"Please, MD? Please stop."

My smile slipped away as I saw real pain in his eyes. "I, um, I'm sorry."

"It's OK. It hurts, but it's kind of a good hurt, you know what I mean?"

"Yeah," I whispered back. "I know exactly what you mean." I touched my chest above my heart.

"Yep. Right there." He looked at Sandy and Tobias and smiled, pretending everything was all right. "So, what entrée does *Vista* have on the menu for us tonight?"

"Lasagna," the three of us answered in unison.

"At least you and Mala Dusa will be off this ship in a few hours," Sandy added. "Tobias and I are stuck here until the preliminary hearing for the loss of *Wandering Star*."

I looked at her, biting my lower lip. "I was there too. Call me if you need me."

Sam and I went to the pool after dinner and sat with our feet in the water, me being very careful not to get my dress wet. We didn't talk much, we just sat and watched Bodens Gate getting larger and then the structure of the space docks blocking out our view of the stars.

I straightened my knee and watched water dripping from my foot. "What are you going to do while you're waiting for *Mesa Vista*?"

"Research and planning. RuComm has a guesthouse at the embassy in Eindhoven. They expect me to stay there and create a detailed plan for Kempner-27 before they arrive to pick me up. Of course, I'm only one third of the biology team, so my plan probably won't amount to much. The senior biologist is on his ninth hop."

"So it's another test? They just want to see what you can come up with?"

"Probably." He put his foot underneath mine to catch the water dripping down.

"I'll bet you surprise them."

"Thanks."

"I'm going to spend one night at the hotel with my parents and Winn, and then it's off to the Warrens with me."

"Stay in the Mission, MD, where you're safe."

"Afraid I'll get kidnapped?"

"Something like that."

I grinned at him. "If they put me up for sale, will you come bid on me?"

"You shouldn't even joke about that. I know you've heard the stories about what happens in the Warrens. It's not funny." He put his hand into the water and splashed my leg.

"Hey! No water on the dress." He put his hand back in the water and looked at me, an evil glint in his eye. "Dress," I cautioned him again, trying to look stern.

"I wish you weren't wearing it tonight."

I raised my eyebrows, expecting him to clarify his statement or maybe blush. He's cute when he blushes. But he just kept staring at me until I had to look away.

He laughed. "Just so I could splash you one last time."

I stood up. "Come on. We need to go get our stuff. We'll be docking in a few minutes." I held my hand out to him.

He took hold of it. "I'm ready, although I don't think we have all that much 'stuff' to get."

He was right. When we met back at the airlock on the outer ring corridor, I had a small bag with a change of clothes and nothing else.

"I had to give my display pad back so I need to buy a new one tomorrow," I told Sam. "That's the third one I've lost or broken since my family moved to Earth."

"I don't think your dad can blame you for this one."

"He won't, but Hannah probably will."

He laughed and bumped my shoulder with his. "I *am* going to miss you, you know."

"Yeah, I know. I'll miss you too. Please don't get eaten by some weird megafauna thing with big teeth or suckers or something."

"And don't get yourself put up for auction. I don't have very much money."

"Do you promise to be miserable for the next few days?"

"I will if you will."

"That's a deal." I smiled at him. "I'm already starting."

CHAPTER 9

BODENS GATE

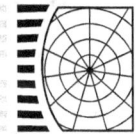

The hatch began to open and Winona slipped through before it could even complete its cycle. I ran toward her and we almost crashed to the deck when we grabbed each other. She was squeezing me hard enough around the middle to make breathing impossible.

"Careful there, Winn, I'm crushable."

She stepped back from me and wrapped herself around Sam while I tried to catch my breath. When she released him, she put her hands on his cheeks and pulled his face down far enough to kiss his forehead.

"Thank you for taking care of my Mala Dusa. I forgive you now for lying to her and her parents when you first met them."

"What are you talking about, Winn? Sam didn't lie to me."

"You are terrible at research. Did you even look him up at all?"

"No." I looked at Sam. He was blushing again.

Winona stared at him, head tipped to the side. "So, are *you* going to tell her?"

He sighed. "I, um, I'm not twenty-one."

"He just turned twenty!" Winn was more excited than I had ever seen her. "Last week, while you were still on *Wandering Star*. He graduated from the Academy at nineteen. The youngest was some girl who was fifteen, and there have been loads that were seventeen or eighteen, but still..."

Samuel Coleridge, child prodigy, was staring at his shoes.

"It doesn't make any difference," he told his shoes. "I'll still be on *Mesa Vista*, you'll still be on Earth, and you're still sixteen."

"Why didn't you tell me?" I asked gently.

He glanced up, looking miserable. "Because I don't want you to think I'm some kind of freak."

"Hah!" Winona was triumphant. "See? I found one for you."

Dad and Hannah had reached us by then and Dad pulled me into a hug. Sam turned and walked away from us toward the hatch. Winn wouldn't let him leave, though. She put her hands on his chest and pushed.

"Back," she ordered. "You can't leave yet. Duse still needs you."

"Why?" he asked.

I pulled away from Dad and ran to him. I whispered in his ear, bracing myself with both my hands on his right shoulder, afraid to hug him. "Because it *does* make a difference. It makes you even more special and more precious." I gave him a quick kiss on the cheek and waited for a lightning bolt from *Mara Vista*.

"Ms. Holloman." I closed my eyes, waiting for it. "I'm sure you can do better than that to say goodbye to Mr. Coleridge. You won't be seeing him again for quite some time."

We kissed. It was our first real kiss, and it was long and gentle. He let go of me and I wobbled a little.

"Buy a new display pad first thing," he told me, "so we can talk every day."

I was still wobbling.

"OK?" he asked.

"Uh huh." He must have left me then, because the next thing I knew Hannah was standing next to me and Sam was gone.

She sighed. "It doesn't always take very long, does it?" I knew she was feeling my emotions. I think everyone within a hundred meters could probably feel them.

"He made me a dress," I told her.

"I see that."

"And underwear." I reached down and touched the hem, lifting it slightly.

"I'll take your word for it."

I could feel that she wanted to be angry with me, but couldn't. I *do* love my mom.

"It's very early in the morning," she said. She took one arm, Dad took the other, and they guided me toward the hatch. "Would you like to come back to the hotel and sleep a few hours?"

"In a bed?"

"Yes. A soft bed."

"OK. I cut my hair. Did you notice?"

"It's very becoming."

"Those helmets, they were so hard to get on with long hair. I was the last one to the rally point."

"That's why I first cut my hair short. I never looked back." She smiled at me. "It makes you look more grownup."

"Thanks, Mom."

The bed was soft and I stayed in it until almost 10:00. By then, Winona had been making an increasing amount of noise, talking, clattering things, and stomping her feet. When my door slammed, I opened one eye and found her face a couple of centimeters away from mine.

"Oh, good, you're awake. Get up so you can swim with me before lunch."

"You woke me up so we can go swimming?"

"They have a slide."

"A slide?"

"One of the twisty ones. With the extra gravity, I can achieve enough velocity to skip on the surface of the pool like a stone on a pond. So far I've only managed two hops, but with practice—"

"I bet we can do three." I sat up and looked around the room, remembering where I was and how I'd gotten there, remembering Sam.

"I need to buy a new display pad first," I told her.

"I knew you'd be this way. There's a new pad on your bag. I've been chatting with Sam all morning."

"Really?"

"Pretending to be you."

I screamed. I didn't mean to, it just came out. "Please tell me you didn't."

"I didn't. I wanted to see how much you love him." She put her hand on my cheek, very gently. "I wish I could feel your emotions like your parents do. What's it like, being in love with him?"

Hannah and my dad came into the room before I could answer.

"Were you screaming?" Dad asked.

"Winona was being mean to me."

"Good," Hannah commented. "It was time for you to get up anyway."

I turned back to Winona. "It hurts. That's what it feels like right now."

Hannah sat down next to me and put her hand on my chest, the glib attitude she had had when she came into the room gone. I could feel her banging around inside my head while she looked into my eyes, then she pulled me into her arms.

"You couldn't tell anyone how you felt," she whispered to me.

"No."

"Or show it in any way."

"That's right."

"You could see him and be with him, but not touch him. You could talk to him, but never say what you wanted to tell him."

"Yes. It was just like that." I felt tears in my eyes.

"I thought I remembered what it was like, but feeling it again... Dusa, I wanted to spare you this." She sniffled, wiping my tears with her fingers while hers ran down her cheeks. "And here I am crying right before a big meeting again."

"I'm sorry, Mom."

"Was it the Tarakana?" Winona asked. "Did they do this to her?"

Mom smiled. "Oh, no. They did this all on their own, her and Sam. That's what I was looking for, to make sure." She let go of me and stood up. "Although we do need to talk about the Tarakana once you're up and dressed."

"Swim first," Winn demanded.

Hannah sighed. "You do know *you* work for *me*, right?"

We both looked at her, pleading.

"A short swim, then Tarakana while we eat lunch, then I need to get to my meeting. This election business is not going like I planned it at all."

"You should use your avatar." Dad's tone of voice told me that it wasn't the first time he had suggested it.

"And *you* should stop worrying. No one remembers me here." She kissed him. "I'm just folklore."

"A composite character, composed of bits and pieces of many leaders of the rebellion," Winona added. "That's the story I put out for you to the local media four days ago, building on the rumors and stories you've been feeding into the population for the last decade."

"See? Perfectly safe."

Winona turned toward her. "I wouldn't say that, ma'am. It would be far safer if you used your avatar."

"Who do you work for?"

"You, Ms. Weldon."

"It's settled then. Go swim and then we'll talk."

I sent a good morning message to Sam and walked to the pool with him looking at me from the screen while we talked. It took Winona another eight tries on the slide before she got her third skip. I was there in the water with my display pad and captured it for her, which was good, because she hit her head when she arched her back coming out and said she didn't really remember much about it. She was all smiles though when we sat on the side of the pool watching it in slow motion.

After viewing it for the third time, Winn announced, "It's lunch time and Hannah will be mad if we're late. She wants to talk to you about the extra passengers you had with you on *Wandering Star*."

"I don't want to talk about them."

"Why not?" Hannah asked from behind me. She and Dad had brought lunch down to us to eat poolside. Winn and I dried off and put on shirts and shorts to be more presentable at the table.

"Is it safe to talk here?" Winona asked.

Hannah tapped a small cube she had brought with her that was humming softly in the center of the table.

"Is that a ..."

Hannah nodded. "Jammer. It will be more private talking here than if we were in our room, which is almost certainly bugged. Now," she said, turning toward me, "why don't you want to talk about the Tarakana?"

"It doesn't seem right to talk about them, you know?" I answered. "There's just something wrong about it."

"So, would you say that the Tarakana are beneficial to us?"

"They scare me a little, but yes. I think the way they amplify emotion and passion is very beneficial. And they're kind and gentle. When I asked them to stay away from Sam and me, they did, although Merrimac just wanted to help me. He's my friend."

"Merrimac again." She glanced at Dad. "What did he make you do, Mala Dusa?"

My forehead wrinkled as I thought about it, trying to cut through the fog. "Something with the engines. We had to stop the ship so they could move on, get on board the *Vista* ships before we reached Bodens Gate. It was very important." The memory seemed incredibly distant now.

"She killed the ship," Hannah told my dad. Her voice seemed far away too, so I concentrated on eating my sandwich and thinking about Sam. I missed Sam, but if I tried, I could almost see him when I shut my eyes.

"Look at her, still in a Tarakana haze." Dad's voice was floating somewhere close by. "But why make her do it? They could have sabotaged the engines just as easily themselves as having her do it."

"I don't know. It worries me. They need her to have that guilt in her for some reason, even though they're suppressing it almost completely now."

"Mala Dusa? Do you know where the Tarakana are now?" Dad asked.

"Are we still talking about them? Um, some on the *Resolute*, some on *Sierra Vista*, and *Mara Vista*, and *Buena Vista*, and soon on *Mesa Vista*, since one went with Sam. They're moving on with us to the empty planets. You need to let them go. You can't stop them and you shouldn't try. The central worlds are too crowded now, that's what Merrimac told me when he was wrapped around and around and around my legs." I took another bite of my sandwich and closed my eyes again so I could see Sam. Hannah asked me a couple of more questions, but I couldn't hear them. It was not as important as Sam or the song I was humming.

"Shit." Hannah's voice, far away. "They shut her down completely. She's just sitting there humming the elephant song to herself."

Winona's hand touched my cheek. "Duse? Tell me about the pool they had on *Mara Vista*."

"Oh, you would have loved it, Winn. It didn't have a slide, but the display screens made it look like we were swimming under an open sky, except the sky was open *space*. Sam and I swam there every night after dinner."

"And she's back, just like that." Hannah was staring at me.

"What?" I asked.

"Nothing. Hurry along with lunch. There's not much time before we have to leave."

We finished lunch and went back up to the suite. I got dressed, casual but nice, better than what I wear to school. Winona came into my room looking ten years older, her hair tied back and a confident air about her that reminded me of Hannah.

"Wow, Ms. Killdeer, you look like someone not to be trifled with. Are you presenting today too?"

She giggled, ruining the illusion. "No, my role is to sit beside your mom and do instant research on anything that comes up so I can pass the information to her. It's fun."

Dad came in, looking like he was ready to teach class. Mom looked like she was ready to run a world; stylish, confident and just a little bit sexy, which was kind of disturbing. She smiled at me, looking just like her statue, and a sudden jolt of fear grabbed at me.

"You shouldn't be here, Mom. Someone's going to recognize you."

"They haven't yet and this is our third day of meetings. Members of the Central Government were pushing for a delay in full enfranchisement for my citizens in the Warrens. They would have gotten away with it too, if I hadn't been here in person to push them back." She shook her head and then had to run her fingers through her hair to get it away from her eyes. "If anything, I should have come here sooner. Stop worrying. I get enough of that from your father."

Winona whispered to me while we walked to the lobby. "She's becoming more Ysabeau Romee and less Hannah Weldon every day we're here. It's incredibly exciting. Yesterday when one of the Central Government politicians was arguing with her, she reached across her chest like this." Winn placed her right hand under her left arm.

I looked at her, not understanding.

"Your dad says she used to wear a gun in a holster just there." She tapped her ribs.

"Great."

"Isn't it?" Winona sighed, completely enthralled.

We entered the lobby, and Dad said to Hannah, "Lots of police this morning." His voice seemed very calm.

"They are called Guardians of the Peace here, or the Guards." Then, too calmly she said, "Mala Dusa, Winona, please return to the room."

Winona stopped and turned. I stopped, but I couldn't turn away from what was happening. When Mom and Dad reached the front door, a man in a dark suit and two women in uniform blocked them. I couldn't hear the question he asked her, but I saw her response, the contemptuous smile and the arrogant way she looked at him.

Her voice carried clearly to me, "And who do *you* say I am?" Then they took my parents away.

Winona was tugging on my arm. "We need to run, Mala Dusa."

"They took my parents." I pointed. "We have to stop them."

"We can't, and we won't be able to help them at all if we don't get out of here *right now*." She pulled me toward a side exit.

"I need to go back to the room first. I need my dress."

"No." She pulled me outside. "The members of the Guard are already searching our room. Sam can make you a new dress."

I let her pull me along the sidewalk and into a coffee shop. We sat and Winona got out her pad and started typing.

"Your mom has a lot of friends on the council and in the Union government. They may be able to get her released quickly. I'm sure Janus Boden is behind this. He was the one pushing to disenfranchise the Warrens." She looked up at me. "There is one problem though."

"What?"

"Your mom. She *is* Ysabeau Romee, and she all but admitted to it when they stopped her." She sighed. "Did you *see* her when they asked her? The pride and grace in the way she was standing there? I think she would almost rather burn than deny who she is and what she did."

"Burn?"

Winona was back typing again. "That's the capital punishment on Bodens Gate; death by immolation. I think that's why your mom decided to call herself Ysabeau Romee in the first place."

I looked at her blankly and she touched my forehead, but gently.

"Research, Duse. Romee was Joan of Arc's mother."

I shook my head, but it wouldn't clear. "This can't be happening."

"And it won't if we stop it."

I looked around at the other patrons in the coffee shop, happily going about their day. "When will it be safe to go back to the hotel?"

"We're never going back, unless you want to burn too."

"What have *I* done?"

"You know who she is and didn't report it. That makes you an accessory after the fact. Me too."

"This can't be happening."

She tapped my forehead a little harder this time. "*Think*, Duse."

"I'll contact Grandpa. He doesn't really like Hannah all that much, but he'll help me. It's going to take two and a half days for him to get my message, though. And Sam. I need to talk to Sam. Maybe RuComm can help us. Maybe we could stay at the embassy with him. Maybe—"

"They'd turn us in. They would have to under terms of the Union charter."

"Well, we can't stay here. Maybe the Mission. We can ask for sanctuary or something. I'll contact Father Ryczek and see if I can come there now instead of tomorrow morning."

Winona looked at me, her head tipped. "I was wrong, Duse. It turns out that the Warrens are going to be the safest place for you on Bodens Gate."

I sent a detailed message to Grandpa and then a simple one to Father Ryczek asking if I could report for duty earlier than planned. I saved Sam for last. I set up our personal encryption and punched in his code.

"Hey, MD, what's up? I thought you were going to be at the Council meeting all afternoon."

"Hush, I need help and I can't talk long. Something terrible has happened and I... I, um." I was losing focus looking at him. The concern filling his blue eyes was mesmerizing. It made my chest hurt. "I lost the dress you made for me," I told him.

"Give me that." Winona pulled my pad away from me and swung it over in front of her. "Samuel, we need you to contact RuComm and make them aware that her parents, Hannah Weldon and Theodore Holloman, have been detained by the Guards. See if there is any aid available because of their years of service to RuComm and the Union. Talk to the Union ambassador too if you can. Do you understand?"

"Not really. Why would the Guards do that? I've been listening to the news while I was working and all they're talking about is the arrest of some woman that killed forty-two people and ordered the killings of like a couple of hundred more back during the rebellion. They said..."

He stopped talking and I pulled the pad back over to me. "Sam?"

The look in his eyes had changed. "Did she do it? What they're saying on the news, it's very detailed."

"Careful," Winona whispered to me.

"I don't know. I just know she's my mom and I have to help her. Those things that happened, that was during the war."

"There are rules, even in war. They teach us that."

"Sam, are you going to help me or not?"

He nodded. "Of course I will. Where are you?"

"On the run." The words sounded unreal even as I said them. "I'm going to try to make it to the Mission. Father Ryczek is a friend. I think I'll be safe there."

"Good. Let me see what I can find out and I'll be back in touch." He disconnected and I rolled up my pad.

"Do you trust him?" Winona asked.

"Absolutely."

"Now answer me using your brain."

"I've known Sam for ten days. He's a RuComm scientist on his first hop and a graduate of the Academy. He lied to me about how old he is because he wanted to impress me and wanted to..." I bit my lower lip. "So I trust him, but I can't predict what he's going to do. Something that he thinks is good for me is about all I can promise."

"We need to move."

"OK, where?" My display pad dinged and I opened the reply from Father Ryczek. "Listen to this, Winn: 'So pleased that you will be joining us early. I imagine even the meager comforts of the Mission will be a blessing to you after a harried day. I will meet you at the Gabriele Restaurant at 18:00.'"

"So he knows what's happened. How far is the Gabriele Restaurant?"

I tapped on the name and the pad gave me a map. "Almost ten kilometers, located in the old customs building on the edge of the Warrens. Looks kind of sketchy. Italian themed food."

"Let's go. It's 15:00 now and it will be a long walk in these shoes and with the extra gravity."

"An autonomous taxi would only take a few minutes."

"As soon as you put your hand on the payment pad the doors would lock and we'd be on the way to the Guardians of the Peace. Think!"

I looked at her, trying to make sense of it. "OK."

We started walking, first past office buildings and little open parks, then apartment buildings and empty lots. The sun was starting to get lower and the buildings we passed were turning to bars, pawnshops, and 'dance' clubs with the apostrophes around 'dance' flashing in lurid colors.

"Are we almost there, Duse? My feet hurt."

"Less than a kilometer according to the map." There was a group of men with a vicious looking dog in front of a building with steel mesh covering the windows watching us walk by. "I think we should have risked the taxi."

"We'll make it. Keep your shoulders back and walk fast."

We walked fast, but Winona was limping and a blood stain was soaking through the outside of her left shoe.

The Gabriele Restaurant didn't look much better than the businesses we had been passing. It was made of crumbling concrete blocks splattered with paint in random designs that might have been intentional, but probably weren't. I felt completely out of place; too young, over dressed, and my body woefully under-designed for the gravity. People were staring at us.

We found a table off to the side and as far away from the bar as possible. Our waitress seemed confused that we were there at all.

"Hi, I'm Tammy." I looked at her nametag, which read Giselle. "So, what brings a couple of city girls like you two out to the Gabby on such an evening as this?"

Winona was busy examining her foot, so I answered for us. "The food, of course. We hear that your lasagna is excellent."

She ignored me, looking at Winn. "What happened to your foot, honey?"

Winona looked back at her, eyes very big. "I underestimated how much walking I'd be doing today. It was a long way from City Center to here."

Tammy / Giselle stared at us, eyes narrowed. "You *walked* here from Eindhoven? Listen kids, I have a tip for you. Sometimes people run away from the Warrens to the city. No one runs the other way, got it? Do your parents know where you are?"

I had a good answer for that. Instead, I decided to stare at the menu.

When I looked back up at her, she must have had some sense of the despair that I was feeling because she sighed and shifted her weight from foot to foot a couple of times as she evaluated what to do with us.

"Fine, what can I get you? You do have money, right? This is a cash only outfit."

"Cash? I've never carried cash in my life." I looked over at Winn and she placed a stack of octagonal coins on the table.

"I'd like to try your lasagna, please."

"And you?"

"Anything but lasagna. What do you recommend for me?"

She smirked. "Other than getting your ass back to Dulcinea where you belong? Try the baked manicotti, it's not bad."

"Thank you, that sounds fine."

When she left, I whispered to Winona, "How did she know I'm from Dulcinea?"

Winn laughed. "Do you own a mirror, Duse? On this planet, you are unique and exotic. You stand out."

I sighed. "At least you had some cash. Why *do* you have cash?"

"I got them as a souvenir. I hope it's enough. I don't think we'd enjoy trying to work off a debt here."

When Tammy / Giselle brought us our food, she also handed Winona a square bandage, maybe ten centimeters on a side.

"Thank you, ma'am, you're very kind."

She nodded. "I've a daughter that's always getting herself into trouble. Maybe someday someone will show her a kindness when she needs it. I'm off in a half hour, so if you need anything else be sure and let me know before then." She smiled at Winona. "You or the princess."

I opened my mouth, closed it again. When she left, I asked Winona, "Was I really doing it again?"

Winona grinned, enjoying my misery. "No more than usual."

We ate slowly, still having an hour to kill before Father Ryczek was supposed to meet us.

At fifteen minutes before 18:00, a waiter we hadn't met brought us refills for our drinks, a sweet bubbly concoction that tasted a little like guava. Winona thanked him and reached for her glass.

"Finally. That lasagna was salty." Before she could wrap her lips around the straw, a very large man sat down with us at the table. He was maybe fifty and completely bald except for the tattoo of a dragon draped across the top of his head, the wings coming down his cheeks and crossing his mouth.

"You're Alice's daughter, that's for sure." He smiled and his teeth made it look like the dragon's wings had claws. Winona never took her eyes from him as she pulled her glass closer to her mouth. The man took Winn's glass away from her and stuck a couple of his fingers into it. Winona watched him, more curious than upset. He touched his fingers to his tongue, made a face and spit into her drink. He turned his chair around, surveying the other patrons, finally settling on a stylishly dressed woman sitting a couple of tables away. She was staring at us and he waved a short fat finger at her.

"These two are mine, Odette," he called to her. She shrugged and waved back at him.

"Did you order a second round?" He asked Winona.

"No, sir."

"Did you know the man that brought it to you?"

"I assumed he was a waiter." Winona sounded embarrassed.

"My name is Cuza. Father Ryczek sent me to pick you up."

"Can you prove that?" Winona asked him.

"Ho! You're a quick one, aren't you?"

"I've heard Hannah and Dad talk about him," I told her. "His illustrations are distinctive."

As he walked us to the door, I asked, "What would have happened if you hadn't stopped us from drinking those refills? What would have happened to us?"

"Oh, Odette mostly fills orders for domestics." He looked at us closely. "But she's not above snatching up a couple of girls for the doll trade if an easy chance comes to her. Either way, you would've been sold by day's end tomorrow." He smiled at us without humor. "Welcome to the Warrens."

It had gotten dark while we were inside, and the soft bed I had slept in the night before seemed very far away. Winona's fingers wrapped around mine as I took her hand.

"Whatcha got there, Cuza?"

Tammy / Giselle was leaning against the wall of the building watching us.

"Evening, Maribelle. Just a couple of new recruits. What you doing out here? Guarding the café?"

"Those two had me worried some so I stuck around after my shift. It's a relief to see they belong to you."

"Yeah, Odette was about to roll them, though. If I hadn't been a bit early they'd be on their way to the block."

Maribelle came up to me and touched my hair, smelling it, and then ran the back of her fingers down the side of my neck. "Jasmine. Odette would've made her nut for the quarter on this one." She turned to Winona. "And the other one. Have you ever seen eyes like hers? It's like she can see right through you. She's special, probably worth even more than the blonde to the right buyer. You need to be more careful with your things."

"Yes, ma'am. And you need to be more careful if you was planning on messing with Odette again. That's a sharp knife she carries in her boot."

"You would know. Go carefully, Cuza."

"And you too."

Winona did something very surprising when we climbed into the truck next to Cuza for the ride to the mission. She started to cry.

CHAPTER 10

THE WARRENS

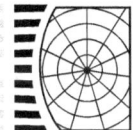

"She always cry so much?" Cuza asked me.

"No, never. And today she was the one in control while my brain was just frozen."

Cuza nodded. "She's one of those. A friend of mine was the same way. He was cold as winter wind when things got interesting, then, once the troubles was over, he'd shake so bad he couldn't stand. Damn, I miss him."

"Was he killed in the war?"

"Naw, third wife got him. I told him having three at one time was a bad idea." He shook his head, remembering.

Winona sniffled and looked from Cuza to me. "I'm done crying now. Our reports about current conditions in the Warrens were grossly inaccurate. I believe someone may be intentionally misleading Ms. Weldon. We have to determine who and why. It may just be underlings trying to enhance their own reputations by painting an unrealistically optimistic picture, but I suspect that it's Janus Boden feeding false information to the commission in order to keep them from wanting to investigate ground truth."

Cuza laughed. "I got no idea what she just went on about, but if you suspect Boden of anything underhanded, there's good odds you're right."

She looked at him. "I believe this man will be invaluable to us."

"And I reckon Maribelle was right about your street value."

"I *know* she was right," I squeezed her hand. "Winn is worth ten of me. Probably worth way more than ten."

"To the right buyer," Winona added. "Anything from Sam?" she asked, ignoring the compliment.

"No. I tried him again just before our 'refills' came. No messages and he's not answering me."

"There could be lots of reasons for that."

"None of them good."

"No, none of them good."

Cuza drove up to the Mission's front gate, actually driving. His hands were on a wheel and his feet were doing things on the floor. I'd never seen a person drive before; it looked like it could be fun under other circumstances. He pushed something that was supposed to open the gate, but nothing happened.

"We just cleaned all the trash and dirt out of the track this morning and it still ain't opening."

The truck's running lights were shining on the gate. "I think your problem is the chain," I pointed. "It looks like there's too much slack. I'll take a look at it in the morning and get it working for you."

Cuza was studying me, eyes narrowed, and then he grinned. That dragon on his head was going to take getting used to. "Mala Dusa, when I look at you I see Alice, but when you talk I hear Teddy."

He got out of the truck with a hammer to get the gate moving again while Winn and I looked at each other. "Teddy?" we said together.

"Now I can't wait to see him again," Winn grinned at me.

"Yeah, me too." I couldn't smile, though.

Father Ryczek met us when we pulled up to the main building. I'd only seen him in videos and pictures that he'd sent to our church when he had been asking for funding or telling about how the Mission was helping the Warrens. He'd seemed an experienced and wise administrator. Seeing him dressed in stained coveralls there in the courtyard, lit by security lights, and with the smells of the Warrens in my nose, he seemed eternal and elemental. Father Ryczek had always been, was now, and would always be there tending to the people that needed him.

He put his hands on each side of my face, his smile making the lines around his eyes deeper than they already were. "Mala Dusa, Little Soul, you've traveled a long, weary road to be here with us. I pray that the yoke ahead for you is easy and the burden light."

"Seeing you makes it so." I replied.

He turned to Winona and greeted her in the same way and then he sighed, looking at us, taking it all in. Two sixteen year old girls, dressed in fine clothes for the council meeting, the bloodstain on Winona's shoe, hair askew from ten kilometers on the road, no bags.

"Fugitives."

"Yes, sir," Winn answered. "We would like—"

Father Ryczek cut her off, holding one bony finger in front of her nose. "I know why you're here, Ms. Killdeer." He turned toward me. "Your parents arrived on my doorstep with secrets and hidden agendas. I took them in knowing God would use them anyway, and he did, although at a terrible cost. I thought maybe your heart was pure, at least until I got that letter from your father begging me to release you from this assignment. Tell me again why you're here."

I tried to hold his gaze, but couldn't. I looked at the ground while I answered. "I came because I wanted to find out what happened to my mother. And to serve God." I looked back up at him, pleading. "I do want to serve God."

"Your family has been a thorn in my flesh for almost twenty years, including all the letters Alice sent me begging to come here. I don't know how God is going to work things out this time, but I've no doubt he will."

Father Ryczek shook his head. "Well, come on then, let's get you inside. You'll have to share a room, and I'll see if I can't find some clothes for you. Oh, I almost forgot. You have a visitor waiting for you in the dining hall."

Sam stood when I came into the room. I wanted to run to him, but there was something about him that made me hesitate. He was pale and seemed very unsure of himself, pulling on the collar of his shirt like it was scratching him.

"Hey, Mala Dusa."

I walked up to him slowly and put my arms around him, resting my head against his shoulder. He held me like he was afraid to touch me.

"I'm sorry I couldn't reply to your messages," he whispered.

"Couldn't?" I whispered back.

Winona and Cuza had joined us by then and we all sat down together, Cuza smiling at Sam. What little color had been in his cheeks drained away.

"Were you able to talk to the Union ambassador?" Winn asked.

"Yes, that part was easy. He brought me right in to his office even though he was in a meeting. He was with, um," he pulled on his collar again. "He introduced me to Mr. Boden. They're all very concerned about you. You need to come back to the embassy with me. Tonight. Both of you."

"Why?" Winona asked slowly, her eyes never leaving his.

"It's important." His collar was bothering him again. "Running makes you look like criminals. It puts your parents at risk. The Guards just want to talk to you, get some things straight."

Cuza leaned close to him. "If Janus Boden is looking for criminals he need look no farther than his bathroom mirror. That bastard needs to burn and I'm the man to light the match."

Sam put his hand to his collar. "You shouldn't say that."

"That buzz you're feeling there is a feedback pulse," Cuza told him. "There ain't no signal getting out of the Mission tonight."

"You have a jammer?"

"If it was any stronger, God wouldn't be able to hear Father Ryczek's prayers."

Sam sighed and closed his eyes. "MD, first *Wandering Star* and now this. Are you trying to get me killed?"

"No, I'm really not." I reached across the table to him and he reluctantly took my hand.

"I've examined events in the lives of her parents and grandparents," Winn told him. "There's a definite pattern of drama and adventure far outside the norms. I'm not even sure what to call it, but I'm developing a working theory that may account for it. Isn't it exciting just being with her?"

Sam didn't look excited. "I was able to talk to Captain Kelang before I talked to Ambassador Killian. What's left of *Wandering Star* should be on orbit in the next day or so. He thinks RuComm may be able to do something, maybe at least get your parents off planet. The Captain said to tell you that this time he'll take action personally, whatever that means."

I nodded. "What about you? Can you keep providing information about what Mr. Boden is planning? We need someone inside the embassy that can—"

"Your mom, *is* she Ysabeau Romee?" he interrupted.

"She's my mom. She needs my help and I need yours."

"You met Boden. Choosing a side here ain't difficult," Cuza added. "Did he threaten you or bribe you?"

Sam was looking down at the table. "He made me a promise that my RuComm contract would be terminated and I'd be stranded on Bodens Gate if I didn't come here tonight."

"What else?" I asked gently.

"If you come back with me, you, Winona, and your father will be deported. No charges will be filed."

"And my mom?"

"A fair trial?"

"Ha!" Cuza snorted.

"It's better than if you *don't* come with me. All four of you will be charged." He took my hands and lowered his voice, "He said you and Winona probably wouldn't last long enough to stand before a judge. He was really graphic about it."

Winn blinked at him. "It's a bluff. No evidence exists that Hannah was Ysabeau. He wants us back under his control so he can put pressure on her to confess. I knew we did the right thing in running. He knows that he'll be forced to release her in two or three days due to lack of proof, pressure from RuComm, lobbying by senior Union leadership, and sniping from his enemies within the Central Government." She ticked the reasons off on her fingers, then reached out and took one of Sam's hands away from me. "Samuel, you should stay here. Don't go back until they're released."

He pulled his hands away from both of us. "No. My ship will be here in a couple of weeks. I have reports to prepare and RuComm is counting on me. Every step I take to help you, it just gets deeper. There's no bottom to it. I've lied for you, defied my team lead, and I'm in technical violation of my contract. That's just from knowing you for ten days. What comes next? Will you have me out in the Warrens with a gun in my hand fighting the Guardians of the Peace and killing your enemies?"

"It ain't a bad life," Cuza told him.

"No." He stood up. "Your family, your friends, you're all crazy. Dangerous. I can't do this anymore. I'm sorry, Mala Dusa, I just can't."

"Well then," Cuza said, standing, "I guess we need to get you back to the border so you can get a taxi and go tell your new friend Boden all about our little chat."

"I won't tell them anything." There was a sullen, stubborn look on his face.

"Uh huh." Cuza nodded, looking at me out of the corner of his eye.

It was the first time I'd heard someone's life being threatened.

"Just take him back, Cuza," I told him. "Back to his clean new starship and clean, simple RuComm life while we stay here and try to save my parents."

Cuza put one hand on Sam's shoulder, making him flinch. "I could introduce him to Odette on the way back. She probably thinks I owe her one."

"No, please don't." I stood. "Goodbye, Sam. Thank you for all you did for me on the ship."

"Thank you for being my friend, Mala Dusa. I'd still like to—"

I closed my eyes and he stopped talking. I didn't open them again until I could no longer hear the sound of Cuza's boots on the flagstones, proud of myself for not crying.

"I'm sorry, Duse." Winn took my hand. "I'll find you another one."

I sighed. "But I wanted *that* one."

Winn spent the next two days talking to Cuza, the teachers at the Mission school, and some of the people taking shelter with the church. She made notes and tried to figure out how the Confederation that Hannah had founded in the Warrens was being compromised, and who was doing it.

I worked on getting the front gate to work, realigning and tuning the communications array up on the roof, and trying to make the hot water boilers work properly. I had no idea what I was doing most of the time, but I think I was more successful than Winona.

I was doing my best not to be worried about my parents. After the initial excitement in the media, there was almost nothing. Winona kept reassuring me that there was no evidence and that Hannah would never admit to anything. I prayed she was right.

I went two days without talking to Sam. I'd like to report that I went more than twenty minutes without thinking about him, but that would be a lie. He haunted me. I found myself losing focus while I was working, seeing his eyes looking back at me instead of the greasy innards of the equipment I was trying to fix. I dreamed about him at night.

"Cuza is taking me to the market tomorrow morning to talk to some of the local merchants. Do you want to come?" Winona and I were eating dinner on Friday evening and I was tired from working all afternoon realigning the stage lights in the sanctuary, Father Ryczek critiquing every millimeter of movement, color overlap, and focus change.

I stared at her, almost choking on the chunk of bread I was stuffing into my mouth. "What happened to 'Promise me you won't go outside the gate, Duse? You'll be ravaged and die a horrible death before you make it five meters.' You threatened me with snow to keep me in here."

"That was different. Now the risk is worth it."

"How's that? Worth more than me finding out about my family?"

"Yes." Winona was studying the contents of her salad bowl, shoving green and purple things around with her fork, looking for the perfect next bite. "I believe your parents will be released day after tomorrow. Hannah will be asking me what happened and I need to have an answer for her, at least a preliminary one."

"What makes you think they'll be released?" I asked it in my best calm voice, but my heart was pounding. I'd been following the news and exchanging messages with Captain Kelang. No one had heard anything yet.

"You're not going to like it."

"If my parents are being released, I'm going to like it."

"Sam told me."

I felt my mouth fall open, like it always did when my brain was stunned into no longer being able to think.

"I helped him set up encryption when he went back to the embassy. The same night you said goodbye to him. He's been telling me everything that's happening there, or at least all of the conversations between Janus Boden and Ambassador Killian."

"They still trust him? Why would they include him in their plans?"

"Um, they're not. I also showed him how to tap into the signal from the bug they planted on him using his display pad. After he told them that Cuza had found and destroyed it, we changed its frequency and he planted it in the ambassador's office the next morning at like 03:00. We've been listening to their meetings the last couple of days."

"He said he wouldn't help. He said I was crazy and dangerous."

"He had a change of heart on the way back to the embassy. He seems to have self-control issues where you're concerned. Or Cuza may have hit him." She considered this while she chewed. "He's scared, Duse, but he's doing it for you. If they find out, he'll be in serious trouble."

"He should come here to the Mission after my parents are released, or right now would be better."

"He's gone too far for that now. It would only make things worse for him. He needs to lay low and just ship out like none of this ever happened once *Mesa Vista* arrives."

"But I want him *here*." Winn reached across the table before I could dodge. "Ow!"

"You're better than that, Mala Dusa."

"Not when it comes to Sam." I rubbed my forehead. "I'm not very good at all."

"I know. I should have waited before telling you, but I'm excited. The agreement is for the Central Government to release them Sunday morning. The terms require them to leave Bodens Gate immediately, and for the Union to bar her for life from participating in the Commission or anything else having to do with planetary politics. They'll come pick us up and then we'll all be escorted to a shuttle."

"I can't leave. There're two new solar arrays arriving on Tuesday that I'm supposed to help set up. I'm under contract."

"And you think you'll be able to sneak out some night for dinner at the Gabriele Restaurant with Sam before he leaves."

"Maybe."

"He's right about you."

"That I'm crazy and dangerous?"

"No, that's why we both love you so much. I was thinking about when he said you were trying to kill him."

It was like strong hands were squeezing my chest. "How come you get to talk to him and I don't?"

"You know the answer to that. Sam recognizes that you're a problem so he plays tricks on himself to keep either of you from doing something stupid. He talks to me and not you because he's pretending that you don't love him anymore. It's an interesting tactic. Maybe you should try it."

"So when is the great and wise Winona going to allow me to talk to my friend again?"

She was using a piece of bread to get the last of her salad dressing and stray bits of onion. "We can't let them know that there's still a connection between the two of you or they might suspect him of passing information, or use it as a conduit to put pressure on Hannah and your dad. My encryption makes it look like he's just sending messages to his parents. Talking to him should be safe once we're off planet and there's no longer any possibility of you seeing him again."

I sighed, or it was supposed to be a sigh. It came out as a whimper.

"Be brave, Duse. He'll be back about the time we're finishing our senior year. He'll come find you, I'm sure of it. Until then, you can send messages back and forth across the light years. It could be worse." She thought about it. "Much worse."

It was Saturday in the Warrens and Winona wouldn't shut up. She was determined to make me less miserable by the force of her own cheerfulness. She was chattering on about the different styles of architecture we were passing and the organic growth of the streets and alleyways. She was even commenting on what was contributing to each new smell we encountered, making me guess what it was.

I wasn't feeling any less miserable. Sam had died overnight, a dozen times in a dozen different ways, each one hideous and vivid in my mind. Winona told me that I had been screaming for the Tarakana to get out of my head, swinging a wrench at the shadows under the beds and in the back of the closet. After she took my wrench away, Winn had laid down next to me, and held me in the dark until I cried myself back to sleep.

Walking along with her and Cuza in the bright sunlight, I was still convinced it was the Tarakana. It had felt just like when Merrimac had shoved me down the twisted future paths to where Sam and I were together. But this had been dark, feeding on my fear and panic, showing me all the ways they would take Sam from me, until only the despair of love eternally lost remained. I woke up angry, wanting to hunt down everyone that might hurt Sam or keep us apart. I wanted to find someone to kill, and that was a feeling that scared me almost as much as losing Sam.

"Do you smell that, Duse?" Winona asked again. "Guess what it is."

It smelled like garbage soaked in sewage. All of the Warrens smelled that way to me, so I told her, "Garlic."

"Nope, it's garbage soaked in sewage." She smiled at me, eyes sparkling. "Being used as fertilizer for the garlic." She laughed and I smiled for what seemed like the first time in a week.

"God, I love you, Winona."

"I know you do. By tomorrow night your parents will be free and all four of us will be on a Union ship thrusting away from here. Sam will be working on his plan for Kempner-27 with your invaluable help via display pad, and you'll be making rude innuendos to each other all through the trip home. With any luck, he'll be back in time to dance with you at the spring prom."

"You make it sound so easy. Do you really think Hannah will just fly away from all this?"

"Of course not. But she's shrewd and subtle. She'll leave, but she'll find a way to stay involved." Winn looked around at the crowds on the street as we neared the market square. "She loves these people."

"She ain't leavin'." Cuza had been ignoring our conversation since we left the Mission. Now he stopped and looked hard at Winona. "Not if she's who she was, not after you tell her what's happening here. You see that stone?" He pointed to a large plinth, maybe three meters on a side that someone had covered with flowers.

"Is that where her statue was?" Winn asked, her voice reverent.

"Yeah, until they made me move it. Those flowers started appearing a couple days ago when the first media reports came out that Ysabeau was alive and the Guards was holdin' her. Folks here remember. They remember what hope felt like and they teach their kids what it was like."

We walked up to the stone and he took a single rose from inside his coat. He held it out to me. I sniffed it and smiled, enjoying the sweet scent after the stench of the Warrens. Cuza took his thumb, intentionally stabbed it with one of the thorns, and then wiped his blood on the petals before laying the rose on top of the plinth. I shivered, glimpsing the depth of devotion and love that he had for her.

Winona took Cuza's hand and kissed it. When she looked at me, there were tears in her eyes. "If Ysabeau stays, I'll stay and fight with her."

An alarm was ringing silently in the back of my head, sounding just like the one on *Wandering Star* that was supposed to send me running to the rally point.

"You'll stay here? Fighting? Like *really* fighting?" The tears in Winona's eyes had turned to cold hatred and I felt like I was back in my nightmare again, the one where Sam had died so many times that the landscape was littered with his broken bodies.

"Oh, God damn it," I said under my breath, and immediately put my hand to my mouth. Dad almost never swears; Hannah does it all the time. Both of them yell at me whenever I do it.

I looked around at the buildings crowded around the square, feeling panic. Left, right, maybe behind us. Forty kilograms, Dad had said. Forty-five on Bodens Gate. Maybe looking like a dog, or something else, or maybe nothing but a shimmer in the shadows. No, there they were under an awning twenty meters away. Three dogs lying in the shade with their eyes open watching us. I wished I had my wrench with me.

I picked up a rock and threw it at them, then another. I charged at them, still throwing. On the fourth throw, they stood up and trotted away from me down an alley. I felt a quick wash of amusement from them, then there was a shimmer, and they vanished while still in the middle of the alley.

"Duse, what are you doing?"

"Didn't you see those dogs?"

"Yeah..."

I put my hands on her face, pushing her hair back, looking at her eyes, trying to see if my Winona was still in there.

She took my hands and pulled them away from her face. "Mala Dusa, are you OK?"

"Those weren't dogs. Think about it. What were you feeling a moment ago, when Cuza was putting the flower on the plinth. Was it normal?"

Her forehead wrinkled. "I wanted to find Ysabeau's enemies and help her kill them. I still do, but—" She paused, looking confused. "When I try to think about why killing is needed, it feels fuzzy inside my head. But it *is* needed, right?"

"I don't think so, Winn."

"So you two comin' to the market or are ya just gonna chase stray dogs?"

"The market," Winona answered, still looking troubled. "I need to give my report to Hannah tomorrow." She squeezed my hand and we followed after Cuza.

The Warrens were a mess. Maybe it was worse before Hannah united the clans into the confederation. Cuza said it was, but it was hard to believe. Before the war, there had been a thousand clans, maybe more. No one really knew. Now there were fifteen. Every merchant we talked to had a story to tell.

Elena Croitoru made custom clothing and sold it in the market every Friday and Saturday. Watching her hand stitching an alteration to a wedding dress while she talked to Winona made my fingers hurt. She had been twenty-five when her clan joined the confederation. She lost her husband to a Central Government ambush. The rebellion had brought her a widow's veil, a small pension, and hope that the daughter that would never know her father might somehow have a better life. Sofia was a year younger than me. She was sitting on the ground next to her mother, learning to sew. During the week, she attended school in Eindhoven learning to program AI systems. She said she was good at it and wanted to start her own business working the Union ships that passed through the docks for resupply and repair.

That could be a problem. The Central Government had imposed rules that would require her to join the Space Dock Affiliation first and there was a waiting list, and examinations, and licensing that could take up to ten years to get through and more money than Elena made in a year. Unless your family had connections, like most of the citizens outside the Warrens had.

But it would be no problem, Elena assured us. Ysabeau was back and she would fight for the Warrens again, fight to finish the revolution and make the people equal to any citizen.

Her smile made me shiver.

Darius Bourean made high-end cookware emblazoned with the sign of an ox on the handles. Before the rebellion, he had dealt in scrap metal and used crockery. In the first months of peace, he built a factory and made contracts with distributors in the capital, establishing a brand that quickly built a reputation for durability and elegance. Then the clan that controlled the section of the Warrens that included his factory wanted him to pay a separate tax to them and the clan that controlled the road leading to Eindhoven wanted money each year for transit improvements that they never made. The confederation had won the war and lost the peace, in his opinion. Fifteen squabbling, corrupt warlords controlled the Warrens. They were supposed to have given their weapons and allegiance to the new government, but instead they had set up private security forces, internal checkpoints, and demanded protection money from local businesses. His contracts with the shops in Eindhoven now flowed through the local clan leader, the Clan leadership council and an official in the Central Government, each layer taking a cut of his profits and delivering nothing in return.

But he was optimistic. Ysabeau was back and the warlords would fall in line behind her or she would sweep them away like the garbage they were. I bought an insulated metal cup from his stall in the market. A line of oxen was engraved on the side, chasing each other nose to tail in an endless circle.

I refused to enter the next shop. The sign said they made sausages and neatly wrapped cuts of meat. The smell made me want to have salad for dinner, maybe for the rest of my life.

"Um, Winona, I'm going to wait out here, if that's OK."

Cuza looked at me and then at Winona, who was already entering the shop. He told Winona, "Let me introduce you to Zimbrean. He's a friend of mine, so you'll be safe enough with him. I'll wait out here with Alice." He closed his eyes hard. "Sorry, Little Soul, 'old eyes are easily fooled', they always say."

I smiled at him and waited for him to introduce Winona before going to stand by a stall selling flowers, letting my nostrils have a break.

I saw the movement out of the corner of my eye just in time. I turned quickly and caught the ball a fraction of a second before it would have hit my head. There was a boy of eight or nine staring at me, just as amazed that I had caught it as I was. I kicked the ball back to him and saw that he wasn't alone. There must have been at least ten kids between eight and fourteen playing in the spaces between the market stalls, chasing after the ball, kicking it to each other, laughing and screaming and being a nuisance to all of the adults trying to shop.

I followed them and soon they were letting me have a turn. I didn't know the rules, or even what game we were playing, but it was fun. After about three or four laps around the market I stopped in front of the butcher shop to catch my breath and all the kids gathered around me asking me questions and staring. *Where you from? Why you so skinny? Have you been sick?* I told them about Earth and Dulcinea and that I was working for Father Ryczek.

A girl of maybe thirteen, and possessing more curves than my body will ever know, touched my arm. "You're very strange," she told me. The rest of the pack had moved on, chasing the ball on another lap of the market.

"And you're very beautiful," I answered.

"Not like you. You're amazing." She held her hand by my face and traced a line straight down to my feet. "All one line."

"What do you want to do when you grow up?" I was suddenly curious about what a child in the Warrens might see as possible futures.

"I want to be an architect." She looked around her. "I want to tear all of this down and build it again the right way. Or maybe an engineer. Or maybe..." She blushed and looked away.

"Or what?"

"I've been dreaming about something the last few nights. I think, maybe, I want to design weapons."

"Weapons? What kind of weapons?"

"All kinds. I think maybe that I won't really be able to become an architect. The waiting lists are so long for the good schools in the capital.

And then you have to join the government guild and they only let citizens join, not us. No one will let us do what we want in the Warrens unless we have weapons, so I want to design them and build them. Then I can help Ysabeau fight. At least that's what I've been dreaming about the last couple of nights. It's kind of silly, isn't it?"

"I don't know," I mumbled, feeling a kind of humming building in the back of my head. The rest of the kids were back, crowding around me again, laughing and giggling, wanting to touch my bare arms and staring at my legs.

There were several adults gathered around me now too. "I really don't know, but what's happening here, it isn't right. The leaders who should be protecting your rights and making your lives easier are just helping themselves to the money in your pockets. It has to change."

More people were joining the crowd now. "This isn't what people died for, that a few men get rich. Your children's future should be limited only by the strength of their desire and the abilities God has given them." I pointed to where the empty plinth stood covered with flowers. "It's not what she sacrificed for. It's not what my mother died for."

"Are you a child of the Warrens?" an old woman called to me.

"I am," I answered. "My mother died here as the rebellion was being born. Her blood joined with the dirt when they shot her down."

There was a murmur in the crowd.

"How much have you all suffered, trying to make a better life for your children?" I asked them. "We can do better than this. We owe it to those that died, and to our children, and to ourselves. Our struggle isn't finished. We've only paused to rest a moment before pushing on into the daylight. Remember the words in the Articles of Confederation. Our rights are from God, not Janus Boden, who chooses to give us only scraps. Our rights are ours to claim and defend."

"Are you starting your own army, Duse?"

I looked at Winona, blinking several times before I realized where I was. "Are we going back to the Mission now?"

"Yeah. I think we should." She grabbed my arm.

"Let her talk," someone yelled.

"Yeah, let her talk!"

"That's plenty for today," Cuza shouted back.

They hustled me down an alley and away from the crowd. Some of the children followed us until Cuza turned and smiled at them. They scattered.

"Why did you stop me? I was just about to tell the kids about my mom. She loved kids. I was going to show them the picture of her at the Mission surrounded by her students and covered in paint."

"Uh huh." Cuza replied.

"And then I was going to tell them *everything* about my stepmom."

Cuza stopped and he and Winona stared at me.

"You do know where you are and what was about to happen, don't you? Who your stepmother really is?"

I felt proud of her, more proud than I had ever felt before in my life. "Of course. I am the daughter of Ysabeau Romee."

CHAPTER 11
PARADISE

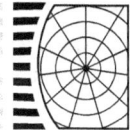

"It would have started right then, you know? Another five minutes and she would have been up on that plinth with a thousand people shouting her name." Winn was talking to Cuza while I sipped cold water from my new cup, my head pounding.

"We'd have had blood in the streets by nightfall." Cuza sighed, disappointed.

"They were inside my head," I whispered to Winona while Cuza started pacing around the room. "It felt *so* good with them in there. The words felt right, and I wanted to hug all of them, they seemed so precious to me. I had such a feeling of love for every single person there. It was like I *was* the Warrens."

"At least you didn't feel like you wanted to kill people the way I did," Winona whispered back.

"Oh, but I did. And not one or two at a time. I wanted... war. With the Tarakana in my head, I wanted to lead them into war. The whole plan was there in front of me. I still feel it. Four months to unite the clans and then we can take the capital in three weeks. Less than twenty thousand dead." I nodded to myself. The cold water felt good on my tongue while I waited for what Cuza had given me to stop my head from aching.

Winona's display pad pinged and she unrolled it on the table. "Samuel," she told me.

He started talking before she could say hello. "Is she *insane*? Boden was just here asking about what it would take to revoke her Union citizenship so he can have her *executed*."

"I should have anticipated that someone was recording it," Winona sighed.

She glanced at Cuza, who just shrugged. "It's all good. I wouldn't mind watching it a couple more times myself."

She turned back to Sam. "Do I need to hide her somewhere?"

"No." Sam sounded frightened and he kept looking over his shoulder like he expected someone to be breaking down his door. "I think you're going to be on a shuttle by nightfall, though. Ambassador Killian wants you gone. All of you."

I leaned in front of Winona, pushing her out of my way. "Sam, I, um, I..." Whatever it was that I had wanted to say, the long explanation and apology that I had been formulating vanished from my head at the sight of him. All I managed was, "I'm so sorry. I just couldn't help myself."

"Yeah, I get that about you." He frowned at me for a very long moment and then he started to smile, although I could see him fighting against it. My head didn't hurt quite so much. "I'm starting to understand a lot about 'couldn't help myself' thanks to you. Promise you'll call me once you're safely off planet."

I nodded, not trusting my voice. Winona shoved me back away from the pad. "I'm tempted to hide her anyway to keep her from doing anything else she can't help."

"Hold on." Sam was touching things on his screen. "Um, her parents have just been released and are in route to the Mission... two special officers of the Guard... armed."

"What are you reading?" Winn asked him.

"Oh, his mail. Ambassador Killian talks to himself sometimes, like when he's entering his password. I've been reading his mail in addition to listening to his meetings."

"Samuel, have you considered that Mala Dusa is a dangerous influence in your life?"

"Yeah. But what choice do I have?" He tapped at the screen some more. "This is odd. There's confirmation of the Guard, but Killian hasn't sent anything to schedule a shuttle. Someone else must be doing that."

"What Union ships are on orbit that are headed to Earth next?" Winona's voice had dropped and her breathing had changed, becoming rapid and shallow.

Sam tapped, looked, and tapped again. "None. They must be routing you through Dulcinea or maybe Pomplamoose."

"Well, the day got a bunch more interesting just now, didn't it?" Cuza rumbled.

The door slammed behind us. Winona touched the icon to disconnect and Sam vanished.

I turned and watched Father Ryczek striding across the dining hall towards us. He was not a large man, and he was old, but the look on his face terrified me.

"Cuza!" he shouted while he was still ten meters away. "How could you have allowed this to happen?"

"It's going to happen, Father, you know that. What you saw today shows just how small a spark it's gonna take to light it off."

He sat down heavily in the chair next to me. "And you, thorn in my flesh, what can I do about you? Or should I call you Joan now?"

"Joan?"

He pointed at one of the stained glass windows. "Daughter of Romee, is that your future self?"

The young woman in the window was kneeling with a large sword in her hands and a halo surrounding her head. There were red flames in the background, hinting at her fate.

"No," I whispered to him. "Please, no."

"You say 'no', but your every action, your every *breath* is taking you down that path."

"I can't—" I was going to tell him that I couldn't help myself, but that would've been a lie.

"They're on the way here, so I'm told, Ted and," he grimaced, "Hannah. Cuza, I know you well enough to know what you'll be planning. Is it in the service of God and of His Mission here in the Warrens?"

"It is, Father."

"There's no other way?"

"No, Father."

Father Ryczek struggled to his feet. He looked around the dining hall and started walking toward the exit. "Clean up when you're finished."

"Yes, Father."

"What does *that* mean?" I asked when he was gone.

"It means that we're probably not going to make it back in time for the fall semester."

133

"It means the two of you should go to your room and I'll call you when I'm ready for you."

"Please, sir," Winona asked. "Let us stay until they arrive. Then Mala Dusa and I can go to our room to get our things. We can provide you with a good distraction." She was staring at him, eyes large, until he smiled back at her.

"Fine."

Cuza started pacing around the room again, stretching, and rolling his neck around in loud circles. "Damn, I'm gettin' old."

"Winn, what are you planning," I whispered.

"There's no shuttle coming for us."

"I figured that part out on my own."

"We'll need to overpower the Guards to make our escape." She seemed more excited than frightened, her face glowing.

"And go *where*? This whole place seems to run on cash and you're the only one with any coins."

"Not any more. I gave you the last of them to buy that cup."

"We should run and there's nowhere to run. I want to hide and there's no place to hide." I looked around the room, searching for an answer, panic starting to fill me. Cuza was leaned against the wall examining a knife he had pulled from his boot. The blade alone must have been twenty-five centimeters.

Winona kissed my lips. "Mala Dusa. Saint Joan." She giggled, making me smile. "Be brave. Your parents will be here in a few minutes."

I took a deep breath and nodded.

"Let's go, you two. There's an office by the foyer and I'd rather have a smaller space for this kind of work. I don't want to mess up the dining hall so close to meal time."

I was shaking while I walked between the two of them, trying to absorb the easy confidence they seemed to share.

The office had a conference table with six chairs and a desk. Cuza moved things around a little and said, "Mala Dusa, you'll sit here, Winona, here next to where I'll sit. Your parents on the other side with one Guard, and that will leave the desk chair for the other one. When I ask you to go to get your things, circle around to the right first."

"Just Mala Dusa," Winona told him. "I have an idea." She went to Cuza and whispered in his ear so I couldn't hear.

"I don't get to know the plan?" I was surprised to hear how badly my voice was shaking.

134

"No. Your part is to stand up and walk to the door. It's going to be OK."

"And no tears from you," Cuza warned Winona.

"Those will come later," she replied.

My tears started as soon as I saw my dad. Professor Theodore Holloman, who would have been home teaching a summer class in stratigraphy if it wasn't for me, had been beaten. His face was bruised on the left side, making his eye squint where it was swollen. They had dressed him in an ugly grey jumpsuit before bringing him to the Mission. When I ran to hug him, he held me at arm's length.

"Gently, Dusa. I've got a couple of ribs that are trying to heal." I rested my head on his shoulder while he rubbed my back for a few seconds. From him I felt sorrow.

Hannah was dressed in the same sort of shapeless gray jumpsuit as Dad. She seemed unhurt, other than a deep cut on one cheek and a look in her eyes colder than I'd ever seen before. I could feel her need for vengeance. It was so powerful that it was like it was echoing inside my skull. She glanced at Cuza, and for a second I thought he was going to kneel in front of her.

He took her hand and kissed it. "Been a while," he said.

"You haven't changed."

"Not much."

She smiled, looking incredibly dangerous. "We'll see."

She held me close and whispered. "I'm sorry for what's about to happen."

I started shaking again so hard it was making it difficult to stand; I couldn't help it or stop it. She kissed the top of my head before letting go.

We all filed into the office, Cuza telling the Guards what they needed to do. "I am Cuza, representing Father Ryczek and the Holy Church of God's Mission in the Warrens. These two children were under persecution and have asked for, and been granted sanctuary. You need to reveal to me why their persecution is at an end, and that their passage home will be secure and free of further threat."

Senior Officer Steiner was smirking. Looking at his face, I think he must have spent a lot of time smirking. "Is it really necessary that we endure this archaic formality?"

"It is if you want me to allow these two young girls to accompany you."

Steiner drummed his fingers on the table. "Fine. These two 'young girls', who fled from the Guardians of the Peace and who, just this morning, spoke words of sedition to an unlawful assembly in the Warrens, are being escorted off this world to a place where they can cause no further trouble."

Cuza smiled back at him. "You'll need to be more specific."

Officer Trilby answered for Steiner. She was late-twenties with a kindness in her eyes that clashed with her body-armor and sidearm. "We will go with the four of them from here to the spaceport, then up to the docks to ensure that they board the merchant ship *Gellhorn*. Once we put them on board, our job is done. Is that specific enough, Mr. Cuza?"

I don't think she knew that no one had requested a shuttle or that no merchant ship named *Gellhorn* was currently in the space docks. I glanced at Winona. She was totally focused on Cuza and Steiner.

"Yes. Thank you Officer Trilby. Children, do you need to get anything before your departure?"

"Yes," I stammered. "I have a bag, and I need my cup from the dining hall." I stumbled to my feet, everyone staring at me.

"Should I go with her?" Trilby asked.

Steiner leered at me. "Naw, although I wouldn't mind going with her myself if I thought we had the time. What a pity." He looked me up and down and my shaking got worse.

Trilby glanced at her partner with a look of disgust. "Be quick, girl."

I nodded and Winona turned toward Steiner. "I need to go with her. Hold this for me." She slid a stone toward him. Steiner instinctively reached for it, his hand grabbing it in the center of the table.

Cuza was quick. The knife left his boot and arced through the air with all the power of his right arm behind it. It slammed down. Steiner's hand was pinned to the table, the tip of the knife buried deep into the wood.

Steiner screamed. I screamed and jumped back. Cuza shoved Steiner hard in the chest a fraction of a second later, driving him to the floor. A significant part of Steiner's right hand was left behind, still attached to the knife. Dad had taken Steiner's side arm at some point; everything was moving too fast for me to see it all. The sharp report when he pulled the trigger made my ears ring and I jumped again. There was blood on me. There was blood everywhere.

Officer Trilby was lying on the floor trying to reach her holster. Hannah had knocked her there and was now standing over her watching her struggle.

Dad handed Hannah the pistol and she aimed it at Trilby's head. I don't know what it was that Hannah was feeling. It was beyond naming. I didn't have to guess what Trilby was feeling; I could see it in her eyes and I could smell it.

"Enough!" I shouted. I pushed past the overturned chairs and got down on the floor next to her. "It's enough."

"Get out of the way, Mala Dusa."

"No!"

"Do you know what they did to your father while they made me watch? Do you know what they did to *me* while they made him watch? Get out of my way."

"'They'. You said 'they'. *They* did it, not this one, not her. You don't have to kill her. Cuza, you must have someplace you can keep her until we're gone and it doesn't matter anymore."

Cuza was wiping the blood and bits of flesh off his knife onto Steiner's pants. "Yeah, I suppose."

Hannah lowered the gun a fraction. "It's an unnecessary risk."

Trilby looked at me and then at Hannah. "Why are you doing this? Why couldn't you just get on the damn shuttle and leave?" Her eyes kept darting over to Steiner's body.

Winona knelt down next to her, staring into her eyes, her head tipped. "You aren't stupid. If you think it through, you will realize that there was never going to be a shuttle. And the Union merchant ship *Martha Gellhorn*? She left Bodens Gate two days ago."

"I didn't know." She looked at Steiner again and dabbed at the blood that was trickling from her nose. "God damn him. He told me this was going to be a quick, easy assignment, that we'd have a little fun. He didn't mention killing children."

She sighed, shivering, and looked up at Cuza. "Get them out of here first. I don't want them to see it."

Cuza nodded. "Alright you two, out. Go clean up and get changed. We've a long walk ahead of us." He turned to Hannah, taking the gun from her. "You should leave too. Go talk with the Little Soul."

"No, you can't do this," I protested. I felt like all the strength was gone from my body. "You said you could hold her for a while."

Hannah took my hand, pulled me to my feet, and out of the office. "He was lying to you, Dusa. There's only one way this can end." She closed the door behind us.

It was almost twenty minutes later that I jumped at the distant sound of the bang. Hannah was wiping my face with a damp cloth. She paused, looking at Dad. "Cuza." She shook her head, rinsing the cloth in the bowl on her lap.

"He killed her," I whispered. "Why, Mom?"

"Twenty minutes? Cuza would never be so cruel as to wait that long. He'll claim he killed her, but she's alive somewhere; somewhere out of our way for now, I hope."

"Because it was the right thing to do," I told her.

"Huh. Tip your chin up a bit." She wiped my throat and frowned. "Cuza spared her because you asked him to. I'll bet he's called you 'Alice' more than once too. He had a soft spot for her. I see it in his eyes every time he looks at you that he loves you in the same way. OK, all done. Winona, stay there, you're next."

Dad sat down on the bed next to me while Hannah started on Winn's forehead. He winced as his ribs shifted. "Almost ready?"

"Ready for what? To live as a fugitive in the Warrens the rest of my life? Hannah told me that you once almost killed a man because he was a threat. It must have been satisfying to finally get it done, to kill someone with the bullet that was meant for her."

When Hannah wants to know what I'm feeling, it's like she's grabbing my brain and shaking it. With Dad it feels more like a hug. He was hugging me hard, so I closed my eyes and let him look.

"OK, I wasn't going to tell you about this, but you need to know." He paused and I could feel him struggling. "Steiner, that man who looked at you when you got up, and wanted to..."

"The man that wanted to rape me?" I had meant to keep my voice calm when I said it. It still broke, thinking about the man that had wanted to follow me back to my room and rape me before he murdered me and then the rest of my family. I was starting to shake again.

"Yes. He was there when they were interrogating us. They would alternate every few hours, working on one while they questioned the other. He was the one that held Hannah down while another man ripped off her dress."

My hand was up over my mouth and Dad continued. "They didn't physically rape her, but they talked about it constantly, using it as a weapon. They kept her naked the whole time, tied up, humiliating her and me. There wasn't anything I could do to protect her. They kept at her, touching her, hitting her, saying they wouldn't stop and that they would rape her if I didn't admit who she was. Do you understand now why I killed him?"

He had said it all very calmly, his voice even and flat. I could feel the rage underneath it though, how he would like to go back and kill Steiner again, and then again and again, over and over until the pain stopped.

I looked at Hannah sitting on Winona's bed, talking quietly with her, gently wiping the blood from her face. "How can she...? How can she even *function* after that?"

"This gift that we share, it's pretty strong between you and me. With Hannah, after all this time, it's almost like we're one person when we want to be. Most of her was inside me while it was happening. I was holding her and we were comforting each other. It'll still catch up with her though, sooner or later. She's trying to push it off for now, until we're all safe again. She's an amazing woman. I had forgotten how strong she is when it's needed."

He smiled at me, touching my hair.

"In a few hours, or a day or two at most, she'll shatter and I'll need to help her put the pieces back together. She's going to need all of our help then."

I didn't realize I was crying until he reached up and touched my tears.

"You need to push it off for now too. No tears yet. We'll get through this together."

I couldn't take my eyes off her. I wanted to run to her and hold her. I wanted to try and make all the badness go away, to ease her anguish the same way she used to hold me and tell me how wonderful and special I was after one of the many bad days at school when everyone had been mocking 'weird Mala Dusa'.

I looked into my dad's eyes and his emotions were closed to me. "What about you, Dad? Are you going to be OK?"

"I'll heal, and we *will* find a way back home." He smiled at me again. "Although, Winona told me what you did this morning. Are you sure you're not planning on staying, Saint Joan?"

"Don't call me that. That was the Tarakana in my head."

"Again?" He sounded worried. "They seem to like you a little too much."

I nodded and my display pad pinged.

"Sam," I whispered, trying to pull the pad from my pocket. I looked at the name on the screen. "It's Captain Kelang." I tried not to sound disappointed.

"Is the connection secure?" Winn asked. Hannah had finished with her face and was starting on her neck.

"Just standard."

"Be careful what you say, for a change."

I tapped the icon to answer him. "Captain Kelang."

139

He smiled. "I had hoped that the reports of your death were premature."

"Am I dead?"

"It seemed a possibility. A message was sent from Ambassador Killian's own account to every media outlet on the planet saying that a militia ambush had hit your party in the Warrens, killing two members of the Guard that were providing escort. Interestingly, it also said that he was requesting permission for special Union transport to retrieve you from the church Mission where he hoped that you were taking refuge. I'm working on fulfilling that request right now, if you still need retrieving."

Winn had her head tipped back, looking at the ceiling while Hannah finished with her. "Bold move, Samuel," she said quietly. "The ambassador is going to be pissed when he finds out."

Hannah sat the bowl on Winona's lap and moved over next to me. I gave her the pad.

"Captain, thank you for your quick response. We really could use your help getting out of here." She had just a trace of a smile on her lips and her tone of voice was a magical combination of gratitude and command.

"Councillor Weldon, are you all right? Have you been injured?" I would swear that had the Captain been there in person, that he would have knelt or kissed her hand the way Cuza had. This man, who had only talked to her for a few seconds, had followed Hannah's career for over a decade. Now he was ready to put his own career, and maybe his life, on the line for her. I glanced at Dad. He had an amused expression on his face, like he had seen her do this before and that he loved her for it. I needed to have her teach that trick to me.

"We're fine for now. How soon can you come for us?"

"That's what I'm working on. The local authorities have given me three answers in the last ten minutes. First, they claimed that they were still holding you and your husband, then that one of the clans had killed all of you. Now they're telling me that you left for Earth this afternoon on a ship that departed space dock two days ago. I've tried to reach Ambassador Killian, but the comms at the embassy are completely down." He smiled ruefully. "I'm about ready to have a shuttle drop right into the Warrens to pick you up."

Hannah's eyes lost focus for a moment. "No, Captain, please don't do that, not unless we have to."

"I will come for you today, Ms. Weldon, one way or another. We'll get your family out of there."

Hannah smiled gently. "Thank you, Captain. I will never forget this."

Kelang disconnected and I put my arms around her. She rested her head on my shoulder for a moment, me holding her instead of the other way around.

"Thanks, Mala Dusa. I'm going to need a lot of hugs for the next week or two."

"How did you do that?" I asked her. "With the Captain. He'd do anything you ask. What's the trick?"

"I should ask you the same thing about Sam. He's taking an awful risk for you."

"Oh, that's just Sam. He's—"

"He's in love with her," Winona interrupted, "because she's a little bit crazy and extremely dangerous. I am starting to believe that some people find that combination irresistible."

Hannah closed her eyes, her head still resting on me. "That's the trick, Dusa. When you find one like that, never, never let him go."

I looked at Winn and had a sudden need to be holding her too. I held out an arm and she joined us.

I glanced at Dad and he shook his head. "Uh-uh. I'd hate to interrupt and, you know, ribs." He tapped his side.

"Coward," I told him.

"You bet. All three of you are extremely crazy and a little bit dangerous."

"Other way around," I corrected him.

"Don't be so sure."

I held out my arms to him until he came close enough to hug.

There was a sharp knock at the door and it immediately opened. Cuza was there, looking freshly showered. Father Ryczek was standing in front of him, profoundly unhappy.

"Ms. Weldon, or should I call you by your *Nome de guerre*?"

"As you wish." Her emotions snapped shut.

"Come to see how your experiment in creating a living paradise is working out?"

"It was never meant to be a paradise, Father, just a place where people could live in dignity with hope for the future. I'm sorry if your Mission couldn't handle the competition."

"God's Mission, not mine. And it still provides the only *true* hope for the people here."

"And thanks to your friend, Boden, it's likely to remain so."

"Not *my* friend. The Bodens are an abomination, and have been for generations." He paused, looking at all of us. His expression softened. "You're not staying to fight though, are you?"

"I don't know where to begin. We've been lied to and misled at every level."

Winona touched her shoulder. "I have a preliminary report almost ready for you. When you have time. We can fix this without bloodshed. Maybe."

In the back of my head the memory of the Tarakana was whispering, *we can be in the capital in three weeks with only twenty thousand dead*. God help me, but I wanted to do it. With Winona by my side, I knew that I *could* do it.

"I'll work with you," Father Ryczek said. "No one knows the people of the Warrens the way I do. I love these people more than life itself. We share that much, you and I."

Hannah nodded, silent. I could feel a crack in her mind threatening to open and Dad in there trying to keep her together. She closed her eyes and her head tipped forward. I held her close to me.

Ryczek glanced at my dad, I think noticing for the first time his physical condition and Hannah's. The corners of his mouth turned down. "So, that's how it was?" he asked.

"Yes," Dad answered, "That's how it was."

"Killing is a dreadful thing, but often understandable and sometimes necessary. Are they both dead?" he asked Cuza.

Cuza's eyes locked onto mine and he winked. "It's been taken care of, Father."

Ryczek nodded, knowing Cuza was lying to him, but trusting him anyway.

"Where do we go from here?" Father Ryczek asked. "The media is reporting that Union transportation has been requested for you."

"We've talked to them. They're having difficulty getting permission to come for us, and the government bureaucracy is going to get organized again if we don't move quickly enough."

"I can get you to the terminal."

"We'd never make it past security if they've been told to watch for us."

"I can get you straight to one of the landing pads. You aren't the first fugitives we've had to move off planet. Tell your Union friends to drop a shuttle onto pad twenty-two in one hour."

Father Ryczek did something next that I will always remember. He knelt down on the floor in front of Hannah and placed his hands on her cheeks.

"Daughter, I walked in the Warrens this morning, and it *is* a better place than it was before you came. Not a paradise, but there's hope. There are flowers piled high where your statue once stood. Let it be enough for now. Go home and rest. Heal. Come back to me again when you are ready to forgive and to talk. OK?"

She nodded and whispered back to him "OK."

"Now get ready to travel. I've brought a bundle of clothes. They aren't stylish, but something in there might fit you."

Hannah stood and helped him to his feet. It felt like the cracks were holding again for the moment, thanks to Dad. "Stylish or not, I am grateful for all you've done for us."

"And my contract?" I asked him.

He chuckled. "Next summer I expect to see you back here or I'll press charges. You still have Bodens Gate citizenship, as I recall."

"Yes, Father. I owe the Warrens a couple of months of service. And I owe you my life."

I sat next to Cuza while he drove. We passed the Gabriella, where I had briefly dreamed of having a secret dinner with Sam some night. It looked dirty and dangerous in the late afternoon sunlight. I sighed. It would have been so perfect. I was chewing on my lower lip, wondering when the next time Sam's lips would be on mine, wondering what his reaction would be if I were to nibble gently on *his* lower lip.

The truck hit a pothole, jarring me back to reality. I shouldn't be thinking about Sam's lips. I should be worrying about whether he was even still safe after what he'd done to save all of us. I should be praying for him. I leaned my head to the right onto Dad's shoulder and closed my eyes.

He took my hand. "It's going to be OK, Dusa."

I squeezed his hand, but didn't say anything. I was too busy praying.

We reached a security gate on the lower level of the terminal. The bored guard glanced at us. "Mission business, Cuza?" he asked.

Cuza passed him a thick envelope. "That's right, Johan. I won't be but a moment."

Johan pocketed the envelope and opened the gate for us.

Sitting in church a few months before, I had watched a video of Father Ryczek detailing how he was using our donations. He had talked about clothes and food and teaching supplies. He hadn't mentioned bribing guards to smuggle fugitives to safety.

"I'm going to have to up my monthly donation, Cuza," Dad commented.

That's Dad. He was still assuming that we were going to make it home and everything would be back to normal.

The truck rounded a corner and climbed the access ramp up on to the landing pad. A beautiful little ship was there, looking clean and new compared to the scorched white of *Wandering Star's* shuttles. The Union and RuComm emblems on her side above the name *Bahia Vista* made me feel like Dad was right; we were almost home.

I got out of the truck, my only possessions the clothes I was wearing, my display pad, and my Bourean cup. I had the lock of Winona's hair still tucked under my watch, and I never took off my watch.

We all hugged Cuza before we boarded. He held Hannah a moment longer than the rest of us.

"I was right about you, Cuza." She told him. "You haven't changed and you don't disappoint."

"Don't stay gone so long next time, and take good care of Little Soul. We need her back here."

We climbed aboard the shuttle, the landing ramp rumbled closed and we waited.

"*Star*?" Dad asked.

"*Vista*," I whispered to him. He smiled at me from across the aisle, embarrassed.

"*Vista*, why aren't we moving?"

"Traffic control has placed a seal on outbound movements. Duration is unknown. They have advised us to stand by."

A shiver passed through me and then the shaking started again deep inside.

Winona nudged me. "Call Captain Kelang."

I nodded and started to unroll my display pad.

"I can contact him for you, if you like," *Vista* offered.

"Yes, he needs to be aware of what's happening." A moment later, I was looking at the Captain on the main display screen at the front of the cabin.

"Good to see you're all safely on board. We should have you underway in a few minutes. The Guard was demanding to inspect all outbound craft, so I told them that RuComm doesn't recognize their authority and that my shuttle will be departing as soon as it's ready. They've gone off to discuss it with their superiors, I believe."

There was a soft ping and a timer appeared at the bottom of the screen, counting down from sixty. "We will be departing in one minute. Please ensure that your restraints are tight and that all items are secure."

"Thank you so much, Captain. I'm looking forward to meeting you in person," Hannah told him.

That tone of voice again. I really needed to learn it.

At eight seconds, the timer stopped and *Vista* informed us, "There are personnel in close proximity to my hull. I will not be able to use my thrusters until they depart."

Captain Kelang frowned. "Sound the claxon for twenty seconds and launch anyway. My authority."

The alarm was loud enough that we could hear it inside the cabin. I had once been told that the claxon of a departing starship was loud enough to rupture eardrums at one hundred meters. Winona whispered to me, "This is how careers end."

I turned my head to look at her, whispering so Dad wouldn't hear. "This is how *wars* start." I could feel my excitement building. "The Central Government is going to blame 'the Warrens' for the deaths and injuries we just caused, including killing that creep Steiner. The Council of Clans will claim they know nothing about it, but they'll find the accusation insulting. Both will blame the Union, since the order to get us off planet came from the embassy. Sam has played his role *perfectly*."

"Duse…"

"Now's the time for the next push."

"Duse…"

"You and I should go back as soon as we can, back to the market. I need to talk to the people there again. We can be in the capital—"

"Duse!"

"What? Don't you *feel* it? We'll never have an opportunity like this again in our lives."

"What are *you* feeling Mala Dusa?"

The hum in my head was roaring. "It's the right time, but I'm in the wrong place. I should be back there. Sam! We left Sam back there. His role isn't finished. I need him. I really, really need him." Winn's eyes were huge looking back at me.

"Mr. Holloman!" She reached across the aisle and grabbed Dad's shoulder. He had been leaning back with his eyes closed, holding hands with Mom.

"What is it Winona?"

She opened her mouth, closed it again, and then smiled at him. "Never mind. It can keep."

She turned back to me. "Tell me more."

CHAPTER 12

SAM

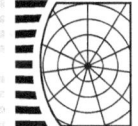

I unrolled my pad across our laps and began sketching. "Before the Confederation, there were thousands of clans and they overlapped everywhere. Now, thanks to Hannah, there are only fifteen and they have defined territories. Which ones are still loyal to the Articles of Confederation and which ones are corrupt?"

Winn stared back at me. "All of them are corrupt. I think the Bovita will follow you because of who you are." She glanced across the aisle. "We need your mom to join us on this. Our odds of success are much greater if she's there, even if it's just to initially provide you with legitimacy."

I looked at her sitting next to my dad and could feel the anguish in her, swelling and then subsiding as she tried to overcome it, then overwhelming her again. It scared me that my biggest concern right then was whether I could use her for what we were planning, wondering if she would hold up to the strain. *They humiliated her*, a voice was telling me. *You need to be with her and hold her and tell her how much you love her.*

"Just one out of fifteen?" I asked.

"Well, the Roho should fall in line if we eliminate their current leadership, and the same with the Feraru. With that core, we can pressure the rest to join or face rebellion within their own populations."

She was studying me. "When your mom united the clans and created the Confederation, she worked in the shadows. I was watching you in the market, Duse. There's no one that looks like you, no one that sounds like you, and no one the people here will fall in love with like you. You need to be highly visible the whole time."

"It's about the ideas, Winona, which is good because I know damn well that no one is attracted to me."

"No, it's about convincing people that *you* can make the ideas *real*. In the Warrens, your appearance makes you rare and exotic; it won't matter that you're not pretty. And always remember that some people are attracted to you."

"Sam." The thought of him started to fill me and the hum in the back of my head receded for a moment. I looked at Winn, pleading. "Winn, help me. What am I doing?"

Then I pushed Sam back. There wasn't time for him now. He had a role to play, but I couldn't have him yet. When we were done and the Government was defeated, then would be the time for Sam, then I could take him.

The shuttle ride was too short to finish even a rough outline of all we needed to do. Our first focus would be establishing a foothold with the Bovita. Finding a way back down to Bodens Gate was critical.

The shuttle docked and I was still talking to Winona quietly as we walked down the ramp, working on alternatives for how we were going to get back to the Warrens.

"Hey, MD."

Sam was there.

The hum that had been filling my head vanished, pushed out by the only thing that mattered to me. I ran to him and wrapped my arms around him so tightly that it was like my body wanted to merge into his. After a few moments of crushing each other, when I finally realized I couldn't get any closer, I tipped my head back and we kissed.

Something was trying to get back into my head, but there wasn't room any more. All I could feel was his mouth on mine and his arms holding me up. I felt like I was falling. It was a wonderful feeling and I gave myself over to it.

"OK, I think she's coming out of it now."

That was Dad talking. I opened my eyes, realizing that I had deck plates under me and Hannah's face over me. The deck plates were cold; Hannah looked amused.

Sam was holding my hand, a little crease of worry between his eyes. He bent down close to my head.

"Don't kiss her," Winona warned him. "She might faint again."

"I fainted?"

"You did," she told me, and then to Sam, "I'm impressed that you could do that."

Sam looked embarrassed as he helped me sit up. I closed my eyes again, my head pounding. After a moment, I opened one eye, squinting at Winona in the glare of the lights in the shuttle bay.

Before the blackness took me again, I managed to say, "Tarakana. Don't let them in, Winn. We have to stop them."

I woke up feeling very comfortable. It took several seconds before I realized that Sam was carrying me.

"Hi, there," I said, looking up at him. "Where we goin'?"

"Infirmary."

"Am I sick?"

"The mobile scanner says you're fine. Your parents wanted to make sure, so I volunteered to carry you while they go to talk with the Captain."

"Where's my Winona?"

"Right here," she answered from behind us.

I lifted my head enough to see her. "Hi, Winn. I'm bein' carried."

I put my head back down and looked at Sam. There was a line of sweat on his forehead. "Sorry I'm so heavy," I told him.

"You're not."

"Oh." I probed deeper, finding I could dimly sense what he was feeling. "I'm sorry I'm scaring you."

"How did..." He paused, looking down at me.

"It's the Tarakana." I could feel his confusion. "You try it. I'll bet you can tell what I'm feeling right now if you want to." I looked up at him with my eyes half closed, smiling. I knew he had reached me when he blushed. "I have some secrets I need to tell you, Sam."

He put me down on the medical bed and I took his hand. "It will get stronger the more we're around them. And they're everywhere, at least everywhere *I* go."

I looked over at Winona while I laid down. "Do ya think they're following me? I think they might be following me."

Something cold touched my forehead and everything seemed muffled while the AI scanned me.

"It's almost like she's drunk," Sam commented.

"She doesn't drink." My Winona stood up for me. "Except for a small glass of wine with dinner sometimes. Or a beer. She really likes margaritas, but not straight tequila."

"Bleah," I added. "Made me throw up."

"What is it, then?"

"Tarakana!" I answered. I tried very hard to look serious. "The colony in the Warrens is *bad*, Winona, not like Merrimac. He might have created the colony here, but they're not like him. He's my friend, but these guys are really, really... Did I say really?" Winn nodded. "Really bad. We're gonna stop them. You can help us, Sam. And then when we're done, you and I can do what I was thinking about." I grinned at him.

"What's a Tarakana?"

I tried to answer. Winn wouldn't let me. "You lie still, Duse, and I'll explain it all to him."

I closed my eyes and listened.

The medical AI pumped something into me that made my headache go away after a few minutes and I stared to feel more like me again. It told me that I had undiagnosed over activity in certain regions of my brain and advised me to drink more fluids and get more sleep. Sam was sitting in a chair beside me, completely numb.

I sat up on the edge of the bed swinging my legs back and forth looking at him. "There were Tarakana on *Wandering Star*. I used to play with them when I was little and they remembered me. They wanted you and me to be together. They do that sometimes, push people together so they can feel their emotions. They did it to the engineers, Tobias and Sandy. They did it to my parents and they did it to Dad and Hannah. I told them to stay away from us. They promised they would, but there was still one in your cabin and one followed you to the embassy. I don't know what they want."

"Don't you? Winona thinks they're controlling you."

I could feel my face getting hot. "What we feel for each other, I want it to be *us* that's feeling it. Merrimac tried to show me what I needed to do for us to be..." I stopped, chewing on my lip while Sam stared at the floor.

"I wasn't interested in that. I told him to get out of your head. I think he was in there making you dream one night on the shuttle, showing you what was possible. But when he was in *my* head, it wasn't like he was controlling me; it was gentle. It's like he shows me what's possible and

150

then suggests what I need to say or do to make it real. At least that's what Merrimac did most of the time."

The thought of what I had done to the engines haunted me, but I wasn't ready to confess that to Sam yet.

"The Warrens colony is very different. The feelings they want to create in us are dark and violent." I thought about it for a second. "Yeah, they're trying to control me, and Winona, and I don't know who else."

I rubbed at my head, wincing. The pain was still there just under the surface.

Sam looked lost. "Every step is deeper and there's no bottom to it." He sighed. "Now we're going to confront an alien species that can hide in plain sight, or look like something else, and can *enter our minds* and make us do things we don't want to do. I thought it was a big step when I decided to help save you from a planetary government that was trying to kill your entire family because your mom is an infamous leader of the insurgency."

Winona smiled at him, trying to be reassuring. "The Tarakana were real before you knew about them. The threat was real, but now you have the opportunity to do something about it. And what you did at the embassy was wonderful. It really did save our lives."

"What I did came to me, almost like in a dream. It was like I *had* to do it before I left. That wasn't me being brilliant though, was it?"

I shook my head. "Nope."

"This morning I contacted Captain Kelang and asked permission to come up and stay on *Bahia Vista*. I told him I could help fit out the biology lab while I worked on my Kempner-27 plans. For some reason, he agreed right away. This ship won't even be ready for service for another four months. Then this afternoon I knew I had to send that message in the ambassador's name and get out fast."

I looked around at the infirmary. "This ship isn't done yet?"

"No, she's supposed to be Kelang's new command. If he survives the investigation into the loss of *Wandering Star*. And the investigation into why he dropped a shuttle into Eindhoven and then brought it back without permission."

Sam was up pacing around the room now while I still sat on the bed swinging my legs. He continued, "It doesn't matter if he loses his commission though, does it? He's served his purpose. It's like all of us exist to keep Mala Dusa alive and in the right place, and then we become disposable."

"Exactly." Winona got up and hugged him. "I knew you were brilliant. That's part of the theory I've been working on. I want to tell you about her parents and grandparents. There's a pattern and I think you're part of it now. I'd like to have a second opinion and then we need to talk about *your* parents."

Sam sat down on the floor and leaned back against the wall with his eyes closed.

"Winona! You broke him." I went and sat down next to him, taking his hand.

"I can tell you about my mom, but I never knew my dad. He was chief engineer on the *Zheng He*. They left space dock two months before I was born, surveying for new worlds."

"And never came back," Winn finished for him.

"That's right. I only knew him from the stories Mom told me. MD, when you talk about why you want to build ships, the way they make you feel and how your eyes light up at the thought of it, you sound just like how Mom says he talked."

He picked up his hand that I was holding and examined our intertwined fingers. "I love you, Mala Dusa, even though I know I shouldn't. Is what I'm feeling because I fell in love with you, or was I pushed?"

"I don't know," I barely whispered. "You love me?"

"Yeah. God help me." He sighed, shook his head, and said under his breath, "Sixteen. Shouldn't even be touching her."

Winona was looking at us. "How come *Bahia Vista* is letting you talk like this?"

Sam looked at her, surprised. "I don't know. We shouldn't have been able to get away with the kiss in the shuttle bay, either. Maybe they haven't integrated that silo yet. *Vista*, are you monitoring RuComm personnel for contract compliance?"

"Yes Mr. Coleridge."

"I just told Ms. Holloman that I love her. That's not a violation?"

"You and Ms. Holloman are exempt from that clause."

Sam and I looked at each other. "On whose authority?"

"That information is not available. It was established at incep."

"Incep?" I asked.

Sam answered. "Inception. It's when her AI became sentient. Like eighteen months ago."

Winona sat down cross-legged in front of us, looking happy. "At least we know we're where they want us to be. Is the ship's mess hall functional or do we have to go scrounging? I'm hungry."

"How can you be thinking about food?" I asked her. "That means the Tarakana knew we were going to be here over eighteen *months* ago. How can we hope to fight against them?" I was feeling hollow inside, like I was doomed to play a role I had no control over. The shaking started again.

She stood and grabbed my hand. "Up. Let's get some food in you so your brain will start working again."

Sam got up too. "The right question to ask is how someone made *Vista* think the exception was created at incep. And why."

Winona looked at him. "I love you, Samuel. You always—"

"Ms. Killdeer," *Vista* interrupted, "please be careful of your feelings for RuComm personnel while on board."

Winona stared at the ceiling for about three seconds with her head tipped before sighing and turning toward me. No sound came out, but her lips said, *princess*.

"It's not my fault this time!" I protested.

"Let's get something to eat. It's already 19:30 and I'm starving."

I took Sam's hand and we followed Winona out of the infirmary. She asked *Vista* to guide us, and I didn't bother to tell her that Sam and I knew the way since the deck layout was the same as the *Mara Vista*. I don't like it when Winn is mad at me; it makes me feel like the world is all munted and higgledy-piggledy.

My parents were already in the mess hall, sitting in a couple of chairs they had moved off to the side and placed face to face. They were holding hands with their eyes closed, leaning forward so their foreheads touched, oblivious to the other people having dinner.

"I don't think we should bother them," Sam said.

I saw the corner of Hannah's mouth twitch upward. "It's OK, they know I'm here."

"Of course they do." Winona was still grumpy.

"Winn, please don't be like that. I need you to figure out my life for me. There's no way I can do it myself."

"You're right about that at least." She still looked unhappy. "I don't like where my theory is taking me. That's why I need Sam —who I'm *not* in love with—" she shouted at the ceiling, "to listen to my logic."

I put my forehead up against hers "But *I* love you, Winn." It was like when Sam was carrying me; I had a dim impression of Winona feeling flustered.

She pulled back. "Don't do that. I don't want to be part of whatever that is. Please promise me, Duse, promise that you won't try to know what I'm feeling. Promise me."

"OK, I promise." I was willing to promise almost anything to keep Winona from being mad at me. "We just need to keep the Tarakana out of our heads. The more they touch us, the harder it will be to *not* know what each other are feeling."

She nodded and we walked past my parents to see what *Bahia Vista* had on offer for dinner.

"Well, at least it's not lasagna." Sam was sniffing at a tray of browned, tubular meat.

"*Vista*, what is this?"

"Mititei, made from a mixture of lamb and pork, then grilled. They make an excellent appetizer for the chicken frigarui. Be sure and save room for a babka for dessert, though." *Vista* lowered her voice. "It's been soaking in a rum syrup all day."

We were about half way through dinner before Hannah and my dad joined us. She seemed much more relaxed, almost at peace. Dad started telling us about what they had discussed with the Captain, something about how we were all going to get back home. I wasn't really paying attention. The engineering team was sitting one table over, going through plans for what the swing shift would be working on that evening to get *Bahia Vista* ready for service. They had a schematic of one of the engines glowing in the air above the table and I couldn't take my eyes off of it.

"Mala Dusa, you should be paying attention to this." Dad was staring at me, not as patient as he sounded.

"Yes, sir. It's just... they have the drawings up, and you know..." I sighed, turned around, and then immediately looked back over my shoulder.

"Tell Sam to kiss her again," Winona suggested. "That seems to hold her attention, at least until she passes out."

"You're not helping, Winn." Sam took my hand under the table, and I hate to admit it, but I lost interest in the schematic for the moment.

Winona smiled at me, looking smug.

"What did I miss?"

"We'll be going back on Tuesday," Dad answered.

"Good. That gives Winn and me a couple of more days to work on plans." I unrolled my pad in front of Hannah. "Here's what we've got so far. The Bovita are the key, then the Feraru and Roho. Consolidating the clans into a single force shouldn't take more than four months if we remove the right people up front."

"Back *home*." Dad corrected. "We're going *home*. The agreement with the Union was for us to leave Bodens Gate. 'How I overthrew a government' is not an appropriate topic for your summer essay."

"This could work, Ted."

Hannah was busy scrolling through my hastily sketched maps, studying the kill lists and armament requirements.

"No, Hannah."

"The Warrens are going to rebel, Mom," I told her, "even Father Ryczek knows that. They'll do it without leadership, without a plan, with nothing but hope and only a dim memory of what things were like at the beginning of the Confederation. When that happens, the CG will slaughter them. Boden will win again and conditions will be worse than they were before you started."

"Are they still in your head?" Winona asked me softly.

"No, I don't think so. But part of their plan is still there, and it's the right thing to do. Winn, you're smarter than I am. Is there a way for the people in the Warrens to claim equal standing with the Citizens that *doesn't* involve armed conflict?"

"There was, but Mr. Boden made it harder, maybe impossible. It would have required Ms. Weldon to bolster the Council of Clans and negotiate from that base position of strength. Boden's agreement with the Union banishing her makes a negotiated solution unlikely. Civil war is almost inevitable. Boden will prevail with few losses on his side. Losses in the Warrens will be heavy. He's pretty good at this game."

"We can't let that happen, Mom."

Sam was still holding my hand. He lifted it up and kissed the inside of my wrist. "You're still trying to get me killed, aren't you?" He sounded resigned. "I'm going to be out on the street with a sword or a gun in my hand trying to kill your enemies. Sooner or later, it's going to happen." He took another bite of his dinner, using his left hand so he didn't have to let go of me.

I was going to tell him 'no', but I couldn't. I wanted him more than anything right then, more than designing ships, more than freeing the

Warrens. I squeezed his hand and he looked at me. He seemed more amused than scared or angry. His eyes were so blue and I was visualizing us back on Bodens Gate, the danger and excitement of him fighting beside me during the day and being with me every night.

"Whoa." He blinked at me. "I could *feel* that. Wow, MD."

"Now, that's enough!" Dad took the display pad out of Hannah's hands and turned it off. He didn't give it back to me after he rolled it up. "We are going *home*. We're leaving *Tuesday*. I've lost too much to Bodens Gate. I won't risk anything more, do you understand? All of you," he looked hard at Hannah, "do you understand? Sam, you get on your ship when it comes. The rest of us, including Mala Dusa, will be back on Earth by then, where we belong."

I could feel Hannah wanting to argue. She looked at Dad and her head tipped ever so slightly. She sighed. "Your father is right. We need to get you home. This isn't our fight."

"But it *is*," I pleaded. "When we were in the market I could see it on their faces, the hope that would flare up in them when they said your name. There's a girl there that wants to be an architect and a man that just wants to be able to make these," I tapped my cup, "and sell them to people that want to buy them. I played with some of the kids. I talked to a crowd of people."

"I saw that part." There was pride in her voice.

"I can't walk away. How many will die each day while I'm safe at home, sitting in class? How many could I have saved?"

She closed her eyes. "That's the path I followed and my friends died one by one, and our followers died by the hundreds and then by the thousands. I watched your mother bleed to death and I came within seconds of losing Ted and you. They say that you're not really part of the Warrens until your blood has joined with its dirt, and I did that too." She touched her abdomen where I knew there were scars. "I sacrificed my own children and it still wasn't enough. It will never be enough. I won't give them you and Winona. Your father killed a man today. That's the Warrens. That's Bodens Gate. It's death, and pain, and torture, and... and..." She couldn't finish and the anguish poured back into her.

When she opened her eyes, there were no tears in them. "We're going home. Don't argue, don't plan, and don't scheme. Just know that it's the right thing to do."

I glanced at Winona. She had her eyes half closed, lost somewhere in her own thoughts. Sam squeezed my hand, letting me know that he was still there with me.

I stood, pushing my chair back loudly. "Sam and I are going to sit by the pool. Winn, why don't you come with us? I have some planning and scheming to do."

Sam stood and kissed me gently because he knew that I needed kissing.

"How can they keep *doing* that?" Hannah asked.

Winn answered for me because my mouth was busy. "*Vista* says she has a record exempting the two of them from the Romantic Entanglements clause. It was established at incep eighteen months ago. I believe Mala Dusa feels it would be wrong not to take advantage of it."

"Shit. I need to talk to Ted privately. Winona, get them out of here, but don't leave them alone, not for a moment. The way she's feeling right now, God knows what she'll do next. Remember who you work for, Ms. Killdeer."

"Yes, ma'am. You should also know that there is at least one Tarakana on board. It came up on the shuttle with us and Mala Dusa is particularly vulnerable to its influence. I think she's safe for now, and I'll stay with her tonight, but I'd like to get on your calendar to discuss the situation."

Hannah nodded. "After breakfast, 07:00 at the latest. I can't do any more today, it's too much." She ran her fingers through her hair, pushing it up out of her eyes. "I need a shower. A long shower."

Winn tapped on my shoulder. "Let's go Duse. Let him breathe for a few minutes."

There was no water in the pool, so the three of us took lounge chairs and moved them to the bottom of the deep end and sat looking up at the display screens. Bodens Gate floated above us, visible between the latticework of the space dock.

"What are we going to do, Winona?"

"We're going home. We'll apply for admission to the Academy together and then we'll finish our senior year." She turned to Sam. "I want the first dance with you when you get back in the spring to take Mala Dusa to the prom, OK?"

He gave her a shy smile.

"I can't go, Winn. Those people there," I pointed, "they need my help."

"Then pray for them. Send money to Father Ryczek and Cuza."

"But the plan—"

"The plan the Tarakana shoved into our heads? It's crap. I was looking at it while Hannah was flipping through what we scribbled on the ride up here. Four months to consolidate the clans? It'll take a year or more, even with everything going our way. I suspect it would collapse into prolonged armed conflict between the clans. Casualties would be in the thousands. You'll never take the capital, not by force. The Central Government controls the air and has assets on orbit. Your twenty thousand dead would be more like half a million. The Tarakana want death and suffering, not freedom for the human population."

"That's not what I felt from Merrimac. They push people together because they want our passion. They want our love."

"Except he's not the one that put that plan in our heads, is he? You said it yourself; the colony in the Warrens is bad. They feed on us, Duse. They're parasites. They want our terror and our lust to kill."

I sighed, not wanting her to be right. "It doesn't matter if the plan is crap. I still need to do something. I know I can help them. How can I leave?"

"You're not the only one trying to help. It's not the only place that *needs* help."

"I touched them. I played with them. I heard their voices and I can still smell the Warrens. You want me to just float away back to Earth after that?"

"For now. It's what we have to do. We lost this round, but you know Hannah won't be able to stay away either. For now, it's time to go home. Your parents need you, especially your dad. He's in more pain than he's letting on. I don't have to be able to feel emotions like you to know that you're hurting him."

I was too tired to fight anymore and I knew she was right. "I'm a brat."

"That's one word for it."

We sat in silence for a long time. I was drifting in and out of sleep, still holding hands with Sam, even though I couldn't feel the fingers wrapped around mine except when he moved.

"Mala Dusa?" Only a whisper. Winona again.

"Sleepin'," I told her.

"What happened on Cleavus?"

I couldn't open my eyes. "Mom and Dad abandoned there. Fell in love."

"How many Tarakana were there?"

Really, Winn? It must have been 02:00. It felt like 02:00. "Don't know. Dad said a bunch of them at first."

"Then what?"

"They all went away except for Merrimac. They hid or somethin'."

"What about before that?"

"Before?" I sighed.

"What happened to the original Union colony?"

"Abandoned three hundred years ago, I guess. No one knows. Buildings still there. Whole cities. No people." I started drifting back to sleep, dreaming about empty buildings.

"The Tarakana destroyed them." Her voice was matter of fact. "They did what they're trying to do in the Warrens. Nation against nation, then group against group, and person against person until no one was left."

I felt cold suddenly and very awake, remembering. "I think I saw that! When Merrimac was in my head on *Wandering Star*, he showed me different paths through the future, but it was all jumbled. He was desperate. His colony was down to seven pieces and he was desperate to move out of known space. I think I'm supposed to go with him and get away from what's about to happen."

I looked at Sam snoring gently next to me. "Me and Sam. It was important that we be together, but I still can't see why."

"Because you don't want to see." Winn leaned back in her chair and closed her eyes as though she was going to go back to sleep.

Now I was uncomfortable and cold and confused. "I want to go to our cabin and sleep. I need to brush my teeth and I want a pillow."

"Sure. What about Sam? Should we just leave him here?"

I leaned over him and gently kissed his forehead. He sighed, a sound that ended in a guttural moan as he wrapped his arms around me and pulled me down hard on top him, kissing my neck and shoulder. My body's response was instant and completely beyond control of rational thought.

"Not a good idea, Duse."

"Sam," I managed to gasp. "Sam, wake up."

His eyes opened and he let go of me, blushing. I love it when he does that.

"Sorry, MD. Dreaming, I guess."

"We're going to our cabin for the rest of the night. Come with us unless you want to sleep here."

"No." He stretched. "I'll walk with you."

We left the chairs at the bottom of the pool and had *Vista* guide us to the cabin Winona and I were to share. We rounded the corner into the passageway and I stopped so quickly that Winn crashed into me. There was a large German Shepherd lying in front of our door. I tried to walk backwards and I was making a sound somewhere between a whimper and a cry.

Sam pushed past me and knelt next to the Tarakana. "Don't touch him, don't touch him," I was whispering over and over, unable to make my voice any louder.

Sam touched him.

He rolled the dog over and then looked up at us. "He's dead." He held a hand up covered in blue that dripped from his fingers. "And it's not a dog."

CHAPTER 13

RUMORS OF WAR

"Vista, did you see what happened here?"

Sam didn't seem upset at all. I was trying not to let myself curl up into a ball on the floor. I don't really have a 'fight or flight' reflex. When I'm scared, I curl up into a ball and wait for death to find me.

"I have no record of any unusual occurrences at this location."

"Do you see a dog lying here dead?"

"Yes. The dog appeared in that condition at 01:24 ship's time."

"Appeared? What killed it?"

"I have no idea. The dog appeared in its current condition. Due to ongoing construction, I have lapses from time to time."

"So your sensors weren't operating?"

"Systems in this part of the ship show no interruptions. However, the dog simply appeared at 01:24. There's no record of its existence prior to that event."

Sam poked at the dog with his finger, looking in its mouth and touching its paws. He lifted up what looked more like a tentacle than part of a dog.

"I only half believed you, Winona." He waved the tentacle around. "This is kind of hard to ignore."

"What do you think killed it?" Winn asked. I still had my arms wrapped around myself, but was starting to recover from the initial shock.

"Well, off hand, I'd say that having its throat ripped out was probably a contributing factor. I need to dissect it to know more."

"I have to let my dad know." My voice was only shaking a little bit. "I hate to wake them up, but they need to know."

"And the Captain." Sam was looking a little lost. "I'm the only RuComm person on board; everyone else is engineering or construction. I wish we had a couple of more biologists here. Let's get a blanket or sheet or something from your cabin first so we can wrap it up and move it to the lab."

"Should we move it at all?" I asked.

Sam shrugged. "*Vista* has a full record of what it looks like now that she can see it. There's nothing we can do with it here."

Winn put her hand on the access panel and our door opened. I kept my eyes up and straight ahead as I stepped over the Tarakana into the cabin. She stripped one of the sheets off her bed and offered it to Sam.

"You and MD lay the sheet out and I'll roll it on since my hands are already covered in blood."

"Blue blood?" I asked.

"Hemocyanin. Copper based blood, I'm guessing."

"Yeah." My brain really wasn't working. I had learned about hemocyanin back in third grade. Most of Dulcinea's native animals ran on hemocyanin. I had a *lacerti hyacinthi* for a while as a pet until I set it free one afternoon. It was a big blue lizard-like thing with six legs and sad eyes.

Winn squeaked when she opened the door. It takes a lot to make her squeak like that. The passageway was empty. Even the carpet covering the deck plates looked clean.

"*Vista*? Sam asked. He was irritated.

"Yes, Mr. Coleridge?"

"The dog that was lying here? The dead dog?"

"That dog was removed at 02:36."

I looked at my watch. One minute ago.

"Who removed it?"

"I don't have a record of that event. It simply was removed."

Sam looked at his hands, holding them up for us to see. "I still have the blood, at least."

"I think we should take you to the biology lab right away," Winona told him.

I grabbed him by the elbow and he smiled at me, surprised.

"I don't want you to be 'simply removed'. I'm not done with you yet." I told him.

"Not disposable?"

I squeezed him tighter. "No."

We walked that way the whole distance to the biology lab, me stumbling a little bit because I was hanging onto Sam's right arm with both hands. Winona helped him open sterile swabs and containers and we managed to get four good samples ready. By the time they had been sealed and slid into the AutoAnalyzer it was nearly 04:30.

Sam washed the remaining blood from his hands and collapsed into a chair, grinning at me. "Is your life always this interesting, MD? Because I'm not sure I can take much more."

"No, it's really not. I'm usually pretty boring."

"Tell him about the cloud of smoke you made in chem lab last year. Or what you did to Brad Jenkins when he called you a—"

"Winn, why are you talking?"

Sam chuckled. "I like listening to the two of you talk. I never really had a close friend when I was growing up. I was a lot younger than everyone else because my mom kept pushing me up through the grades. I got lonely sometimes."

"Some of my teachers wanted to push me up a grade," I told him. "My parents refused because they said my social skills were already terrible."

"Mala Dusa and her folks saved me from being lonely all the time. I don't think my parents have ever met any of my teachers. They're just happy when I'm away at school every day."

I smiled at her. "I love my Winona."

"And I love my Mala Dusa."

Sam tipped his head back and closed his eyes. "I suppose I need to call the Captain now. I don't know how I'm going to explain this."

"*Vista* has the video," I reminded him. "The sight of you lifting that tentacle up should convince him."

"*Vista*, can you please display the images from when we first saw the dog until we went into the cabin?"

"What dog is that, Mr. Coleridge?"

"The dog. The dead dog that was in the passageway."

"I'm not aware of there ever having been a dog on board."

Little shivers chased up and down my arms. "Show when the three of us went in to my cabin."

We watched ourselves come around the corner, pause a moment and then go in. A few minutes later, we came out and walked away. No dog.

"There wasn't any blood on me in the video." Sam put his hands over his eyes, looking like he was in pain. "*Vista*, how long before the blood analysis is completed?"

"I'm not showing that any blood analyses are currently in work."

"That's it, then." He turned to Winn and me. "Anyone want to explain what just happened, because I've got nothing."

"The Tarakana are very impressive." Winona sat down next to him. "I'm starting to understand why Hannah hates them so much."

I sat down on the floor and leaned back against her knees. She started making little braids in my hair. "I told you Merrimac was my friend. This proves it."

"Come again?" Sam asked. "That wasn't Merrimac?"

"No, all of the Merrimac colony are darker than that and have really dark faces except for a couple of tan spots above their eyes. The dead one was lighter. He was probably the one from the Warrens that came up with us. Merrimac killed him and wanted to make sure I knew about it."

"Then he made everything disappear so we'd look like idiots if we told anyone about it."

I laughed out loud. "Of course. Although I guess it's not funny. Hannah and my dad chased them for over two years while they were hiding alongside us on the same ship and playing with me every day." I hummed a bit of the elephant song to myself.

"Why are they doing this? Are we just pets to them? Do they *feed* on us? Are there good ones and bad ones fighting each other with us in the middle? It's like they have more control over our systems than we do."

I had never heard Sam scared before. I didn't like it. It made me feel cold all the way through. "Merrimac is my friend," I told him again, as much to reassure myself as him. "The bad Tarakana is dead and we're safe for now." I looked at my watch. Almost 05:00. "We need to talk it through, but not now. Too tired now to think any more." I tipped my head back to look at Winn. "Need to sleep," I told her.

She stood up without warning me and I toppled onto my back, staring up at the ceiling. Sam's face appeared over me and I put my arms around his neck.

"I like this view," I told him, giving him a sleepy smile.

"Do I need to carry you again?"

"Tempting, but no. Just help me up."

Sam walked with us back to our cabin. I found myself shaking again as thoughts of the Tarakana started to fill my head and I worried about what Merrimac was trying to tell me by leaving a dead one in front of my door. By the time Winona put her hand on the panel, I wasn't sure I wanted to go in. There were shadows under the beds and in the closets plenty big enough to hide a half dozen Tarakana. I hesitated, looking back and forth between Winn and Sam.

"Oh, fine." Winona grabbed Sam's arm and pulled him inside. "We have four bunks in here. Samuel, this is yours. Stay in it or I will know." She pushed me onto my bunk. "Head goes on pillow. Keep it there."

"Yes, ma'am," I told her. I slipped off my shoes and slept fully dressed, watching Sam tossing and turning for a few minutes before drifting away.

I was dreaming about when I was little, playing in the tide pools on Dulcinea. I was happy, exploring, and being daring while knowing that my parents were there and would always keep me safe. There were so many wonderful things to find and look at before the tide came back in.

I didn't want Winona to be waking me up, but she was doing it anyway. I struggled against it, trying to stay by the tide pools. Then my blanket was gone.

"Winona!"

"Hush, Samuel is still asleep. You need to come with me to have breakfast with your parents."

"Why?"

"Do you remember last night at all?"

All the happy tide pool feelings evaporated. I got up, went to the lavatory and looked in the mirror. It was hopeless, so I threw cold water on my face, brushed my teeth —finally —and joined Winn in the passageway still wearing the donated clothes I had worn when we had fled from the Mission, and then slept in.

Winona looked bright and alert, clothes fresh from the printer, face scrubbed and hair combed. "How come you look beautiful this morning and I look like this?" I asked her.

She looked at me and shook her head. "You're fine. Tousled is a good look for you."

"Thanks."

Watching my parents eating breakfast as we picked up our food made me feel a little better. Hannah was telling Dad a story, waving her fork around, endangering the piece of sausage she had stabbed and forgotten about. Just like home. I still couldn't feel any emotions from Dad. His face looked better and he seemed relaxed. I wasn't convinced.

I sat down, clattering my tray, and Hannah regarded me closely. "Ms. Killdeer, I thought I told you to keep her and Sam away from each other last night."

Watching the two of them looking at each other with their heads tipped to the side would have been funny if I'd been more awake. "It wasn't Samuel," Winn replied. "She looks this bad because we spent most of last night chasing Tarakana."

"You said I looked fine."

"You look like you should be asleep for another couple of hours."

"You could have left me in the cabin sleeping with Sam." Hand went to mouth. Too late.

"So they did spend the night together."

"No! Well, yes, but I slept between them," Winn explained. I had never seen her quite this rattled.

Dad was staring at me now too.

Winona continued. "I mean after the Tarakana, when we got back to the cabin. I mean they were in separate bunks and mine was between them. We were scared." She paused and took my hand. "I'm still scared, if you want to know the truth."

"Oh, I want to know the truth, Ms. Killdeer. Maybe you better start at the beginning."

While Winn told them how we had spent the night, I had the opportunity to finish my breakfast, steal two of her sausages, and drink most of Dad's coffee. By the time she was done, I was feeling much more alert.

"You actually had blood samples?" Dad asked. "That's impressive. We never even got close."

Hannah was looking at her plate, but not seeing it. I think she was trying to figure out the same thing I was: What was Merrimac doing?

"Mala Dusa," she asked sharply, "why didn't you wake us?"

"Wurthuhmphumph." I answered around a mouthful of Winona's French toast. I swallowed. "We were busy with getting the samples collected and then after that everything was gone. It was the bad Tarakana that was killed, so we weren't in danger any more, and, well," I looked at Dad, still trying to feel something from him, "I thought the two of you could use some sleep after everything that's happened."

"Well, you're not wrong, but you still should have gotten us up," he told me. "Some Tarakana may be worse than others, but they're all dangerous. Don't let them fool you, Dusa."

"I don't think that's true. Merrimac is my friend. He's been kind to me, other than..."

"Other than destroying a starship? Other than trying to get Sam into your bed?"

I chewed on my lip. "Yeah. Other than those things."

"Those two things are related," Winn whispered. I heard her, but I don't think my parents did.

"Why do you think he killed the other Tarakana, the one from the Warrens? What is he trying to protect you from?"

When Dad asked, the crack opened a little and I finally knew what he was feeling. I felt his shame from being unable to protect Hannah from Steiner, his fear and determination to protect all of us now, no matter the cost. It left me speechless for a moment. I had never known him to be anything other than confident and strong, someone who always knew what to do. This was the first time I'd seen him as a man. A good man, one of the best, but sometimes unsure, sometimes wrong, and sometimes vulnerable.

"I love you, Dad."

He sighed. "Thanks, Mala Dusa. I need to hear that from you occasionally. Now stop trying to get inside my head and tell me what Merrimac did to you, and what he told you."

"I'll try, but it's confusing. The way they think, it doesn't make sense to me. It's like all of them are thinking at the same time and the 'what might be' and the 'what is' get all jumbled together."

Hannah smiled at me. "Just like your dad. I've only been in close contact with them a few times and it's wondrous. I try to think like that, exploring all the possibilities at once. It made perfect sense to me being in that group mind. It was just too easy to get lost in there. Alice was the same way as me. She hated touching them because she thought she wouldn't be able to find her way back out."

"When Merrimac first touched me on *Wandering Star* he was disappointed," I told her. "He thought I would think like my mom. It was like I had failed him, or no, it was like I was flawed."

"That would make sense." Winona was looking at me. "I think they were hoping that you'd have Alice's mental patterns and your dad's bravery.

But you don't, and that's probably why you get such a headache and go all loopy whenever they try to control you."

"You think they're *breeding* us?"

"Well, *your* family certainly. Several others too, including Sam's. I just can't quite see what they're trying to accomplish. The colony in the Warrens wanted to use you to start a war, but Merrimac stopped them. Why?"

"Because I would have died," I told her. "I saw that very clearly. He doesn't want me to die. He's my friend."

"He's not your friend, Duse."

Dad interrupted before I could yell at Winona. "You think Alice, Hannah, and I are all part of a Tarakana breeding program?"

"You and Alice, yes. Not Hannah." Winn was looking at her, studying her. "You were supposed to fall in love with Alice when your lives were in danger on Dulcinea, but Hannah did something to you before you met, something unexpected."

"It was the way she smiled back at me after I kissed her cheek," Dad replied. "I've never wanted anything more in my life."

Well, I could feel *that* from my dad. It made me blush.

He smiled, looking a little lost in the memory. "I'm going to get some more coffee. Someone drank all of mine."

"The Tarakana hate you, I think," Winona continued after dad left.

"Mutual hatred," Hannah replied.

"I can understand that after what they did to your careers."

"Actually, that has very little to do with it. I could have forgiven them for hiding from us." She closed her eyes. "It's what they did to Ted."

"What did they do?" I asked.

"I'm not going to talk about it. Ask him sometime."

I didn't push, not with what she had been through, not with the pain swirling under the surface of her mind.

I got up and kissed her and she held me close to her for a minute.

"Um, I seem to have missed something." Dad was back with a couple of cups of coffee.

"I love her," I told him.

"That's good." He handed me a cup. "I think you need this."

"We still have no idea what Merrimac's next move will be, why Mala Dusa is so important to him, or how we should be responding," Winona added, trying to get us back on track. "I'm truly terrified."

"I'm terrified too," Dad replied. "I don't think this is just about Mala Dusa."

"It's not. It about the Mala Dusa and Sam combination."

"Sam." I sighed as the thought of him filled me. Winn looked at me, irritated, and I tried to focus before she could tap my forehead. "It's about a lot more than Sam and me. Something is going on with all the Tarakana colonies, not just in the Warrens. I can almost see it, but it keeps slipping away. All I get is a vague feeling and then it's gone. I think we need to run."

"Run where? Run from what?"

I shrugged. "Winn, why don't you tell them what you think happened on Cleavus. That's reason enough to run."

Winona told the story and Dad kept trying to punch holes in it; trying to tell her how the Tarakana had helped him and Alice stay alive.

"So," I interrupted, "you're saying that Merrimac was your friend?"

He scowled at me. "It seemed like he was at the time."

"That's what I—" The sound of my display pad chiming stopped me. I reached in my pocket. Empty. I stuck my hand out to Dad, wiggling my fingers impatiently. "It could be Sam."

It wasn't. "It's from Grandpa. I sent him a message when you were arrested, asking for help. I kind of forgot to tell him you were free now." I unrolled my pad, hoping he hadn't done anything too drastic.

I scanned the first couple of paragraphs and then slid it to Hannah. "He can't do anything to help us. There's, um, Dulcinea is..."

"Dulcinea is at war with itself," she finished for me, scrolling through the message. "The Oceanus Protectorate has occupied the northern archipelago, Union attempts to mediate have been rebuffed by both sides and all interstellar commerce has been halted." She looked up at Dad. "Thousands are already dead. The University has been closed because of conscription."

"That's insane. There's nothing in the archipelago but poor quality iron ore and sheep."

"What about Marcus Wright? Did Grandpa mention the Margo Islands?" I asked.

"Marcus. The man is unkillable, although I was tempted to try a couple of times after he'd had one too many beers at our house. He's stuck on that island with his students. Transportation has been cut off, but he's safe. Why?"

"I think I was supposed to be there. If I'd followed the plan Grandpa gave me, I'd be there right now. And if *Wandering Star* hadn't been destroyed, Sam would be there now too. Helping with the survey was supposed to be his first RuComm assignment. We would have been stranded together with war going on all around us."

Hannah shivered.

"If you had stuck with that plan," Winona added, "you'd be well on your way to becoming pregnant by now."

I turned toward her, about to protest, but I couldn't. I knew she was right.

Hands touched my shoulders, rubbing them gently, making little tingles run down my arms.

"You should have woken me. What have I missed? Tarakana mysteries all solved?"

I stumbled to my feet and turned toward him. "Hi."

"You look nice this morning," he said shyly.

"Tousled," Winn whispered. "Told you so."

Hannah was staring at Sam with her eyes narrowed. I think she was imagining him getting me pregnant and wondering where to hide his body after she killed him. "Go get some breakfast, Samuel. I don't think you're going to like what we've come up with so far."

"I'm not surprised. I spent twenty minutes this morning arguing with *Vista* about what happened last night." He shook his head. "It's like someone punched holes through her memories and replaced them with something else."

Hannah smiled at Dad while Sam went to pick up his food. It was odd sort of smile, a little crooked and she had the look in her eyes she always gets when she wants Dad to do something crazy with her.

"Hannah... no. In forty-eight hours we'll be on board the *Orso Ipato* headed for home."

"A lot can happen in forty-eight hours. And I just want to look. It can't hurt just to look."

"She's a totally new class of ship; it's not like *Wandering Star*. The underlying language and syntax will be completely different."

Her smile became more of a smirk as she leaned toward him, knowing she'd already won. "Won't know till I look."

Sam came back carrying a cup of coffee and a couple of hard rolls. "Let me grab a chair."

"Don't bother," Hannah told him, standing. "I need your help talking to *Vista*. You're going to help me find her lost memories."

"OK." He glanced at me, disappointed.

"Go help my mom," I told him. "I need to take a shower and print some new clothes."

"You may not need to print anything. When I was at the embassy, the CG delivered all your personal belongings that had been left at the hotel. I had them sent up here yesterday. They should be in my cabin."

"Blue dress?"

"I don't know. I never made it back there last night." He blushed and glanced at my dad.

"It's OK," I told him. "Winn explained everything."

"Not really," Hannah took a step toward him and Sam retreated. "But I'm sure Sam will be spending the next couple of nights in his own cabin. Right?"

"Yes, ma'am," he assured her. "My cabin. All night. By myself."

"Good. Let's see what you've got."

My stuff was fine —including my precious blue, hand made by Sam dress —and so were Winona's things. Hannah's clothes had been shredded and Dad's were completely missing.

He shrugged it off. "I always travel light. But I guess now I'll need to get a new pack and rock hammer."

"You brought your hammer?" I asked.

"Always," Hannah sighed.

Winn walked back to our cabin with me while Sam and my parents went off to do whatever they were working on to find *Vista's* missing memories. I took a quick shower, the warm water relaxing me and reminding me that I was very short on sleep. At the same time, the two cups of coffee were working hard to keep me awake. This was a feeling I was going to have to get used to if I was serious about attending the Academy next year. Wasn't that what Sam had told me? Five hours of sleep a night when he was lucky. I got out and looked longingly at my pillow.

Winona was sitting on her bunk, face buried in her display pad.

"It's not just Dulcinea. There are reports of problems on half a dozen planets; Montecito has announced plans to leave the Union, there's been a coup on Meeker, Calisto has seized Union ships on orbit there." She stopped with her mouth open and looked up at me. "Duse, nuclear weapons have been used on Piermont. Fifty *million* dead, probably more."

"I think this is why we need to run." I sat down next to her. "Merrimac told me he needed to escape *Wandering Star*. He said the central planets were getting too crowded and making it hard for the Tarakana colonies to remain hidden so he wanted to move outward with us, past the known worlds. He was desperate."

Winona still had her head down, scrolling through the news feeds. "I think the other colonies have agreed on a different strategy. They're going to destroy the Union, isolate each planet and reduce the populations to whatever size is optimal for Tarakana survival."

I stood. "Come on. We need to find my parents."

"Do you plan to get dressed first?"

I looked down at myself. "Um, I suppose I should."

"Sam would enjoy seeing you like that, but I imagine your mom would be unhappy."

"Yeah." I rummaged through my box of clothes, the thought of Sam seeing me in my underwear stuck in my head. I briefly caressed the blue gauze dress, then put on a t-shirt and pants.

"*Vista*, where's my mom?"

"Ms. Weldon is in the starboard shuttle bay."

I looked at Winona. "Shuttle bay?"

"And in the mess hall, and in the infirmary and in the outer ring corridor near the port aft engine—"

"Pause." I pulled out my display pad. When Hannah answered, I asked her, "So, where are you, *really*?"

There was a wild look in her eyes. "*Vista* having trou-ble pinning me down?"

"Mom..." I swallowed hard, unable to talk.

"What's happened?" She sounded worried now. "We're all in the main science lab."

"Winona and I are on the way. Things are worse than we thought."

Winn kept her head down while we walked, unable to tear herself away from the news. "The Central Government on Bodens Gate announced that they are investigating collusion between factions in the Warrens and the Union. Someone attacked a CG patrol near the central market and six people were killed. CG security forces are threatening preemptive strikes if the Council of Clans fails to cooperate in the investigation." She glanced up at me. "The Council will never cooperate and the Warrens will rebel. Without strong leadership..."

I closed my eyes. "The plan isn't even there anymore. I know it was worthless, but it died completely with the Tarakana that shoved it into me. All I can do is pray for them."

Winona held my hand the rest of the way to the lab.

Sam gave me a gentle kiss on the cheek when we arrived, and then one to Winona. She smiled at him, took my hand, and passed it to him. She walked away from me to where Hannah was typing rapidly at a terminal. Winn still had her fingers up to her cheek, touching where Sam had kissed her.

"Do you have a brother?" I asked him. "Or maybe a friend that's as wonderfully freakish as you are?"

He glanced back at her. "For Winona?" He smiled at me, looking amused. "I don't know. I'll have to think about it. I'm freakish?"

"Yeah. You are. Wonderfully."

"Thanks, I think." He was watching Winn talking to Hannah. "Your mom's brilliant, by the way. She's been manipulating *Vista's* sensors to produce the same sort of gaps that might be hiding the images of the Tarakana. *Vista* even admits to analyzing blood samples now, she just doesn't know where they are. It must be amazing having a mom like that."

He had that look in his eyes, the same as Cuza and Captain Kelang. I needed to spend some time with Hannah when we got home and learn how to do whatever it was she did to them.

Winona was busy showing Hannah everything that was happening in the Union.

I stood behind them and said softly, "We need to run."

Hannah was scrolling through the pages and I could glimpse the pictures; plumes of smoke rising over ruined cities, men and women holding onto each other trying to provide comfort, children crying, angry people yelling, bodies lying still in the streets. Lots of strong, dark emotions for Tarakana to feed upon.

"It might be too late for that." She zoomed in on a story for me to read.

'Trapped Between Worlds', the headline read. 'The Reunification Commission ship *Sierra Vista*, en route from Bodens Gate to Ratatoskr, became stranded last week when two of the three Deep Space Holes between those worlds were found to be missing. RuComm and Union officials do not know when they will be able to send a rescue mission. Without use of the Deep Space Hole network, the crew's transit time could be in excess of seventy years, according to a Union spokesperson.'

I stepped back and looked at Sam. "Seventy years trapped on a ship with Mr. de Sande."

"Huh," he snorted. "MD, maybe you should try to focus on something other than the trivial, but horrifying."

"Like why, or even *how* someone could destroy one of the DSHs?"

"Not destroyed; missing."

"Ms. Weldon," Winona asked, "can a DSH be used as a weapon?"

Hannah looked troubled, like she didn't want to consider the question. "I don't know. We create them on-site and I don't remember hearing about any being moved afterwards. It's no accident that they're kept so far away from the worlds they connect. I think the only way to use them as a weapon would be if you wanted to destroy an entire planet."

I felt the terror flowing into her, like cold water running down my back.

"Winona, have you seen anything about unrest on Earth?" she asked, trying hard to keep the panic out of her voice.

"No. Almost everywhere else, but the communication lag is considerable."

"I need to find Ted. *Vista*, where's Ted?"

"Mr. Holloman is on the bridge," Vista answered. "And in the mess hall, and in the infirmary."

She closed her eyes. "Always too damn clever for my own good."

CHAPTER 14
LEAVING SOON FOR HOME

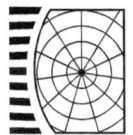

"He's not actually on board," Winona had her pad out and Dad's face was looking back at her. "He's on *Wandering Star* with Captain Kelang."

"What's he doing there? Tell him to stay put and that we're on the way. *Vista*? How do we get to *Wandering Star*, and you damn well better give me a straight answer."

"Of course, Ms. Weldon. *Wandering Star's* remains are docked next to me. I've been helping the team recover what we can of her systems and of her memories of almost fifty years of service to the Reunification Commission."

We started walking fast, following the blue orb that *Vista* was using to guide us. Hannah stopped for a moment and placed her hand on the wall. "I'm sorry, *Vista*. She was a good ship and she served me faithfully. I'm sorry this happened to her."

"That's kind of you to say so. I'm learning a lot from what she experienced."

Hannah patted the composite wall plate a couple of times and we walked on at almost a run.

When I was little, whenever Hannah would catch me being rude to our household AI, she would sit with me on the floor teaching me to have respect for non-human life, and even respect for things that we owned. I anthropomorphize almost everything because she raised me that way. I even apologize to my toys if I drop them. It's a little weird, but I think I'm a better person because of it.

I patted the wall in the same place she had when I passed, and said a silent prayer that *Vista* would never find out what I had done to her sister.

We found Dad in what had been the bridge. All of the equipment was smashed. The framework that managed the matrix for the big display screens was shattered against the wall along with the remains of desks and other equipment. Part of the wall was missing and more debris was scattered in the passageway. It made me want to cry.

Dad was with the Captain and Sandy Williams. It had only been a week since I had last seen her on board *Mara Vista*, but it seemed like a lifetime ago. I wrapped my arms around her in a tight hug even before I said hello.

She patted my head and kissed me. "You've had quite the time of it, haven't you honey? Your dad was telling me some of it."

"How's Tobias? Is he here with you too?"

"Down talking to the engines. We'll both be here a while yet. The investigation will take another month at least and there've been some troubles on Meeker. The new government there is restricting immigration from the Union and I'm not sure we'll be able to move there any time soon."

"Why would they do that?"

"Something about wanting to maintain their 'planetary identity', whatever that means."

"That's stupid. Their identity is a bunch of people that moved there from somewhere else."

"Yes, it's stupid, but there's not much we can do about it. There was a group that wanted to close Meeker off a couple of years ago, but no one was much interested. Now, with other planets blocking Union ships, they were able to convince enough people to be stupid along with them. Everywhere people go, there's always some that want to tell everyone else how to live and are willing to use force to make it happen."

She smiled at the look of confusion on my face. "You don't follow any of this that happens off Earth, do you?"

"Not as much as I should. It always seems so far away. My Grandpa sends me stuff about Dulcinea sometimes, and I went to school there so I knew about the OP and Palma Federated States always wanting to fight, but not all this. It scares me."

"You're leaving for home tomorrow?"

"That's the plan," Dad answered. "But now with what's happened to *Sierra Vista* I'm not sure I want to risk it."

"So, you've already heard about the missing DSH and have been here discussing it?" Hannah asked him.

Dad answered carefully, feeling the same irritation from her that I was. "Yes, I was just about to come find you so we could decide what we need to do."

"Good answer. Any ideas on how a DSH could be moved like that?"

Sandy's forehead wrinkled. "Well, that's just it. It can't be. We build them in place and once they're activated they're anchored by their own gravity."

"Destroyed, then?"

"If someone's figured out how to do that, I'd like to hear about it."

Dad got kind of a goofy smile on his face. "If you want to stop people from using the DSH network, and they can't be destroyed or moved, they must be—"

"—hidden," Winn finished for him. There was awe in her voice.

"Yes."

Sandy was shaking her head. "You can't hide that big of a gravity well. The ships sense it and guide on them."

Winona looked at me and silently mouthed, "Tarakana."

Hannah quickly changed the subject. "Tonight will be our last on *Bahia Vista*. Why don't you and Tobias join us for dinner? I know Mala Dusa would enjoy having someone to talk starship engineering with."

"Yes, I would." I smiled sweetly at Sandy, trying to look as if a pleasant technical discussion over a plate of Janjetina was upper-most in my thoughts.

"Sure. I know Tobias would enjoy seeing you again."

"Ted, we need to go."

"OK. My new hammer should be ready about now anyway, if you don't mind stopping by the shop on the way back. They said it would only take about an hour for the sintering." He picked up a backpack that looked remarkably like the tan fabric and leather bag he always carried, just cleaner.

Hannah grabbed his arm. "That's fine. Captain, Sandy, we'll see you for dinner then."

"What's the hurry?" Dad asked once we were off the ship.

"You didn't see that shimmer in the corner of the debris field? He was there, listening. If the Tarakana have found a way to hide the Deep Space Holes, I want time to think about what we're going to do about it before they know we know. Let's get your damn hammer and then find some-place quiet to talk."

We stopped by one of the scruffier shops along the space dock's main corridor. There was a glowing sign in the window displaying a short loop from what looked disturbingly like a real, fatal knife fight. Above it, the shop's name flashed in lurid red—*Strong Blade, Limited.* The shelves were full of edged weapons, and not the kind that you just hang on the wall.

Hannah browsed while we waited with Dad at the counter for his new rock hammer to cool.

"How much for this one?"

The proprietor looked up at Hannah from her display pad, smiling indulgently. "That one may be a bit heavy for you. Are you looking for something for defense or more of a decoration?"

Hannah accepted the challenge. "Neither." She lifted the sword from the rack and held it in her right hand, her left fist planted on her hip, and smiled arrogantly. "I need a good arming sword for offensive work. The balance on this one is a bit off for me, but it might do if the price is right." She moved her wrist and the sword's tip moved gracefully through a series of cuts.

The woman at the counter swallowed hard. "You didn't by chance live in the Warrens once long ago?"

Hannah came close to her and took her hand, squinting at a small tattoo of an eagle next to her thumb. "You're Baderca clan. No, I've never been to the Warrens. A dangerous place, so I'm told. How much?"

The woman closed her eyes and her lips moved as she prayed or maybe said an incantation to ward off evil. She kissed her thumb at the end. "You may have the sword. Your enemies are my enemies."

Hannah bowed her head. "Evil must be fought wherever it is found."

The woman nodded, satisfied that the right words had been spoken. "Perhaps my lady will need a scabbard?"

"Yes, and a good belt and frog."

Hannah didn't bother to haggle on the price of those items and the woman seemed content when we left. Hannah insisted on wearing the sword at her side on the way back to the ship, making Dad look uncomfortable. Winona had serious love in her eyes.

Sam whispered to me, "One more step closer."

I looked back at him with raised eyebrows.

"To being out on the street with you, killing your enemies."

I put my arm around his waist and smiled as gently as I could. There was nothing for me to say.

We were almost a hundred meters from the shop before Dad said quietly. "You do recall that we're leaving tomorrow night, right?"

"If the Tarakana will allow it."

"You need to be more careful. That woman remembered you. I saw it in her eyes."

"She should. If you were to look at her back, you would find the scars where her *ex*-husband burned his name into her flesh."

Sam's hand found its way around my waist, maybe because he loves me, maybe because he needed something to hang on to.

"So," Hannah said brightly, turning towards us, "is everyone ready for lunch?"

Dad talked about *Wandering Star* while we ate. I'd seen him do this before, trying to cover over what Hannah was doing by talking about something else, something normal. I think it's the way he copes with being in love with one of the most dangerous women in the Union. He seemed more desperate about it this time.

"How are they providing environmental control?" Winona asked him. "I assume even the auxiliary engines are inoperative."

"Everything is being powered by the space dock. Her engines are useless even for salvage. They'll be scrapped along with most of the rest of her once they've recovered what data they can."

Sam and Winona seemed just as fascinated as he was with what forty-six g of acceleration had done to the crew spaces. He was showing them pictures of unrecognizable objects that had penetrated walls and punched through deck plates. I slowly lost my appetite.

The *Orso Ipato* was due to dock at 15:00. We wouldn't be getting on board until late the next afternoon in preparation for a 22:30 departure. Underneath Dad's cheerful banter, I had the impression of a door closing, and his fear that it would click shut before we could pass through. I was pushing what was left of my pasta salad around with my fork, not listening to him anymore.

"Duse, look at this picture of what's left of your old cabin."

"No."

"You don't want to see it?"

"No, I don't want to see it." I pushed back from the table. "I need to go for a walk."

Sam stood and I think he was going to go with me until Hannah stopped him.

"If you're done, Sam, we can get back to work finding those blood samples."

"Yes, ma'am," he replied obediently.

"And, Ted, I could use your help too. We have things to talk about."

"Yes, ma'am," Dad answered, sounding just like Sam.

I looked at her, not smiling.

"Enjoy your walk, Mala Dusa. I don't need you or Winona just yet."

I turned and walked out of the mess hall without a word, Winona following close behind me.

"*Vista*, are your trail sims loaded yet?" I asked.

"Yes, they are, Ms. Holloman. What would you like to see?"

"Dulcinean Heritage Trail, please. Can you set gravity to Dulcinea local?"

"Of course."

We were standing in a subalpine meadow and I was light again, fifteen kilos gone in an instant. It made me laugh.

Winn smiled at me. "That sounds better. What was wrong with you back there?"

"Nothing's wrong with *me*. The Union is falling to pieces, Tarakana are doing God knows what, and in twenty-four hours we're leaving for Earth. I don't know when, or *if*, I'll ever see Sam again. I just wanted to walk with him, but Hannah speaks and he obeys. And Dad. He always obeys, even when she's crazy. He always tries to cover for her."

"Ah. Princess Mala Dusa is jealous of her mother."

"Am not." I looked at her and her eyes were studying me. "If we leave, I may never see him again. If we stay, Hannah's going to get him killed."

"The Tarakana won't let that happen."

"That's comforting."

"And I thought you wanted to go back and fight."

"I do."

"But without Sam."

"Yes." I sighed. "No. I can't have both?"

We stopped where there was a view down a steep cliff to a small creek winding across the valley floor. The illusion was nearly perfect. Air was blowing across my face and there were birds above us, riding the thermals. "And Sandy; she's stuck here now. She and Tobias are supposed to be on Meeker being happy and in love with each other."

I sat down on the trail, the feel of cold deck plates under me despite it looking like dirt. "What's wrong with people? I can understand the desire to own things, like land or stuff that you make. Property rights are the foundation of human rights. But those people on Meeker are acting like the land owns *them* and they have to protect it from everyone that isn't already living there."

Winona stared at me until I put my hand up to my mouth. "Oh. I'm sorry, Winn. Your ancestors had their land stolen from them, didn't they? Stolen by *my* ancestors. We destroyed your entire way of life."

"You can't choose your ancestors." She sat and took my hand. "Duse, do you see those two big sticks on the sand bar in the middle of the creek? How do you suppose they came to be there?"

"Well..."

"I mean if they were real."

"OK. They were washed there by some storm and then left next to each other when the water level fell."

"Where are your people from, Mala Dusa?"

I played along. "Mom was from Dulcinea. Before that, her family was from Australia and England and before that maybe the Netherlands and Scandinavia. Before that, no one knows. Dad's family has been in the southern Rockies for like five hundred years, but somewhere in Europe before that."

She nodded. "My people were mound builders along the Mississippi for a thousand years. They lost that land and way of life long before your people came to North America. Then we were in the Dakotas for a couple hundred years, and people came and took that land and way of life from us too. My folks lived on the west coast until Dad took a new job and we moved down the street from you.

"That's you and me down there on the sand bar, Duse. Some unknown storm brought us together and there we sit. The only thing that's certain in our lives is that another storm will come someday. Moving around is what people do. It defines us as a species."

I touched my watch, thinking about the lock of her hair that was nestled under it. "I'm going to tie my stick to yours so I don't get lost."

She squeezed my hand. "That's a good idea. I'll do the same."

I stood and pulled her to her feet. "Run with me."

"I'm not dressed for..."

I didn't hear the rest of it, because I was running. She caught up, of course. Winn has always been faster than me. We spent most of the afternoon running, talking, laughing, and getting blisters on our feet. Or at least I got blisters. Winona had the sense to take off her shoes and run barefoot. We had worn ourselves out by the time Hannah called me and asked us to come to the biology lab. We found the nearest cross passageway and opened the hatch.

There was an engineering team installing something in the plenum just outside, and they looked down at us in surprise when the hatch opened.

"Where did you two come from?"

"Sand bar," I told them. "We got stuck there together after the last storm."

That made Winona laugh, a sound I hadn't heard enough of lately. I smiled at their confusion and we took off running before they could ask us any more questions.

We stumbled through the door to the lab together and Sam was staring at me.

Winona whispered, "You're tousled again. Look at his face. Just don't let him get close enough to smell you."

I nodded, trying to be serious.

Hannah sighed. "I don't know which is worse, the way you were or the way you are. Sit down and I'll show you what we've accomplished; those of us who've been working while you were goofing off."

I sat down at one of the desks and Sam sat down close to me.

"You're not going to believe this, MD." He looked at me, his eyes kind of scrunched up. "Have you been running?"

"Yeah, sorry. Didn't have time for a shower."

He took my hand and whispered, "That's OK. It's worth it to be close to you. I'm just sorry I wasn't there to help you get sweaty."

I smirked at him, thinking he hadn't realized what he had said. He held my eyes in a steady gaze until I blushed and looked away.

Hannah and Dad were standing at the front of the room and I tried to concentrate on what she was saying.

"This is the blood sample that you collected. Mala Dusa, you should recognize these markers from your sixth grade science project." The screen was showing the results of the mass spectrometry analysis.

"I do! That's almost a perfect match for *lacerti hyacinthi*! Tarakana are *Dulcinean*?"

"Maybe." She pushed her hair back up out of her face. "I'm worried that finding the blood samples was too easy. Part of that is because the new *Vista*-class AI system is really the old *Star*-class AI with a fancy wrapper around it. The RuComm acquisitions group got taken if they thought they were buying something new. Bottom line is the analysis might be bogus."

Dad was smiling. "I do love the Tarakana."

"How will we know if it's real?" I asked.

"We won't. We can't. Maybe we have a clue. Maybe it's misdirection."

"It's a perfect Tarakana thing to do, isn't it?" Dad added. "But let me show you something a little bit more concrete."

He cleared the screen. "*Vista*, can you detect the Deep Space Holes that are closest to you?"

"Yes I can, Mr. Holloman." They appeared on the screen.

"What about the first one between here and Ratatoskr?"

"That DSH is not in the prescribed location."

"How are you searching?"

"I'm feeling for the gravitational field that should be at that location. It's not there."

"Please check optically for distortion at that location."

"There is distortion there."

"Is it consistent with the gravitational lens effect produced by a DSH?"

"Yes, it is."

"So, the DSH is still there?"

"No, I'm certain that it's missing."

He smiled at us and spread his hands.

Winona had her arms crossed. "Ms. Weldon, I now fully understand your feelings toward the Tarakana."

"Two years of this crap," Hannah replied.

"But now people are dying."

"Yes, they are. And the Warrens are next."

"How do we stop them?" I had my arms crossed too.

"We? 'We' don't stop them. I'm looking at two young girls that need to be back in school in a few weeks, and a young man with a ship to catch."

I hadn't noticed before that she had her new sword lying on the table next to her. Her eyes kept drifting over to it.

"Mom, what are *you* going to do?"

Dad was waiting for her to answer, his arms crossed now too. I think they had already had this fight and Hannah had lost. "We're going home tomorrow," she answered, locking eyes with him. "We're going to let the people die."

"What is the commission doing?" Winona asked. "Have you been in contact with them?"

"They're not allowed to talk to me. Janus Boden has bribed or threatened them into silence. Right now it looks like their strategy is to wait for the Warrens to be beaten into submission and then try to pick up the pieces."

I was feeling sick. All I could see were the faces of the children that had let me play with them in the market. How long before they were all lying dead in the street, just like in the pictures we had seen on the display pad? There had been stray dogs slinking around in the shadows by the ruined buildings in those images. I wondered how many of them were real dogs.

I got up and walked toward the door. Hannah sighed. "There she goes again. Winona, please make sure she's at dinner on time."

Winona followed me back to our cabin. By the time she caught up, I was already sitting on the floor of the shower fully dressed, letting the warm water pound on my head while I cried. I could see her sitting on the floor, waiting for me.

After a few minutes, she asked, "Do you need help washing your hair?"

"No."

"Because it's going to be hard to wash much else while you're still wearing your clothes."

"Shut up, Winn."

"What do you think we can do down there?"

"We can fight!"

"We would all die. Are you ready to watch your mom and dad die? How about Sam and me?"

"We can at least try. We have to at least try."

"Sometimes doing nothing and waiting for the right time takes more courage..."

"Than doing the wrong thing right away," I finished for her. "I don't deserve you as a friend."

"You don't, but you're stuck with me. Hand me your wet clothes and get cleaned up. I want to take a shower before dinner too."

I dug through my box of clothes while Winona showered. My blue gauze dress was the obvious choice for our last dinner together, but I wanted something else, something Sam would remember. The dress I chose was white, with a row of twenty buttons holding it closed from its relatively modest V-neck to the hem just above my knees. I left the top two buttons undone.

Winona looked at me when she got out, head tipped and water still dripping from her. "Interesting."

"I thought I'd surprise him by not wearing the dress he made for me."

"That ought to do it."

"You think he'll like it?"

"How does it make you feel, wearing it?"

I looked down at myself and blushed.

"I can assure you that it'll produce the desired effect. Do you know what you're doing?"

"No, but I want to do it anyway."

"Your mom's going to order me to stay by your side all night again after she sees you."

"Will you?"

"I should."

"But will you?"

"I haven't decided yet. It depends on how stupid I think you want to be."

"Just a little bit stupid?"

She hugged me and whispered, "I'm jealous. I'm trying not to be, but I am."

I squeezed her tightly. "We'll find you a freak of your own. I promise. Please let me have this last night with him. I promise I won't be too stupid. And you're the one who found him for me, remember?"

After a moment, she whispered, "Princess."

She pulled away from me and closed my top buttons.

"Do you think that will keep Mom happy?" I asked.

"Maybe. And it'll give Sam something more to do later."

"Winona!"

"It's why you're wearing it, isn't it?"

I chewed on my lower lip. "Maybe. I don't know." Winn was still looking at me. "OK, yes, the thought crossed my mind."

She nodded. "Help me pick out something to wear. I think I'll go talk to one of the engineers tonight. The younger one that was working outside the ring corridor this afternoon was kind of cute."

Sam was wearing buttons too. A dark blue shirt and standard issue RuComm khaki pants. The shirt looked soft and it made me want to

185

touch it. Did he know that when he picked it to wear? By an unspoken agreement, we didn't so much as hold hands during dinner. I was worried about the questions it would raise with the Captain, and I knew it would be painful for Tobias and Sandy to know that Sam and I could do what RuComm had forbidden to them.

I also had a dim hope that it would convince my parents that we planned to keep our hands off each other. With normal parents, that might have worked, but the two of them spent dinner bumping around in my head trying to gauge my feelings. That convinced me that I needed to find the most remote part of the ship I could as soon as possible after dinner.

I couldn't finish dessert, and when Dad settled in with a cup of coffee and a long story to tell, I excused myself and asked Winona and Sam to join me for a walk on one of the trails. My heart rate was already up. When Sam stood next to me, the back of his hand touched mine and I could feel my cheeks flush.

"Ms. Killdeer..." Hannah's expression was more amused than I would have expected.

"Yes, ma'am, I know."

"I would like to review a couple of things with you in regard to the situation on Bodens Gate. Could you please stay here with us?"

Winn's eyes went huge and she kept looking back and forth between us. "I don't think... What if she..." Winona sighed. "Certainly, Ms. Weldon."

I gave Hannah a quick hug. "Thanks, Mom."

"For what?" she whispered.

"For trusting me."

"Huh," She chuckled and looked over my shoulder. "It's Sam I trust. Have a good walk, Little Soul. And go *carefully*, OK?"

"Yes, ma'am."

When I turned to leave, Dad asked her, "Are you sure about this?"

"Not even a little bit. But... she needs to say goodbye. You know what it's like not to have that closure."

I didn't stick around to listen to the rest.

Sam took my hand as soon as we were out of the mess hall. "Where would you like to walk?"

"You pick."

"I wish we had your dad's mods for the Sonoran desert."

"You think you'll need a thunderstorm to cool you down later?" I teased.

We entered the ring corridor and Sam seemed unsure of himself. "Let's try this one. *Vista*, Carlsbad Caverns, eighteen degrees C, and diffuse lighting effects, please."

We were underground and I could hardly see Sam next to me until my eyes adjusted. There was the sound of water dripping somewhere in the distance, making hollow echoing sounds.

I squeezed his arm. "I didn't know she could do this."

"I thought we might go for a walk, so I asked her for a full list. This one sounded... special."

I kissed him, then I pressed up closer and kissed him again, letting my lips linger on his.

"Let's walk a bit, do some exploring."

"OK." I really didn't feel like walking, but his arm went around my waist and the feel of his hand there made up for it.

We walked a few hundred meters, past deep pools and masses of flowstone, until we rounded a corner and found a small tent pitched square in the middle of the trail. I almost walked straight through it, thinking it was part of the simulation.

Sam pulled me back. "Careful there, MD. The tent is real. I, uh, put it there. Maybe I shouldn't have, but I thought that we might..."

I got on all fours and crawled in through the door. Soft blankets covered the floor, making it feel snug and secluded. I turned around and looked up at him. "Are you coming inside or not?"

Sam crawled toward me, his head nuzzled up against mine and he pushed his shoulder against me until I was lying on my back with him smiling down at me.

"What if someone else comes to the ring corridor?" I asked.

"*Vista* will warn us if that happens."

My hand was on his shirt. It was as soft as it looked. "You've thought of everything, then."

He was still staring at me, his hand caressing my hair, down my cheek, fingers rubbing gently on my collarbone.

"I don't know what gives you that idea. This is all kind of new to me."

My hand was on his chest, feeling it under the softness of his shirt. "Really? It's new to me too. Everything in my head is from things I've read or stuff I've watched without my parents knowing about it. My heart and the rest of my body seem to know more about what they want than my head does. Parts of me seem positively confident, but most of me is scared to death."

"Scared of what?"

My fingers undid the top button on his shirt. I didn't remember telling them to do that. "Scared I'll disappoint you because I'll do something stupid."

He wasn't looking at my eyes anymore. After a moment, he leaned forward and kissed the hollow of my throat, very softly, then lower down my chest, following the buttons that were coming undone.

I could feel his breath warm against my skin after the first five or six, and he said, "I'm just as scared. Will you promise to tell me when I do something stupid tonight? Because I have no idea what I'm doing and I don't want to disappoint you either."

We spent a lot of time kissing after that, talking a little bit, exploring and trying to understand that slow and gentle was better than most of the lies we had been told. It was a long time later, I don't know how long, that Sam paused and looked at me. All of the buttons were undone by then and his shirt was lost somewhere in the tangle of blankets. He was leaning on one elbow, his hand on my belly, his fingers moving gently back and forth.

"Mala Dusa, I love you."

"Really? I had no idea."

He grinned, his eyes watching his fingers. "I have to stop."

"Why?"

"If I don't stop now, I won't be able to stop at all. Do you understand? I don't want to stop, but we should."

I took his hand, kissed the palm, and put it between my breasts. "Because I'm too young."

"Yes, that's part of it." He moved his hand to the side, dragging the backs of his fingernails in slow circles. "It would still be wrong, even if you were older."

"I know," I whispered, closing my eyes as shivers ran through me and my body pushed against him. I took his hand again and held it against mine, palm to palm. "Can we go just a little further? I *need* to go just a bit further." I put his hand where I wanted it to be. "Please."

He was looking at his hand, moving it gently over me. He shifted then, moved his hands underneath my legs, and kissed me. "Yes, ma'am."

I put my fingers in his hair and moaned.

My Samuel is wonderful. We went just far enough that night, touching, kissing, and finding ecstasy in each other arms, without going *too* far. I slept with my head on his shoulder for a few hours afterward, and didn't think about the Tarakana or the shadow of war in the Warrens or anything at all other than the man who loved me and whom I loved.

I woke to a kiss on my forehead. "You're beautiful when you're asleep."

"Just when I'm asleep? Maybe *that's* why I've never seen it."

He kissed me again. "You believe too many lies about yourself."

"Thank you for being blind."

"Uh huh."

"What time is it?" I was feeling too comfortable to look at my watch.

"Almost 03:00."

I sighed. "I should get back to my cabin. Winn is going to be worried about you."

"About *me*?"

"Yeah. She thinks I'm a bad influence on you."

"Probably true."

I snuggled closer to him. "What's going to happen?"

"What do you want me to say?"

"Tell me everything's going to be OK." His hand was caressing my bare shoulder. It felt so good and natural that we were together like that, like I was right where I was supposed to be.

"Of course everything's going to be OK. The ship that's going to take you home is already in dock and you'll be on your way later today. *Mesa Vista* will be here in five days. When I get back to Earth in a few months, after having incredible, exciting adventures, I'm going to come dance with you. After that, you'll go to the Academy with your best friend, Winona, and become the most brilliant ship designer in history. They'll build a statue of you on the Academy grounds, and all the pigeons—"

"Stop! Skip the part about the pigeons. Tell me about us."

"You and I will carry on the most loving," he kissed my shoulder, "romantic," *kiss*, "passionate," *kiss*, "erotic," *kiss*, long distance relationship imaginable. And when you graduate, first in your class naturally, we'll find a way to be together."

"Together."

"Yes, maybe on Earth, or a ship, or some planet no one's heard of yet. It won't matter. Do you know why?"

"Because we'll be together."

"Exactly."

I kissed him, climbing on top of him to do it. "You better walk me back to my cabin now."

"OK."

"Because if you don't, I'm going to do something stupid."

"OK."

Moving off of him and helping him pack up the blankets and the tent was one of the hardest things I've ever done. Knowing it was the right thing didn't make it any easier. I looked around one last time at the simulated cave.

"*Vista*, close Carlsbad Caverns, please."

We were standing in a brightly illuminated corridor of gray metal. I sighed and looked at Sam. "Thanks. You're going to have a hard time topping that."

"I've got a few months to plan before we have an evening together again."

He took my hand and we walked back into the main body of the ship.

I didn't tell him about what I had seen for an instant when the illusion of the cave had vanished and the lights had come back on. For a moment, there had been something close by where the tent had stood, something about the size of a big dog, something that was feeling very satisfied and content.

CHAPTER 15

FIGHT OR FLIGHT

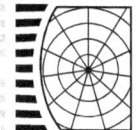

Sam kissed me goodnight at my door, a process that took longer than I expected, but was still too quick. After the door closed behind me, I leaned against it trying to gather the energy to brush my teeth and undress for bed. Parts of me felt sore, and parts were weak, but all of me was happy. I took one silent step forward, being careful not to wake Winona.

"How's Sam? You didn't break him, did you?"

"Shush, Winona's sleeping," I told Winona. "We don't want to wake her."

"Come sit beside me. I want to hear everything."

I sat on the edge of her bunk. "It's private."

"Uh huh. Your buttons are misaligned."

I looked down. "Oops." I undid five or six and started trying to put them in the right holes. I gave up. "It was dark, and there're *so* many of them."

Winn patted her pillow. "Come on. Lie down and start talking."

I put my head on the pillow next to hers. "OK, but I'm not going to tell you everything."

Between the giggles and the prodding and Winona knowing me better than anyone else, I told her *almost* everything. "Now let me sleep," I said at the end. "*Really* need to sleep."

"What about brushing your teeth?"

I heard the question, but couldn't answer. I slept with my head on Winona's pillow until morning.

"Get up, Duse. It's almost time for breakfast."

"You go."

"Come on. They'll have waffles."

"Waffles?"

"And Sam will be there."

My eyes opened. "Right. I should change."

"And take a shower. You smell like him."

"I do?" I sniffed my arm and smiled. "I do."

I showered quickly and dressed simply. A t-shirt and pants were on the top of the box and I didn't want to waste time digging. Sam wasn't in the mess hall when we arrived, but they did have waffles and coffee. I was starting to appreciate what a wonderful thing hot caffeine could be in the mornings.

Winona was less pleased with the breakfast selections. "No hash browns this morning?"

"I'm sorry, Ms. Killdeer," *Vista* explained. "There was a theft overnight of almost two thousand kilos of fresh vegetables. All of my potatoes were taken."

"Who would steal vegetables?"

"I wish I knew. My sensors did not record any intruders."

Winn was still grumpy about it when my parents got there a few minutes later.

"Oatmeal and toast. No hash browns."

When Winona explained why, Hannah blushed and looked at Dad. I had never seen her blush like that. I didn't know she *could* blush.

"Oh, God, Ted. I knew we shouldn't have done that last night. It was stupid." She put her hands over her eyes. "And you with your ribs still healing. Are they OK this morning?"

"They're fine. We checked, remember? Every shadow, every corner. We were alone last night."

"What are you talking about?" I asked.

Hannah sighed, looking uncomfortable, but she pressed on. "There's part of the Tarakana life cycle that requires very intense human emotion." She looked at Dad. "The kind that only comes when two people who love each other are together. It triggers something in the Tarakana and they start reproducing by binary fission. Let me tell you, it's not pleasant to watch. They eat a lot during that stage. Mostly vegetables. And they really love potatoes."

My hand had come up over my mouth. "There was one with Sam and me last night in the ring corridor."

"What did you *do*, Mala Dusa? Last night, how far did you go?" Hannah had gone pale.

"Um, not *too* far. We didn't.... I'm still..." I wanted to be angry with her for asking, but she was obviously scared and that was rare enough that it carried me right along with her.

"You knew it was there and you didn't do anything about it?"

"I didn't see it until afterward. What happens now?"

"Two thousand kilos of food are missing. We never were able to quantify how efficient the conversion process is, but there are probably more than fifty of them on board now." She was pushing her hair off of her face and then letting it fall back across her eyes, then pushing it back again. "They're going to try to follow you onto the *Orso Ipato* this afternoon. I don't know how to stop them."

"But they're Merrimac's colony, so it's OK. Merrimac is—" They were all staring at me, daring me to say it. I sighed. "It could be worse."

Sam came into the mess hall then and gave me a quick good morning kiss on the cheek. "Hey, MD. Did you sleep alright?"

I had no control over the happy emotions that flowed from that single, simple kiss. It was powerful enough that even Winona felt it; I saw it in her eyes. I swallowed hard. "Yeah, fine. How about you?"

Winn didn't give him a chance to answer.

"Wow!" She turned to my parents. "Did you *feel* that? That *can't* be a normal, average human response for the emotions to go that deep." She looked at us with her hand on her forehead. "That was... blinding. That must be what the Tarakana are trying to select for. If Sam and Duse can produce that intensity from a quick kiss on the cheek, what must they have created last night?"

Sam was confused and angry. "You *told* them about last night? How could you..."

Hannah interrupted him. "She hasn't told us anything. She wouldn't do that. Two young people in love about to be separated for almost a year? She didn't have to say a word. Believe me; we remember what that's like."

"There was a Tarakana in the cave with us last night," I told him as he sat next to me. "Now they're stealing all of *Vista's* potatoes and making a bunch more Tarakana."

193

"It scares me that those things could be related."

"It should." Hannah still looked pale. "I don't see a way to resolve this. Your 'friend' Merrimac has won. He's beaten me at every turn. I tried to trap him on *Wandering Star* and instead ended up in prison on Bodens Gate with Steiner." She paused a second with her eyes closed. "Then I almost got us all killed. We think we have a blood sample, but that's almost certainly fake. Will we make it back to Earth if we take *Orso Ipato* tonight? Sure, if it serves the interests of the Tarakana."

She pushed back from the table. "I'm going to the gym with my new sword. There's a combatives sim I've wanted to try."

After she left with Dad, Winn turned to me, "I know you're not related by blood, but I can tell she raised you."

"Thanks."

"What should we do with the rest of the day, Duse? We aren't scheduled to board the *Orso Ipato* until 15:00."

"Try to stay out of trouble?" I answered.

Sam started laughing. I looked up from my coffee at him.

"Admit it, MD. That was funny."

Winona smiled at him. "Come on, Mala Dusa. Let's get out of here and cause trouble somewhere. It's what you're good at."

"Wait a minute. I want to finish my last sip of coffee first, and..." I reached across the table, "eat your last piece of toast." I stood and ate the toast while we left the mess hall.

Winn lowered her voice and told Sam, "That's why I always take extra. You should too, if you're going to be around her at meal time."

"You're really funny today. Where do you want to go?"

"Space dock. I need a new souvenir since you spent all my coins." She tipped her head. "Maybe a sword."

"Great. Do you even know which end to hold?"

"Hannah will teach me. You should get one too, and then she can teach both of us on the trip home."

"OK. And one for Sam, so he can defend himself from me when he gets back." I grinned at him. "Because I'm going to attack you."

"I had fencing at the Academy. You better practice a lot if you want to beat me."

"I'll have Winn by my side. Think you can take both of us?"

"It sounds like it would be fun to try. Maybe I'll bring reinforcements."

I took his hand. "That won't be until we're graduating. God, how will I make it that long? It's an eternity. Winona, how many months are there in an eternity?"

"Nine or ten, in this case."

I looked at Sam smiling at me. Blue eyes. Then everything went dim and there was a voice in the back of my head. I stopped walking and listened.

"That might work," I whispered. "Are you sure they wouldn't just... Oh. Of course. But I don't want to have to choose, please don't make me choose."

Something cold was pressing on the back of my neck and I squinted at Sam. "Blue eyes," I told him. I was sitting at a table near a sidewalk café. "Again?"

"Again," Winona confirmed. "You were talking, but not making any sense. Tarakana?"

I nodded.

"What were they telling you?"

"I don't remember," I lied.

"Damn it, Mala Dusa, they are *not* your friends. I'm your friend." She took her hand and seemed about to tap me hard on the forehead, then frowned and leaned forward and kissed me instead. "Say it; tell me I'm your friend."

"Winona Killdeer, you are my best, and until Sam, only friend. You're the *only* one in the universe who I know will put up with all the stupid things I do. I love you more than life."

She put her arms over my shoulders and pressed her head against mine. "That's my Mala Dusa. Now, what did they put into your head?"

"I promise I'll tell you," I glanced at Sam, "both of you. Let me sort it out a bit first. When they do that to me, it gets all jumbled and I need to think about it, OK?"

"No, not OK. You see that look in her eyes, Sam? That's the look she gets when she thinks she's her mom, her *real* mom and can come up with some complex plan that manipulates all of her *friends* in to doing what she wants. She forgets that all she has to do is ask." Winn turned her back to me.

"Sam? Please give me a few hours. When we get lunch I'll tell you everything, I promise." I smiled at him, trying to look as desperate as I felt.

"Will a couple of hours make a difference?" he asked Winona.

"We should take her somewhere and force it out of her." She sighed. "Fine. But I want to buy a sword. I think I'm going to need it."

We walked for a while, exploring the main concourse of the space dock and window-shopping.

"Why no firearms?" Sam asked. "Swords are so..."

"Archaic?" Winona finished for him.

"I was going to say messy. Personal. I'm pretty good at hitting a target hundreds of meters away with the right rifle. Being close enough to," he reached his arm out, twisting his wrist "... you know? I'm not sure how I'd react to that."

Winona looked around at the different shops and people hustling by on their way on or off planet. "They're probably available, if we knew which unmarked door to knock on."

"I don't doubt it. I imagine they worry about the type of ammunition too. Punching holes through the walls would be bad."

We stood in front of Strong Blade, Ltd. for a couple of minutes, watching the video clip that was looping underneath the sign. It was of a young woman talking to a crowd of people in the Warrens. There were captions at the bottom of the display, translating her words. I didn't need to read them though, because I still remembered what I had said.

Winona turned to me. "Well, that should get us a discount, I would think."

I pushed past her and entered the shop, standing up straight with my shoulders back, just like Winona always told me to do when I wanted people to take me seriously.

The proprietor smiled at us. "Ah, I had prayed that you would return, and now here you are. My lady is not with you, or the handsome man who loves her?"

"No, my mother," I paused just a fraction of a second for emphasis, "told us to come. My friend and I have never used a sword, but she wants to teach us. She said you could suggest what would be appropriate for each of us and give us a fair price."

I glanced at Winona, who was looking proud of me, and at Sam, who was trying to look fierce and determined. He was adorable.

"And what about you?" she asked him. "Certainly you know how to hold a sword in your hand and put it to good use."

He blushed, but gave her a straight answer. "I have four years training with the foil."

"Earth," she sighed, "and Dulcinea. Such peaceful, civilized places they must be."

"Not at the moment."

"So I've heard," she nodded. "*A time to love and a time to hate, a time for war and a time for peace.* Here, it seems, there is always plenty of time for hate."

She squinted at me, took my right hand, and pulled on my arm. "For you, I think the rapier. Your arm is long; that will make it longer. And for your friends, the gladius." She looked at Winona and Sam. "With practice, it will become part of you, and you will feel naked when it's not close by your side. Let us see what I have in stock."

It took more than an hour for her to find the right sword for each of us, show us how to hold and care for it, and tell us something of the history and lore of each one's use by the clans in the Warrens.

When I put my hand on the reader to pay for it all, Sam whispered in my ear, "Your mom's going to kill you, you know."

"Now I can defend myself," I smiled back at him.

He kissed my cheek. "She'll probably just settle for killing *me* instead, and maybe Winona for not stopping you."

"No one can stop *me*." I had meant it as a flippant remark, but the woman grabbed my hand before I could pull it away.

"Are you going back? The clans are close to uniting, but they need someone to lead them, someone to stand where *her* statue once stood and say the words they need to hear. You've no idea how close you came."

I tried to step back from her, but she held tight.

"No, I can't. I just... can't right now."

She squeezed my hand hard. "Soon, then. Go carefully, you and your friends, and tell her that I took proper care of you."

"Thank you," I said softly. "I will."

She kissed my hand, and we left.

"Is that what they put back in your head," Winn asked before we'd gone a dozen steps. "To go back down there and lead us all into a bloodbath?"

I shook my head. "I'm hungry. Lunch first. I'll tell you while we eat. Afterward, you can tie me up or sedate me or something and carry me on board the *Orso Ipato*."

Winn nodded. "Pretty much what I was planning."

We found lunch in the central atrium where a dozen restaurants competed for attention under a view of Bodens Gate. We stared at the ceiling for a while, trying to tell if the effect was from display panels or actual transparent plates built into the space dock.

I smelled hamburgers and grilled onions, and lost interest in the view. Sam found something that was supposed to be a tamale, but came in a bowl, and Winona smelled something else altogether and wandered off.

We found a table where we could watch for her, and Sam stole one of my onion rings while I tried a bite of his food. It wasn't bad.

"The onions rings are decent, MD. Good choice."

"No choice. They said they didn't have any chips." Sam's face went pale. "What?"

"That means…"

"The Tarakana have gotten into the supplies here too?"

He nodded. "There could be hundreds of them up here now. Do you feel anything?"

I thought about it while I took a bite. "No, nothing."

When Winn joined us, she was carrying a large bowl and had a contented smile. "Buffalo stew with fry bread crust." She sat down and put her nose right above it. "They told me it's been simmering since yesterday." She poked a hole through the crust and smelled it again. "My Granma used to make this for me when I lived with her. Smelling this, I remember her, and the house, and the barns." She sighed and took a bite, her eyes closed and her face happy.

I looked back at my burger. "I think I should have gone with Winona."

"Does it have potatoes in it?" Sam leaned over, looking into her bowl.

She stabbed one and held it up for him to see. "Last batch till they get resupplied tomorrow. But I'm not going to worry about how many Tarakana are here with us now, just what they're trying to shove into my Mala Dusa's head." She pointed her fork at me. "You talk, I'll eat." She put the fork in her mouth and closed her eyes again.

I ate another onion ring and looked up at Bodens Gate. Part of the *Orso Ipato* was visible nestled in to the far side of the dock. There was a winged lion a hundred meters long painted on its side.

"I don't have to go home with you. I could go on *Mesa Vista* with Sam if I want to." I looked at Sam so he could see in my eyes that I wanted to.

There was a quick flicker of joy there before reason blotted it out. "Really? What makes you think you can do that?"

Winona had stopped chewing and her face went blank. I turned back to her before I answered Sam.

"I'm not going to do it, Winn. The vision they tried to push into me isn't as strong as the one that's already there. You and I are going home, we'll finish our last year at John Kinsel, and then we'll go to the Academy next year together and become so famous that they erect statues to us on campus."

Sam smiled gently at me, amused that I had used the fantasy he had told me. I continued talking to Winn, but I couldn't take my eyes off of him. "I have nine or ten months of eternity to get through and I'll die if I don't have you with me."

She took another bite of stew. "Tell me how you were going to do it."

"Oh, easy. One of the Tarakana was going to go in my place."

"I think your mom and dad might have noticed."

"Not if you helped. The Tarakana are only about eight kilos lighter than me and they can look like anything they want. Put some clothes on one after it's assumed my shape and no one would notice. Especially if I wasn't talking and was being all grumpy, the way I really *will* be when we leave. Hannah would never notice as long as she didn't get close enough to sense its emotions. And Merrimac told me he could get me on *Mesa Vista* with no problems. Once a ship is in full boost toward the DSH, there's no turning back. By the time we reached Kempner-27 it would be like I was part of the crew."

"Great. You'd be back on Earth just in time to give birth. You really think RuComm will let you attend the Academy after stowing away on one of their ships? And you'd get Sam fired. I keep telling you, Duse; they are not your friends."

"I'm not going to do it. It's just... an interesting idea."

"They can really look like one of us?" Now Sam had stopped eating. The thought seemed to trouble him.

"I... um. I saw my mom when we were on *Wandering Star*, my real mom."

"Oh."

"They seem to like the dog shape, and Merrimac showed me what they looked like on Cleavus. When I was little, sometimes they would turn into small elephants or other animals and they would play with me."

I looked away and took another bite of my lunch. "It doesn't matter. I'm going home, and Winona will keep me alive until you come back in the spring." I gave him a brave smile that didn't work and tried to concentrate on my food.

"You're not afraid of them at all, are you?"

"Not of Merrimac. I know I should be, but I'm not. He makes me feel safe, like everything's going to work out. You don't feel that from them?"

"Maybe a little." He didn't look happy about it.

"Winona?"

"They terrify me. They've manipulated your families for generations. Everything *is* working out. For them. Or almost. I don't think they planned for your dad to be in love with Hannah or for your mom to die."

"It's strange," I said between bites. "I came here to learn about my real mom, but I don't know much more than before I left." I reached my fork over to her bowl and stole a piece of carrot.

"Have you managed to learn anything about Hannah?" There was a bit of an edge to her question.

"I'm still trying to put those pieces together. There's the Hannah I grew up with, who was always there when I got home from school, took me camping every summer with Dad, and yelled at me for not cleaning up my room. And there's the Hannah that overthrew a government, the Hannah that Cuza worships. Then there's the Hannah that would go back down there right now if Dad would let her. I don't know."

Sam stole another one of my onion rings. "Have you always called her Hannah? Even when you were little?" Winn had her head tipped, waiting for me to answer.

"No, not until I was like eleven or twelve. I was starting to understand that Alice had given birth to me and that *she* was Grandpa Vandermeer's daughter. So one night, when Hannah was tucking me in, I asked her if I could stop calling her mom. She said that would be OK. After that, I kind of became obsessed with finding out more about Alice, wondering how my life would have been different if she had raised me, wondering if my dad had loved her as much as he does Hannah."

I was reaching my fork toward Winona's bowl when I realized her eyes where all scrunched up.

I glanced at Sam and his eyes were scrunched up too.

"That must have broken her heart."

"No, she said it was OK." I looked back and forth between them. "She really did. She said it was OK."

Winona touched her finger to my forehead and sighed. "That's because she loves you."

I leaned back, Winona's stew safe for the moment. "But it wasn't OK, was it?"

"Just call her mom more often. She likes it when you do that."

I took a bite from Sam's bowl, feeling miserable. "I need a lot of work. I'm not a very good person."

He chuckled. "Wait till you get to know *me* better. Growing up without a dad? No friends? I did terrible things to my mom when I was growing up. I'm a mess too. Maybe you can try to figure me out while I try to understand you."

I kissed him. He tasted like tamales, so I kissed him again.

"Stop!" Winona protested. "We only have about three hours before we leave and I'm not going to spend it watching that."

"Let's go back over to *Wandering Star* after we drop off the swords. I want to say goodbye to Tobias and Sandy again and thank Captain Kelang. I kind of feel bad about ignoring them last night at dinner."

"Notice this, Samuel? It takes a lot to get her attention, but once you do, there's a really nice woman inside."

He was staring at me. "Yeah, I've noticed that. Do you think she's worth all the trouble?"

"There *are* days that I have my doubts," my best friend continued, "but in a frighteningly real sense, you were made for each other. I suppose that means that you can't help how you feel about her. I just want you to know that she's worth loving."

"Thanks, Winn, I'm still sitting right here, you know? And nothing to say about Sam?"

"I don't know him well enough yet to do a proper critique. He may be a little slow to do what's right, the same as you're a little quick to do what's wrong, but he seems solid so far. What the Tarakana are doing horrifies me, but they *are* producing some interesting people, and not just you and Sam. I'm talking about your dad and his sisters, and Alice and her father."

She reached across me and took the rest of my hamburger, still thinking. Winona is always thinking. "The Tarakana are not infallible. I need to keep reminding myself of that. We can beat them."

"Or at least understand them," I added. "Not all of them are bad."

"You worry me." She ate the last bite of my hamburger and made a face. "That was terrible. Let's talk your dad into barbecuing next week." She took my last onion ring. "I suppose you'll want your room back."

Home next week. Sitting there with Bodens Gate hanging above us, it seemed impossible. I looked at Sam. I wanted to go with him so bad it hurt. And I wanted to return to the Warrens with my new sword to try to make things right, and I wanted to go home with Winona.

Less than three hours left. I wanted to spend all of it in a small tent in a cave pretending nothing else existed. I wanted to listen to the sound of water dripping and echoing in the distance, talking quietly with Sam. I wanted to feel his hands touching me and to experience the softness of his skin under my fingers.

"Mala Dusa?"

"Uh huh."

"Are you with us?"

I opened my eyes. "Sorry. Day dreaming. Let's go drop off the swords."

Winona didn't want to drop off her sword. She wanted to wear it. "Look," she pointed, "lots of people are wearing them."

I looked around the concourse. "I see *one*, and I don't think he's bathed in the last year. That's your role model?"

She smiled. "Yes. And what about that group over there?"

"Those are Guardians of the Peace, and those things by their sides are called guns."

"They won't let me have a gun, so a sword will have to do."

"Fine, but if you cut your fingers off, I'm not going to help you find them. Sam?" I could see it in his eyes. "Don't you cut your fingers off either. I like your fingers."

"I won't."

They opened the boxes right there at our table. I touched the hilt of mine and was tempted, but decided to wait until I knew what I was doing. One of us still needed to have fingers.

People stared at us when we walked back to the ship. I was the Princess Mala Dusa, now with armed escort. Winn made a point of bowing to me while we waited for the lift to take us up to *Vista's* outer ring, making Sam snicker.

"I hate you, Winona Killdeer."

"Yes, my lady."

"The next stranger we meet, I'm going to introduce you as Witasna o Killdeer, heir to the Lakota matriarchy."

"I never should have taught you that word."

Mom was standing in front of us when the doors opened.

She grabbed my arm and pulled me in with her. "Quick. All of you. I was afraid I'd have to search the entire dock." She kissed my head as the door closed. "And you had the good sense to buy swords. You know how to use them?"

Sam shrugged. "How big of a difference can there be between a foil and a gladius?"

"Why didn't you just call us, Mom?" I opened the long box with my rapier in it and struggled with the unfamiliar belt, trying to get it to sit properly on my too skinny body.

"Can't. All Union comms are being jammed. I came down here as soon as we realized it. Ted is on his way to the *Orso* to see if we can board now and maybe break orbit early if this means what I think it does."

"That wouldn't make any sense." Sam had the little crease between his eyes he always gets when he's confused. "Bodens Gate gets most of its revenue from interstellar trade. Seizing Union ships would bankrupt the government."

Sam and my mom seemed perfectly calm, working the problem. My brain was going fuzzy as panic started to fill me.

"The door is closing," I whispered. "Just like Dad was afraid it would."

"Not yet, not if we hurry."

We got off the lift and Mom moved us quickly onto the ring transit car that would take us to where the *Orso Ipato* had docked.

"My stuff. Did Dad get my box?"

Mom was watching the markers showing our progress with a worried look on her face. "What? No, of course not. No time."

Sam took my hand. "I'll take care of it for you."

"You're not coming with us?"

"Only to kiss you and Winona goodbye. You knew that."

Mom was still watching the markers, I think willing us to move faster. She didn't seem surprised when the lights flickered briefly and the transit car coasted for a second or two. There was a jolt as we shunted onto what looked like a maintenance track and entered the darkness of a long shed build over the rail.

"Winona, Dusa, please get behind me. Sam, I've no right to ask, but could you please stand beside me?"

"Yes ma'am." He moved in front of me, shielding me with his body from whatever was to come. He grinned at her. "I've been telling Mala Dusa that this was inevitable."

She smiled back at him, looking confident and very dangerous. "Follow my lead. I can probably talk our way out of this. Don't touch your sword or even look at it unless I do. Understand?"

He nodded, but none of that mattered once the doors opened. There were four members of the Guard waiting for us, standing about three meters back with their weapons already drawn. Behind them, a fifth man was smiling cruelly at Hannah.

"Swords, Ms. Weldon? Really? Is that the best you could do?"

The man with the Guards was older and fatter than his pictures, but I still recognized him.

"I like swords, Mr. Boden. They force you to look at a man in the eyes before you kill him."

He chuckled. "Foolish words from a foolish woman. And stupid, when you're standing there with your daughter to protect."

I was looking at the Guards and the small maintenance room we were in, trying to find some weakness or way we could get past them. I recognized the one pointing her gun directly at my head. I said her name out loud, surprised. "Officer Trilby." A slight smile touched the corner of her mouth.

"Come now, Ms. Weldon. Please step out of the car. Nice and slowly. That's good. I've not had the pleasure of meeting your daughter and her friend. Mr. Coleridge, why am I not surprised to see you with this group of fugitives? No, not surprised, just very disappointed."

Sam didn't answer.

"So you seized all the Union ships in dock just to have the pleasure of saying goodbye to us? I'd no idea I was so important to you." Mom sounded confident, but I could feel the fear in her.

"Is that what you think? No, this meeting is just a happy byproduct. With all the unrest in the Union right now, it seemed an excellent opportunity to renegotiate our contracts on more lucrative terms. The CG has seen fit to put me in charge of finding a solution that will better serve the interests of our constituents. Putting a temporary hold on outbound traffic seemed like a good way to get the Union's attention. But when I learned you were leaving, I just had to arrange one *final* meeting."

He gestured at me. "You, child, step out from back there. I can hardly see you."

A shiver passed through me. I had not been shaking up until then, but now it started, deep inside. I took one hesitant step backwards.

"Oh, that will never do." He snapped his fingers.

Officer Trilby holstered her weapon and pushed past Mom to come around behind me. She grabbed my upper arms and pulled back hard while shoving me forward. It hurt. I stumbled forward two or three steps and stood facing him.

"That's better."

Trilby was holding my arms behind me so tightly that my hands were already starting to tingle.

"Let's get a good look at you." Boden walked all around me with a hard smile on his lips, studying me like a biological specimen. He touched my hair, took a handful of it and pulled my head back, making me gasp.

"Let her go," Mom told him. "Please."

"Please, is it? I wish she had come back to the embassy that night. Things would have been so much simpler."

He turned his attention to Trilby, but kept his grip on my hair. "So this is the girl Steiner found attractive?"

"Yes. I've no idea why. It was disgusting." She pulled my arms back just a little bit more. "She got him killed."

"Yes. I'm very sorry for your loss. He was one of our best."

He tugged my hair again and I closed my eyes, trying not to cry out. I was whimpering though. I couldn't help it, and I was ashamed.

"Boden, please." Mom's voice sounded desperate. "Write down whatever you want. I'll sign it right now. Just let her go."

He ignored her. "Tell me." His mouth was right next to my ear. "Are all the girls on Dulcinea as ugly as you?" Trilby laughed and she leaned me forward, making it hard to breathe. Boden slid his other hand up inside my shirt, cupping my left breast. "And so malformed?"

He grabbed hard, twisting, and I screamed. Through the pain, I felt Sam sharing my agony. He was about to do something stupid and noble, and I readied myself to watch him die.

I opened my eyes, squinting through the tears. Winona was whispering something to Sam and he nodded. I couldn't feel anything from him anymore, just somewhere close a cold anger, powerful, overwhelming. Boden let go of me, looking momentarily confused.

"I have more important things to attend to. Officer Trilby, take them all in to custody and get them back down to Eindhoven. We'll work on getting charges filed sometime, oh, in the next month or so. That should give us time to get to know each other a little better."

He stopped in front of my mom and smiled. "Ms. Weldon. I'm sure I'll be seeing much more of *you* later."

After he left, Trilby let go of my arms and shoved me toward Sam.

He held me while Winona took a couple of steps toward her, angry. "How could you?"

"What? You think I *owe* you something? You cut off my partner's hand and then shot him in the head. This is what I owe you."

The back of her hand hit Winn square across the face. I caught her before she could fall and she looked at me, one eye closed. "My face exploded, Duse. I felt it explode. Not sure how I can still talk without a face." She started to cry.

CHAPTER 16

BODENS GATE

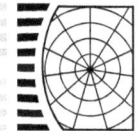

Officer Trilby had her weapon back out and was pointing it at Sam.

One of the other Guards said, "Trilby, I believe we were ordered to move these folks down to the surface. There's a shuttle waiting for us."

She glanced at him. "I don't remember him saying we had to take all of them, Franklin."

"It was kind of implied."

"Whatever. How does delaying it a day or two really make a difference? Dead by the flame, dead by torture, or dead by a bullet to the head, is still dead. Franklin, you stay with me and we'll transport them. The rest of you go catch up with Boden and make sure he stays safe."

"What should I do about their swords?" Franklin was looking at Mom, uneasy.

Trilby smiled. "Let them keep them until we're on planet. I'm kind of hoping they try something stupid so I can kill them all right now. 'Killed while trying to escape' always looks good on a report."

Franklin shook his head and motioned for us to precede him through the door. I helped guide Winona. Between the tears and the swelling around her left eye, she was nearly blind.

I kept watching Mom, waiting for her to make a move or signal or something. She just walked, head held high, not talking, not even looking at me. No one had said anything about Dad, and I didn't want to bring him up, but I was worried. And hopeful. I kept expecting him to suddenly appear behind us, kill the guards, and whisk us off to the *Orso Ipato* for a daring escape.

We reached the shuttle and Franklin attached our arms and legs to the manacles that were part of the seats. Trilby's gun never wavered and Dad never came.

Trilby turned to Franklin when he was done. "Go catch up with the others. I'll take it from here."

He hesitated. "Are you sure?"

"Oh, yeah, I'm sure. I need to have a little time alone with them before I turn them over on the ground." She smiled. "Don't worry. They won't be dead."

"That's not procedure. There should be two of us at least."

"Go." She put a hand on his chest. "I *need* this. I'll cover for you if there are any repercussions."

"I don't know..."

She shoved him backwards out of the hatch. "I'll make it up to you. Personally." She kissed him hard on the mouth.

"You're crazy. I'm not sure I can deal with crazy."

"Yeah, I *am* crazy. Tonight you'll find out how much fun that can be." Trilby put her hand on the panel by the hatch and it slid shut. She strapped herself into one of the seats facing us. The shuttle was larger than I had expected, with room for maybe a hundred prisoners and eight guards. The gravity wobbled a few minutes later as we passed through the field around the dock.

Trilby finally holstered her weapon and smiled at us. "That was close. I was afraid he really *was* going to insist on coming. Franklin's a stickler for procedures."

She unstrapped and knelt in front of Winona, unlocking her manacles. "Sorry about the slap, kid. I had to make it look real."

"Yes, it definitely felt very real."

Trilby touched her cheek. "A medical AI should be able to fix that right up."

She knelt in front of me and looked into my eyes before undoing the locks. "I didn't know he was going to do that to you, but I should have guessed. I'm sorry."

"If this isn't just another trick, then you've already made it up to me. But how can I trust you?"

"Huh. Am I that good at playing a psychopath?"

She unshackled Sam. As soon as he was free, he stood and drew his sword in one fast smooth motion. He held it to her neck and looked at Mom, silently asking her what to do next.

"Mala Dusa, take her gun and then get these chains off me. Where's this shuttle going?"

Trilby's eyes were staring at the blade resting against her throat. "Um, empty field about three klicks from the Mission. Your friend Cuza's supposed to have transportation waiting."

"And then what happens to you?"

"Cuza fixes it so it looks like you overpowered me and stole the shuttle. Assuming the Guards believe it and don't arrest me, he said it should earn me a medical discharge. I think I'll find a nice desk job somewhere."

"What's he going to do to you?" Sam had moved the blade away from her now that Mom had the gun. She dropped the magazine, looked at it, and put it back in.

"I didn't ask for specifics, but I'm sure it won't be pleasant, if that makes you happy."

"Why not just stay in the Warrens?"

Trilby sank back into her chair. "No, not a chance. I don't like the chaos and disorder. Or the way it looks or, especially, the way it smells." She closed her eyes. "The people are violent, uneducated, and have been bred for brutality for generations. Given the proper guidance, they *might* be ready to participate in our civilization in fifty or a hundred years. Maybe. I know they can't help being inferior, but that doesn't mean I have to like them. Actually, I *hate* the people in the Warrens." She paused and looked at each of us. "And I hate all of you too."

"If you feel that way, why are you doing this?" I was standing in front of her, my hand braced on the bulkhead as we passed through turbulence in the upper atmosphere.

"It was better than having Cuza kill me or turn me over to be sold. And, well..." She sighed. "I did owe you something. I'm not a psychopath."

"You just work for them."

"Not after today."

The shuttle spoke to get our attention, a stern male voice. "Ten minutes to landing. Please secure loose items."

"Dusa, bring me the first aid kit." Mom held her hand out.

I grabbed the box from the wall and gave it to her. "For Winona?"

She removed all of the gauze bandages and a small tube, and then tossed the kit back to me. "No, Officer Trilby."

Mom shot her point blank in the stomach.

I jumped at the sound and my hands went up over my ears.

Trilby was already going into shock. "What...Why?" She was looking down at the blood soaking through her shirt.

Mom opened the tube from the kit, smeared the clotting agent on the gauze and pressed it onto the wound. "Now you don't have to be concerned about whatever Cuza was going to do to you. Don't worry, I don't think I hit anything vital and the Mission's medical AI should be able to 'fix that right up' for you. If Cuza's waiting for us, you should be there in twenty minutes."

"What..." She licked her lips, "What if I had been lying about that part?"

"Oh. Well, then you'll be dead in about forty-five."

Trilby looked up at me. Her eyes were glassy and scared. "I wasn't lying. Promise you'll tell him to take care of me. Promise you'll tell him. I know he'll listen to you. In case I can't speak for myself when we get there."

"I promise."

Hannah frowned at me. "Go get strapped in."

I sat next to Sam and cried all the way down to our landing in a muddy field. It was a cold afternoon in the Warrens, and I could smell it immediately when the hatch opened; sewage soaked garbage and wood smoke.

Cuza glanced at Officer Trilby and then Hannah when he entered the shuttle.

"I shot her," she explained, "That should be enough to keep her from being executed, and the time line will match up better."

"That's generous. If I didn't know better, I'd think you was goin' soft."

"Yeah?" She pushed past him down the ramp. "Explain that to Mala Dusa for me."

He knelt and examined Trilby. She moaned a little, but didn't open her eyes. "Little Soul, you know this is softer than what I was plannin', right?" He looked down the ramp to where Hannah was waiting impatiently for us to join her. "She's a fine, gentle woman at heart. Where's Teddy?"

I sighed, not knowing what to think, so I settled for kissing Cuza's cheek "He's still up there."

"That ain't good."

"What're we going to do?"

"Do you trust God?"

I nodded while he wiped my tears.

"Keep trusting him and do what you think is right. It'll work out. And love on your mom. She needs it, especially if Teddy's gone and gotten himself into trouble again."

"You'll take care of Trilby? We'd be in a lot worse trouble right now if it wasn't for her." I touched her hand. It felt cold.

"Just like Alice. Yes, Little Soul, she's going to be fine. Hannah was careful."

He walked down the ramp with us and I turned back to him. "And Winona. I need to get her to a medical AI."

"There's no time," Hannah answered. She kept looking at the open sky above us. "We've already been standing around too long. Where am I going, Cuza?"

"Number twenty-six. You still remember the way?"

"Like it was yesterday. Medical supplies?"

"In the usual places."

She kissed him on the lips. "How many times have I owed you my life?"

"Aw, I don't count such things."

She touched Winona's chin, moving her head back and forth in the fading light, looking at her eye. "Can you run?"

"I am the wind."

Mom chuckled. "Sam, I'll lead, you bring up the tail. The path is complex, designed to reveal anyone following us on the ground, and fool those watching from above. Stay close."

Complex was an understatement. We went into people's apartments and out through their kitchens. We were underground part of the time and once leaped from rooftop to rooftop. Mom never slowed and never spoke until we entered an abandoned building, ran up the stairs and stopped.

She was out of breath, but still managed to gasp, "Made it."

It was cold and all the blinds were down. I put my hand on the light switch but nothing happened.

Mom smiled at me in the dark. "I helped pull all those connections out seventeen years ago. The CG was tracking us and we thought they might have been using the building's wiring as a listening device. They were." We were on the second floor landing and she was looking around at the gloomy hallway, remembering.

I moved closer to Sam and touched his fingers. "What do we do now?"

She seemed to be surprised that we were still there with her. "I need to find Ted." She shivered, pulling herself back from wherever her thoughts had wandered.

Mom took out her display pad and opened it. "I shouldn't do this, but I have to know he's all right. It's risky. They could find us." She waited, wanting us to give her permission.

I looked at Winn and then at Sam. Winn answered for us. "Do it. I won't be able to enjoy my time here if he's still in danger."

She nodded, touched a few keys, and then disconnected.

"What did you tell him?"

She held the display up for us to read.

"Running through the snow?"

"He'll understand. He'll know right where we are and that we're safe for the moment." She started to shake her head, but it turned into another shiver. "Don't ask me how."

"No lights. Is there heat?"

A crooked smile touched her lips just before the light from the display pad winked out. "No. But there're lots of blankets."

Sam squeezed my hand to reassure me. I know that's how he meant it, but God help me, all I could think about was being under a stack of blankets with him.

I think Sam blushed. It was getting easier for us to feel each other's emotions. I know Mom felt it too because the way she looked at me, head tipped.

"Let me show you the room you and *Winona* will share, and then I'd like to put something on her eye before we try to find dinner."

We examined our room with its bare floors, single bed and one desk with a hard chair. I was about to protest that I didn't want to share a bed, but stopped myself. It seemed very petty given the circumstances. We examined Sam's room, Mom using the light of the display pad to show us that it looked the same.

"There're candles in the drawer if you want a little light and to save your display pad power. Keep the shades down though if you do. Don't even peek out. There's a bathroom down the hall that shares a wall with the apartment next door. We steal a little hot water from them. Use it sparingly."

Her pad dinged and she smiled when she opened it.

I read it aloud when she showed it to me. "I'm buying the beer?"

"That's a good sign. He's safe and we have new allies. Remind me to tell you about how we talked our way out of New Palisade some time." She sighed. "It took a lot of beer and a *lot* of dancing."

Winona leaned forward. "Dancing? You were a dancer on New Palisade?"

"Ms. Killdeer?" Mom warned her.

"Yes, ma'am. I work for you."

"Good. Now let's get your eye tended to."

Watching her putting salve in Winona's eye and touching healing sticks to her cheek by candle light made me feel like I'd stepped backwards in time a thousand years. Winn claimed it didn't hurt anymore, but I think that was just her being brave.

"What happens tomorrow?" Sam was still holding the candle while Mom finished with Winona.

"Cuza will be back in the morning. He's trying to set up a meeting for me with the leadership of the Bovita and then with the Council. If the political situation in the Warrens is as fractious as I'm afraid it is, we have a hard fight ahead of us. And I need Ted."

My heart skipped a beat. "I thought we were going home."

"You didn't notice when Boden changed that plan?" She glanced at Sam. "At least for some of us. *Mesa Vista* will be here in four or five days, if the CG lets them dock. I'm going to do everything I can to get you back up there."

"Thanks. There're times when I catch myself starting to feel like Winona, that I work for you."

She smiled at him with her eyes catching the candlelight and he blushed. I added learning how to smile like that to the list of things I wanted her to teach me.

We ate a dinner of cold, prepackaged synthetics while we sat on the stairs, a single candle providing light. I had wrapped myself in a blanket with another one on top that I was sharing with Winona. The cold didn't seem to bother Sam. Mom had a blanket, but it had slipped off her shoulders and she hadn't bothered to wrap herself up again. She shivered a couple of times while we ate. I don't think it had anything to do with being cold.

Winona was picking at the brown lump of 'food' in her hand, tearing off chunks and sniffing at each one before putting it in her mouth. "I've been thinking about the plan that the Tarakana put into Duse's head. It was flawed, but there might be some elements that we can build on. I wish I had seen more of it."

I nodded. "Most of it's gone, like a half remembered dream. I should talk to the Tarakana again. They may have a better plan now."

Winona and Mom stopped chewing and stared at me. "I don't mean the *bad* Tarakana colony, I mean Merrimac."

"Part of the Merrimac colony is down here?" Mom spoke quietly.

"I thought you knew. You didn't feel him on the shuttle?"

She shook her head.

"Really? There were—" I thought about it for a second, "—eighty-three of them on board. I thought you felt them."

Winona's eyes had gone large. "Are they here with us now?"

"A couple somewhere in the building, I think. I was going to try to find one after dinner and chat with him a bit. I suppose I'll need to touch him to get what I want."

I looked at Sam for support. He was looking at his shoes. "See!" I pointed. "Sam knew they were on board too. Can you feel the ones that are here?"

"One in the bathroom and one up on the roof."

"Yeah, I think you're right. That's even better than me. You're getting good at this."

"It's important that I go with you, MD. I need to talk to him too. And touch him. I'm not sure why, but I think it's *really* important to touch him together."

"Like hell you will." Mom interrupted before I could agree with him. "I don't have time to keep the two of you from doing the stupid things that your 'friends' keep trying to convince you are so important. Not if I'm going to keep us alive for the next forty-eight hours, or even until morning. Please," she took my hand and stared hard at Sam. "Please promise me that you won't do what they're trying to get you to do."

I stole a quick glance at Sam. He had the same defiance in his eyes that I was feeling. I swallowed hard before answering.

"No, I can't promise that. You *need* what Merrimac is offering. He can help you unite the clans and reach a settlement with the CG that doesn't involve mass murder."

"It's called war."

"And he needs our help to eliminate the bad Tarakana colony that's making things here even worse."

"Ah, now we're getting to it. What else does he want? You and Sam?"

"Yes. But I've convinced him that he has to wait for that."

Mom laughed. "Really? And you believe him? OK, then, let's *all* go touch the damn Tarakana."

She stood and there was a hooting sound that came from somewhere in the building. A sort of panic started to fill me. "That's not a good idea. They don't want you to touch them."

"So, he's still afraid of me?" She was smirking.

"Uh huh."

Winona was staring at her. "If they're afraid of you, how are you still alive? He seems to have no problem eliminating family members, or allowing them to die, once they've served their purpose. Alice's mother, Ted's mother, Sam's father. There's more."

Mom sat and took another bite of her dinner before answering. "I don't know. I guess he still needs me. For Mala Dusa's sake, I suppose. I know they don't like me connected to their group mind. I understand them too well. The last time it almost felt like *I* could control *him*."

"Really?" Winn was excited. "Now I want to touch him too. The way you've described the group mind, all thinking as one, the twisted passageways of thought... I want to see it, explore it."

"Too late." Sam shook his head. "They're gone."

"But not for long." Mom was squinting at Sam like he was a threat that needed to be eliminated, and soon. "And not very far away. Not while the two of you are here. Finish dinner." She pushed her hair back away from her eyes. "God, I need Ted."

After we finished eating, Mom excused herself to go 'think about how to pull off a miracle'. I wasn't sure if she meant uniting the clans or just surviving long enough to find a way home. After a few minutes, I excused myself too and followed her. I tapped gently on her door and then opened it. She was sitting at the desk with her head down resting on her arms. She had her display pad out, but left it turned off.

"I can help, if you'll let me. I still remember most of the plan, more than I want to, more than I admitted to Winona. There was so much blood that I've been trying *not* to remember it."

She lifted her head and smiled wistfully at me. "I can't think. I thought I was over this, being so dependent on your father being close by. When I try to think through what we need to do next, the only thing that comes into my head is that Ted's not here, that he's in trouble, and that he's not here."

"Is that from what you experienced when you touched Merrimac together?"

"No, I had this problem before that. Ted told me it's part of being in love. I think it's part of a deep personality flaw."

"If it is, I'll bet it's a flaw that he loves about you."

She tipped her head, studying me. "That sounds so much like something your mother would have told me, if she hadn't hated me."

"Did she really hate you?"

"No. I think she wanted to, just like I wanted to hate her. We couldn't quite do it."

I laid down on her bed. "Tell me what it was like when you and Dad touched Merrimac together."

"Why?"

"You know why. I'm *going* to do it. I have to. It's... inevitable."

"You really believe Winona is right about you and Sam?"

I waited a moment before answering, pretending to think about it. If Winona believed it, then I knew it must be true. Winn was never wrong. "I do. We've never touched Merrimac together, but I can feel Sam's emotions better than I can feel yours or Dad's. I can feel him right now, actually."

"At what range?"

I put my arm over my eyes. "He and Winn are exploring the apartments. They're downstairs now where the old kitchen used to be. Sam's happy, laughing at something she's telling him."

I could feel what Mom was feeling too. I opened my eyes and grinned at her. "And *you're* worried about what your grandchildren are going to be like."

She rolled her eyes. "Grandchildren. You're sixteen, Mala Dusa. Don't talk to me about grandchildren."

I blushed, breaking the connection with Sam, who I knew had been aware of me touching him. "Not for years. I'm not stupid. So what's it like, being inside the group mind with someone?"

"He'll be able to see your soul."

"Oh."

"Not ready for that, are you?"

"All of it? It worries me enough when I think about God seeing into my soul."

"All of it. Every bit of darkness, every scar from things you've done. When he sees what a monster you really are, you'll wonder how he can even stand to be in the same room as you."

"But Dad loves you more than anything."

She chuckled. "He's a bit of a monster himself. It makes him forgiving."

"So he and my real—He and Alice, they did it too?"

I felt all the doors in her mind slam shut and I was sorry I'd asked. "Of course."

I felt the hatred in her, not for Alice, but for the Tarakana. "That's going to make it hard for us to work with them, you know."

"I *won't* work with them."

"What did they do to you?"

"Ask your father."

"He's not here."

She took a deep breath and held it a moment before it came out in a ragged sigh. "Ted's not perfect, but he's perfect for me. I love him more than life. On Dulcinea, on the ship afterwards, I was willing to die rather than not be with him, and I knew he felt the same way about me. He loved me despite what I had been and despite all that I'd done. No one has *ever* loved more than we love. Yet three months after we were separated on Cleavus, he was in love with Alice, married to her, and with a child on the way."

"Me."

She looked at me. "Yes, you, who I love. But that's what the Tarakana did; they took Ted's heart away from me and gave it to your mother because they wanted, no because they *needed*, you. I never got him back, not all of him."

"Because of me."

She shook her head hard. "Dusa, I love you completely. You share my emotions so you know it's true. This wasn't your doing, or Ted's, or even Alice's. Merrimac did this. And I'd kill him if I could. The whole colony."

After a moment, I told her, "Let me help you think, if I can. You always say my brain works like Dad's. Maybe if I tell you what I remember it will help you."

"OK." She unfolded her pad. "We can try."

"You should get a new one of those."

"Why? This one still works fine."

"It's so bog standard." I shook my head and propped the pillow up behind me. "OK, the first thing you need to do is take over the Bovita clan. In the outline they gave me, that involves eleven murders." I looked over at her, hoping she would disagree.

"That does seem a bit extreme. How about we try it with none? I still have friends in the Bovita."

Some of the tension left me. "Good. I just got that new sword. I don't want to get it dirty." I grinned at her.

She chuckled. "Where *is* your sword, anyway?"

"Back in my room."

"You should keep it with you. We aren't really safe here. And we should start your training tomorrow."

All the tension came back.

"Let's assume the Bovita are on our side," she continued. "What comes next?"

"Ambush at the Council of Clans. Forty-two more murders."

"Hmm. 'Ambush' is a good word for what I have in mind, but I don't think we'll have to kill anyone. Well, not more than one or two. Maybe three."

I laid on my back and walked through the rest of the plan with her. The body count kept going up, but slowly, and the timeline kept stretching away. Two months became five, and finally six. Every day in the Warrens, every step in the plan was a risk; a chance taken that one of us would die. Mom seemed happy or at least satisfied when we were finished. I was praying that Dad was somewhere working on a better plan, one that would see us back home.

The apartment was colder when I made my way back to my room three hours later. Winona was already in bed, wearing a t-shirt that she had found in a box in the closet.

"Left you something on the desk," she said sleepily.

I looked next to the candle. "Toothbrush?"

"Toothbrush."

I bent over and kissed her.

"Bleah. Go brush your teeth. You smell like that gunk we had for dinner."

"Yes, ma'am."

I rummaged through the box when I returned, settling on something almost soft and with long sleeves. I slid under the covers next to Winn.

"I am on my side of the bed," she informed me. "This is your side." She traced an imaginary line down the pillow and across the top blanket.

"Uh huh." I put my feet against her leg to warm them up and snuggled against her shoulder. "Mom and I are going to overthrow a government. Want to help?"

She rolled her head over to look at me, good eye open. "OK, sure." She yawned. "But sleep first, overthrow government in the morning." She kissed my forehead.

I closed my eyes and felt for Sam, wanting to touch him one more time before I slept. He was dreaming something happy, so I slid in and joined him, falling asleep while we held hands and walked through an alien landscape.

CHAPTER 17

PLANS AND REALITY

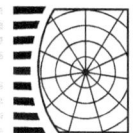

"Where ya goin', Duse?"

I had spent the last fifteen minutes working on extracting myself from our bed without waking her. Move foot, listen. Lift blanket, listen. Put foot on floor, listen. I was pulling my pants on when Winn's sleepy voice stopped me.

I sighed. "Go back to sleep."

"You know Sam needs his sleep too. Yesterday was kind of stressful for him. Come back to bed. You need sleep more than you need what you were planning on doing with Sam."

I smiled to myself. It wasn't often that Winona misread my intentions.

"It so happens that I'm not going to Sam's room." As soon as I said it, I knew it was a mistake. My hand was on its way to cover my mouth. I redirected it to my forehead. Winn probably would have let me go to visit Sam.

"Thought so." There was a smug smile in her voice.

I finished pulling up my pants and sat in the chair looking at her, or at least looking in the direction of the bed. It was too dark to see anything other than dim shapes.

"Fine. Merrimac is up on the roof of the building next door to us and I'm going to go talk to him. Why he's next door and not on our roof, I have no idea."

"And you want to be an engineer?"

I blushed. "Heat signature."

The sheets rustled softly as she climbed out of the bed. "I better come with you. What time is it?"

"A little after 03:30."

She yawned. "Cold out here."

I tossed a heavy sweatshirt that matched the one I was wearing in her direction. "Hush. We still have to make it past Mom's room."

"Give me a minute. Need my sword. Do you have yours?"

"Yeah, but the belt doesn't work for me. It keeps sliding."

"You need hips."

"I need a lot of things."

We made it out into the hallway, moving slowly.

"Don't step there," she warned me with a whisper.

"Why not?"

"That one squeaks. Don't you remember?"

Winona remembered because she had stepped on it once and now had a mental map of every squeaky board she'd stepped on in the entire building. I paused near Mom's room and tried to feel if she was awake. It was risky, since she usually was able to feel my emotions before I felt hers. I took a step closer, concentrating. Then another step and another, until I was touching her door.

I shook my head, looking at Winn in the candlelight and whispered. "I should be able to feel something even if she's sound asleep."

I opened her door, worried now, and entered carefully. Winona followed close behind me. Mom's room was empty.

I held the candle high. "Her coat's gone. And her sword."

"She snuck out. Are you sure you're not related by blood?"

I ignored the question and spoke quietly to the empty room. "Mom, where *are* you?"

"Come on, let's go see Merrimac." Winn wiggled her fingers at me. "I want to touch him."

"I don't think that's a good idea. They're afraid of Hannah because her mind is complex, like theirs. I think having you on the inside would terrify them. You're liable to take over and never come back out."

"I think that's the nicest thing you've ever said to me."

"I meant it as a warning." I tried to sound stern. "If Merrimac knew what you are, the way you remember everything and *know* everything, I think he might kill you."

"I've considered that, and he might. You don't need me as much as you do your mom."

"I think I need you even more than her, that's why I don't want to risk you."

She smiled. "You love me enough to keep me safe."

"You won't go back to bed now even if I beg, will you?"

"Nope. I'm going to touch him. It's up to you to keep him from eliminating me afterwards."

I sighed. "At least Sam's still sleeping."

"Are you sure?"

I thought about it for a moment. "Yeah, sleeping..."

Winn was holding my arms. "You were swaying."

I blinked at her. "Was I?" I swayed, not able to help myself. "We were... dancing."

"Sure you were. Come on, we have Tarakana to touch. How were you planning on getting over there, anyway?"

"I don't know. Let's try to find some stairs or a ladder in here that provides roof access."

"Then what? The other building's a couple of meters shorter than this one, or don't you remember that either?"

"There's probably a ladder that connects them. Or we could jump."

"We'd break our legs in this gravity, and even if we didn't, how do we get back if there's no ladder?"

I sighed. "There's a ladder."

"He's already been in your head tonight, hasn't he?"

"I didn't want to worry you."

She looked at me in the dim light, worried. "How often do you hear him?"

I bit my lip. "All the time, at least since we were on the shuttle yesterday. I think he's worried about me too. He never leaves me anymore."

"No wonder you hear Sam's dreams."

I walked to where I knew there was a steep staircase leading up. "That part's kind of nice. I think he was in one of my dreams tonight too." I closed my eyes, remembering. "I need to be more careful what I dream about."

"You should be terrified that this is happening. It's not normal. It's not *human*."

I stopped at the top of the stairs where a narrow door opened out onto the roof, and looked down at her. She looked pretty in the candle light, her face all scrunched up with worry.

"I know. Instead, I feel excited, like I used to when my dad would take me adventuring when I was little. I can't wait to see what comes next."

She just kept staring at me. I tried to smile at her, but it was a weak effort. "Don't let me get lost, Winn. Now blow the candle out and we'll run to where the ladder leads down to the other apartment block. Ready?"

She nodded and we were in complete darkness when I pushed with all my weight against the door. The creak of the hinges was louder than I expected and it wouldn't open all the way. We squeezed out and ran.

Chairs, makeshift awnings, and children's toys littered the roof of the other building. Laundry floated above it all, hanging like flags from long ropes. I collapsed into one of the chairs and tried to catch my breath, more winded than after five kilometers on one of *Vista's* trails.

Winn was standing next to me, looking at the stars. It was a clear night for the Warrens; it didn't even smell very bad.

"That's Alnitak," she said, pointing. "And Alnilam, I think. I don't know where Mintaka is. Everything's so different. Orion was the first constellation my dad taught me. I want to see it again, with the stars all back in the right places. I miss my parents."

"I thought you didn't get along."

"We don't, not always. That's as much my fault as theirs. They don't understand me and I do everything I can to be difficult. But I love them and I know they love me."

I looked at her next to me, her face still turned upward to the stars. "We're going to make it home, Winn. Don't worry."

She sat in the chair across from me. "So, where is he?"

I shrugged, examining my feet. "Waiting for something, I think. I don't know what, but he's close by."

"Why aren't you wearing shoes?"

I wiggled my toes at myself. "I wanted to be stealthy. I'm stealthier when I wear just my bare feet, don't you think?"

"I think you're planning to warm them up by putting them against my legs once we get back to our room."

"Good idea."

We sat and looked at the stars for a while, waiting. I was drifting, almost asleep again, when I felt him close by, almost next to me. "Sam," I whispered, my eyes popping open.

A blanket dropped across my lap. "Maybe this will help keep you warm."

I jumped out of the chair and almost fell onto Winona. "How did you do that? You were sleeping and dreaming about... well, you were dreaming. How could you sneak up on me?"

He blushed, so at least that was some compensation. "I heard you open the door. I think everyone in the Warrens must have heard it. After that, I followed you. I saw you from the other roof and you looked cold sitting there, so I went back and got a blanket."

I sat down, my heart still pounding.

"We're waiting for Merrimac," Winona told him. "Now that you're here—Ah, there he is."

I felt something warm covering my feet. Merrimac was there, big brown eyes staring at me while warmth moved up my legs.

I scratched his head, feeling the welcoming hum of the Tarakana inside him. "Now I have my Sam with me and Hannah's off chasing phantoms."

Winona frowned at me and asked, "Mala Dusa, do you know where your mom is now?"

The question confused me. "She died, Winn. They shot her, not far from here, and she died. Merrimac was there, I see it in their memory. He tried to stop it from happening, but mom stepped in front of Hannah at the last second and... and she died. I never did get to meet her."

She took my hand and leaned toward me, pressing her forehead against mine. "I know that. What about Hannah? Do you know where *she* is?"

"Oh, Hannah!" Joy pushed all my sadness away. I leaned forward and whispered to her. "Not gonna tell ya. It's a secret."

Winona sighed and her head tipped just like Hannah's always does when she looks at me. "Can you tell me anything about her?"

"Merrimac is a little afraid of her. You should see her use a sword, and she knows dozens of languages. She plans the most perfect picnics and camping trips. You've *got* to try her waffles sometime."

Winn was smiling at me so I kept talking. "She loves me, and my dad, and I love her." I twisted my fingers in Merrimac's fur. "But I'm afraid of her a little bit too, aren't you? She hates these guys a lot, but I forgive her for that. I understand now. They're going to keep her safe for me anyway because she's almost like my mom."

"She is your mom."

"No, I mean her *soul* is like my mom's."

Sam was sitting next to me, looking worried, like Winona. I leaned toward him and said gently, "You can touch him too, if you want. Just don't look at me too closely, OK? You might not like me very much anymore."

"How much bad could you have done in sixteen years?" He put his hand on my cheek and I leaned into it. "I lied to you when we first met because I was embarrassed, and I walked away from you when you needed me most. I'm a terrible person. Maybe when you see it, you'll finally be able to dump me before it's too late."

I smiled, loving him so much. Something wrapped around us, warm where it touched my skin. I think I heard Winona gasp and then all I could see was the group mind of the Tarakana. There were hundreds of pieces now instead of the seven that I had felt on *Wandering Star*. And that's what they were; just pieces of a single organism connected by thought, making one Merrimac.

Sam was there with me. I tried to hide from him so he wouldn't see who I really was. I didn't want him to see all the bad, selfish, cruel, things I had done. But there was nowhere to hide, just like Hannah had warned me. So I stood there in that other world, feeling naked and exposed, and let him look into my soul while I marveled at the glowing, beautiful Sam that seemed to, somehow, still love me.

I touched him, trying to forgive where he felt ashamed for walking out of the Mission that one night. There were other scars too, older and deeper. I wanted to touch them all and help him heal.

Before I could, there was a voice calling to me from far away, insistent and angry. "Damn it, Duse, stop humming that stupid song and come back to me." It was quiet for a moment and I started to fall back into Sam. "OK, if you won't come out, I'm coming in."

Looking at Winona inside the group mind was blinding. I felt tiny and pale in comparison. She was only there for a moment before she broke us free. Or maybe Merrimac pulled away from her, I'm not sure which. He was gone when I could see again and Winona was crying while Sam held her.

"Why did you make me do that?" she sobbed.

"You said you wanted to touch him!" My head was pounding.

"But not with *you* in there too. Now you know what kind of person I am. You could see *all* of me."

I opened and closed my mouth a couple of times before I could answer. I pulled her away from Sam and wrapped my arms around her. "I'm in awe of you, Winona Killdeer," I whispered in her ear. "You're amazing and I love you."

She looked at me like I might be mocking her. "Really?"

"Really. Even if you did frighten Merrimac away."

She shivered while I used my sleeve to wipe her tears and her nose. "I did, didn't I?"

"You did. What else did you see in there? Sam and I were kind of distracted. I was hoping to find a battle plan or escape plan or something. Instead, all I saw was a blinding bright Winona."

"Which do you want, battle or escape? There were at least five or six of each that they were thinking about at the same time. I think we need your mom to sort them all out. There's parts even *I* don't understand; dependencies on the seasons, and clan affiliations, and somehow it's about Venice back on Earth. There's also something about how your mom first took over the Bovita clan and how she, she... Oh." Winona's eyes were getting big again.

"What? How she what?"

Winn shook her head. "Doesn't matter. Where's Hannah?"

"Merrimac made her think I was going to sneak off to the market tonight. She was camped out there waiting to intercept me. She should be back by..." I glanced at my watch. "Ten minutes ago?"

I turned and gave Sam a hard kiss on the mouth. "We gotta run. Do you still love me?"

"Stupid question. Race you to the door?"

I ran, Sam right behind me, but the wind was faster than us both. We stomped down the stairs, heedless of the noise we were making. Mom was waiting at the bottom, burning precious display pad power to better look us over.

I could feel the relief in her, buried somewhere behind the expression on her face that was promising us all a slow death.

"Look at you three, enough guilt on your faces for a hundred vásárló."

I stepped forward, feeling brave. "It's my fault. They just followed me."

Her head tipped slightly. Was that a flicker of pride?

"Good. Then you can explain to them why they're going to miss breakfast while we try to make it to the next safe house *without dying*. Do you have anything in your rooms that you need?"

"Just my shoes," I mumbled.

She glanced down at my feet, laughed, and rolled her eyes. "Run and get them. Meet us downstairs."

"Yes, ma'am." I ran.

The path was less convoluted than the one we had taken the day before. The sun wasn't quite breaking the horizon when mom dodged into a small workshop and led us to an apartment above it. It smelled like old oil and dirt.

"That was longer than the route we took yesterday." Winona was examining her shoes, pealing something black and sticky from one of them. "Almost four kilometers?"

"Complaining, Ms. Killdeer?" Mom sounded like she was still angry. If she was, I couldn't feel it. She was just tired. And... lonely.

"I miss him too," I told her.

"It doesn't help me when you do that. I've about had enough of my brain being poked at today."

"Sorry."

She sighed. "I was sitting in the market square for over an hour, convinced that you were on your way there, in mortal danger. Then I suddenly realized that I had no idea where that thought had come from. I hadn't even checked your room before I left. Damn Tarakana. I hope it was worth it for you."

"Ms. Weldon, please tell me about the Trade Guild of Venice and how they're involved."

"Huh." Mom was looking at Winona, a bemused grin on her face. "If you got that out of them, it may well have been worth it. You were in there too?"

"Yes, ma'am, but only for a moment. I'm still trying to integrate everything I saw. I need help."

Mom nodded. "I don't doubt it. The group mind is a chaotic place."

She rubbed her eyes with the heels of her hands. She'd been doing that a lot lately. "Mala Dusa, there's a bakery a block and a half south of here. Go get us something for breakfast."

"But you said—"

"Are you hungry or not?"

"Hungry," I admitted. "But I don't have any money, not like they use here."

"You won't need any. There's always a basket out front. And take Sam with you. You don't need his protection with the damn Tarakana following you everywhere, but I need to talk to Winona alone. The emotional leakage coming from your brain is giving me a headache. I talked to your dad while I was waiting for you at the market. When you get back I'll tell you about the Trade Guild and—"

"You talked to Dad? Where is he? Is he all right? What's he doing to get us out of here? When—"

"He's fine, Mala Dusa. He's safe. Breakfast, then we'll talk."

I forced myself to shut up. "We'll be back soon."

"Oh, and before you go, look around downstairs for a rag, not too dirty, but maybe a little oily. I need to clean this."

She removed her sword from its sheath and laid it across a table. Drying blood stained the tip.

I had my hand over my mouth, so Sam asked for me. "There were troubles this morning?"

"A couple of optimists stopped me on the way back to the safe house. I didn't hurt them as badly as this looks, but they'll remember me. Good for my reputation." She grinned, like it was no big deal, almost as if she'd enjoyed it.

Sam took the hand that wasn't covering my mouth. "Let's go, MD. I'm hungry too." He was smiling while we walked down the stairs.

"I might have gotten her killed." I had my eyes closed, perching on the edge of a desk while Sam was rummaging through workbenches and looking in cabinets. He finished peering behind a lathe before answering. "Not likely. I can't imagine your mom ever losing a fight like that."

"She has scars," I whispered. "One here," I touched my stomach, "that lines up with one here." I touched my back.

"Oh. She always seems so confident, so powerful, like she could never be defeated. She makes me want to, I don't know..."

"Join her on a noble quest? Fight by her side, vanquish her foes?" He blushed. Ha!

"She's amazing. I like her. She's done a good job raising you. You're a lot like her."

My turn to blush. "I'm *nothing* like her. I'm not confident, or powerful, or brave, or..."

He kissed me, which I needed. I put my arms around his waist and pulled him into me. It turned into a long kiss.

He pulled back from me after a moment and smiled, his eyes looking into mine. "I, uh, I should run these rags up to your mom now before she comes down and sees what we're doing. I'm not sure which of you is more dangerous."

I glanced down to where his hips were pushed up against mine, biting my lip. "I am. Hurry back."

We walked out into the morning sunlight holding hands. No one paid any attention to us other than the merchants calling to the passersby to come see the treasures they had for sale. Our clothes were like what everyone else was wearing; a little old, a little worn, a lot stained, not quite the right size. My sweatshirt looked like something I would have tossed into the collection box at church back home. I put the hood up, not wanting anyone to see me.

"Worried about being recognized?" Sam smiled over at me, I think. My peripheral vision was impaired.

"Something like that."

He stopped and tipped his head to look at me inside my hood. "This emotional connection thing we seem to share now, it's, um, I can tell what you're really feeling, you know?"

I sighed and tried to continue down the street. He wouldn't let me. "You're embarrassed. About what?" He answered himself after a moment when I refused to speak. "More than embarrassed. You're ashamed, ashamed of the way you look?"

He pulled me out of the flow of traffic into a doorway and pushed my hood away from my face, lost in the wonder of being able to feel my emotions. I tried to block him, but I could never do that, not with my parents, not with Sam.

"I can see it in your head, you think you look... poor."

"Shut up."

"Why? Why do you feel that way? You're an amazing, caring person. You left home to do Mission work here, to help these people."

I felt him reading me, boring deeper, and it was worse than when we had been in the group mind, more personal than when Hannah tried to know what I was feeling. "Get out," I managed to whimper, and he was gone so suddenly that I swayed.

"Mala Dusa, you're better than that."

"No, I'm not."

"Rich girl, privileged and caring. You *do* love these people, but you want to do it from a position of power. It makes you feel good to help them when you're in control. But now... Now you're one of them, not knowing where your next meal will come from, wearing donated clothes, and unsure if you'll see the next sunrise."

I slapped him. Not hard, but I could feel the shock and pain it caused. He reached for me, and for a moment I thought he'd hit me. Instead, he pulled my hood back up.

"Let's go. Winona and your mom are expecting us to come back with breakfast for them."

We walked in silence the rest of the way. Sam's emotions were ragged, churning. I didn't know what he was feeling and I don't think he knew either. I was feeling miserable.

The bakery had a basket on the side of the building with loaves and rolls that had gone stale or were slightly burned, free to anyone in need. There was part of my brain that was yelling at me not to take any, that there was *no way* that I was in need. I had been hungry when we'd left the workshop. Now I had no appetite.

I picked up a loaf and looked at Sam with one eye, the other one hidden behind my hood. "I really *am* that bad."

He took the bread from me and added to the others in his arms. "I had no right to say those things to you."

"Give me a couple." We split the bread between us and started back the way we had come. "I told you that you wouldn't like what was inside my head."

"I think Winona's right about you."

"She usually is. What specifically?"

"She said there's a good woman inside you, once we get her attention. And that you're worth loving."

"Even Winona's wrong sometimes. I *hit you* for no good reason."

"You had a reason."

"No, I didn't. Just stupid pride." I looked around at the people on the street. "I'm not sure I care about them at all. Maybe Trilby was right about the brutality here. It's infecting me. I've been scared almost every second since mom told us comms had been cut and I'm tired of it. And I'm cold." I tried to pull the hood closer around my face. "Cold all the time. I *need* friends like you and Winona. I need you too much to be pushing you away."

"How about if I promise to be more subtle and you promise not to hit me again."

I stopped and wanted to cry. I kissed his cheek, very gently, and pulled my hood down. "I'm sorry. I don't care how I look anymore as long as you don't mind being seen with me."

"Proud to be by your side."

"I *do* love that you're crazy."

"Uh huh. Maybe tonight I'll show you how much fun crazy can be."

I gave him my best shy grin, balanced the loaves on my left arm, and held hands with him while we walked.

"Trilby. I've been thinking about what she said to your mom when we were on the shuttle."

"Right before Mom shot her?"

"Yeah. That's something I'll always remember. But what Trilby said really wasn't much different from what I heard from the people at the embassy. I think that's what pissed off your mom so much. It's easy to fight against Boden and those like him. It's the citizens that she needs to win over. Most of them pity the people in the Warrens, some even want to help them, but none of them want these people as part of their society."

"They're like me. They help because it makes them feel good about themselves."

"You *are* better than that. I feel your heart."

I glanced up at him, doubtful.

"It's a good heart. It glows."

"You see what you want to see, but thank you." I squeezed his hand. That was when I finally understood a little piece of how Hannah and my dad stayed so much in love. It was impossible for me to stay mad at Sam when I could feel everything he felt. No secrets, no misunderstandings, and this vision he had of me in his head. I would never be able to live up to it, but I knew it wouldn't matter. He was going to be in love with me even when I was mad or frustrated with him. I knew there was more to learn and I was looking forward to exploring all of it with him.

When we got close to the workshop, he whispered to me, "Just keep walking."

"Why?"

"I should have let you keep your hood up. We've got a tail."

I felt like all the air had left my lungs and I couldn't catch my breath. I stumbled over the next crack in the jagged pavement because my legs were shaking. Sam caught my arm.

"Careful. She's probably just a fan of your video. Let's cut down this next alley and see what she has to say for herself."

I nodded slightly, terrified, trying to rest in the calm I felt in Sam's mind.

We turned sharply to the right and stepped back into shadow, waiting. Sam handed me the bread he was carrying and pulled his short gladius out.

My sword was still in its sheath. I had no idea how to use it other than as a pointy club.

A figure came around the corner hesitantly. Sam grabbed her shoulder with his left hand, the gladius ready in his right. He paused, and the girl's eyes looked as terrified as I felt.

"Who are you?" he demanded, sounding fierce.

I glanced at him. Yes, fierce, not adorable anymore.

"Katarina, sir. I want no trouble." She looked at the sword that was touching her stomach. "Please don't."

"Why were you following me?" I asked gently.

"You're her, the girl that was in the market. They say you're going to unite the Warrens." She touched one of the loaves of bread in my arms. "I thought maybe I could help you."

"How?"

Some of the confidence was coming back to her. "You're the daughter of Ysabeau Romee. You've more important work than gathering poverty bread. Come stay with my family if you need food and a warm place to sleep."

I was starting to like her, but Sam shook his head. "Not yet, Katarina. Thank you for your kind offer. You'll know when the time is right."

I frowned at him and he lowered his sword.

"I can go?"

"Yes, you should go."

She bowed slightly to Sam and left us.

"*Now* will you let me keep my hood up?"

Sam sighed and his hand was shaking as he sheathed his sword. "Yes, put it up. I want to circle around a bit before we go back into the workshop to make sure no one else recognized you."

I covered my head and was ready to go when I noticed Sam was still leaning against the wall. I touched his cheek.

"MD, I almost killed her. I was ready to. That was my plan; grab her shoulder as soon as she came around the corner and thrust as hard as I could just below the ribs. When I saw her face I hesitated."

"Good. She was a friend."

"If she had been an assassin, that moment of hesitation would have been enough for her to have put a bullet through your head." He looked around at the narrow, garbage-strewn alleyway. "I don't belong here. *You* don't belong here."

"And yet here we are. It's going to be OK. Mom promised to get you back up to your ship in two or three days. Then you'll be on your way to a *real* adventure."

He gave me a crooked grin. "Right. I keep forgetting."

I took his hand again, both of us shaking, and we walked around randomly for fifteen minutes before entering the workshop.

I laid the loaves on the table and smiled at Winn. She had her hair tied back and was looking very sharp and professional despite her stained sweatshirt.

Mom barely glanced at me. "Good, you had the sense to keep your hood up. We don't want anyone to recognize you out there."

I pushed my hood back and sighed heavily. Mom didn't look up from the chart she was creating, but her eyes closed like she was in pain.

"Tell me."

Sam told her.

She listened without comment until the end, and then nodded. "I can understand why you didn't kill her."

She turned back to her charts, and all I could hear echoing in my head was the unspoken second part of her sentence: *but you should have.*

She and Winona went back to working on their plans. How many deaths were in there already, line items on a to-do list?

"I'm cold." I told her.

"No heat. Put a sweater on under your sweatshirt. I think there're some downstairs."

Winona handed me a stale roll. "Eat, and then help us. No one knows the Tarakana like you do."

I looked at the roll like it was poison. "No, I can't." I pulled my hood back up and walked toward the stairs, feeling numb, the girl's terrified eyes haunting me. Sam would have killed her for me. Next time he wouldn't hesitate. "I can't."

He grabbed my elbow when I passed him and started to follow me.

Hannah called to him. "Samuel, I could use your help too. Let her go."

"Mala Dusa, they need help. It's important. Stay, and at least hear news about your dad."

"I can't, not even for that." He released me and I felt a new emotion from him, strong at first, then fading as I walked down the stairs—disappointment.

I didn't care. I rummaged through the old workshop, looking for a sweater at first, then finding other things, wondrous things.

234

CHAPTER 18
TRYING TO STAY WARM

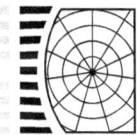

A couple of hours later, I tromped up the stairs carrying two heavy buckets of paint. I let them slam down on the floor, my shoulders aching. Ten percent over Earth gravity doesn't sound like much until you have to live with it.

"What you got there, Duse?" All three of them were staring at me.

"Paint. I'm going to paint the walls and ceiling in that back office and then I'm going to heat it up. Anyone that wants to sleep in there with me will be warm tonight." My eyes darted to Sam. I didn't want them to because I was still mad at him, but my eyes weren't listening to me.

Mom sighed. "Paint?"

"More than paint. The shop down there must have been in the pressure suit business, among other things. It looks like they built and maintained the kind of suits used in putting together structures in open space. There're big containers of the ceramic micro glass bubbles that they use for insulation, so I dumped a bunch into some paint and about broke my arms stirring them in. This stuff should provide enough of a barrier that we can actually be warm."

Winn was looking at me with her head tipped. "What will you use for a heat source?"

"There's a box of chemical heaters down there, but if this is as thermally reflective as I think it is, just body heat might be enough. Assuming we put enough bodies together in there." I was looking at Sam again.

Mom's emotions were hovering somewhere between amused and irritated. "I'd rather have you helping with planning than slapping paint around. You and Merrimac are a bigger part of this than I want to admit."

"I've been thinking about that while I was down there exploring and stirring. I can't do it. I *won't* do it." I sat down on one of the buckets. "I'm defective, that's what Merrimac thinks, and he's right. He's hoping to fix the line in the next generation; it's why he's brought Sam and me together."

Sam was staring at me, a little shock on his face. "What?" I asked him. "It's what we are to the Tarakana, breeding stock. It'd be wrong to pretend that their way of thinking, or even their motives are remotely human. He's fond of me, but it's not human fondness, not even the way we're fond of pets. I love you, Samuel. Knowing that I have *no choice* but to love you doesn't make me love you any less."

"You're not defective."

I laughed. "Oh, yes I am. I feel it all the time. They mixed together Ted and Alice and they got me. I think in straight lines like Dad, and everything scares me like my mom. Better luck next time, Merrimac."

I turned to Hannah. "I won't fight. I won't kill. I won't help you plan to fight and kill. I know it's necessary and I know it's the right thing to do, but not for me. That girl this morning that you think Sam should have eviscerated? I looked into her eyes. She was terrified that she was about to die, but only for a moment. Then she offered to help us unite the clans so we could go do," I waved my hands at the table where they were working, "all that. Fighting, killing, it's what the people here want, and in the end, there will be a better life for those that survive. Me? I'm defective, so just let me go paint and try to stay warm until Merrimac gets tired of me, or the clans or Boden find me and kill me, OK?"

I stood and looked around. "Damn, I forgot the brush."

Hannah laughed. "You see that, Winona? Sam? If you've ever wondered what her *real* mom was like, that's it, right there. She's just one step away from being full-on Alice, and I blame myself for her falling short."

I waited for it, waited for her to insult my mom and me. "What step is that?"

"Alice would have found a way to unite the clans, defeat Boden and get us back home without shedding a single drop of blood. All your life I've fought against you learning how to manipulate people the way she did, but it's in you. It's why I want your help now. I can't do this without killing a few people, more than a few, to be honest. Maybe you can find a better way?"

"You said I think in straight lines, like Dad."

"That doesn't mean you can't be a shrewd, manipulative... person, like Alice."

I shivered. "OK, sure. But can I do it while I paint? I'm still cold. And I want to know what Dad told you last night."

She tapped her watch. "It'll be lunch time soon and I have business in the market. You three paint to your heart's content and I'll bring back something to eat in an hour or so. Winona can fill you in on what Ted's been up to. Ms. Killdeer, if I'm not back after *two* hours..."

"We'll come looking for you."

"No, you'll work on finishing that sub-routine that gets you back up to the space dock. Are we clear?"

"You know we'll come looking for you."

"You've spent too much time with my daughter. Just lie to me."

"We'll abandon you to your fate and catch the next shuttle out."

"Perfect."

She looked at me, head tipped, studying my face. "I love you, in case I haven't said it recently."

"Thanks. I'm not very easy to love."

She chuckled. "Loving you is the easy part. Are there any more sweatshirts like that downstairs?"

"A few, hanging in the exercise room, outside the showers."

"There're showers?"

"Yeah, but no hot water." I shivered, remembering how cold the water had been when I'd put my hand in it.

She touched my cheek and whispered, "Now's the time, Dusa. Scheme and manipulate and help us find a way out of this mess. Use Merrimac and anything else you can think of."

I was shaking while she disappear down the stairs. She was scared. "I love you too, Mom," I said out loud even though she was already gone.

Winn was standing next to me. "What color?"

"Color?"

"Yeah, what color's the paint?" She kicked one of the buckets. "Did you at least make it pretty?"

I sighed. "It was the only color I could find." I tipped the bucket so she could read the label.

237

"Zinc chromate. So it's green?"

"Kind of like the mashed up peas they serve us at lunch sometimes."

"Bleah."

"Bleah," I agreed, smiling at Sam and sticking out my tongue.

He just shook his head. "I'll go find us some brushes. We need to be done by the time she gets back. That plan needs *a lot* of work." Sam was scared too.

He went down and I asked Winona, "We're not going to make it, are we?"

She shrugged. "The plan's not done yet, but Sam should be fine. We'll get him out of here as soon as *Mesa Vista* docks, so like three days at most. And there's always your dad. He's been busy."

"Tell me."

She thought about it for a moment. "I should start at the beginning. The Venice Trade Guild traces its origins to the founding of the Most Serene Republic of Venice in the eighth century."

"Winn? *Please* don't start at the beginning."

She frowned at me. "You won't have context, but OK. Your dad reached the *Orso Ipato* in time to warn them that the CG was about to impound all Union ships in dock. They were able to seal up and unlatch before Boden and the CG could seize them, the only ship to do so. The Guild was grateful."

"I don't imagine Boden was too happy about it. I'd like to have seen his face as he watched them drifting away."

"He wasn't pleased. He wanted your dad as much as he wanted that ship and her cargo, and he wasn't going to let a couple thousand meters of vacuum keep him away. He and his security detachment shuttled over there and demanded entry. Captain Checchi let them board, but they never made it past the shuttle bay."

"Then where's Boden now?" I was hoping he was still up there, imprisoned in a small room with bad synthetic food and recycled water to drink.

"Your dad said Checchi didn't respond well to being threatened, so she, um, well Boden's still there, tethered to the side of the ship."

"How did they get him to put on a pressure suit?"

"They didn't. The Guild doesn't mess around, Duse. It's how they've lasted this long. They'll keep him strapped to the side of that ship all the way back to Earth as a message to anyone else that might mess with them.

238

I've heard that Guild ships that were seized on a couple of other planets have already been released."

I had my hand over my mouth to hold it in, but I giggled anyway.

"Are you OK?"

"Uh huh. I shouldn't laugh."

"Yes you should. I've been trying to find a picture of him, but the Guild hasn't posted one yet. Probably waiting for him to become a bit more desiccated."

I tried to feel sorry for him, but couldn't. I turned my back to Winona so she wouldn't see the way I was smiling.

"Your dad did another favor for the Guild too. He showed them how to use an optical telescope to find the DSHs."

"Did he tell RuComm too?"

"No, that was the favor. The Guild will sell the information to RuComm and the other merchant companies. In return, they gave him a discount on our tickets back home."

"Not free tickets?"

Winona laughed. "No, just getting a discount from them is a pretty rare event. *And* they gave him a full refund on the tickets you held for the *Orso Ipato*. That must have really hurt. Now he's trying to convince the Guild to negotiate with the Council of Clans instead of the CG for terms and fees at the Bodens Gate dock. It's a tough sell, though. The clans don't have much of a reputation for stability, and the Guild prizes stability over almost everything else other than profit."

"Enter Mom."

"Yeah. Hannah doesn't have much time to pull it off." She stared at me. "You may want to try supporting her."

I nodded and leaned forward, pulling the hair away from my forehead. "Hit me there Winn, I deserve it."

"Well, that could have gone better."

"What are you talking about, Winona? It's perfect." We had started with the ceiling, worked down the walls, including the door, and finished in just under an hour. Fortunately, there hadn't been any windows to cover.

"I'm not sure you're supposed to get this stuff on your skin." Sam was trying to wipe some of it off his arm. I think he was just spreading it out.

"I wouldn't worry about your skin," Winona comforted him. "I think the fumes will kill us all first."

"It says that it comes off with soap and water. See?" I held the empty bucket up by their faces.

"We don't have any soap."

"And you said the water is like ice."

I looked around the office. "You know, I think it's getting warmer in here already."

"Come on." Winona grabbed my hand.

"Where we goin'?"

"Shower. This stuff stinks and we need to get it off of us."

"You're kidding, right? And besides, I like that green in your hair. It's a nice contrast to the black. Sam? Tell her, Sam. We don't need showers."

My Samuel betrayed me. "I'll wait outside with a couple of towels for you, if I can find any. I'll at least try to find some sort of clean rags. And there're coveralls in about twenty different sizes in the lockers."

I undressed while I whimpered and then screamed as soon as the water hit me. Winona was there with me, scrubbing my head and hands and face, while I tried not to shake too much to get the pretty green highlights out of her hair.

Then, after four or five minutes of agony, the most miraculous thing happened. The water started to get warm, then became almost too hot. I closed my eyes and let it pound on me.

"Share." Winn pushed me out of the way. I put my arms around her and we grinned at each other like we'd never had a hot shower before.

"This can't last." Winn was clean now, and I assume I was too since she'd stopped trying to rub my skin off.

"Right. We need Sam in here." I leaned away from the water briefly, and yelled. "Sam, we need you in here!"

"Really, Duse? I know he's seen all of you, but…"

Sam came in looking at us to see what was wrong while he tried *not* to look at us. My Sam is always a gentleman. Mostly.

"Is that steam?"

"It is," I answered. "Get in here quick before it goes away."

He blinked at me. "Um, OK."

"We're just leaving," Winona gathered what dignity she could, along with a small towel and a dusty looking coverall. Sam started to get undressed.

She took my hand, pulling me out into the main workshop.

"Wait. I want to stay a minute. Or two or three. What if he needs something?"

She closed the door behind us and tossed me a towel. "You'll have plenty of time to watch Samuel take showers. Years, probably. Now get dressed. You're already starting to get cold again and your mom will be back any minute. You want her to find you in there naked, watching Sam?"

"Don't care," I huffed, pulling a pair of coveralls on over a thermal shirt and pants. "He's pretty."

"Yes, he is pretty."

The way she said it sounded sad. "Winn, why can't I feel your emotions? I should be able to since the Tarakana connected us. You sound sad."

She had a smug smile on her lips while she bent over to put on her shoes. "I'm blocking you. If you want to know what I'm feeling, ask me."

I sighed. "I can't block anybody. Dad tells me that I've always been that way, I broadcast." I took her hand. "Am *I* making you sad?"

She kissed me. "Not sad, more worried, maybe jealous. I'm happy that you're happy. I can feel it whenever you look at him or he looks at you. I still don't believe Merrimac is your friend, and I don't like him, but he's a hell of a matchmaker."

"I'll ask him about you next time I see him. I'm still keeping an eye out so you can have a freak of your own."

I felt *that* in her, the sharp flash of fear. "I'd prefer that he forget that I exist. Just keep me in your prayers, OK? I think God listens to you."

"Constantly," I assured her.

Sam joined us, already completely dressed.

He looked at me and I wouldn't have blocked him from knowing what I was feeling even if I could have.

He swallowed hard and looked at Winona. "Hannah's not back yet?"

"No, you'll have to wait a bit longer for lunch."

"That wasn't the only thing I was worried about."

"I know, but I'm trying not to know everything you're feeling. It's distracting, and we should be back upstairs planning."

"OK, I'm hoping MD can reduce our body count. What were we up to, fifteen?"

"Fifteen for the initial consolidation, assuming no collateral damage. Then the messy work starts."

"At least that's less than what the bad Tarakana colony here was trying to get us to do." I followed them up the stairs, still trying to get my sword to sit properly. "I should return this thing."

Winn turned, her face too close to mine for me to focus on her. "Your mom is starting us on pell training tonight. You need to learn to use it because there might come a time when you have to save my life, or Sam's. Please don't argue with her anymore about it. It'll be good exercise for you, if nothing else."

I nodded, barely moving my head. Winona gets a little intense when she's scared.

We worked through mom's plan for clan unification and I was able to save the lives of eight people I'd never met. It increased the risk, playing them off against each other, finding ways to earn their support rather than killing them outright, but if it worked, we'd have eight allies that would be dead otherwise. And I began to see a broader plan and my role in it along with Merrimac's. Hannah was right about how none of it would work without us.

When I looked at Sam and Winona going through each detail, I realized they couldn't see it. It was brilliant and subtle and the more I looked, the clearer it became. Winona had been right next to mom when she'd created it, but Winn couldn't see it. Only I could.

When we finished, I pulled my sleeve back and looked at my watch. "Two and a half hours. I'm going out to find her."

I put my hand on the pommel of the sword and pulled it out, slow and awkward.

"Just leave it here, Duse. Having Sam and me escort you might bluff someone into thinking you're more important than you are. It could work to our advantage."

I laid the sword across the table. "I'm nobody."

"You're the Princess Mala Dusa, and we will defend you to the death." Sam was smiling, but I knew he was serious.

"Keep your shoulders back and your head high. Now let's go get your mom."

"Not dressed like this. There was a duster coat down there, and, damn it, I'm going to be warm."

Once we were downstairs, I stripped off the coveralls and put the coat on over my shirt and pants. It was heavy leather and reached almost to the floor. It was perfect.

We got out on the street and Sam warned me, "We should find a hat for you. You don't want to be recognized."

I smiled at him, feeling a familiar hum starting in the back of my head. "Oh yes, I do." I started walking, shoulders back, almost swaggering. "I want them *all* to know who I am and why I'm here."

Sam sighed and whispered to Winona, "Hang on, here we go."

By the time we were half way to the market square, we'd picked up a tail. More than a tail, it was like a parade.

"Duse, why are you doing this? This wasn't part of the plan."

"Sure it was. You just couldn't see it till now." I glanced back at her. "You *still* can't see it, can you? My mom, Alice, would be *so* proud of me. And so impressed with Hannah."

"Do you know what's going to happen?"

"Sure. I'm the bait. Your job is to get me to the market and up on the plinth where the statue used to be." I glanced back at them. "Where Hannah's already speaking."

"That was in the plan?" There was doubt in Sam's voice. I think he was doubting my sanity.

"Between steps four-twelve and four-thirteen, right before the escape branch."

A light went on in Winona's eyes. "You should have told us. This is *insane*. That means Hannah stayed out past the two hour mark intentionally, knowing we'd come. Why didn't you tell me when you saw it?"

"Because you would have tried to stop me. Because I'm the bait."

"The bait for what?"

"You'll see. It's why I had to be unarmed."

"But you were terrible even pulling the sword out of its sheath! Leaving it behind was my idea."

I gave her a quick grin.

"Wow." Sam was impressed.

Winona was more like horrified. "That was Alice? She manipulated and misled her *friends*?"

"She was worse. Much, much worse, so my dad tells me. He says it was part of why he was so attracted to her."

"I could see that." Sam was still impressed, and something more, something that would have to wait.

Winn looked over at him, eyes narrowed. "That's stupid."

He shrugged and I wanted to kiss him, but not yet. He had a role to play.

243

"When we get to the market, go straight to the plinth. There's going to be a crowd, so you may need to push people out of the way. Don't be gentle about it. Sam, I need you to lift me up there so I can stand next to my mom. Can you do that, and make it look graceful?"

"Sure, you weigh next to nothing, even here. Then what do I do?"

"Stand in front of us and look fierce, like you did this morning with the girl."

He nodded and gave me a test scowl. I tried not to smile. Maybe it would work better when he saw the crowd.

"And what am I supposed to do?"

"Winn, you stand next to him and look—" I turned toward her. "Yeah, that's perfect. You even scare me."

"I wish I could. You should be terrified instead of giddy. I can feel him in you, making you calm."

"I know. There're a lot of pieces of Merrimac nearby."

"Wasn't talking about Merrimac. So you're the bait. What are we supposed to do when the CG shows up to kill you? Swords against guns? Or maybe they'll just obliterate the whole market."

"The CG's not coming. They learned that lesson last time, about not creating martyrs. At least that's mom's assumption. I pray she's right."

"So who's coming?"

"Did you even look at Mom's overall plan or were you too focused on each individual step?"

Her eyes lost focus while she reviewed it in her mind. "She's paying off Merrimac and setting the hook for the Trade Guild at the same time." Her grumpy expression faded to adoration. "When I grow up, I want to be Hannah."

"What does she owe to Merrimac?"

I came to a complete stop when Sam asked that, because I realized that I knew the answer.

"She's buying back my soul." I looked at Winona. "Isn't she?"

"Keep walking or your followers will catch up to us."

I started walking, trying to feel the confidence again. "She and Dad could have convinced the Guild to support the Warrens behind closed doors with the Clan leadership if it wasn't for what I did."

"I suppose so," Winona replied.

"Oh, damn it."

"You seem to be swearing a lot lately, Duse. Relax. Your mom's got this. Get up there and be Joan, the crowds will love you. Then, after Merrimac finishes off the bad Tarakana colony that's coming to take you, we can sit in the back of the council chambers while your mom meets with the representatives of the Trade Guild and the Council of Clans. It'll be fun."

Sam was confused. "I still don't see why she owes anything to Merrimac."

"Because of me. I did something on *Wandering Star*, something terrible that I can't tell you. Mom's risking all of our lives so no one will ever find out. The bad colony is here, following us. All of them. They'll try to take over and use me to turn this into a blood bath. Merrimac will try to stop them and wipe them out. He's got a pretty good numerical advantage now, but if I go off the rails when I start talking..."

"What? What are you expecting Winona and me to do?"

I lifted my head. We were almost to the market now and I could hear the noise of the crowd.

"It's why I'm unarmed, my love. If you have to do it, do it fast. Don't hesitate like you did this morning, OK?"

"You ask too much. Find another way."

"If I'm that far gone, putting a sword through me would be a mercy. Winona, you'll know if the time comes. *Make* him do it, or do it yourself."

"Why didn't I see that in the plan before? In between step five-twenty and twenty-one. Damn it."

I grinned at her. "Now who's swearing?"

"You know we won't last long after we kill you, right? The crowd will tear us apart."

"I know. If that happens, we'll be the first of the five thousand that will die before nightfall. But we'll be together and only five thousand will die, not fifty thousand or five-hundred thousand."

"Find another way."

"There *is* no other way. We've placed our bets; on Merrimac and the Trade Guild and the Warrens." The crowd was huge and volatile. I couldn't hear my mom over them. I could see her though, and my dad standing on her left and a bit behind her. It would make a great statue someday.

I stopped and turned to look at my friends. "And we've bet on each other, that the two of you can hold me together long enough for us to win."

"You mean for Merrimac to win."

"Yes. That's the first step." I stopped and pulled up the sleeve of my coat. "I still have this with me too." I took off my watch and slid the lock of her hair out from under it. "I'm going to need every bit of courage and wisdom you can give me."

She took my hand, turned it over and kissed my wrist. "I'll always be with you."

I put the lock of her hair back under my watch and fastened it tightly. "Now you and Sam get in front of me and clear a path. The Princess Mala Dusa needs to make a grand entrance." I tried to smile.

Winona had her head tipped, staring at me. "It's going to be hard to tell whose puppet you are, you know?"

I smiled at her. "Please be certain before you do anything irreversible."

She nodded and turned her back to me, smashing her elbow into the man in front of us. "Make a hole! You there, move!"

It took only a few meters for the crowd to realize what was happening and shift out of our way, opening a path to where my parents were standing. The people started to fall silent as I passed, then a general hush came over the crowd. I knew Mom had been talking, because I had seen her gesturing. Without amplification, I doubted if anyone past the first few rows could hear her. That thought had comforted me, knowing that only a few people would be able to hear whatever nonsense I might be able to come up with.

Then I could hear her talking, speaking a language I didn't know. I heard my name somewhere in the flow of her words, Mala Dusa, little soul, and the rumble of the crowd repeating it.

I was doomed.

They were *all* staring at me and then the clapping started, rhythmic and slow, matching my pace toward the plinth, like a funeral march. Sam and Winona were both in my head, trying to keep me calm, trying to keep me from turning and running for my life. Sam was being brave because Winona was brave, and whenever I felt Winn start to falter, Sam's bravery reinforced hers. That was me in the middle, praying that God wouldn't allow the pounding of my heart to crack my ribcage wide open.

I don't remember how Sam got me up there, just that I felt light in his arms and then I was standing on the platform, my arms raised above my head, one of my hands in Mom's hand, the other in Dad's while the crowd made my ears ring.

After what seemed forever, they stepped back from me and I was alone. But I was *not* alone. I might never be alone inside my own head again. Sam and Winona were touching me gently, Mom was trying to be gentle, but she wasn't. Dad was distant, waiting, watching. And there was the hum of Merrimac suggesting what I needed to do next.

I went with Merrimac, and started slowly undoing the oversized buttons on the coat I was wearing. When I was finished, I let it slide off my shoulders into a pile around my feet, letting the crowd see me in the tight long sleeve undershirt I was wearing, letting them see the arms that were too skinny and legs that were too skinny and the face that would never be pretty. They cheered me.

I picked the coat up and threw it as far as I could. It didn't go far. "Are you ready?" I yelled to them. "Are you ready to throw off the dead weight that Boden's been making you carry here in the Warrens? Are you ready to be free?"

That bought me another couple of minutes to gather my thoughts and try to understand what Merrimac was asking me to do. At least I thought it was Merrimac. There were other voices, other paths calling to me. I glanced back at Hannah, looking for reassurance. She and Dad were gone.

I could do it, I knew I could. Sam and Winona, just children, would never be able to reach me in time. The fate of the Warrens balanced on the head of a pin. My destiny was blood, my future the pyre. I was ready to speak, to push us all into darkness.

Merrimac was an outlier, going contrary to the will of the other Tarakana colonies. Even if he won here, it wouldn't matter. The Union would fall, Bodens Gate would be isolated and the Warrens would descend into chaos and death.

Do it now, attack and rule. Wasn't that always the answer? Be part of the gang that won, repress the others as long as possible, and accept death with the changing fortunes when they came. Boden was dead. Now was the time for a new ruler to rise and reward her friends and supporters.

That's when I saw her. Katarina, the woman that Sam had almost killed, was standing a couple of rows back. A girl of maybe three years was holding her hand and looking excited and confused by the noise and the people packed shoulder to shoulder. I smiled at her and blew the little girl a kiss. Katarina jumped up and down and whispered to the man next to her. I knew what I needed to do.

The crowd had grown quiet again and my head was clear. "Boden is dead," I told them. "His body is lashed to the side of one of the great merchant ships that are the foundation of our wealth, the wealth he stole from us and paid out to those that kept him in power. No more!"

I waited for quiet, pacing around the small plinth. "Death in the vacuum of space. A fitting end for a man with no soul. So, now is it time

247

to fight?" Cheering. "Now is it time to kill?" Less cheering. "Is it time to attack and destroy and take revenge?" Murmuring and whistles. I nodded. "You're right! You see it, don't you? We've all seen too much of death, but it's made us wise. Enough blood, enough killing, enough death. Now is the time for your wisdom, the wisdom of the Warrens."

I held my hands out to the side, palms up. "Don't you see it? You've *already* won. It's time to reach out and take hold of the prize. Equality. Respect. Honor. Prosperity. Peace. The freedom as individuals to make your lives better, and make a better world for your children. Is that what you want? Because you've earned it."

I sighed, trying to stop the shaking. Merrimac was winning. It was an invisible battle, unless you were looking for it. I saw the shimmers on the edges of the crowd, occasionally a dog running, or something that almost looked like a dog. The dark paths were starting to close.

I kept talking. A few sentences, and then I would wait for the cheering to stop before I continued. Forty-five minutes passed and I think I only had said ten minutes' worth of words. The crowd was happy, I was happy, Merrimac was happy. I stepped to the edge and looked at Winona and Sam. They were happy too.

The first bullet hit my left shoulder when I stepped back to the center of the plinth. It spun me around, knocking me off balance. The second bullet missed. I heard it go past my ear, loud. An angry *wizzz* sound. A touch of heat.

Then I was down, Sam lying on top of me. There was yelling close by, but I couldn't understand what was being said. I was looking at Sam's eyes, blue and so close to me. I wanted to kiss him one more time before I died, but I couldn't move. Frustrating.

Winona leaned in next to me, looking worried.

"Hey, Winn. Think I got shot."

"You did. I told you that would happen if you left the Mission."

"I guess you were right. Sorry we never got lunch today."

"It's OK. I think this rally is starting to break up now anyway. We'll get you to the medical AI at the Mission and have something to eat in a little bit."

"OK. Good plan." I closed my eyes and drifted. I dreamed about my real mom. She looked nice, wearing a blue t-shirt while we hiked together on the DHT. She was proud of me, but I could tell she was worried.

CHAPTER 19

DOING MY BEST

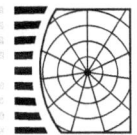

There was a dragon right in front of my face when I woke up, sharp teeth making the claws sparkle in the dim lights.

"Cuza." I tried to smile back at him and I felt a tear sliding down my cheek. "Didn't die?"

"No, Little Soul, you didn't die, not even close. It's good to see your eyes open again, though."

I thought about it for a few minutes, trying to put the pieces back together. My head was empty, no Tarakana, no Sam or Winona, just Mala Dusa.

"Where is everybody?"

Cuza chuckled, a low, dark sound. "It's three o'clock in the morning, so sleepin' I would hope."

"All except Cuza."

"Bah. I don't sleep most nights, not much anyway."

It was pleasant, lying there talking to Cuza. I felt warm finally, and safe. I shifted a little, feeling something pinching me. My left shoulder was covered by a cuff with wires and tubes running in and out of it. I looked at it, trying to remember why it was there.

"Who did this to me?"

"Don't know his name, or much else about him. We found what was left of him up on one of the rooftops. A pack of dogs had gotten to him and ripped him up quite a bit. I guess the critters didn't like the sound of gunfire. Or maybe they're on your side now too." He smiled at me again, like it was absurd.

"They are," I assured him. "Those dogs have to keep me safe. I haven't had my babies yet."

"Oh, is *that* what it was?" He nodded, the gentle smile making the dragon look less fierce.

"Yep, that's exactly what it was." I closed my eyes and slept a little bit more.

Cuza was still there when I forced them open again. "What day is it?"

"The sun will be rising on a beautiful Saturday morning in an hour or so. Why? You got somewhere to be?"

"It *was* Thursday. Sam leaves... tomorrow. I lost a day with him. Is he still here? Still in the Mission?"

"Where else would he be?"

"I want to see him. And Winona. Where's my Winona?" My heart was pounding hard in my ears.

He tapped something on the screen behind me and I was suddenly sleepy again, dizziness starting to overtake me.

"Cuza! Really?"

"Sammy was up past midnight sitting here with you. Let him rest. Winona and your folks are in Eindhoven with the Clan leadership. Big meeting later this morning, so I'm told."

I rolled my head over and looked at the thing on my shoulder that was knitting me back together. "Want to get up now. Eat waffles."

"I know you do. Sleep a bit more first."

"Oh, fine." I closed my eyes and looked for Sam. I found him, not too far away, dreaming about being lost in a big house full of dark corridors and stairs that descended into blackness where there was only fear. I took his hand and together we changed the dream, opening windows and letting in the sun.

I woke to the feeling of fingers gently moving the hair away from my forehead. I smiled and waited for the kiss that I knew would follow. Nothing. I opened my eyes a slit. No Sam, only Cuza and an older woman with her gray hair tied back, nose to nose with me.

"Ah, there she is. Feeling better without that cuff on I suspect."

I looked at my left shoulder. There was a pink area two or three centimeters across near my armpit, but no hole, no blood. I turned back to Cuza, feeling sudden panic. "What day is today?"

"Saturday. Almost 13:00."

"Is it the same Saturday as the Saturday it was last time that it was Saturday?"

"Cuza, what were you thinking dialing her up so high? It's a wonder I was able to wake her up today at all. *Now* listen to her."

Cuza looked embarrassed. "But, Doc, she needed a good *long* sleep. It's hard the first time you get shot, scary even, not knowin' that you'll be OK."

I was looking back and forth between them, feeling empty and panicky. I couldn't feel Sam or Winona, or my parents.

"You let him leave! I was asleep for a week and you just let him leave without me having a chance to say goodbye." Tears started and I wasn't sure if they'd ever stop.

Understanding came into Cuza's eyes. "Same Saturday, Little Soul. Peace. It's only been a few hours. Sammy's in Eindhoven with your parents. Hannah called and asked for him, so of course he had to go." Cuza smiled at the doctor. "Young lovers."

She gave him a sideways grin before turning back to me. "How did you know he was gone?"

I was awake enough to just shrug. "If he was still in the Mission, he'd be here with me." I was furious with him. Hannah had called, so *of course* he went to her, leaving me to die in the infirmary.

She patted my arm. "You should get up and dressed now. Get something to eat, you'll feel better. I have some exercises for you to do that will help you get the strength back in that joint." She poked at the pink spot, squinting at it. "I'll send them to you. You do have a display pad, right?"

I nodded while Cuza shook his head. I raised my eyebrows at him, then, "Oh! It was in the pocket of that big coat I was wearing. The one I threw into the crowd." My left hand came up to my forehead, and I winced at how sore my shoulder felt. "Dad's going to kill me."

"We should have a donated one you can borrow."

I sighed. "Thank you."

It took me a while to get dressed. All of me was sore and every time I moved my left arm it hurt, sending little tingles racing down my fingers. I carried my tray through the line in the nearly empty dining hall, feeling wobbly, settling for a small bowl of soup and a couple of rolls.

Father Ryczek was sitting at a table by himself and he waved me over. I sat with him, not sure what to expect. He let me eat in silence for a while, but I could feel him watching me.

251

"Alice, your mother, sent me dozens of letters asking to come here." He took a folded piece of paper from his pocket and handed it to me. "This is the one that convinced me to allow her to come. I printed a copy years ago and I look at it from time to time when God sends difficult people to my door. This is the one where she tells me the truth. You see? She was running away; running from Dulcinea, running from the memories of her first husband who she felt had abandoned her by dying, running from her father, and mostly running from herself and who she had become. She wanted to come here to be reborn.

"Funny thing, though. By the time she got here, she didn't need to come any more. Ted had already saved her, or was in the *process* of saving her. Everything in life is a process, a journey. She stayed because Ted was on a journey too, trying to find out what kind of man he was going to become."

"He's a good man."

Father Ryczek nodded. "He tries to be, and that's all anyone can do. And now there's Mala Dusa, who came here to find her mother. Have you found her yet?"

"And to serve God," I reminded him.

"Yes. Have you found her?"

"I'm in the *process* of finding her. It's complicated." I bit into one of my rolls, letting the crumbs fall into the soup. "Hannah's my mom, isn't she? More than Alice ever can be." The thought of that made me sad. I touched the paper, tracing the words Alice had crafted into sentences, begging for redemption in the Warrens. My mom. I had made her sick in the mornings and made her waddle around with me in Bodens Gate's high gravity.

I knew she had loved me, but all I had of her were other people's memories.

"There's no right answer. Do you love Hannah?"

"More than I knew. Being here with her, seeing what she can do, how strong she is, *and* how vulnerable..." I shook my head and finished the last of my soup. "She's Mom, and more than Mom. And less. It's strange."

I found him staring at me when I looked up, holding my eyes with his.

"Ah. You no longer see her as you did when you were just a little girl." He smiled softly at the way I was frowning.

"It's OK, Little Soul. There's more to be gained in growing up than is lost, if you do it right."

I looked back at my plate. "Then I don't think I'm doing it right. I'm selfish and cruel, even when I try not to be. I'm probably not living up to either of their expectations. I do terrible things when I don't have my friends around to make me better."

"Pray to God every day that he keeps those kind of friends close to you." He touched my chin and lifted it so I had to look at him. "You'll be fine. There's *a lot* of Alice in you. Alice raised by Hannah." He started chuckling. "God help us all."

He stood, taking my dirty dishes and stacking the trays. I walked with him to the recycler.

"Now, then, about those new solar arrays that we're still waiting for you to install and integrate into our power grid."

"Nobody's touched them yet? They're still waiting up on the roof?"

He nodded, a bit of a smile crinkling his eyes.

"What's the weather today?"

"Snowing right now, but tomorrow's supposed to be sunny. You'll have the walls around the roof to keep the wind off you."

I was chewing on my lip, wanting to get started prepping the grid and updating the control software right away. I could get that done while the weather was bad. "I need to talk to Mom. I don't know what her plans are."

Father Ryczek sighed. "I'm to keep you hidden here while you heal and until she's 'ready for you'. Whatever she means by that."

"I used to think she always had a plan. Now I'm not so sure. I think she improvises a lot and depends on her own brilliance to keep her out of trouble. And Dad. He keeps her out of trouble a lot of the time too."

"He's rescued her more often and in more ways than they'll probably ever tell you."

That was a troubling thought, and it reminded me of something important. "Sam." I whispered his name out loud, touching my pockets, looking for my display pad. Empty.

"Cuza said you might have a display pad I could borrow. I need to talk to Sam and then Mom and then I'll start the install process for getting the panels integrated." I rolled my shoulder around, listening to the clicks and pops. "And I've got to do some kind of exercises this afternoon that the doctor was supposed to send me."

Father Ryczek held his finger up in front of my nose. "One thing at a time, thorn. Focus. Serve God, then other people, then yourself. Got it?"

I nodded, knowing that what he was saying was profound, but I wasn't really listening. All I could think about was contacting Sam.

"And don't neglect your shoulder. I can't have you wandering around here complaining about how your body hurts all the time the way Cuza does."

"Yes, sir."

I followed him back to his office where he opened a cabinet and gave me a box.

"This looks brand new."

"It may well be. Sometimes we get donations of things that have never even been unwrapped. People get things, and then decide they want something better. The wealthy are not understandable, not by me anyway."

I unrolled it in my hands, looking at the screen coming to life. "It's even got a charge. I promise not to lose this one, and I'll get it back to you before I leave."

"How many have you lost?" He looked mystified.

"Lost or destroyed?"

He closed his eyes and held up his hand. "Never mind. Do your best."

"I always do. Mostly."

"Go. And remember what I told you."

I left, wondering what it was he had told me. Something about focus.

It only took a few minutes to sync to the Union net and enter my credentials. I punched Sam and waited. Nothing, so I punched him again. And again.

Finally, text came back. *Meeting going on, your mom presenting, can't talk now.*

I stared at it. No '*how's your shoulder, MD?*' No '*I miss you.*' No '*I'm sorry I left you in the infirmary to die.*'

I closed the session without replying and wandered around the Mission for half an hour before I could trust myself to start coding the power grid. The pad chimed a few times while I was working and each time I'd say out loud to myself, "Sorry, busy writing code, can't talk now."

I was feeling better as I worked, and I finished all the updates by late afternoon. All I'd need to do on Sunday was the physical setup on the roof and connecting the power link.

Father Ryczek came into the control room just as I was finishing the last simulated load.

"All done," I told him, feeling like I'd accomplished something good. My anger had dissipated.

"Did I give you a display pad this afternoon?"

I bit my lower lip. "Yes, Father."

"And you've been ignoring it, God alone knows why." He unfolded his pad and held it up to me so I could see Mom's unhappy face.

"How was the meeting?" I tried for innocence, but I could hear the defiance in my voice.

"I want you here for dinner, if you're not too busy. Representatives from the Council of Clans, the CG, RuComm and the Trade Guild will all be joining us. Wear something nice, something professional, something that leaves your left shoulder bare, do you understand?"

Father Ryczek's chin came up a little at that last part, and a disapproving glint appeared his eyes.

"Sure, I understand. I could print a new shirt for myself with an arrow pointing at my shoulder with letters that say, 'Look at me! I got shot fighting for the Warrens!' if you think that would be better."

She said something that the display pad edited out and I found myself looking at Winona. She kept glancing off screen and finally told me, "She says to tell you to wear something appropriate and to be at the hotel by 19:00. Would you like to talk to Sam?"

"Oh, does he have time for me now?"

"Duse, you don't know what it's like here." She tapped her forehead and stared at me. "We need your support, remember?"

A miserable looking Sam leaned into view. He opened his mouth to say something, then closed it again and settled for just looking at me. I could feel him. Over ten kilometers away, and I could feel every bit of his pain and longing. I wanted to be mad at him and say something cruel, but couldn't.

I sighed. "I love you *so* much, Samuel. I'll be there as quickly as I can."

He nodded and I started to reach for him. Father Ryczek slammed the pad shut.

"Are you going to wear the kind of ridiculous outfit Hannah suggested?"

"No, sir." I blinked a couple of times, trying to clear Sam out of my thoughts for a moment. I could still feel him. "I'll need your help. I don't have anything of my own to wear, and I don't think I've *ever* owned anything that would be appropriate. Maybe one, but I don't have it anymore."

"My help? With clothes?" He looked down at his coveralls. "Let's see if Leticia is about."

Father Ryczek took me to a part of the Mission where his staff had small apartments. He tapped on a door and a woman about the same age as my mom answered. "Little Soul." Leticia patted my cheek fondly. "You were just a big bump between Alice's hips when I saw you last. Now look at you."

I smiled at her. Another link to my mom's past, more memories that I could share, but never own.

Father Ryczek told her, "She needs a dress for tonight. Something nice, but that the Citizens from Eindhoven will recognize as being from the Warrens. And something that the Clans will find respectful, maybe even elegant."

I grinned shyly. "Is that possible? And I need to leave in about an hour."

She tipped her head, looking at me from different angles. "How's your shoulder? Does it hurt?"

"It hurts," I admitted. "But my friends will help me and I'm going to be OK."

"Spoken like a child of the Warrens. Let's see what we can find for you."

She chose a dress made of light overlapping layers of soft cloth, subtle, subdued colors and leather boots that covered my ankles. The boots were a little loose on my small feet, but they stayed on when I walked slowly enough. The lines of the dress accentuated my thinness rather than trying to conceal it. I swallowed hard looking at myself in her mirror.

"Will that work for you?" she asked when we were done. "It was my daughter's a couple of years back till she outgrew it. Her first grown-up dress. She's fifteen now."

I shook my head at myself. "It's much prettier than I deserve. I can never thank you as I should."

She hugged me close and whispered. "Keep fighting for us. That's all the thanks I need." She let go, touched my hair, and looked me up and down one last time, not seeing me anymore, lost in a memory. "And don't get shot any more, promise?"

"I'll do my best."

Cuza drove me to the edge of the Warrens, saw me safely into an auto-cab, and kissed me gently on the cheek.

"You comin' back tonight?"

"I don't know. Mom has plans for me."

"Let me know if you do. I'll come fetch you."

I kissed him softly on the lips the way I'd seem Mom kiss him. I put my hand on the pay screen and the door slid shut. "Central Hilton," I told it.

There were Guardians of the Peace waiting outside the hotel with slung rifles and wearing full body armor. I was suddenly afraid that I'd stumbled into a trap and that Boden himself would be there smirking, waiting to grab me. I could almost hear his voice, so real was my fear. I got out of the autocab ready to run as fast as I could in my too big boots. Maybe the dark and the snow would hide me.

"Why so afraid?" Dad wrapped my hand around his arm, supporting me.

I glanced around at all the guards. They looked more bored than threatening now. "I don't know. There are just so many of them."

He grinned at me while we walked into the lobby. "Welcome to Bodens Gate. Yesterday's enemies are today's protectors."

I was still afraid, but having him next to me was keeping me from shaking or sprinting down the street. "What will they be tomorrow?"

"Well, that's what we're working on tonight. How's your shoulder?"

"Better. Still hurts when I use it."

"Doing your exercises?"

"No, not yet. But I got everything ready for the new solar array. Do you know how many patches I had to apply first? It's a wonder the Mission had power at all."

"What was the last rev date?"

"Like five *years* ago."

He chuckled. "At least it wasn't from when I was last here. But that's Father Ryczek, always assuming that if it's working today then it'll be fine for another year." He glanced down at me. "Nice dress, by the way."

"Thanks. I'm not sure what Mom will say."

"Go easy on her. She's not as calm as she appears."

"You're helping her, I can feel it."

"As much as I can. It's why I need to get back near her soon." He patted my hand that was on his arm. "I'm not as calm as I appear either."

"Dad, at what range can you feel her emotions?"

"It gets a little easier every year. Maybe thirty or forty meters now, depending. About twice the range I have with you. Why? Can you feel Sam already?"

I nodded, biting my lip.

"That's not a bad thing, Dusa. He's right there talking to your mom."

I looked up at Dad, wondering if I should give him something else to worry about.

257

The gentle smile he'd been wearing since I'd arrived slipped away. "When did you first feel him tonight?"

I shrugged. "I don't know. I feel him all the time now, at least when I want to. It was strong, even from the Mission. At this range, I feel him whether I want to or not."

We had stopped walking and Sam was staring at me from across the room. I gave him a shy wave, wiggling my fingers. I could tell he liked the dress.

"Are there Tarakana here magnifying the effect?"

I shook my head. "No, surprisingly enough, there's none inside the hotel. A few out on the street, but none here."

"Unless they're hiding from you."

"Good point. I don't think so, but it's possible. Merrimac is usually honest with me because he's... Well, he's honest with me."

"Let's not mention this to your mom just yet, OK? She has enough to worry about tonight."

"I thought the meetings were over. This is just a celebration, right?"

He looked at me with a touch of disappointment. "The meetings are for posturing. The real work happens over drinks and dinner."

I shivered as the ground under me shifted. Not a dinner party. "I'll try to be who she wants me to be, who she *needs* me to be."

We started walking again. "Just be Mala Dusa. That should get the job done." Dad took my hand and placed it on Sam's arm.

I glanced into Sam's eyes, smiled, and then focused on Mom. She was examining me, physically and emotionally, inside and out.

"Well, look at you, daughter of the Warrens." She tugged on one sleeve, adjusting it. "I would prefer that you back my play and not argue with me over every damn thing." She touched my hair, moving it, fluffing it a bit and sighed. "But this isn't bad. I can work with this."

She glanced at a man that was standing near us, then pulled me into a tender hug and whispered in my ear. "This is probably better than what I had planned, actually. Good job, Dusa."

I rested my head on her shoulder and closed my eyes.

"Thank you, Ms. Weldon. That was perfect."

I opened one eye watching him leave. "Was that the pose you wanted?" I kept my head on her shoulder, listening to her chuckle.

"He's been haunting me and your father all afternoon waiting for you to show up. Maybe now I can get some work done."

"So I'm just a prop for you this evening?" I pulled back from her, trying to gauge what she was feeling.

"I think it might be the other way around. *You're* the one they all want to talk to. *You're* the one that convinced the Trade Guild and RuComm that the clans were serious about peace and stability. You're the one they won't *shut up* about."

I smiled, feeling lost. "I got shot. That demonstrated peace and stability?"

She held my face between her hands, pleading. "Mala Dusa, promise me that you will at least *glance* at the headlines in some news source once a day, OK? I'm not surprised Father Ryczek kept it from you, but I thought Cuza—No, he would have sworn Cuza to silence too."

She let go of my head and I wobbled. "What? What's been happening?"

"Flowers," she answered. "And candles. People marching together in the streets singing. Citizens have been joining in. It's damn weird, but it's good."

"Oh. It's probably—"

"Here. You look like you need this." Winona handed me a glass of wine before I could make Mom mad by telling her what I thought was causing everyone to feel so loving toward each other.

"Can I have this? I thought I was too young."

"Sixteen," Winn reminded me. "Bodens Gate treats you as an adult at sixteen."

She smiled and I wondered how many glasses she'd already had.

"That's sixteen *Bodens Gate* years, of course, but you'll be seventeen in six weeks, Earth weeks, so... you're good!"

I tried a sip. "Not bad." I swirled it in the glass. "What is it?"

"Pinot Noir, I think. Boden's personal family label." She smiled an evil Winona grin at me.

The red liquid in my glass suddenly reminded me of blood. "Really?" I took another sip and noticed Sam staring, probably reading the darkness in me. "I might need a bigger glass."

Dad took my hand, I *know* reading the darkness in me. "There are some people we'd like you to meet. And I'd suggest you go easy on the alcohol this evening. Just because it's legal doesn't mean it's wise."

"Yes, sir." I winked at Winona and tapped my glass, thanking her.

Watching Mom working her way through the crowd was incredible. And it was *work*, there was no doubt about that. I stayed with her for the first hour, letting people shake my hand or hug me, but it was Mom doing the heavy lifting. She focused on the representatives from the Council of Clans and from the CG, making introductions, answering questions and laughing at stories that weren't funny, eyes sparkling.

Dad was there with her, supporting her, encouraging her and catching anyone that tried to get away. There was one woman from the CG, a delegate from Heusden I think, that would have happily followed him for a more private conversation. He somehow managed to get her hands off his leg long enough to introduce her to a leader of the Boucher clan, mentioning the clan's desire to open a new factory making high speed injectors for food printers. He slipped away once negotiations started, with a grin in my direction.

"Your dad," Winona handed me another glass, "is remarkable." She smiled at Sam and me, and then giggled.

"No more wine for Winona," I told her, taking her glass away from her.

"My job here is to provide Ms. Weldon and your father with facts, figures, and analysis. My ability to do so is unimpaired." She took her glass back and stared into it.

"Right. We need food." I led us over to where Dad was busy talking to a Trade Guild officer.

"Hungry," I told him.

Dad ignored me. "Ah, Ms. Killdeer. How deeply penetrated are residents of the Warrens into space dock operations?"

"They account for nearly eighty percent for the unskilled and semi-skilled taskings, but only eighteen percent for skilled positions. The Central Government has only certified one Warrens based firm to provide starship servicing, and they have been required by CG edict to maintain rate parity with existing service providers. Otherwise, their rates would be substantially less. Six firms in the Warrens have attempted to gain certification, but have been denied, often for patently fabricated or arbitrary reasons."

Winn glanced at me, smirking.

The Trade Guild officer was staring at her. "How much less? How much is 'substantially'?"

"It is difficult to be precise, and of course it would depend on what services are needed, but if the market were truly open and competitive... I think you could conservatively expect a drop in full service fees of between twelve and eighteen percent, not counting the cost of fuel."

The officer did his best to hide his glee.

"Hungry," I said again.

Dad sighed. "Mala Dusa, there are tables full of food *everywhere*. If you're hungry, take Sam and go eat, but I need Winona a bit longer. Look," He pointed at a big man with a grey beard sitting at a table with a group in RuComm and Union uniforms. "That's Captain Cradock from the *Galla Lupanio* talking to some folks that you and Sam should meet. Get some food, introduce yourself, and tell them about the Warrens."

"OK, just don't let that man kidnap Winona." I glanced at the officer whispering in Winn's ear. "I think that's love in his eyes."

"It's love alright, but not for Winona. I'll take good care of her."

Sam took my hand as we walked across the room. "You're afraid."

"Poor social skills. I'm not good at meeting new people."

"Says the girl who stood up and talked to thousands of strangers for almost an hour."

"And hated every minute of it. Especially the getting shot part." The group Dad had told us to talk to was watching us approach. "Why do I feel like I'm about to get shot again?"

"You're not. Do you want me to distract them while you get something to eat or do you want to lead the attack?"

I had my shoulders back and my head up. "I am the Princess Mala Dusa. I always..." I looked at him and smiled. Then I stopped. I knew what he was feeling and desiring and it was overpoweringly dangerous, because I was suddenly feeling and desiring the same thing. I had to take a couple of deep breaths before continuing. "I'll lead the attack, and I'll do everything Mom and Dad expect of me. Then you and I need to get out of here."

He nodded. "I'll get you something to eat."

"Something simple," I told him. "Something I can eat with my fingers."

All of them stood when I approached their table. "Captain Cradock?" I held my hand out. "I'm Mala Dusa Holloman. My father tells me that you are captain of the *Galla Lupanio*."

He took my hand gently, but his eyes were looking at me hard. Do all captains have eyes like that, that seem to be able to see straight through to your soul? It was comforting knowing that he had no idea what I was feeling.

"I have that honor. And I am very pleased that you, your parents, and your friend will be joining us on Tuesday for your journey home."

That was news to me, but I think I hid it well. I smiled as he introduced me to the other captains at the table, two men, one woman, all with the same eyes.

We talked about the Warrens and the people that lived there. I tried my best to dispel the myths, misconceptions and prejudices that they had always believed, while Sam brought me an endless supply of crunchy little bites of dough full of cheese and spicy meat. They were addictive. I think the only thing I convinced them of, other than my appetite, was that they couldn't trust the opinions and reports from the CG.

"Go there," I insisted. "Spend a few days, or even a few hours talking to the people, learning what they want out of life. It's the same things you want, opportunity and the freedom to pursue it, to make a peaceful life for their families, and to build a better life for their children. Ground truth, my friend calls it."

I was quiet for a while after that, enjoying Sam sitting next to me, wondering how to make a polite exit. Then the conversation shifted, and Captain Cradock started talking about how the *Galla Lupanio's* engines had recently been updated and that he was looking forward to testing them now that the DSH network was visible again.

For the next hour, we talked starship design while I ate and had another glass of Boden's wine. The *Galla Lupanio* was an older *Doge*-class ship, but the Guild had continually upgraded her in ways that RuComm never seemed to be able to afford. I ran out of food at some point because Sam had left me, but it was still another twenty minutes before I could pull myself away to go find him.

He was in the bar, drinking a beer, and flirting with a woman that was at least five years older than him. Well, *she* was flirting with *him*, that much I could see. Sam was feeling interested, but in a strangely detached way.

I stood between them and kissed him on the mouth, doing things that should have left him with little doubt about my intentions. A quick glance over my shoulder showed that, yeah, she was definitely too old for my Sam. I think she recognized me because she looked a little frightened. Good.

I ignored her. "I got three more letters of recommendation. Can we get out of here now?"

"Sure. Did you let your parents know?"

"I'll let Dad know while we're en route. I don't dare get within twenty meters of him or Mom. They'll lock me up." We left without saying good-bye to his new friend.

"En route where? I have a very nice room upstairs that I'd like to show you."

"I'll bet you do. We're going to the Warrens."

"MD, it's almost 23:00."

"I know. I've already sent a note to Cuza to pick us up at the border."

"We're spending the night at the Mission? My last night here. Our last night together for a very, very long time."

"Yes. Trust me. I have a plan."

We walked out into the snow. "On Dulcinea," I told him while we waited for the autocab, "the snowflakes are *huge* and they float in the low gravity forever. Here, it's like little snow pellets that are angry at the ground. They smash into it and try to cover it up as quickly as possible." I tipped my head back to catch some of them in my mouth.

"How much wine *did* you have tonight?"

"Just the right amount, I think. So, who was she?"

"Sarah. She's an aide to one of the CG delegates. You wouldn't like her."

"Well, that's pretty much a given."

"She was at your rally when you got shot and she marched with a candle in her hand last night, praying for peace in the Warrens, but she's like Trilby. She believes the people in the Warrens are to be pitied and helped with generous charity and sympathy. Maybe someday..."

Sam stopped and kissed me. It was a good kiss.

"Someday?" I managed to ask.

"This is a long fight." He glanced over his shoulder. "I don't know how Hannah's going to be able to just pack up and leave with you on Tuesday. Then there's everything else going on in the Union. It's all one big fight and it's all falling apart. I don't see how we can win it."

I kissed him, trying to do for him what he had done to me. "I know, but we won this round. Tonight, maybe just for tonight, we can celebrate."

CHAPTER 20

MERRIMAC IS MY FRIEND

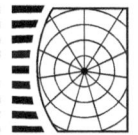

Sam and Cuza were standing in the mud and broken stone parking area outside the Gabriele Restaurant staring at each other. Sam wasn't backing down.

"Cuza! Is something wrong?" I had to shout the question over the low frequency shaking coming from the Gabriele. It might have been music, but it was mostly just a beat pounding against everything. Little bits of stone were spalling off the concrete block walls.

Cuza started to turn toward me, then changed his mind and grabbed Sam's right hand with his. "You gonna take proper care of her?"

"Yes, sir."

"No takin' advantage? No treatin' her bad?"

"I would never do that to her."

"You'll treat her like she was your very own sister?"

"No, sir. I will treat her like the woman I love."

Cuza sighed, unhappy, and I prayed that he wasn't breaking Sam's hand. I had plans for those fingers.

"You make her cry... No, I don't suppose you will. You know how to use that sword you're toting around?"

"Yes, sir. And I won't hesitate if the time comes to use it."

Cuza let go and I breathed a sigh of relief.

"OK, you two. Let's go for a ride. There're heavy coats in the back seat. Put 'em on."

I wrapped a long wool coat around me, turning up the collar. It smelled like real wool, and I wondered briefly if there were sheep on Bodens Gate. A Winona question for some other day. I pulled a wool hat down low on my forehead, tucked all my hair in, and smiled at Sam. Yeah, just the response I'd hoped for.

"Cuza, will you teach me to drive sometime, please? This looks fun."

"I don't know about fun, but sure. Your dad picked it up pretty quick, I'm sure you will too."

I smiled to myself, rocking back and forth as we navigated the rough street, one shoulder bumping against Cuza's, the other resting against Sam.

After a few minutes, Sam looked over at me. "This isn't the way to the Mission."

I tried to stifle a giggle.

Cuza shook his head at me, a wry grin flexing the dragon's wings. "Girls and their secrets."

Sam wanted to ask me where we were going, I could feel it. I just kept smiling to myself with my eyes straight ahead until we pulled over to a stop.

"I need to let you off here. Too hard to turn this thing around once the road narrows and with all these people out on the street."

I got out and he hugged me.

"You be gentle with him, Little Soul."

"Yes, sir."

"And don't tell your mom I did this."

"What about Father Ryczek?" I teased him.

"Oh, that'd be OK. He's used to me doin' stupid things and *he* won't kill me."

Sam and I helped him get turned around and then followed the crowd moving along the street.

He took my hand. "OK, where are all of us going?"

"You should look at the news feeds once in a while. Didn't you know there's a big rally in the market at midnight? Live music and dancing, flowers and candles. I want to see it."

"You're not, uh, planning on getting up on that plinth again, are you?"

I smiled and then the horror of it hit me. "God, no. I'm in disguise and plan to stay that way." I took my hand and put it into the pocket of his coat. "We'll only stay a little while. After that, phase two of my plan."

"Humm. How many phases are there?"

"You'll see."

I could hear the music already. It was swaying in the air instead of pounding, and I wanted to sway with it.

Sam danced with me, holding me and twirling me while I looked up at the snow coming down on us. After that, we chanted slogans with our fists in the air. Then we held candles while we prayed for the brave girl who'd almost lost her life there a couple of days ago. God help her heal quickly.

The music slowed after that, and he held me close while we rocked back and forth. My head was on his shoulder and I smelled damp wool and Sam.

"Did you pray for me?" I asked softly, not moving my head from where it was resting comfortably.

"Uh huh. I prayed that you were sufficiently healed."

"Sufficient for what?"

He squeezed me a little closer, hands low on my back.

"Oh, that. Let's go find out."

I led him away from the crowd, down a narrow street past a bakery.

"I think I know where you're taking me now."

"Hush. Act surprised. Phase three is a secret."

We entered the old workshop, the access panel still keyed for my hand, Mom or Cuza not having reset it yet. It was too dark for me to see if Sam was surprised. We made it upstairs, dim light from the street making all the shapes mysterious and frightening.

My sword was still lying on the table where I'd left it.

"Put it on." Sam demanded. "I want to see something."

I complied and then stared up at him, defiant.

"Pull it. As quickly as you can."

I did, fast and smooth, then grinned at him.

"You manipulated Winona and me perfectly."

"Are you objecting?"

"No. Winona says I'm an idiot for feeling the way I do, but no. Put it away, unless you want to duel."

"Not with swords." I put it down and laid it back on the table.

"Now then, let's get down to why we're here."

"Right! The paint. I have to know if it would have worked." I grabbed him and pulled him into the back office, slamming the door behind us.

It was dark. I opened the door again and Sam started to follow me out.

"Don't move! I just need to find some candles."

"So, what phase are we on now?"

"Three, almost four, if I can find a match."

I found what I needed and closed the door gently. I tried not to notice that the candles were shaking in my hands as I put them around the office.

"We could have just used the light from my display pad."

"No," I corrected him. "We need a heat source."

"Right. How foolish of me."

I shrugged out of my coat and sat on the edge of the desk, feet swinging back and forth while I looked around. "I think this is going to work."

Sam stood in front of me, pushing closer between my legs, not saying anything.

"What do you think, Sam?"

He shook his head and kissed me, first on the mouth, then down the side of my neck.

I twisted my head and found one of his ears to nibble on while he worked on kissing his way down.

His hand was on my left hip, which felt wonderful, and his fingers started to work up inside the dress, counting my ribs with his thumb, moving upward, sending happy tingles through me. Then it all fell apart.

I pushed him back from me, hard. He stood there, staring at me, and I stared back at him.

"I'm sorry, did I hurt you?"

I shook my head, unable to answer. He looked like he wanted to hold me, but was afraid to come any closer. I could feel the concern in him as well as the frustration, the desire, the *need* to continue with what we'd been doing.

I took a deep breath. "*He* touched me there. He grabbed me and he *hurt* me."

"Oh. I'm sorry, I wasn't thinking. It's still sore?"

I shook my head. "No, not anymore. It's the memory of what he did that hurts." I sighed. "Damn him. I *want* you to touch me. It feels *good* when you touch me. It's just... Oh, damn it, I feel like I'm letting him win. He's dead and he's still winning. I can't push what he did out of my head." I could hear his voice, taunting me. *'Are all the girls on Dulcinea as ugly as you? And as malformed?'*

I reached out to Sam, took his hand and placed it over my heart, refusing to give in. "Be patient with me for a bit, OK?"

"Sure."

He pulled a chair over and sat in front of me, gently massaging my legs while I stared at the ceiling, trying to sort through what I was feeling.

"It's getting warmer in here." Sam's voice was soft, almost a whisper.

I chewed on my lip and watched the shadows flickering against the ceiling. We'd missed a spot near the door.

"It was a brilliant idea, mixing the bubbles into the paint."

"Thank you." I ruffled his hair with my fingers. "Thank you for not being angry."

He kissed my knee through the dress. "It's 02:30. What do you want to do?"

"Hold me, please."

"I can do that."

He lifted me from the desk and held me for a while, swaying gently to the memory of the music we'd danced to. "You're right," I told him. "It is getting warmer in here. Help me pile up some of these blankets."

We made more of a nest than a bed, blankets heaped on blankets until most of the floor was covered. "Help me with my dress? I don't want to mess it up, it's borrowed."

Sam didn't say anything, but I could feel what he wanted to do. Instead, his hands gently undid the buttons when I lifted my chin. I stepped out of the dress and stood in front of him in my thermal shirt and underwear.

He knelt in front of me and kissed my belly, making me gasp even though I had known what he was about to do.

"Samuel, will you be able to stop if you keep doing that?"

"No."

I was still swaying a little.

"Are we past that point already? No more safety nets?"

Sam didn't answer. Feeling what was churning in his head, I don't think words were an option for him any longer.

"Yeah, I was afraid of that." I was almost to that point myself. My head tipped back as I pushed up against him, lifting my shirt, trying to give him more bare skin to kiss. There was a moan building somewhere deep inside me and I knelt with him, kissing his mouth.

Now, Little Soul? Now?

The voice hummed into my head. Merrimac was close by. Of course, Merrimac was close by. I didn't care anymore. Let them watch, let them feel it and enjoy it. *Yes, now!* I wanted to scream the answer to him. *I've waited long enough.*

The thought was sharp and clear inside the Merrimac group mind, the vision of the child Sam and I were about to create. There were glimpses of the possible futures, him growing up, playing with Winona and me, the love shared between us, and the... sadness? There it was again slipping past me. Me and my son and my friends, but no Sam, Sam no longer needed, Sam as surplus, Sam discarded.

I tried to pull back. *No, Merrimac, not yet, not ready yet*! The hum was filling all of me and I wasn't able to stop. I toppled over onto my back, Sam still with me, Sam on top of me, arms wrapped around mine, holding me.

I woke to a gentle kiss on my shoulder, my bare shoulder. I opened my eyes and looked at a very contented sleeping Sam. I swung my head around to see who was kissing me.

"'Morning Duse, ready for breakfast?" Winona was sitting on the floor beside me.

"Oh, Winona, I killed him." I was crying.

She looked over me at Sam. "He doesn't look dead, and if he is, at least it looks like he died happy."

"I'm serious. I think, um, I think I'm pregnant." I lifted the blanket and looked down at myself. All naked. I sighed. I couldn't remember it happening. I couldn't remember anything after we had fallen onto the blankets, arms and legs all tangled together. "If I am, the Tarakana don't need him anymore. They'll let him die. I saw it in the group mind." I looked back at Sam. "I can't live without him, Winn. I'd rather die too."

"Really? You'd rather be dead with Sam than live to raise your child? Your son will be remarkable; you know that, don't you? And you'll have people that love you every step of the way."

"Not without Sam," I whispered.

Winona leaned close to me, big eyes studying my face. Not quite right for Winona's eyes, though, too brown, and the hair...

"Oh, Merrimac, you can't take Sam from me. I'm not ready."

"No," Merrimac sighed agreement in my head, *"not ready yet."* The false Winona pulled back from me. She was talking, but her mouth wasn't moving. *"You take so long to grow to maturity. Next year, perhaps?"*

"Still not without Sam."

"Sam's going on a long journey, many dangers. Do you see all the paths? It would be better to make your baby now."

I closed my eyes and tried to see all the paths, but they went by too fast.

"No, I only see Sam." I put my head down next to him and watched him sleeping.

The candles were still burning when I woke up again and Sam was snoring softly on my shoulder, drooling a little on my shirt, his head right where it had been after we had first toppled over into the blankets. My shirt. I touched the fabric, feeling the roughness.

I whispered into the darkness. "Thank you, Merrimac. You *are* my friend." I could hear a hooting sound from somewhere in the shadows and I slept a little longer, my arms around Sam's shoulders, vowing never to let him go.

"Morning Duse, ready for breakfast?" Winona was sitting on the floor beside me and I felt a moment of sheer terror.

She leaned in close to me and her eyes were almost black, just like they were supposed to be.

"Sorry, I didn't mean to scare you."

"It's alright. How did you find us?" I could feel Sam waking up, stretching, his toes playing with mine.

"Well, I suspected you might come here. That and the display pad you borrowed still has the tracker turned on. I've been following you that way since you left the hotel." She looked around at the office. "That paint really works. When I opened the door it must have been close to twenty in here."

I yawned. "What time is it?"

"06:30. If we hurry we can get back to the Mission before your mom does and then she won't have to kill Cuza. And you. And Sam."

"Good morning, Winona." Sam leaned up on one elbow and looked at her.

"Are you dressed in there, Samuel?"

"I am. What you see is pretty much how we spent the whole night."

"Excellent. I was worried about what would happen with Merrimac controlling everything."

"Merrimac is my friend," I assured her.

"Of course he is. I'll wait downstairs while you get more fully dressed. Be quick about it."

"Yes, ma'am," we answered together.

It took a few minutes to find everything, and I needed Sam to help me with the top button on the dress.

271

"You're very quiet this morning." His hands were warm when he touched my cheek. "I can't even tell what you're feeling. It's all a big jumble."

"That's because it *is* all a big jumble." I was looking down chewing my lip. "I think I saved your life last night, after I killed you."

"Really? I don't remember that part."

I told him what I remembered, all of it, including the Tarakana that had looked like Winona and talked to me without moving her mouth.

Sam kissed me. "You know what I think? I think you're still healing from the physical and psychological effects of being shot, general stress, too little sleep, and too much wine. Last night, when we were together," he smiled and kissed me again, "when we were *almost* together, I think you fainted again. We were so fully and intimately connected that I fainted right along with you. So instead of doing what we were planning on doing, we slept in each other's arms all night." He kissed me one more time, longer, softer. "I'm not complaining. It was wonderful."

"Humph. That's your opinion as a biologist? You've seen what the Tarakana can do."

"I have, and they terrify me. The explanation I just gave you makes me feel better, because it's human."

"So what do you really think happened?"

He took my hand and we walked down the stairs together. "I think you saved my life."

Winona was looking desperate. "This is taking too long. Can you run?"

I looked down at my boots. "Nope. Mom's just going to have to kill us."

She sighed as we stepped out into bright morning sunshine, but I was happy. Sam was holding my hand, Winona was with me and even the Warrens felt like it was at peace.

"Maybe I can tell her we were just out for a walk." Winn was walking behind us working on contingency plans.

I greeted a couple walking the other direction and they smiled and wished us a fine good Sunday morning. I turned to look at Winona without letting go of Sam, walking backwards with his arm across me. "Don't bother, Winn. I'm going to tell mom *everything*, including where we were and what we did. I'm going to tell her exactly how many times Sam kissed me and *where* he kissed me, because I remember each and every one of them and I regret nothing."

She blinked at me. "You're serious. You'd really do it."

"If she asks me, but she won't. My point, Winn, is that I don't regret one second of what we did. I'm proud of my Samuel. If she wants to know that we spent the night in each other's arms, then that's fine. Even if we'd had sex, I'd tell her that too if she asked me, and I'd be proud that we'd done it. If there was enough time before he had to leave, I'd marry him."

Winona came to a full stop and I stumbled a little as I pulled Sam back to her. I could feel him smiling at me.

"Are you OK, Winn?"

She touched my face and then Sam's. She was still blocking me from her emotions, but I could feel a mix of sad and happy fighting for dominance in her. "This is going to be difficult."

"What is?"

She shook her head. "Since we're not in a hurry any longer, do you mind if we stop somewhere for coffee? I chased the two of you most of the night. Kind of forgot to go to bed."

Winona was sleeping with her head tipped on my shoulder. Father Ryczek was close to the end of the service, so I'd have to wake her soon. It was too bad, really; she couldn't block me while she was sleeping. I suppose I should have been listening to the sermon instead of exploring the complex swirl inside her brain. There were so many worries in there, and love kept appearing too, and a sense of relief. Mostly though, she was full of the comfortable, snuggly feeling she had from sleeping leaned against me.

She woke to the final 'amen' during the benediction, stretching cat-like and yawning.

"What'd I miss?"

"God."

"Again?"

"It's alright. I'm sure the two of you will get together eventually."

"What's next?"

"Lunch and then rest. Father Ryczek won't let me work on the solar arrays today because it's Sunday."

"He must not know you very well. Messing around with high voltage systems *is* rest for you. And it would be safer than messing around with Sam until he leaves." She glanced at him and they smiled at each other. "Where're your folks?"

"Working. They left half way through the service to resolve something that came up during negotiations. And please don't remind me that Sam is leaving. I want to enjoy the next three hours, thirty-two minutes and twelve seconds.

"Be brave. Let's get some lunch and then I want to see the array up on the roof."

After a lunch of potato Moussaka, I was ready to rest and maybe nap. I wanted one last chance to lean my head on Sam's shoulder and wrap his arms around me. Maybe pull a warm blanket over us so no one could see where his hands were.

Instead, we were on the roof looking at composite mounting struts and silver-blue solar power elements. It didn't take long for Sam to lose interest and find a spot along the wall where he could sit in the sun on the flagstones. I joined him a few minutes later and Winona sat in front of me, leaned back against my knees so I could braid her hair.

"Can you stop time, Winn?"

"Stop it?"

"Yeah, I want to stop it, right here. I have you and Sam and a warm spot to sit in the sun on a cold winter's day. Give me another minute and I'll be asleep, another hour and I'll be obsessing about how soon Sam is leaving, so stopping right now would be great."

"There's war everywhere else. The Union is tearing itself apart, undoing generations of work and sacrifice."

"Their time can keep going. I want a bubble. I want a Winona, Samuel, Mala Dusa bubble. Can you do that?"

She tipped her head back to look at me. "I wish I could. Enjoy every heartbeat, Duse, and have faith in tomorrow."

"See? I told you that you and God would get together."

It was two seconds later that Cuza found us and told Sam it was time to go. It might have been closer to two hours. Time had stopped having any meaning for me. There was only the time with Sam, and the time without Sam. The time without Sam was about to begin.

Cuza drove him all the way to the terminal so that I could ride along. Sam and I held hands and then I kissed him until Cuza forced us apart.

"MD?"

"Yes, my love?" I wasn't crying. I had promised myself that I wouldn't cry.

"Let's see how long we can keep this connection, OK? And I'll call you as soon as I'm settled on board."

I nodded. I wanted to reach for him again, but it was too late. He was walking away from me and I could feel the excitement building in him the closer he got to the RuComm shuttle on the other side of the door. He was also miserable and I could feel his love for me, but the mission was calling to him and I was so proud of him for not turning back to look at me one last time.

I climbed back into the truck and Cuza glanced at me as we started back toward the Warrens. "You doin' OK, Little Soul?"

I nodded.

"I can take you to find your folks if you want."

"No, that's fine." I tried to put the image of Cuza at the Hilton out of my head. "Winona's spending the night with me and then I'll get your new arrays on-line tomorrow before we go to the hotel."

I put my head back and stared out the side window at the office towers of Eindhoven in the distance. I hummed to myself while I tried to guess what Sam was doing based on what he was feeling.

"What's that you're humming?"

I had to think about it before answering. "The Elephant Song. Do you know it?"

"Sure. Your mom taught it to her students when she was here. She had them marching all over the Mission singing that song for a month." He chuckled at his memories of her.

I wondered if Sam could feel how sad I was, and I was sorry. I was going to have to keep myself happier while he was still in range.

Winona helped. We played hard the rest of the afternoon, having discovered a population of little kids living at the Mission that were just as bored as we were.

After dinner, Winn and I went back up on the roof to sit with our backs against the high wall and watch the stars come out. Or at least the few we could see through the smoke and haze. I was also practicing how to control my connection to Sam, everything from full intimate sharing to just an awareness that he was there. Sometimes it was like I was all alone inside my head. Maybe I was finally learning how to block.

"You seem pleased with yourself, Duse."

I rolled my head over to look at her. "It's not fair that you can do that."

"Seems fair to me. You and Sam are still connected?"

I nodded. "It's like he's sitting right here with us when I want him to be." I smiled at her. "He's trying to be very serious about something right now. Can't you just see the expression on his face?"

"That's over five hundred *kilometers*. How far did you say your parents could touch each other? Like thirty or forty *meters* after being together seventeen years?

"I know. It's like we're one person."

"One soul," Winona whispered. "One soul shared across different pieces, connected by thought." She shuddered.

"I am *not* becoming a Tarakana." Those solemn, big eyes were studying me. "Winona Killdeer, I'm just as human as you are. Do you think I'd still look like this if I could change shapes?"

She touched my cheek and her eyes traveled from my face down the skinny length of my body. "And still you believe that lie. Even with the way Sam loves you? Even with the way *I* love you?"

"Sure. You're both freaks. Like me."

She stood and grabbed my hand. "Come on, freak. It's way past your bedtime. We're going to have a busy day tomorrow."

I let her help me up and we walked back down the stairs into the Mission.

"Can't find it. Can't find it." I was in full panic and I was furious with myself that I couldn't find it.

Winona grabbed my shoulder, spinning me around. "Mala Dusa, what are you looking for?"

"Winn? What are *you* doing here? I have to find..." I sat down hard on the floor, suddenly realizing what was happening and that I was in the Mission, not on board the *Mesa Vista*. I started laughing.

Winona sat down on the floor next to me.

"Sam. Middle of the night safety drill." I managed to catch my breath. "He's trying to find something, his helmet I think, and he's mad at himself, probably because he didn't check where everything was before he went to bed."

I let the emotions fade into the background and we climbed back into bed.

"Are you going to be doing this for the next year while he's gone? And please keep your cold feet to yourself."

I kept my feet where they were. "I don't know. *Mesa Vista* transits the first DSH in about three and a half days. He'll be over fifty million kilometers away then. We're going to hold this connection for as long as we can. After that?" I shrugged and pulled the covers up higher. "Maybe I'll be all alone inside my brain after that."

"Sounds restful," came the sleepy reply.

"Yeah. Restful," I yawned, snuggling into the warmth. "But lonely."

CHAPTER 21

GALLA LUPANIO

Father Ryczek met us in the courtyard to see us off. I was wearing clothes I'd taken from the donation box and I didn't have a bag to carry other than a small clutch for my toothbrush and the few coins that Father Ryczek said I'd earned. The display pad was back in its box inside his office and I planned to give the coins to Winona once we were on our way. She was carrying my sword for me while I said my goodbyes.

"Did you do your exercises this morning?"

"Yes, Father. I'm going to be OK. I left some instructions in the control room for whoever does your system updates next. You shouldn't have any troubles with it though, and I'll check everything when I'm back next year."

He shook his head. "You've fulfilled your obligation here. Come only if you feel God is leading you back to us." He held his finger up in front of my nose. "But warn me first."

"I will, Father."

I hugged him and he whispered, "Go carefully, thorn. There're more dangers in the Union now than I've seen in all my years."

Cuza drove us to the hotel, the old truck seeming almost as out of place parked by the front pillars as Cuza did standing in the lobby. Mom didn't seem to think so, though. She embraced him despite the stares they were getting.

"You're leavin' tomorrow?"

Mom glanced at Winona and me, frowned at Dad, and answered too cheerfully. "That's the plan."

"It's a good plan. Little Soul needs watching. Trouble seems to follow close to her heels if you don't."

"That it does. We'll make sure she's well cared for."

He nodded, and Mom really noticed us for the first time as he left.

"Look at you two, dressed like fugitives. I suppose you'll want to go shopping today."

"Not really, except maybe something for swimming. And do you suppose my box of stuff is still onboard the *Bahia Vista*? I'd really like to have some of those things back."

"I'll talk to Captain Kelang and have everything transferred to your cabin on board the *Galla Lupanio*. We're going out to dinner tonight. Maybe something nice for that?"

I looked at Winona, dressed like me in threadbare pants, the tip of a scabbard visible below the bottom of her oversized, stained sweatshirt. "I think we look fine. Better than fine."

I could feel Mom getting frustrated. "No, you don't. One new dress apiece and no more arguing."

"Swim first," Winona argued.

Mom's head tipped slightly. "Fine, swimming for an hour would be acceptable. Ms. Killdeer, I wish you could stay with me to help with the negotiations next week."

"Next week?" I asked. "Won't we be almost home by then?"

"Right." She took Dad's hand and kissed it. "We'll all be on board the damn *Galla Lupanio* on the way home."

Mom and Dad joined us in the pool and then sat on the side while Winona and I tried to drown each other. I noticed Mom staring at me while I dried off afterward.

I smiled at her. "What?"

She shook her head. "Are you planning on doing swim team again this year?"

"Sure, if I can get my shoulder back to one hundred percent by then."

"What are you going to tell the other kids?"

"About what?"

She touched the scar on the front of my shoulder, then on my back.

"Oh, that. I'll tell them I got shot trying to overthrow a government."

No answer.

"I'll tell them I hurt myself rock climbing?"

"Better."

"While trying to overthrowing a government," I finished with a smile.

She sighed.

"Just rock climbing then. How are things going with the overthrowing the government part?"

"If you mean *building* a government, surprisingly well. So far, everyone seems willing to cooperate and compromise. Your friend has been at every meeting, so I imagine that's part of the reason."

I looked up at her, not sure what to say, so I tried, "You hate the Tarakana."

"I still do. I've never seen them take such an active, almost open role, but I suppose he needs to because Bodens Gate is so critical to fighting what the other colonies are doing."

"You've... talked to him?"

She nodded. "Extensively. I'll never get used to that hum coming into my head. They still scare the hell out of me, but I think I understand what he's trying to do here and across the Union. We're on the same side for the moment."

Her eyes narrowed as she looked at me. "*And* I understand why he's so interested in you and Sam. He didn't mean to show me that part, but the group mind is pretty easy for me to read. Let's just say that we're *not* on the same side as far as the two of you are concerned."

I swallowed hard, wondering if she knew how close Sam and I had come to giving Merrimac exactly what he wanted from us. I felt Sam touch me. He didn't know why I was worried, but I could feel him trying to tell me it was going to be OK.

"What was *that*?"

Mom had been inside my head too. "Um, Sam. He wanted to make sure I was alright."

"You can still feel him?" She glanced at Dad sitting next to her. He was looking up at the glass ceiling, staring at nothing.

"Space dock is over five hundred kilometers from here."

Winona was sitting next to me, fluffing and drying her hair. "Actually, *Mesa Vista* left dock ten hours ago. Assuming normal thrust, they should be almost four hundred thousand kilometers out by now."

"You knew about this?"

Winona decided that she needed to look up at whatever Dad was finding so interesting. I could feel the swirl in Mom's brain, the frustration. She felt as if I was forcing her to revisit a decision she'd already made.

"It doesn't matter. Merrimac is going to be one step ahead of me no matter what I do." She turned toward Dad. "Ted, how much did you know about this?"

"I knew they could read each other ten klicks out, not four-hundred thousand. But I'm not sure it really changes anything. From what you told me about the plans you saw in the group mind it's not even really all that surprising."

Mom doesn't get overwhelmed or afraid, and only rarely had I seen her not know what to do. I saw all of it right then for a brief second before she shut me out.

"Need to learn how to do that," I mumbled to myself.

She stood. "I need to go." She looked at us, distracted. "Ted, can you please help them pick something out for tonight?"

She turned and walked away before Dad even answered. I think she was talking to herself.

Dad usually doesn't block me. He can if he wants to, he just chooses to let me in, like it would be rude not to. He was worried about a lot of things, but mostly about Mom.

"Should I go with her?" Winona had a towel wrapped around her shoulders and looked ready to run.

"No. She..." he sighed. "She's gone to talk to Merrimac again."

"Again? How often does she do that?"

Dad chuckled, but without humor. "I'm worried that she's going to become part of the colony. They seem to have formed a bond; a temporary one I hope. I'll go check on her in fifteen minutes to make sure she finds her way back out."

"Have you been going in there too?"

He nodded. "I don't get as much out of it as she does, but being in there with someone you love... God, it's wonderful."

He shook himself. "Let's get you two dressed and then find something for you to wear tonight to The Gate."

"Nice restaurant?" I asked while we made our way to our rooms.

"It's not bad. Pretentious, but the steaks are decent and there's a good selection of beer on tap. They also have a spiced honey drink called krupnikas that your mom likes. It's powerful. If you behave yourselves, I'll let you each have one after dinner if you want.

Winn and I grinned at each other.

I ordered a dress, soft blue-grays to match my post Samuel mood. Winona chose something in greens that made her look adorable in the sim. I also ordered a new display pad, dreading when Dad would notice. We laid down on one of the big, soft beds while we waited for the dresses to print. Winn and I talked and giggled for a few minutes and then she started to fall asleep.

"I can feel your emotions while you're asleep, did you know that? No block at all. You go all warm and snuggly inside."

Her eyes stayed closed and she wrinkled her forehead at me. "You're not a very nice person."

"I know. I don't think you're really comfortable though until you get a good fistful of blanket in each hand. Then it's like... bliss."

She opened one eye to look at me. "Someday, when I'm mad at you, I'll tell you what goes on in *your* brain while you're sleeping." She closed her eyes and drifted away into bliss.

I put my head on the pillow next to hers. "I love my Winona."

"They look so sweet, don't they? Almost innocent."

Mom was standing next to Dad, looking at us with her head leaned against his shoulder. "It's a shame really, to wake them up and unleash what they really are."

"Hey! We can hear you, you know."

"Good. Enough napping. It's time to wake up and get ready for dinner. And this came for you." She tossed a box to me that landed on my stomach. "What happened to the last one?"

"Lost it," I sighed. "It was in the coat I was wearing at the rally."

"The heavy coat you took off and threw into the crowd as a symbol of Central Government oppression? I might have to forgive you that one."

"Thanks."

The Gate was in the midst of a transformation. Formerly known as Boden's Gate and Tap Room, the staff had covered most of the signs and removed the wall decorations, but our waiter was the exact mix of arrogance and condescension that I would expect in Eindhoven.

He stared at me while he took my order, judging me, and correcting my pronunciations. He made me stammer when I was trying very hard to seem sophisticated.

Mom's eyes narrowed and she asked him, "Je tam nejaky problem?"

He seemed startled. "Ziadne Madam. Máte krásnu dcéru."

She smiled and he scurried away. Mom took a sip of wine before explaining what had just happened by tapping the back of her left hand. "Clan tattoo. He's a child of the Warrens. We'll have excellent service tonight, I think."

Dad leaned over and kissed her cheek.

After dinner, Dad helped Winona and me back to our rooms, providing an arm for each of us to lean on. He had been right about the strength of the krupnikas, and I would have been wiser to have settled for a bowl of ice cream instead of the two small shots that were now warming my blood.

"So," he asked as we wobbled down the hallway, "are you enjoying being back in civilization?"

"Nope," I answered a little too emphatically. "Don't belong here."

Winona leaned around Dad to look at me, using both hands on his forearm to retain balance. "You'd rather be at the Mission?"

"Don't belong there either, but it's better than this. I made a difference in the Warrens. I think I did. Didn't I?"

"You did," Dad reassured me.

"Here? Nothing matters. I'm just krásna dcéra, whatever the hell that means."

"Language," Dad warned.

"How does Mom do it? She makes a difference everywhere she goes. She's back there now," I tried to turn to look over my shoulder and almost fell. Dad kept me vertical. "What's she saying to our waiter? Something that makes a difference, I'll bet. I have so much to learn from her, and now I'll only be with you for one more year before I go to the Academy."

"Mala Dusa!" Winn tipped forward again to look at me. "Hush. You don't want to tell your folks about the Academy yet, remember?"

I put my hand over my mouth. "Right. I forgot."

I smiled up at Dad trying to pretend nothing had happened.

"So, the Academy. That's where you belong?"

I shrugged. "Don't know. But I'm pretty sure it's the door I have to pass through to get to where I do belong."

Dad kissed the top of my head. "Surprisingly, that makes a lot of sense."

"It does? Yeah, it does."

We dropped Winona at her room and then Dad helped me collapse onto my bed.

"Don't forget to brush your teeth."

"Uh huh."

"And get undressed."

"Uh huh."

"Beautiful daughter."

"Thanks."

"No, that's what krásna dcéra means. The waiter told your mom that she has a beautiful daughter. And he's right."

"Oh. Thanks."

Winona tottered into my room wearing a t-shirt and shorts and tucked herself under my covers.

"Something wrong with your room?" Dad asked her.

"Mala Dusa was lonely."

"It's true," I told him. "I was."

Dad left me lying there with my legs hanging down off the side of the bed. "Fine. Make sure she gets her teeth brushed. And we have to be out of here by 06:00 to make it to the space dock on time, so go straight to sleep."

I would have answered him, but I was already asleep.

I woke a couple of hours later to a pounding headache. I took something for it, brushed my teeth, stripped off my dress and put on a soft t-shirt. Winn didn't wake up when I slid in next to her. Somewhere, far away, I could feel Sam sleeping. I touched him gently and dreamed I was in his arms.

We entered the *Galla Lupanio* through her shuttle bay, which was large enough for the ship's shuttle and not much else. She was more than five times the mass of RuComm's new *Vista*-class ships, so I had expected her to be spacious on the inside. Instead, she was unbelievably cramped. I had to flatten myself against the passageway wall on the way to my cabin whenever a member of the crew came running by, which they seemed to be doing all the time. No one walked. I looked into my cabin where there was barely room for a bed and a desk. Winona's cabin shared a bathroom with my cabin, connected by a very narrow door.

"Good thing we're friends," I told her. "And thin."

"Merchant ship. If it doesn't make money for the Guild, then it's not here." A crewman ran by outside the door. "I think that goes double for the crew."

There was a box sitting on my bed and I peeked into it, holding my breath. I touched the blue gauze, enjoying the feel of the texture between my fingers for a moment.

"I want to go back to the shuttle bay and find my parents."

"Why?"

"Because I don't trust them."

"You think they'll ditch us?"

"Mom might. I'm not sure about Dad, but he has self-control issues when it comes to her."

"Ya think?"

We ran, then skidded to a stop just inside the hatch where we could see that my parents were talking to a man in uniform.

"Looks OK so far." I glanced at Winona. "We're supposed to break from the dock in just a few minutes. If either one of them makes a move toward the outer hatch…"

She nodded. "We drag them back in or we go with them."

We waited. They kept talking. There was a barely perceptible flicker of the lights and change in gravity as the ship transitioned to internal power and then the outer hatch slid shut and sealed itself. A moment later, the *Galla Lupanio* announced that we were clear of the Boden Gate docks and maneuvering for home. I liked her voice, there was something warm and sultry about it.

"*Galla Lupanio*," I asked, "What should we call you?"

"You may call me by my full name if you wish, Ms. Holloman. Most of the crew calls me *Schiava*, and I will answer to that as well."

"*Schiava*. That's a pretty name. You may call me Mala Dusa if you like. I'm looking forward to traveling with you and I have a bunch of questions, but first, I think I should go fetch my parents."

"That would be difficult, Mala Dusa. Mr. Holloman and Ms. Weldon departed back to space dock twenty minutes ago."

"But they're right…" I started to point. There were three very handsome German Shepherds sitting by the shuttle."

"*Schiava*, do you have any dogs on board?" I asked the question even though I knew the answer.

"Dogs? No dogs, but I do have six cats that help me police the cargo holds. Would you like to meet them?"

I couldn't say anything. I was too busy trying to decide whether to laugh or to cry.

"Maybe later, *Schiava*," Winona answered for me. She wrapped me into a tight hug. "Choose to laugh, Duse. You'll feel better."

I did a little bit of both and after a moment I could feel Sam holding me too. I let go of Winona and unrolled my new display pad.

"What are you going to say to her?"

"Mom? Nothing. I'm calling Sam. I think he might be afraid that I'm in real trouble."

"Then you're calling your mom?"

"Maybe."

I brought Sam up to date on how my parents had fooled us. He seemed inclined toward laughing it off and forgiving them, but he'd follow my mom into battle even if it meant his own certain death, so I wasn't sure that really helped me.

I went back to my cabin and sat on the bed staring at the display pad, not sure what I wanted to do with it. Winn sat with me, not saying anything, just being there with me.

It was finally starting to seem funny, the three Tarakana sitting there staring at me, getting a free ride with us back to Earth. I tapped the icon for Mom and she answered immediately. One look at the anguish on her face, mixed with guilt, pain and longing, and I had to forgive her.

"Nice one, Mom. When are you and Dad *really* coming home?"

"There's a series of meetings over the next six weeks. After that I should be able to leave."

"So, we could have stayed with you and still made it back in time for school?"

"If this was just about Bodens Gate, I'd have let you. With the rest of the Union tearing itself apart we decided it would be safer to get you back home as soon as possible."

"You could have told us. Explained it."

"We talked about it and decided that there was too high a chance that you'd refuse to go and there wasn't any time to argue."

"You're right, we would have refused."

"Your dad joked that we'd probably end up putting a pair of Tarakana that looked like you two on the ship. It gave us an idea."

"Great. Well, at least it's only for six weeks. I think I can avoid burning the house down for that long."

Dad leaned into view. "Anna and Corinne will be meeting you when you get off the shuttle."

"Your sisters? Both of them? I don't need, I mean, I'll be fine on my own. Really. Winona's folks are just down the street." Aunt Anna was all right. She was a geologist, like Dad. Reasonable, logical. Aunt Corry might be her twin in appearance, but she went through relationships and professions faster than I did display pads.

"It's just for a few weeks," Mom assured me. "This is your last year living at home and I don't want to miss any more of it than I have to."

She disconnected and I sighed. "Can I move in with your parents for the next few weeks?"

"Why? I like your Aunt Corry. She's crazy."

I laid back on the bed with my arm over my eyes. "I'm doomed. She'll have me making clay pots or mosaics or something while we chant ancient Sumerian poems."

At exactly 10:52 ship's time the next morning, I lost my Samuel. We were on the display pad together and I was as close to him emotionally as we could possibly be. At just a bit over fifty million kilometers apart, we were talking over each other because of the comm lag, waiting for *Mesa Vista* to make her jump through the first Deep Space Hole. One moment he was there inside my head, and then it was like he was ripped out of me. The image of him kept talking for almost three minutes before the pad reported that the comm link had been lost.

I sent a message to him, knowing that it would take twenty hours before he saw it, then I rolled up the pad and cried on Winona's shoulder for a time.

"By tomorrow morning you'll have a message from him." She pushed the hair back away from my eyes. "You're going to be fine. Let's get an early lunch and see what there is to do on board this big ship."

"OK. I'm going to be a mess for a day or two, but I'll make it." I tried a brave smile, but it was such a failure that Winn laughed at me.

"Just go ahead and be miserable for a little bit and get it out of your system. I have too much I want to do to have you being all mopey. Like trying to figure out how the emotional connection seems to operate outside normal physics. It cut off as soon as he made the jump?"

I nodded, letting Winona comfort me in her own way.

"So here's the plan. We'll spend a few weeks with your aunts—"

"Doomed."

"—and then your parents will be home and we'll be back in school. As seniors." She grinned at me. "And then, in the spring, we grad—"

"Sam will be back. In the spring, Sam will be back."

"Huh. I think you're right. You *are* doomed."

"If I am, it's a happy sort of doom." I stood, willing myself not to be mopey. "Come on, I'll race you to the mess hall."

"Do you even remember where it is? You got us lost this morning."

"I have no idea where it is. It's the *not* knowing that makes the race more fun, don't you think? Are you ready?"

"I am the wind."

The End

www.ingramcontent.com/pod-product-compliance
Lightning Source LLC
Chambersburg PA
CBHW060408260626
47160CB00006B/2476